The Crooked Elm Partnership

PAMELA A. KELLEY

.

ISBN: 1523474955
ISBN 13: 9781523474950
Library of Congress Control Number: 2016900952
CreateSpace Independent Publishing Platform
North Charleston, South Carolina

For

William, James, and Mardell

1

Heat rising from the center court concrete, Mike and Jake Girardi were on the verge of closing out their doubles match with United States District Court Judge Mitchell Best and his son Andy. As usual, it had been a close, tense battle. The Girardis had won the first set 7-5 and lost the second 4-6. About a dozen racquet club members sat around watching them with various levels of interest, some cooling down from matches and others preparing to begin their own.

The third set had reached a tiebreaker, and Andy was about to serve to Jake in the ad court. Wiping the sweat from his brow, the tired Mike Girardi watched the judge leaning ever so slightly on his left foot as Andy announced the score, "3-6."

Mitch is going to poach, Girardi thought to himself, taking a deep breath and feeling ready to run out of steam at any moment. *Come on, Jake, blast him down the line so we can go to breakfast.*

Andy's serve sliced hard toward the center of the court, landing several inches outside the ad court box. Jake, a lanky seventeen year old, hit the ball softly to the side and shook his head in the negative.

"That was wide."

Mike Girardi nodded his agreement. He didn't know it, but his phone was buzzing away on vibrate in his gym bag, draining the last of the battery's energy. With his law firm partners vainly trying to reach him, he remained blissfully consumed with his match.

Adjusting his cap in frustration but offering no objection to the call, Andy pulled a ball from his pocket and bounced it hard on the ground three times. He wound up his compact body and offered his second serve, this time a looping ball far to Jake's left. As Jake swung his left arm back, the judge broke for the center of the court, ready to pounce on any ball within his substantial reach.

Down the line, Jacob, Girardi urged silently once more.

The left-handed Jake opened his racket face and shot his forehand straight ahead to the judge's right, just as Girardi had hoped. Best lunged back, but was not quick enough. All four watched the ball bounce six inches inside the line—a perfect shot.

"Son of a *bitch*," Best bellowed as he banged his racquet on the ground. Andy Best stared at his father in disbelief, hands on his hips.

Girardi turned away from the Bests and pumped his fist in exultation. "Good job, son," he said as Jake ran up to him and the pair clasped fingers in their accustomed bonding handshake. They then jogged to the net to shake hands with their opponents.

"You got me, Jake," the judge said ruefully as he offered his hand.

"Yes, sir," the young man replied quietly. He had been taught years ago never to gloat or show too much exuberance in front of Mitch Best. "You got me plenty of times today, too."

"Let's pick up those balls," Girardi said quickly to his son. "I'm starving."

"Loser buys, so breakfast is on us," the judge said, working to regain his good cheer.

At the back of the court, Jake stood next to his father as he removed a ball that had become stuck in the fence.

"They were cheating, you know," Jake said quietly.

"There were a couple of close calls."

"Why do you let them get away with that? You would kill me if I tried to cheat."

Girardi nodded firmly. "Worse than that, I'd be ashamed of you if you cheated—and I wouldn't play with you any more, either."

"Why does he do it?"

"Mitch hates to lose," Girardi offered as he eyed the Bests sulkily putting on their warm-up jackets and placing their racquets in their bags. "He's been that way as long as I can remember."

"You hate to lose, too," Jake pressed in frustration. "In this case, taking a few calls back would just have evened the playing field. I don't get it."

"There's a lot that you don't get yet. This isn't the time for a philosophical conversation about fairness in the universe. Mitch has been a friend of mine since the first day of law school—we take our friends flaws and all, Jacob. It's not easy to find someone who will stick by you through thick and thin."

"You're just afraid to offend him because he's a federal judge."

"That's not it," Girardi rejoined, the glow of victory fading as he squinted up at his son and then headed toward the Bests.

"I finally got a new car," Andy offered a couple of minutes later. "Do you want to see it?" he asked Jake.

"Sure."

"You boys go on out to the parking lot," Judge Best ordered. "But don't be too long—we'll meet you in the dining room."

The judge had been a member of the Newport Racquet Club for well over a decade, and he was a fixture among the local elites there. The Girardis came regularly as the judge's guests, but were not members themselves. They belonged to a small gym with a swimming pool near their home in Tustin.

In the clubhouse, the judge paused to check his messages while Girardi headed for the dining room to request a table. Wearing his tennis whites, navy pullover, and designer sunglasses, Girardi looked every inch the successful law firm partner that he was. In his mid-forties, the trim Girardi wore his dark hair and beard close-cropped.

The judge soon caught up with Girardi, and the young hostess led them past several long buffet tables heaping with food to a prime table by the window.

"Thanks, Veronica," Best offered with a wink as he sat down and took the menu from her. He was a large, barrel-chested man of fifty. He wore his salt-and-pepper hair in a crew cut, a holdover from his four years in the Marine Corps between college and law school.

"How's Andy doing at school?" Girardi asked as they settled into their seats. "Is he finding a routine this term?"

"I think he's improving this semester." Andy was a freshman at USC, his father's undergraduate alma mater. The younger Best had struggled his first term, landing himself on academic probation, much to his parents' disappointment. Best's daughter Brianna was a sophomore at a liberal arts college back east. To his pride, she was a straight-A student.

"How's Jake doing on the baseball team?"

"So far, so good," Girardi offered with similar caution. "The new coach seems like a good guy—he's still getting to know the players. Jake wants to play in college, you know, and so his junior year is key."

"It's all about the stats, isn't it?"

"He can get attention by putting up good numbers, that's for sure."

"He's a gifted athlete."

Girardi shook his head proudly. "Thanks, Mitch."

He's also a great kid, Girardi added to himself.

Judge Best leaned back in his chair and folded his arms. "It doesn't look like either of our boys will follow us into the law."

"Probably not—but you never know. They're still young."

"Hell, I'll be lucky if Andy makes it through college. He's majoring in keg parties right now. He can't afford to screw around like that—he needs to study hard just to get by. He's not as intelligent as his mother and sister. I had to pull a bunch of strings to get him into USC to begin with. While his high school classmates were deciding between Harvard and Stanford, my son was looking at USC or Cal State Stanislaus."

Girardi shook his head sympathetically. "I can't get Jake to spend as much time with his books as I'd like. He's always just fine with a B."

"Just a B?" Best repeated ironically. "I'd do a somersault of pure joy to see a B on my son's transcript."

"Andy's at a university, Mitch. Jake's at a public high school—it's not the same thing."

A waiter wearing a white shirt and black bow tie came over to take their drink order, and the pair then fell silent as they looked over their menus. Girardi could smell the sausages and potatoes at the nearby station.

"I think I'll just have the buffet. That way I can eat right away."

"Sounds good."

As they each folded their menus, a young woman around thirty suddenly appeared at their table. She was tall and slender, with shoulder-length black hair and lovely porcelain skin. She wore a white tennis dress under a form-fitting pink jacket that showed off her trim figure to great advantage.

"Your honor!" She spoke loudly, despite the fact that she stood close by at the edge of the table. "Why, I had no idea you were a member here!"

"Miss Bailey," Best bellowed, looking at the racket that rested against her chest, "I had no idea you were a tennis player."

"I'm not very good," she allowed confidentially, keeping her attention entirely on the judge and not even looking at Girardi. "I'm thinking of taking lessons here—my friend is a member."

"By all means you should take some lessons; tennis is a fine sport. Despite what they say, it's every bit as good for networking as golf—and it's much better exercise."

"Can you recommend a pro?"

"All the staff pros are great here. I work with Gaspar."

"Gaspar?" she repeated slowly with a thoughtful nod. "I'll have to remember that name."

There was something about this exchange that made Girardi uncomfortable as he took out his phone, which was by now dead. He pretended to check his messages, keeping a careful ear on his friend's conversation.

"Do you take lessons often?" she continued.

"Thursday afternoons—I have an hour and a half each week with Gaspar. We're working on my backhand right now. Pretty soon we're going to do something about my serve—it was terrible today."

There was an awkward pause.

"You and I can't seem to get rid of one another," Bailey said with a laugh and smile at the bemused judge.

Girardi shot his friend a quizzical look. "Won't you introduce us, Mitch?"

"Miss Bailey was in my courtroom last week on a removal motion."

Uh oh, Girardi thought at the news that this woman had a case assigned to Best.

"It's my opponent's motion," she interjected forcefully. "I filed suit on behalf of a single plaintiff in state court—you wouldn't believe the injustice that poor man has suffered. It's a heartbreaking story."

Girardi cut her off. "And of course you can't share that story with us now because that would be an *ex parte* communication with the court, which we all know would be against the rules."

Bailey narrowed her eyes at Girardi and continued. "I know the rules. The defendant corporation naturally is seeking to remove the matter to federal court, where defendants always have an advantage. I'm hoping that the good judge here will kick this little case right back down to state court where it belongs. I'm Michelle Bailey."

She offered her hand.

"Mike Girardi."

"Mike's an old law school chum of mine from Davis."

Bailey seemed to size up Girardi. "You're with a firm here in Orange County, aren't you?"

"Marshall, Lufton."

"The New York firm?"

"Yep." Girardi by now had decided that he did not care for Michelle Bailey. *Where are Jake and Andy*, he wondered.

"You big firm lawyers have no idea how good you have it."

"Are you a solo, Ms. Bailey?"

She frowned at the characterization. "I have my own practice, yes."

Just then, the waiter returned to take their order.

"Two buffets," Best growled, apparently annoyed by the interruption.

The waiter nodded, made a notation on his card, and discreetly moved away.

"I should be going," Bailey said, "my girlfriend looks impatient over there in the corner. It was delightful to see you, your honor." Bailey offered another bright smile as she took the judge's hand and held it for a couple of moments.

"The pleasure was all mine," the judge replied.

With a crisp nod to Girardi, she left the table. The judge followed her with attentive, longing eyes until she was out of the room. Then, he leaned forward eagerly and whispered to his friend.

"She wants me," he said with a firm nod. "It's obvious, isn't it?"

Having been a litigator for twenty years, Girardi had excellent command of himself. It now took every bit of his self-control not to let on what he was really thinking.

"I was checking my messages," he lied. "I wasn't really paying attention."

"You weren't?" The judge sounded disappointed. "There's a strong attraction there," he continued. "I noticed it when she came to court on that motion last week. The way she looks at me—God."

"Careful there, cowboy."

"What do you mean?"

"You know what I mean, Mitch."

"It's just a little fun—no big deal. Women love a powerful man."

"But they rarely love him *for him*," Girardi cracked.

"I don't know—I think there's a real chemistry between us. Is that so impossible? I'm not a hundred years old, you know—I'm fifty."

Best had recently celebrated this milestone birthday, and he had yet to come to terms with the fact that his life was entering its sixth decade.

"I think I'll order another hearing and then grant that removal motion," he continued. "That way, I'll get to spend some more time with Michelle."

"Mitch, get real. You are a married man and a federal judicial officer. Think of how hard you worked for that appointment. There's no place for chemistry with some," he paused, searching for a phrase that would get the point across without being vulgar, "some chick with an angle in your courtroom. Stay away from her, Mitch, and don't you dare grant that motion unless there's a good reason."

"But the adverse party would prevail on the motion—no harm, no foul."

Girardi shook his head. His friend never spoke in this way about his work at the court. This woman had obviously gotten to him. Either that, or the job had gone to his head. Federal judges are sometimes compared to kings and queens, ruling in their marble palaces with no one, save the appeals court, daring to question them. For some, it was tempting to get a little carried away.

As Girardi mulled this over, Best leaned back in his chair and folded his arms unhappily. "I'm not sure that you are the man to lecture me about chicks with an angle."

"What's that supposed to mean?"

Best leaned forward and came in for the kill. "Two words—Mona . . . Phillips."

Always with Mona, Girardi thought angrily as he pushed his chair from the table. After about a year of casual dating, Girardi and Phillips had broken up nearly two years earlier. Still, his friends and family seemed to bring her up constantly. *What would everyone do if they couldn't needle me about Mona?*

"I'm going to get my food."

"Good idea."

The boys came in and joined their fathers at the lavish buffet tables. All four piled their plates high and ate heartily. To Girardi's relief, there was no more mention of Michelle Bailey or Mona Phillips, and they passed a pleasant meal together.

As they were preparing to leave, the hostess Veronica approached the table. Her expression was serious.

"What is it, Veronica?" the judge asked.

"There is a message," she said, fingering a small note.

"I'll take it," Best replied, holding up his hand.

"The message is for Mr. Girardi. I'm so sorry."

"What is it, dad?" Jake asked with concern.

Girardi's face went pale as he read the words once to himself and then repeated them out loud. "Jackson Tremont has collapsed and is gravely ill. He's at Hope Hospital—come right away."

2

Half an hour later, Girardi arrived at the intensive care waiting room and looked around for a familiar face. To his surprise, he saw no one he knew. He pulled out his phone, which he'd charged in the car, and listened to three messages, each of which said roughly the same thing—that his law partner and mentor Jackson Tremont had suffered a stroke in his office that morning, that Tremont had been transported to the Hope Hospital ICU, and that his condition was very serious.

Reeling, Girardi plopped down in a stuffed chair in the corner by the window. In the distance, he could see boats with large numbers on their sails racing just outside the harbor. Hope Hospital catered to a wealthy clientele, and the fact showed even in the comfortable, well-appointed waiting room.

As Girardi sat, he thought about his mentor. Jack Tremont was a southerner who boasted direct familial ties to not one but *two* Civil War generals. He'd left South Carolina to attend Columbia Law School, and by his early thirties, he was a partner in the New York office of Marshall, Lufton, Harding and Bruce. He had married his southern belle college sweetheart Celeste, and the pair now had three grown children and several grandchildren.

In the late-nineties, Tremont had spent a year in Southern California working on several criminal matters involving one of his biggest clients.

He and Celeste fell in love with the climate and purchased a spacious home on a big lot in Corona del Mar that soon became known as "The Plantation." Celeste joined the symphony board and several charities, and in no time, Orange County's smart set was clamoring for invitations to the lavish parties thrown at The Plantation. Tremont convinced his New York partners to let him open an Orange County branch office, despite the fact that the firm had no other California presence.

When Girardi first met Tremont, he had been a young prosecutor in the district attorney's office. Tremont was defending a client in a fraud trial opposite Girardi and a team of other DAs. After the trial was cut short by an eleventh-hour plea bargain, Tremont had offered Girardi a job with the nascent Orange County office of Marshall, Lufton.

"Why are you wasting your time as a DA?" Tremont had asked him in the courthouse parking lot. "You're a damned good lawyer—you shouldn't let yourself get pigeon-holed. If you come help me open this office in Newport, I can almost guarantee that you'll be a partner in four years—provided we make a go of it, of course. The money would be fantastic. We're paying New York salaries."

Tremont turned out to be as good as his word, and although it took five years instead of four, Mike Girardi did make partner at Marshall, Lufton. At first, he worked exclusively on matters for Tremont's clients. Tremont began to teach Girardi about client development, and by the time he was named partner, he could boast a small but growing clientele of his own. Girardi knew that he would never generate as much business as the flamboyant Jack Tremont, but he was a gifted lawyer who knew how to run a case, to listen to clients, and to instill confidence. Girardi worked hard and took great pride in his professional success.

Girardi looked up and saw three of the six partners in the Orange County office, Hugh McDaniel, Louis Cox, and Jean Dewey-Martinez. Years ago, an associate had secretly dubbed the trio Huey, Dewey and Louie.

"How's Jack doing?" Girardi asked with genuine concern.

"We were just in with Celeste for a few minutes," replied Dewey-Martinez, the office's lone female partner. She, like Girardi, was in her mid-forties. Tall and stylish, she wore her dark hair in a short, dramatic cut. "Apparently, he's in surgery now. We won't know anything until he gets out—it will probably be hours."

"What happened this morning?" Girardi asked. "The messages said that Jack was in the office."

"We don't know much," she replied. "Apparently Jack was yelling at Spence about something, and all of a sudden, he keeled over."

"With as much extra weight as he was carrying, something like this was bound to happen to Jack sooner or later," Cox interjected.

Ignoring Cox, Girardi spoke up in surprise. "Spence was with him?"

Randall Spencer was a mid-level associate with the firm who had graduated from UC Berkeley's Boalt Hall. He was intelligent and capable, and Girardi liked him. From time to time, Spencer had struggled with the intensity of the practice, but this was the case with plenty of young attorneys. At the moment, Spencer was the litigation department's only mid-level associate. This made him an essential go-between for the partners and younger associates.

"Did Spence say what exactly set Jack off?"

Jack Tremont was known for his temper, and so the fact that he'd been yelling did not entirely surprise Girardi. The three partners exchanged uncomfortable looks at Girardi's question.

"Not exactly," McDaniel broke in. Tall and lean, with thinning red hair, McDaniel was a corporate law attorney and managing partner of the office. "You see, when the paramedics arrived, Spencer apparently fainted from the stress."

"Fainted?" Girardi repeated in surprise.

"Wimp . . .," Cox said under his breath. Cox was the shortest of the trio, with a pudgy red face and a restless, uncomfortable manner.

"Is Spence okay?"

"They checked him into a room upstairs just as a precaution. They say he'll be fine." McDaniel hesitated and looked down at his shoes before fixing eyes with Girardi. "We were hoping that you'd go in there and talk to him."

To what do I owe the honor of this thankless task, Girardi wondered.

"Me?"

"You're the one the associates like, Mike," Dewey-Martinez chimed in, assuming the part today of the good cop to McDaniel's bad cop. Over the years, she had proven herself equally adept at either position. "You've always been the nice one."

Looking at the trio before him, Girardi knew this to be faint praise indeed.

"Alright, I'll talk to him."

"Thanks, Mike," Dewey-Martinez said with obvious relief as the others nodded.

"Do you know the room number?"

"423."

"I guess I'll head up there."

There was an awkward pause as the other three again exchanged uncomfortable glances.

"Mike, there's one more thing," McDaniel continued.

"What's that?" Girardi asked, wondering how these three had found the time to confer together without him on such short notice.

"Since you're the only other litigation partner in the office . . . ."

Girardi immediately disliked the sound of this.

"And you and Jack are close," Dewey-Martinez interjected.

"Will you call Jack's clients right away and reassure them that everything's under control?"

"We don't know yet whether everything is under control," Girardi replied.

"It will be under control if you take over his caseload, Mike."

"Isn't that a little premature?"

McDaniel took a small step forward. "Jack's not getting out of here any time soon—if ever. You're a terrific lawyer, Mike. If you go down to the office and get started today, you'll have command of everything on Jack's desk by Monday morning."

Girardi was dismayed. *They don't want to be bothered by this,* he thought cynically. *Jack's illness is a nuisance to them. They want me to handle it so they can get back to whatever it was they were doing when they got the call this morning.*

"It's too soon for me to presume to take over Jack's matters," he said, knowing how carefully Tremont guarded his clients. "But I will talk to his people and get a sense of what's happening and whether any big deadlines are looming."

"That's a start," Dewey-Martinez said.

"The clients should be reassured," McDaniel pressed.

"That can wait until Monday morning. Let's meet first thing—we should know a lot more by then."

"Will you brief us on Jack's cases then?" asked Cox, speaking up for the first time.

"No, Louis, I will not promise to 'brief' you on anything. I do not work *for* you, I work *with* you—remember the org chart? We're partners."

Cox frowned unhappily but said nothing further. He had become accustomed over the years to following the lead of McDaniel and Dewey-Martinez and rarely asserted himself with his peers. And when he did, it never went well for him.

"I think I'll take off," McDaniel said. "I have a tee time in twenty minutes. There's nothing we can do here. Celeste promised to call me when Jack gets out of surgery."

"I promised my wife that I'd go to *Whole Foods* for her." This was Cox.

"I've got work to do on a new deal," Dewey-Martinez said, "and it's not going to get done here. And, we're finalizing the plans for Jaime's fundraiser. It's coming up on Friday. I expect to see all of you at the Ritz-Carlton with your tuxedos on."

Girardi was impressed by Dewey-Martinez's ability to multi-task so efficiently. She was not only a mother and a law firm partner but was also deeply involved in her husband's congressional campaign.

"And," she concluded, "thank you for taking care of this, Mike."

In another few moments, Girardi was alone in the hallway, shaking his head in dismay. He asked after Celeste Tremont at the information desk and was told that she was waiting in a private room upstairs with her daughter. He stopped in to see them briefly. Celeste cried dramatically on his shoulder and made a few sarcastic comments about the hypocrisy of Huey, Dewey and Louie. Jack Tremont had never cared for these three, who frequently joined together in opposition to Tremont's ideas for the Orange County office.

When Celeste's phone rang, Girardi excused himself, urging her to call him on his cell if there was anything he might do for her.

Girardi then reluctantly made his way to room 423. When he arrived, he found twenty-nine-year-old Randall Spencer wearing a blue dotted gown, reclining on top of the bed with an IV in his arm. His brown wavy hair was disheveled, and his face was pale and sullen.

He looks like the one who had the stroke, Girardi thought as he pulled up a chair next to the bed and extended a hand to the young man.

"How you doin', Spence?"

"I'm doing poorly, Mike," Spencer replied, looking wanly out the window after a weak handshake with his boss.

"Are they planning to keep you for long?"

"Nope—when this drip is finished, they'll probably let me go."

"That's good news."

Suddenly, Spencer sat up straight and began to speak rapidly, his demeanor transforming in an instant. With the color now rising in his cheeks, he explained that his wife was on her way back from a baby shower in Los Angeles, and that Girardi was the only visitor who had been in to see him.

"They told me I was dehydrated. What a bunch of crap! I freaked out—that's what happened. I'm not ashamed to admit it. I feel like ripping this thing out of my arm and ejecting."

"Don't do that, Spence," Girardi replied soothingly. "Let the doctors do what they want. Then you can go home, have a beer and forget the whole thing."

"Forget the whole thing? Are you fucking kidding me? I'll never forget this nightmare as long as I live."

Girardi was unaccustomed to hearing such language from the excitable but normally well-spoken Spencer.

"I'm sure it's stressful, Spence, but do you mind telling me what happened?"

Spencer shook his head in disgust, apparently realizing that Girardi had not called merely to check on his well-being. "I suppose you won't leave unless I do?"

At this, Girardi paused. Spencer was obviously agitated, and it might have been best to leave him be. But Spencer was the only one who could tell him what happened, so Girardi decided to press on anyway, his curiosity prevailing over his concern for the young man.

"Jack was yelling when this happened?" he ventured.

"Nothing new there."

"Worse than usual?"

"Yes. For the past few weeks he's been on a tear—don't you hear him? You work there, too."

Over the years, Girardi had nearly perfected the technique of focusing on his own work and ignoring ninety-five percent of what went on in the office. While such an ostrich approach occasionally had its drawbacks, Girardi believed it to be a central factor in his success at Marshall, Lufton.

"What was the matter with him?"

"How should I know?"

"So, he didn't seem to be upset with your work?"

Spencer shook his head and folded his arms unhappily, tugging on the IV line. Girardi leaned over and rolled the IV stand closer to the bed.

"Jack has criticized my work since day one—but he keeps giving me more. And so do you. I work all the time. I doubt Jack's anger had anything to do with me. Who knows what set him off? The old guy's probably miserable. It's got to be tough being such an asshole."

Wow, Girardi thought to himself, hardly believing his ears. While he knew that partners were frequently disparaged by associates behind closed doors and nowadays even on Internet gossip websites, he'd never directly heard any such name-calling. It came as a bit of a shock. *If he wants to keep his job, he'd better put a lid on it.*

"Last night," Spencer continued, "Jack called me on my cell. It was Friday night—Janet and I were on the sofa. I don't get a lot of sofa time with my wife these days, if you know what I mean."

Girardi nodded sympathetically, thinking back to his married days. "Yeah, I know what you mean."

"Anyway, like an idiot, I picked up because I knew it was him. He proceeded to talk to me for an hour about how his clients keep pressuring him for things. They've never understood how hard he works. All they ask is more, more, more. He must have been drunk—what he said didn't make any sense. At the end of the whole thing, after wasting an hour of my time and ruining my evening, he had the nerve to order me to come in this morning. *But*, I did as I was told."

"Did Jack explain why he wanted you to come in?"

"He said there was some research he needed done for that new CEP matter. It's a government audit involving a subsidiary called Pope Electronics."

"Pope Electronics?" Girardi repeated. "I've never heard of it."

"I hadn't heard of it either."

"I didn't think that CEP was even a Marshall, Lufton client anymore," Girardi ventured.

"Jack told me on the phone that he'd been working *Pope Electronics* alone but needed some associate help. So, I thought we were going to talk about the *Pope* case this morning. But when I arrived, Jack started talking about something he'd done for CEP years ago. He tossed an old memo at me across the desk. At first, I thought it was something I'd worked on. But, to my relief, it was a matter I'd never heard of." He paused to think. "It was called *Trinity Hills*, I think. Anyway, he went off on how sloppy Marshall, Lufton associates were; then it was just blah, blah, blah. I actually calmed down for a while, because my work was not involved."

"You figured you'd just let him rant?"

"Exactly—isn't that what *you* do?"

Girardi squirmed at this, but pretended to ignore the question and its implication. He was determined to maintain control of the conversation. "What happened next?"

"He was yelling and then all of a sudden, his face contorted. He grabbed at his head and he fell over. It was awful."

"And you called 911?"

Spencer wrung his hands and cast his gaze toward the window. "Yep—and the rest is history."

"I'm sorry he yelled at you that way," Girardi offered mildly.

"With all due respect, Mike, no, you aren't sorry."

Girardi was once more taken aback. "You're agitated, Spencer, so I'll let that go. Get some rest and I'll see you next week at the office."

Spencer shook his head violently as he wiped the sweat from his brow onto the sleeve of his gown. "Next week? There's no next week for me at Marshall, Lufton. I'm done."

"Don't be hasty, Spencer. You shouldn't do anything you'll regret later on."

"The only thing I'll regret later on is letting someone talk me back into that hellhole. Look, Mike, I know that you don't yell at your people—and I respect that. But you know how it is with some of the partners in that office. It's not just Jack Tremont, either."

"Why didn't you come and talk to me about this?"

"And be pegged as a whiner? No thanks. We're supposed to put up with the crap and keep our mouths shut. But times are changing, Mike, and things are out of hand at Marshall, Lufton. The younger kids coming out of school won't put up with the abuse. You've been losing associates for years. I was warned back as a summer associate that I'd be miserable if I took that offer—but I thought I could handle it. I was wrong."

Girardi wondered who it was that had warned Spencer.

"Just think about it for a few days before making anything final."

"Too late—I've had my moment of clarity, Mike. If I have to, I'll go back to working at *Starbucks*. I'll be a house husband and let Janet go back to work. Whatever. I'm done with you guys. I'll call Cliff next week and have him send me my things and my last paycheck. Don't screw me on the money, either."

At this, a nurse came in to check on Spencer's IV. This was Girardi's chance to escape, and he did not hesitate to take it. He stood and headed for the door.

"I wish you'd think about this, Spence, but I'll respect whatever choice you make."

"Good bye, Mike. And good luck—you're not a bad guy."

Thanks a lot, Girardi thought miserably. As he crossed out into the hallway, he was convinced that Randall Spencer had worked his last day at Marshall, Lufton.

3

Girardi was at his desk by eight the following morning. It was Sunday, and the place was dead quiet. He had four hours to work before Jake picked him up at noon for their much-anticipated first Angels game of the season. Despite all that had occurred, Girardi was not about to cancel their trip to the game. Time with his son was too important. Sipping on a latte, he stared at a text message from Jack Tremont's daughter. Tremont had made it through surgery and survived the night. The doctors were vague about the long-term prognosis.

Girardi's office was large and comfortably furnished. There was no art on the walls or tables, unless you counted the vintage Brooklyn Dodgers posters behind his desk and the 19th century maritime sketches next to the bookcase. When an attorney made partner at Marshall, Lufton, he or she was traditionally given a generous budget with which to furnish a new office. It was a rite of passage of sorts. But when it came his turn, Girardi bucked tradition by simply purchasing some new cabinets, a comfortable guest sofa and a few items of baseball memorabilia. To the surprise and delight of the managing partner, he had given back most of his decorating budget.

He pushed several buttons on his cell phone and looked at his schedule for the week. Leaving aside Jack Tremont's matters, his week looked full but manageable. But there was no telling what might be on Jack's desk. As he leaned over and flipped on his desktop computer, he was startled by the appearance in his doorway of Clifford Conroy, the Marshall, Lufton office manager. The tall and trim Conroy was in his late-fifties. He wore his mostly gray hair neatly clipped, and was dressed immaculately this morning in a brown tweed coat and tan slacks. The usually dapper Girardi felt a bit underdressed in his jeans and red Angels polo.

To Girardi, Conroy had always carried an air of mystery about him. Girardi knew nothing about his professional or personal background, or how Tremont had come to hire him. Of the partners, only Jack Tremont really knew anything about Conroy, who in some respects functioned more as Tremont's personal business manager than as the firm's office manager.

Some around the office joked that Conroy must have spent time with the CIA on account of his secrecy, but this was said in jest. Still, the joking was evidence of the discomfort some felt with Conroy. Since the beginning, Conroy had been Tremont's right-hand man when it came to the business side of the practice, and Girardi had always appreciated the efficient professionalism with which Conroy ran the office. With Conroy in place, Girardi had been allowed to focus almost exclusively on running his cases, and that suited him just fine.

"I didn't hear you come up, Cliff. Thanks for coming in so early on a Sunday."

"Of course, Mike, it's not a problem."

"You flew in last night?" Girardi asked. He considered asking where Conroy had been, but he figured it was none of his business.

Conroy nodded. "Tell me. How can I help you?"

"I need to get a handle on Jack's caseload so I can look after things until . . .," he hesitated.

". . . until he recovers."

"Exactly."

Conroy nodded his understanding. "You'll want his billing records, of course. How far back?"

"To start with, let's say back to January 1."

The cool Conroy adjusted his stylish rimless glasses and jotted a note in a small tan notebook. His movements were fluid—he always seemed to expend just the amount of energy necessary and not a bit more.

Girardi continued. "And I'd like to see the most recent correspondence and pleading files—and the docket sheets."

"I'll email you the billing records and docket sheets—and I'll assemble the paper files in the small conference room."

"Thanks, Cliff."

"I'll get on this right away—it shouldn't be too tough to find most of these things. Plenty of the files will probably be in Randall Spencer's office."

As Conroy stood from his chair, Girardi rubbed his hand uncomfortably on the back of his neck.

"Cliff—before you go, I'd like to mention one more thing."

"Of course." Conroy resumed his seat and placed his hand on the notebook he'd just slipped into his breast pocket, ready to pull it out, but only if need be.

Girardi hesitated, unable to shake the mental image of the distraught Randall Spencer in his hospital gown, waving his arms and tugging on his IV line.

"It's Spence. I want to give you a heads-up that he might quit."

Conroy let go of his notebook. "I'm ahead of you there, Mike. He quit yesterday afternoon. I'm planning to cut his check and clean out his office today. By the time everyone arrives tomorrow morning, there will be no sign that there ever was a Randall Spencer."

In spite of himself, Girardi opened his eyes in some surprise. *This can be a cold, cold business.*

"I see," Girardi replied. "It's too bad."

"Not really. Jack always had his doubts about Spence."

Conroy's tone was matter-of-fact, not cruel. To Conroy, this was the nature of big firm practice. It was survival of the fittest.

"There are plenty more where Spencer came from, Mike. I can call a headhunter. Perhaps you can look at some resumes next week."

Conroy excused himself, promising to have everything gathered for Girardi within the hour. Girardi thanked him and, feeling restless, followed him out into the hallway. Conroy headed off to the left toward the file room and Girardi to the right, in the direction of Jack Tremont's spacious corner office.

When he reached the doorway, he hesitated, not certain he wished to see the scene of Tremont's collapse. Pressing on, he was surprised to find the office looking very much like normal. The chairs in front of the desk had been pushed aside, presumably by the paramedics, and there were a few small pieces of medical debris on the carpet. Otherwise, the office appeared as it always did.

Girardi took a seat at Tremont's desk. Like everything else in Jack Tremont's life, his office was elaborate and multi-layered. Every inch of wall was covered, with tapestries and fine art prints, awards and diplomas. Tremont was the only partner in the entire firm with eighteenth-century French inspired office furniture. A bookcase near the door brimmed over with pictures of Tremont wearing his trademark suspenders and posing with the various politicians, Republican and Democrat, he had supported over the years. His support had always been strategic, not partisan. The photos, going back over a quarter century, documented Tremont's evolution from a lean, ambitious litigator to a perpetually red-faced, overweight senior citizen.

Next to the telephone rested a large, glamorous photo of Celeste taken at a charity ball the prior Christmas. There were several case files and administrative memoranda in neat piles. Girardi's eyes fell on a document lying askew next to a stack of newspapers. He picked it up and saw that it was an internal firm memorandum dated several years earlier. The client was the same one mentioned by Spencer at the hospital, a private, family-owned corporation, CEP. In years past, CEP, named for its Depression-era founders Charles and Ernest Peck, had been one of Tremont's biggest clients, with billings in some years exceeding half a million dollars. At the height of the CEP years, Tremont had brought Girardi in to cover some of the CEP work. But that had been years ago, and Tremont now did almost no work for CEP. And although his partners were curious as to why, Tremont had never explained what had changed. Even Girardi had been kept in the dark. This loss had been a big hit to Tremont's portfolio, and he had yet to recover from it.

This must be the memo Jack tossed at Spence yesterday, he surmised, picking the document up and looking it over. According to the caption, the name of the matter was *Trinity Hills.* The attorney names listed were Tremont and former Marshall, Lufton associate Elizabeth Stowe. Upon a first perusal, Girardi saw nothing unusual, but he decided to make himself a copy and review the memo more carefully later on. In the shock of Tremont's illness, Girardi was striving to make some concrete sense of what was happening. Everyone knew that Tremont had suffered from health problems associated with his weight, and perhaps the stroke was something bound to happen. But why did it happen now, he wondered.

He picked up the case files on Tremont's desk and carried them over to the small conference room. Conroy soon arrived with more documents, and Girardi settled into his task. He looked around for the file on the new CEP matter Spencer had mentioned, *Pope Electronics,* but it was not in the conference room. He asked Conroy about it, and Conroy jotted a short note into his book and promised to track it down. He also asked Conroy to look for the old files on *Trinity Hills.*

Girardi soon lost track of time, and before he knew it, Jake was calling from the parking lot downstairs. It was time to go to the game.

4

They arrived at their seats just after the national anthem. The centerfield fountains were flowing at full force, and a round of fireworks marked the opening of the first regular season Sunday game of the year. The early-April sky was clear, and there was a buzz of anticipation from the sea of red-clad fans in the stands.

On a stop at the snack bar, they had picked up four hot dogs, two pretzels, a bag of peanuts and two large sodas.

"This should get us through the first couple of innings," Girardi laughed as they took their seats on the aisle and placed their cups in the plastic holders.

Handing his father the food, Jake quickly opened his well-worn pad of scoring sheets and began to fill in the day's lineups. Girardi helped Jake with a couple of the names from the opposing team, the Oakland A's, as he wolfed down his first hot dog. *I'll have to swim some extra laps if I eat all this food*, he told himself as he wiped the mustard from his chin and tore open the peanuts. Glancing at Jake and then watching the home team take the field to an appreciative roar from the crowd, he felt some of his tension easing. For a few hours, he would put behind him his worries about Jack Tremont, for there was nothing Girardi loved more than spending an afternoon at the ballpark with his son.

Girardi had grown up a Dodger fan in the era of Tommy Lasorda and the famous infield of Garvey, Lopes, Cey and Russell. His boyhood room had overflowed with Dodger memorabilia, and his boyhood heart had bled Dodger Blue. But since Jake had been a young child, it had always been more convenient to attend Angels games close to home in Orange County. And, in 2002, when the Angels had won the World Series, Jake's tender young baseball soul had been irretrievably captured by Mike Scioscia, Troy Percival and the Rally Monkey. Each year, Girardi purchased a 25-game ticket package. He and Jake usually made it to half of the games together. Jake and other family members took in another quarter or so, with the remainder of the tickets being shared with Girardi's clients and colleagues.

As play began, Jake meticulously kept score pitch by pitch. The elder Girardi had been an avid score-keeper as a child, having been taught the practice by his father and grandfather, who were Brooklyn Dodgers fans. Girardi's family had moved from New York to California within a few years of the Dodgers and they had always joked that this had been because the family could not live without the team, and vice versa.

Mike and Jake said little to one another for the first few innings, paying close attention to the game, which was shaping up to be a surprising early season pitcher's duel.

At the end of the fourth inning, Jake handed his father the scorecard and shook his left hand. "Your turn—I need a rest."

Girardi happily took the pad and mechanical pencil from Jake, whom he sometimes thought hogged the scorecard.

"Mom called this morning," Jake offered quietly as a couple of women in red Angels tank tops climbed over them on the way to the snack bar.

"Can we get you two a beer?" one of them asked Girardi.

"A beer?" Girardi growled, "he's seventeen." The last thing Girardi wanted to do was encourage the pair, whom he remembered from last season as being very chatty with the men in the section. With his height, people were beginning to mistake Jake for an older fellow than he was.

Intent on his subject, Jake ignored the women. "Mom wanted to know if we'd purchased our plane tickets yet for the wedding."

There were a few subjects that brought an immediate ache to Mike Girardi's heart, and that of Jacob's mother was most certainly one of them.

"I forgot about that," Girardi rejoined. "We need to get you a ticket." He pulled out his phone and handed it to Jake. "Why don't you check Southwest and see what you can find?"

"So, you aren't coming?"

"No, son, I don't think so."

"Don't you want to see mom happy?"

At this, Girardi squirmed in his seat and tapped the pencil hard against the scorecard. He could always tell when Jake was repeating his mother's words, and he hated it.

Girardi had married free-spirited Cassidy the year following his law school graduation, when he was a young assistant district attorney. The two had met back when Girardi was a law firm summer intern and Cassidy was waiting tables at a small cafe near his apartment. Jake had come along a few years into the marriage. When Jake was in grade school, Cassidy had taken a two-week trip to visit her family in Montana. But two weeks had extended into two months, and Cassidy eventually sought a formal separation. Cassidy had told Girardi that she would always love him and reminded him that she had never wanted to be the wife of a law firm partner. She'd been happiest when Girardi was a DA and the two of them, and then the three of them, lived in an apartment in Seal Beach. The big house and fancy lifestyle they'd slowly assumed were simply not for her.

She also made clear her desire for Jake to remain in California with his father and paternal relatives, with whom Jake was close. Mike and Jake had been devastated. Things dragged on, and there were several attempts at reconciliation. But eventually, the couple had divorced. Jake had lived continuously with his father, visiting his mom for two months each summer, first in Montana and then in Arizona, where she had at last put down roots.

To Girardi's surprise, Cassidy had recently announced plans to remarry. During their divorce, Cassidy had said repeatedly that she would never marry again because her freedom was too important to her. Girardi did not know what had happened to change her mind. Cassidy's fiancé was an Arizona ranch owner whom Girardi had never met.

Girardi let out a long breath and then hesitated as he recorded the first out of the fifth inning, a fly ball to left field. "F7," he scribbled.

"That ball was pretty well hit," Girardi offered.

"Not really," Jake rejoined, not to be distracted so easily. "What about mom?"

"Jacob, of course I want your mother to be happy," he continued after some thoughtful silence. "But that does not mean that I want to watch her marry another man."

"But she wants you to come. Why won't you?"

"That's between the two of us, Jake. I promise I'll talk to her about it. You should not be the man in the middle here."

"I've always been the man in the middle of you two—and I always will be."

Girardi rubbed the back of his neck as the batter struck out. He recorded a simple "K" in the proper box.

"Sometimes you are in the middle, Jake. But your mom and I should try not to put you there more often than necessary. Now, seriously, I want you to find yourself a ticket. You'll probably want to leave on the Friday, right?"

"Yep. I've got a game on Thursday, so it will have to be Friday."

"Good—get on the Southwest site. We can book it right now."

Jake let out an unsatisfied sigh, but he soon turned his attention to the phone and in no time had located flights to and from Phoenix that suited his needs. Girardi handed Jake back the scorecard temporarily and proceeded to book his son's flights. To his relief, the subject of the wedding was then dropped.

After the seventh inning stretch, with the score tied 2-2, Girardi handed the scorecard back to Jake for good.

"It's about time," the young man joked.

"You had it four innings, I had it for two and a half, minus the time booking your flights. Sounds more than fair to me. Say, I almost forgot. Your Aunt Valerie invited us for dinner tomorrow night. She's making lasagna."

"Sounds good so far . . . ," Jake offered cautiously.

"She wants you to swing by after practice and pick up Jesse and her friends from ballet class."

"I knew there was a catch," Jake rejoined, shaking his head unhappily. Jesse was his cousin, a fifteen-year-old sophomore at a local Catholic high school.

"That's not much of a catch."

"Oh, dad, come on. Have you seen Jesse and her dorky friends lately? They talk a mile a minute and squeal every twenty seconds for no reason. They are immature and embarrassing. I don't want to have anything to do with them."

"You can set a mature example for them, Jacob."

"Do I have to?"

"Yes, you have to. Val is counting on your coming—and she needs help with the driving. I'll head over there after work. I'm not sure what time I'll get there, because I'm driving to San Diego to prep a witness."

"But I'll have homework."

"Val knows—she promises to find you a quiet place to study."

"A quiet place to study in that house? I doubt it."

"Then bring your earphones and keep focused on the lasagna. You'll pick up the girls at 4:30, okay?"

"Okay, but you don't know how big a favor you're asking of me."

The crowd groaned in disappointment. "Another strikeout—mark that down son and pay attention to the game."

When the Angels had been retired in the seventh, the stadium music went up and the home team resumed the field. There was a pitching change announced, which lengthened the break in play. Girardi leaned over toward his son.

"Listen, be patient with Jesse and her friends, okay? With Frankie deployed, you are like her big brother, now."

Jake looked over seriously at his father. Frankie, Girardi's eldest nephew, was currently on his first tour of duty with the Marine Corps.

"Okay, I'll try to be patient. But you don't know how they act when there are no adults around."

"You can be the adult, Jacob."

"I'll try."

The two then turned their attentions back to the game, which ended in a walk-off home run in the bottom of the ninth. Enlivened by the exciting Angels victory, the two left the stadium in high spirits, hoping that this was a sign of things to come for the home team this season.

5

At nine o'clock Monday morning, Girardi met with office manager Cliff Conroy and Huey, Dewey and Louis in the firm's main conference room.

"So, Mike," Cox ventured when they'd all taken seats, "what can you tell us about Jack's files?"

Girardi shifted in his chair and shot Conroy a sideways look. In the office, there had developed over the years two factions among the partners. One faction consisted of the "old guard," Tremont, Girardi, and Richard Dayton, the now semi-retired corporate partner who had come out from New York and opened the Orange County office with Tremont. Dayton was no longer a significant presence. Conroy, although technically not a partner, had in his own way slipped into Dayton's part of the Tremont triumvirate. Huey, Dewey and Louie formed the other faction.

Girardi launched into a cogent description of the majority of Tremont's workload. He went over key deadlines and case staffing, which was a significant stumbling block at present.

"We really need to replace Spence. And it would be great if you could spare some of your corporate associates to help pick up the slack in the mean time."

McDaniel cast Dewey-Martinez an unhappy glance. "Corporate associates don't know litigation, Mike."

This protectiveness hardly surprised Girardi; big firm partners are notoriously territorial. "They can help with some of the discovery and draft simple motions. A little litigation experience is good for a corporate attorney. Can I call Stacy this afternoon? I worked with her during her 2L summer here."

Stacy Franklin was a second year associate from Stanford known for her intelligence and hard work. She was the most promising of the current crop of young corporate associates.

"Not Stacy," McDaniel rejoined firmly. "We can't spare her. You can have Ed."

"But Stacy's hours were low last month. I checked," Girardi said sharply. "She needs the work."

"Not now," Dewey-Martinez interjected. "I have a new real estate deal coming in. She's going to be swamped by the end of the week. Take Ed—he's all we can spare."

"Ed's in Bakersfield for me this week on due diligence," Cox said quietly. Among the three corporate/real estate partners, Cox was the least senior. He routinely complained of being saddled with the fewest resources and weakest associates.

"You guys are going to have to cough up somebody for me," Girardi pressed. "You can decide amongst yourselves and let me know this afternoon."

"Perhaps we can borrow a litigation associate from the New York office," McDaniel offered.

"Maybe—can you call them, Hugh?"

"Sure thing." As managing partner, it was McDaniel's role to interface with the headquarters back East.

"There's one more thing—then I need to hit the road," Girardi continued. "Jack's apparently been working on something for CEP lately."

"I thought the CEP business had dried up," said Dewey-Martinez, who looked up from the e-mail she was typing on her tablet with momentary interest.

"Apparently, it's heating up again. He's working something called *Pope Electronics*. Cliff is looking for the file. The interesting thing is, Jack has also been looking at files from an old CEP matter called *Trinity Hills*. But, so far, Cliff can't find that file in storage, either."

Conroy leaned forward. "We'll find the files," he said in a tone that suggested he hoped Girardi might drop the subject.

"Who was the associate on the old CEP matter?" McDaniel asked.

"Elizabeth Stowe."

"Lizzie Stowe?" Louis Cox ejaculated with red-faced delight. "She's the one who quit on you without saying goodbye, isn't she?"

"That's not exactly it," Girardi rejoined mildly.

"That certainly *is* it," Cox pressed, his small eyes suddenly glowing in recollection. "That was great! Someone finally gave the middle finger to Mike Girardi . . . Mike the nice one, Mike the great boss . . ."

"Shut up, Louis," Dewey-Martinez interjected.

Girardi turned to the office manager. "Cliff, has Beth had any contact with the firm lately? I wouldn't mind talking to her about CEP."

Cox stared at Girardi. "Yeah, and while you're at it you can ask her why she quit on you that way."

The office's most junior partner was apparently not ready to let the matter rest. But if Cox's commentary bothered Girardi, he did not let it show. Over the years, Girardi had developed an outstanding game face.

Meanwhile Conroy shook his head. "We haven't been in touch with her as far as I know."

Dewey-Martinez looked up once more from her tablet to offer a comment. She was almost never without an electronic device in her hand. "I heard she became a nun or something like that."

Each of the men looked at Dewey-Martinez incredulously.

"*Yes*," she affirmed, "that's what I heard."

Doubting that there could be any truth to this rumor, Girardi made a mental note to ask his assistant Janice to see if she could track down some contact information for Elizabeth Stowe.

"I'll keep working on those CEP files," Conroy offered. "We'll find everything. When she's up to it, I'll ask Celeste to check if there is anything at The Plantation."

"That's a good idea. Thanks, Cliff." Girardi turned to the others. "I'll call Jack's clients in the next couple of days and let them know I'll be the contact person for the time being. And, *please* let me have some associate hours this week. That would be a big help. Now, I'd better get going."

Girardi then drove himself to San Diego, where he met for nearly three hours with the CFO of a high tech firm that was going to trial in a serious civil fraud case in the late summer. The CFO was scheduled to be deposed the following week, and Girardi feared he would be a terrible witness. He talked too much, rarely listened, and was convinced he knew more than the lawyers. Girardi and the company's in-house counsel spent their time together peppering the witness with questions, discussing strategy, and reviewing key documents. The trio shook hands wearily in the afternoon, planning to meet early in the office on the day of the deposition.

By the time Girardi reached Interstate 5, the traffic was heavy despite the fact that it was only three o'clock. He put on his Bluetooth and spent the next hour and a half on the phone, speaking with clients and associates back at the office. As he approached the large domed reactors at San Onofre on the threshold of south Orange County, Girardi's assistant Janice rang in. They went over his latest phone messages, and as they were wrapping up, she mentioned Elizabeth Stowe.

"I found that contact information for Lizzy Stowe."

That was quick.

"Okay, I'm ready."

"Her number was listed in the phone book, but there was no address. So I cross-checked the number and it's for a place off of Ortega Highway called Emanuel Prayer and Retreat Center. I called the number, and sure enough the receptionist told me she lives there."

Holy cow, Girardi thought to himself, *maybe Jean was right about Beth after all.* Shaking his head in dismay, he asked her to text him the address and phone number.

"You said to be discreet," she continued, "so I didn't leave any message, but if you talk to her, please say hello. I always liked her."

"I will—thanks, Janice."

Of all the things he might have guessed, it would never have occurred to Girardi that Stowe, or any of his former associates for that matter, would go into a religious line of work. A few minutes later, he plugged the address into his GPS and saw that the exit for the retreat center was only a few miles ahead.

That's a weird coincidence, Girardi thought, wondering if he ought to seize the moment and look for Stowe. With Jack Tremont ailing and the CEP files missing, she might be his best chance to learn something quickly about the old *Trinity Hills* matter. Why would Tremont get worked up over a case that had ended years before? The whole thing gave Girardi a bad feeling.

At the same time, Girardi had mixed feelings about seeing Elizabeth Stowe. She had departed the firm under unusual circumstances, leaving while Girardi was out of the country on vacation and never saying good-bye to him, despite the fact that they'd worked closely together for four years. Her loss had been a setback, professionally and personally, for he had respected her ability and had gone out of his way to be a mentor. He'd seen the makings of a fine attorney in her—perhaps even a partner some-day. But she'd essentially vanished, and he'd never heard from her again.

Girardi weighed his options, and as his BMW inched along the free-way at a snail's pace, he decided he should take the detour. *I'm not getting anywhere in this mess,* he thought to himself. *I may as well give it a shot. What is there to lose?*

But then, as he flipped on his blinker to change lanes to the right, he reconsidered. Stowe might not appreciate him showing up out the blue after all this time. Watching a large SUV jam into the spot he'd planned on taking, he turned off his signal, remained in the so-called fast lane, and then dialed the number for the Emmanuel Center and asked for Stowe.

"May I ask who's calling?" asked a pleasant elderly voice.

"Mike Girardi."

"And what is this regarding?"

"I'm a former colleague of Ms. Stowe. I'm calling to let her know that another former colleague is gravely ill."

"I'm sorry—do you mind repeating that?"

Girardi obliged her, wondering if the old woman was hard of hearing. "I'll see if I can find her—she may be out in the garden. Just a minute." "Thank you."

She put down the phone with a thud, and Girardi thought he could hear voices in the background. Then, nothing—the line was so quiet that he almost suspected they'd lost their connection. But he hung in there, endeavoring to be patient and wondering what was accounting for the delay. Could they simply not find Stowe, or was she perhaps refusing to speak with him?

Girardi was about to hang up when a familiar voice at last came on the line.

"This is Elizabeth Stowe."

It was strange to suddenly hear the pleasant voice that had been part of his daily routine for years.

"Beth, hi, it's Mike Girardi," he began, his own voice cracking. "How are you? It's been a long time."

There was silence on the other end for some time. "I didn't know it was you calling. Ida said she thought it was someone from the insurance company."

Insurance Company? How did they get that from what I said?

"Nope, it's me, Mike. Listen, I'm sorry to call like this out the blue, but I wanted to let you know that Jack Tremont had a stroke on Saturday."

"I'm sorry to hear that," Stowe replied without emotion. "What happened?"

Girardi had not spoken to anyone outside the firm about the details of Tremont's stroke or his interview with Randall Spencer. Suddenly eager to unburden himself, he told Stowe the story. She listened without interrupting him.

"Did you know Spence?" he asked at last after sharing the scene in the hospital room.

"Of course I knew Spence." Girardi detected hint of exasperation in her tone. "I was his mentor when he was a summer associate and we overlapped for at least a year. I helped you train him. I always wondered if he really wanted to be a big firm lawyer."

"Well, he quit right then and there in the hospital."

"Can you blame him?"

Girardi drew a deep breath and then spoke with meaning, recalling Stowe's own abrupt departure. "I don't like it when anyone makes a precipitous career decision—especially without seeking input from more experienced attorneys and mentors."

"Was Spence working primarily for Jack?" she asked knowingly.

"Maybe two-thirds of his workload was on Jack's cases, one-third on mine."

"You know how hard Jack can be on people. Are you really surprised? In the long run, Spence will be the better for making a clean break of it."

"Maybe . . ."

"Tell me," she ventured, her tone uncertain, "why did you call to tell me this? We haven't spoken in a long time."

That's not my fault, Girardi thought as he considered which tack to take.

"It seems that Jack has resurrected an old CEP matter lately. He was talking about it with Spence when he collapsed. It might sound odd, but I'm trying to figure out if something with CEP was bothering Jack enough to make him sick."

"Jack did tons of work for CEP over the years, and their cases were always stressful for one reason or another. It wouldn't surprise me if he had at least an ulcer or two thanks to CEP. Which matter are you talking about?"

"*Trinity Hills*—do you remember it?"

Stowe hesitated. "I'm sorry, Mike. I've changed my life completely since leaving the firm. I have no interest in recalling anything from that period."

During the time Stowe was referring to, she and Girardi had worked closely, and in spite of his motto that business was business, he felt a sting at these words. But still, there was information he needed, so he pressed on, hoping to appeal to her sympathy.

"To tell you the truth, I'm concerned about taking on all of Jack's work on top of my own. And my nose tells me that something's not right about that CEP work; some of the files aren't where they should be in the office." He paused a moment for effect. "And the worst of it is, I don't have anyone like you anymore that I can rely on. With Jack and Spence gone, everything's on me."

"That's too bad," she said evenly, "but I can't help you."

"Did you take any case files with you when you left Marshall, Lufton?"

"Case files? Are you kidding? Cliff barely let me have the box of Kleenex from my desk when I left."

Girardi nodded knowingly. *That sounds like Cliff.*

"No, I meant personal chron files."

A chron file was a compilation of correspondence and other work of an attorney, usually kept in chronological order.

"I tried to maintain an electronic chron over the years, but it was quite spotty. It depended upon who my assistant was at the time. I did take some electronic files with me when I left the firm, but not many."

"Could you look to see if there's anything on *Trinity Hills*?"

"There probably isn't anything that would help you. I told you, I put everything behind me when I left Marshall, Lufton."

Obviously, Girardi thought glumly to himself as the conversation came to a halt. It seemed plain that she was not interested in helping him. He had no idea what to say next.

"So, what are you up to these days?" he ventured, trying but failing to sound casual. "Do you work at the Emmanuel Center?"

He immediately regretted offering such lame questions.

"I live and work here," she replied as Girardi heard what sounded like a gong in the background. "I'm sorry, but I have to go. Evening prayers are about to start. I can't be late. Good luck with everything—I'm sorry I can't help you."

"If you ever come across anything on *Trinity Hills*, could you give me a call?"

"I really must hang up. Goodbye, Mike."

■ ■ ■

Later that evening, Mike Girardi sat alone with his sister Valerie at the corner table in her spacious kitchen. Stuart Egan, Mike's college roommate and Val's husband of more than twenty years, was a successful software engineer who ran his own firm in Irvine.

The Egan family had moved into the 3,000-plus square-foot home nearly ten years earlier, when development in Irvine had been going strong. For Val and Stu, who had each grown up in modest circumstances, this was their dream house. The place had five bedrooms, four baths, a great room and a state-of-the-art kitchen. Val loved to cook, and the kitchen and attached dining room were the focal points of the house.

While Mike and Val huddled in the kitchen, the others were distributed throughout various room upstairs doing homework and watching a baseball game.

"Val, this lasagna is delicious," he offered gratefully as he took a long sip of beer.

"Thanks, Mikey," she replied, fingering her wine glass. "That's my mission—making the world a better place through Italian cooking."

"Your mission is a lot more than that," he replied supportively, "but your cooking is superb."

Val gave a dismissive wave of the hand, but Girardi could see from her smile that the compliment had its intended effect. She was wearing a yellow retro *Go Go's* tank top and denim shorts—Val was an aficionado of all things '80s, the decade of her youth. With her thick dark hair, toned body and tanned skin, Valerie Egan was a striking woman, even when dressed casually.

"You look tired," she ventured, peering into his face in concern.

"I am tired—and worried."

He proceeded to share an abridged version of the events of the past three days.

"I'm going to be swamped with work," he concluded. "And there's no telling when things will slow down. Can I get you to help me look after Jake?"

"You know I love to have Jake around—he's my unofficial fourth child. But he's older now, and doesn't want to be looked after anymore."

"I know—but he should be with family after school."

"It's baseball season. There's no time for Jake to get into trouble, even if he were inclined to it—which he isn't. Are you coming to his game tomorrow?"

"Are *you*?" he countered.

"Yes. I'll need to juggle some of the driving, but I should be there for most of it. Tommy has team photos, but I think he'll be done early. I spend my life constantly driving around in the same ten-mile radius—it's nuts."

Girardi was relieved to hear that Val was planning to attend the game. He would make every effort to be there, but with things in such an uncertain state at work, he could not be sure.

Val spooned the last of the lasagna onto his plate and leaned forward confidentially. "I think Jake's having trouble with a girl. He told me he doesn't understand how women think."

"Did he give you any details about her?" he asked.

"Of course not."

"Names?"

"Nope."

Girardi combed his memory. "He mentioned someone named Morgan a few weeks ago; she's a vegan."

"Cheeseburger Jake and a vegan?" Val laughed.

"He swears they're just friends."

Val let out a long, wistful sigh. "I remember being just friends . . ."

Girardi laughed. "Those were the four worst words in high school, 'let's just be friends.'"

"I know what you mean."

"So, what wisdom did you give my son on the secret workings of the female mind?"

"Nothing that seemed to satisfy him," she replied with disappointment. "I want to be here for the kids, but some days I feel like I don't have anything relevant to say to them."

Girardi nodded. "It's been so long since we were their age—we think we remember what it's like, but the details are fuzzy. It's probably just as well."

"I kind of liked high school."

"Sure, because you were popular."

"Me? Popular?" Val laughed. "I wish."

"You had a ton of friends."

"In my own way, I was like Jesse. I had lots of friends, but we were the goof-balls, not the cool ones. Always a little bit on the outside. The difference is, Jesse and her friends are A students."

"You could have been an A student if you'd applied yourself, Val."

"You don't think Jesse gets her intelligence just from her father?"

"From Stu? Nope."

"Oh, Mikey, I hated to study. I don't even know how I passed my classes. So far, Jesse doesn't seem to be boy-crazy. And she's not in a big hurry to grow up."

"Good."

"Very good," Val replied, wrapping her knuckles on the oak table.

"How's everything else?" he asked as he finished his third helping. He wanted to ask about Frankie and his deployment, but he hesitated to inquire directly.

"My god, you were starved."

"I skipped lunch."

"You need to take care of yourself, Mikey."

"I will—so tell me, how are things? Any word from Frankie?"

At this, Val's eyes welled up. "I had an email from him last night. He can't even tell me where he is—it's nuts. He says not to worry because he's doing just fine—and that he loves me and his dad and everyone in the family except for Jesse. He's always on her like that—she loves it." Now, her voice choked. "Don't worry? Who is he kidding? I haven't had a decent night's sleep since he left—and I won't until he's back home. It's torture."

"You've got to try and let go a little bit, Val. He's well-trained, and he has excellent commanders. And, it's not as bad over there now."

These lawyerly arguments did little to console the frightened mother who, in nearly twenty years of parenthood, had never been away from her children for more than a few nights at a stretch. That was before Frankie's deployment.

"It all goes back to that damned war—and that president *you* voted for who got us into it to begin with."

Girardi took a patient breath, not interested in debating politics. "Young guys get restless, Val. I've never seen Frankie so motivated—I think this is good for him."

"It's good for him as long as he doesn't come home in a box."

Girardi opened his eyes wide at his sister's bluntness. Val always could get to the heart of the matter. He thought about reviewing with her the steep decline in the casualty figures he'd meticulously studied since Frankie's enlistment. These numbers brought him solace, but he knew it would not be so for Val.

Gathering herself, Val carried the dirty dishes over to the sink and began to rinse them.

"Do you want another beer?"

"No, thanks," he replied, taking the rinsed dishes from her and finding places for them in the full dishwasher.

Val deposited the soap and flipped on the machine.

"Listen, Mikey. I'll help you keep an eye on Jake. Don't worry—he's such a good boy. And sensitive—like his father."

Val hugged Girardi tightly and rested her head on his chest. "Thanks for talking to me," she continued. "I'm a little emotional lately, and I don't want to unload too much on Stu. He's dealing with Frankie's deployment, too."

"No problem—thanks for the lasagna."

"I'll see you at the game tomorrow, right?"

"Hopefully. I'll call you."

And after finding Jake, Girardi and his son headed home. When they arrived, they sat down to watch the rest of the Angels game. The Girardi home was neat and comfortably furnished. It had been built forty years earlier, before the McMansions of more-recent decades. By Orange County standards, the place was relatively small, but for Jake and Mike, there was plenty of room.

When the game was over, Jake headed upstairs as Girardi decided to bite the bullet and call his former wife.

"Hi Cass, it's Mike," Girardi began, trying to summon a cheerfulness he did not feel.

There was music in the background and hesitation on the other end. "I can't really talk now—I'm out with friends. Call me tomorrow."

Girardi was eager to get this particular conversation over with, and would not be put off. "That's okay, I won't keep you. I just wanted to let you know that we bought Jake's ticket for the wedding."

Another hesitation. "You're not coming, then?"

"No."

"What's this about, Mike? You know I want you to be here."

Girardi drew a deep breath and weighed his words. "You know I wish you all the best, but I can't come and watch you marry someone else. Jake will be there for you, Cass, and that's what matters most."

"I think you're being selfish."

Selfish? Clearly, she was hoping to get a rise out of him. But, tired as he was, he held his calm.

"Maybe so, but I've made my decision. You should get back to your friends. Have a good evening."

At this, Cassidy clicked off the line without another word.

6

On Thursday morning, Reverend Susan Mountjoy arrived early at her office daunted by the workday ahead. Mountjoy was the rector of St. Mark's Episcopal Church, a small, half-century old parish situated in the shadows of the Newport Beach office tower where Mike Girardi worked. Like her church, the locally-born and raised Mountjoy would soon mark her fiftieth year. When interviewing for the job years earlier, she had taken this coincidence as a sign that she was meant to be at St. Mark's.

The prior evening, she had been at the church late for Wednesday Evensong. So-called alternative worship was all the rage now in the diocese, and St. Mark's had received a small grant to hire musicians for this special evening service. The idea, of course, had been to attract new members. But the reality was that Evensong was attended mostly by a handful of her most loyal Sunday worshippers. A few newcomers attended from time to time and some of them eventually became regular members of the congregation, but this was unusual.

This morning, her full calendar was to begin with a young couple who wanted the Reverend to marry them at St. Mark's in the fall. Another appointment was with the president of the Women's Guild, who had pushed her way onto Mountjoy's calendar to go over summer programs. A third meeting was with the parish's outside accountant, who would review with her the church's finances. For years now, Mountjoy had buried more parishioners than she'd baptized, and the financial report for this aging congregation was not likely to be encouraging.

Back when she had been a young seminary student, Mountjoy had naively believed that the job of a parish priest was to preach the gospel of Jesus Christ. And, of course, it was. But as rector of a busy parish, Mountjoy was as much as anything an administrator, and her daily routine was often dishearteningly disconnected from her spiritual core.

A bright spot on her morning calendar was her twice-monthly appointment with Elizabeth Stowe. Mountjoy had met Stowe nearly two years earlier, when out of the blue, the young woman had appeared at the Evensong service. From her dress, Mountjoy had assumed correctly that she was a professional from the office tower nearby. That evening, Stowe had seemed distracted and jumpy when Mountjoy had introduced herself at the end of the service. These traits were not uncommon in the professional set, however, and so they had not particularly surprised the Reverend. One thing, however, had struck Mountjoy as odd. Along with a designer briefcase, Stowe had been carrying two overstuffed, reusable Wal Mart shopping bags.

After a brief conversation, Mountjoy had given Stowe her business card and encouraged her to return to St. Mark's. In her business, Mountjoy routinely had such conversations, and most often she never saw the visitor again. She presumed that it would be the same with Stowe, but she could not have been more mistaken.

A few months after their first meeting, Stowe had contacted Mountjoy for an appointment. Over tea one afternoon in the St. Mark's courtyard, she had shared some of her story. Stowe had attended an Episcopal church with her mother as a child, but had drifted away from her faith in college and hadn't attended church regularly since that time. She also revealed that she had quit her law firm job and was in the process of finding a new career for herself. Although Mountjoy had dropped more than one hint, Stowe declined to provide specific details of her departure from Marshall, Lufton.

"It was all a terrible mistake," was all that Stowe would say. "I should never have gone to law school in the first place."

"Why did you go?"

"Like so many others, I went by default. I wanted a good career and didn't know what else to do with myself."

"Do you know what you'll do next?"

"I haven't a clue."

To Mountjoy's delight, Stowe soon began attending Sunday services. Then, she participated in a newcomers' bible-study group. Stowe's interest in the faith had continued to grow and deepen, and she was clearly benefitting from her return to the church. She embarked upon a serious course of self-study under Mountjoy's guidance, reading the Bible and many of the religious and spiritual classics. For Mountjoy, it was heartening, and challenging, to guide this restless, searching soul. The questions of faith Stowe presented were sometimes the very ones Mountjoy struggled with herself, and so both women benefitted from their time together.

Through this process, Mountjoy had come to believe that Stowe might have the makings of a minister herself, but despite her encouragement in this direction, Stowe had yet to embrace the idea of attending the seminary. She had, however, agreed at Mountjoy's suggestion to spend a year as a lay associate at the Emmanuel Center, where Reverend Mountjoy was chair of the Board of Overseers. The center was run by four elderly nuns from a small Episcopal order based in the Midwest. It seemed win/win. Through their talks, Mountjoy knew that Stowe desired an environment where she might do some intensive personal and spiritual discernment. At the same time, the center badly needed someone to go through the finances. A formal outside accountant would have cost money and likely caused suspicion and distrust among the sisters. Although Stowe was not a trained accountant, she had gained enough financial knowledge in her legal practice to take on the project.

Stowe arrived a few minutes early for her meeting, just as Mountjoy was wrapping up with the St. Mark's accountant. The Reverend greeted Stowe with a hug, and the two decided to have their meeting over tea out in the parish garden.

"So, I take it that Sister Agnes let you out of her sight so that you could come and see me?" Mountjoy joked wryly as they took their seats a short time later.

"Yes, but she made me promise also to do some shopping for her on the way back."

"So that the trip wouldn't be a total waste?"

"Oh no, Agnes understands that it does me good to come and see you. But she seems happiest when we're all at the center together."

Mountjoy nodded her understanding and the two went on to share a few minutes of small talk. The Reverend was tall and large-framed, with dark brown chin-length hair, brown eyes and pale, clear skin. She had a commanding presence and a cultured charm that drew people to her. She dressed well, but conservatively, in keeping with her position. Today she wore a charcoal suit and black clerical shirt. As a member of the clergy, she labored to suppress all personal vanity. Her one indulgence in this regard was that she had a few years earlier begun to dye her still-lustrous hair to cover the encroaching patches of gray. Although she never said a thing about it, Mountjoy had always been proud of her hair, which she kept cut and well-styled.

"So, tell me Elizabeth, how is everything at the center?"

"Things are fine," Stowe replied carefully, "the same as always."

Mountjoy's mind was so full of everything happening at St. Mark's that she did not catch Stowe's hesitation.

"Good."

"How are *you*, Susan? When we spoke on the phone you sounded very busy."

"I'm swamped, and there's no end in sight."

"What's happening with the concert?" Stowe asked, recalling prior mention of plans for a fundraiser to benefit the St. Mark's music program.

"It's all arranged. The principal violinist from the symphony has agreed to play a full concert here. It's a big coup to get someone so talented. I'm delighted."

"You should be."

"Naturally, though, I'm worried that no one will show up."

"Why do you say that?"

"Classical music is not to everyone's taste these days, you know."

Stowe smiled with encouragement. "I think the place will be packed."

"I hope you and the sisters will come."

"I'll mention it to them. When is it?"

"The first weekend in May."

"I'll be there—we'll see about the sisters. They don't travel much these days, and the van is in terrible shape."

"We're going to need all hands on deck to make the evening a success."

Stowe looked surprised. "You always seem to have plenty of volunteers."

"I used to have more than I do now. Some of the ladies who used to do everything for the church are in poor health and just can't do as much as they used to. They've volunteered in the church for decades and it's a real loss not to have them. These days, younger women just can't do it—they work and have kids to take care of." She let out a long sigh. "I worry about our future. The average age in this parish is around 60."

Stowe nodded. "Come to think of it, I was the youngest person in the new member bible study."

Mountjoy's mind bounced between subjects. "I saw the accountant today, and Evensong may have to go."

"Not Evensong! That's such a lovely service—we met at Evensong."

"I know. I wish we'd gained more members like you from that service, Elizabeth. But something is going to have to give. I'm praying that this benefit concert will bring in some extra revenue so that I can keep paying my musicians."

"I'm certain it will," Stowe offered optimistically.

Mountjoy's mind moved on to a related subject. "Speaking of money, how do the center's finances look?"

"Honestly—we're struggling."

At this, Mountjoy's heart fell. All she needed was more bad financial news.

"It has taken me a long time to just straighten out the books," Stowe explained. "Sister Margaret was probably a wonderful nun, but she had no business being a bookkeeper, especially toward the end before she died."

Stowe continued. "I still don't think Agnes fully understands why you placed me with her. She thinks it was a lucky coincidence that I can keep the books."

"Agnes is a good and simple woman. For the time being, I'd like her to focus on your spiritual needs and nothing more."

"But if she thinks we're pulling a fast one, she'll be hurt. It doesn't seem right to me." Although Stowe frequently joked about being under the dominion of Sister Agnes, there was genuine concern in her voice now. In her time at the center, Stowe had formed an attachment to the nuns and was quite loyal to them.

"We need to get a crystal clear picture of the center's finances," Mountjoy rejoined firmly. "Then, we can go to the diocese and ask for some money when we know how much to ask for."

As she said this, the rector hesitated. In these difficult financial times, there was no guarantee that the diocese would help even if they wished to.

"*However,*" Mountjoy continued, "we must be realistic. If the situation becomes too dire, the sisters might be forced to close the center and return to the order's home base in Minnesota. Lots of the orders are consolidating these days, you know."

"They're too old to go back to the cold in Minnesota," Stowe offered sympathetically. "Two of them have arthritis, and another has a bad heart."

Mountjoy ignored this. "For the time being," she said, assuming an officious tone, "will you start putting together a formal financial report?"

They were now far from the intellectual and spiritual matters that she most enjoyed discussing with Stowe, but with all that was on her mind, Mountjoy barely noticed. These days, the subject of money was often more present to her than the gospels.

"I can start on a report," Stowe offered. "But it will take me a while to finish. We have a retreat group coming this weekend, so I can't start until next week."

"That's fine, but the sooner we have the report, the sooner we can take some action. I want to discuss this at the next board meeting."

They were soon interrupted by the parish administrator, Miss Clemens. There was an urgent call from Doris Weeks—her husband Elmer was at Hope Hospital. Might the Reverend be persuaded to come over and pray with her?

Mountjoy decided to go to the hospital, asking the office manager to reschedule her other appointments. Doris and Elmer had been married at St. Mark's only a few years after it opened, and had loyally attended for 45 years since. Mountjoy turned to Stowe and apologized for cutting the meeting short.

"I really should go over and see them. Doris is probably frantic. Next time we'll meet for twice as long," she promised.

"Of course you should go—I understand."

As the two dashed back toward Mountjoy's office, Stowe posed a question. "Do you know anything about personal rules?"

With her mind so full of other matters, Mountjoy didn't have much of an answer for her.

"Not really—some religious orders require their novices to write rules for themselves before they take holy vows. It's like a statement of values, I think. Why do you ask?"

"Agnes wants me to write a rule for myself, and I'm not sure where to begin."

Mountjoy let out a long sigh, for she did not always understand or agree with the sister's methods. When she reached her office, Mountjoy headed straight for her overflowing bookshelves. Stowe, who was also a book lover, sometimes teased her mentor that the entire history of Christendom was contained on her shelves.

Mountjoy went through her collection, pulling out various volumes, perusing the tables of contents and then replacing them in frustration. Glancing at her watch, she thought of poor Doris and knew she needed to leave. At last, she settled upon two of the very first volumes she'd considered.

"These two are about monastic orders," she explained, "and I'm almost certain they at least mention personal rules. I'm not sure how helpful they'll be, but it's a start. If we don't find anything here, we can order some books online. Maybe we could do some Adult Education in the parish on the subject of personal rules; perhaps Agnes would come and make a presentation."

Then, she handed over the books and hugged Stowe goodbye.

"Thank you, Susan."

"God's peace to you. And please send the sisters my best wishes."

And with a wave, Mountjoy headed for the parking lot.

7

Girardi sat outside in the plaza courtyard directly below his office tower. It was a gorgeous day, and as he soaked in the sun, he fiddled absently with the buttons on his phone. It was only Thursday, but he was already worn out and frustrated by the state of things in the office. He was managing double the case load now without his mid-level associate Randall Spencer. As was too often the case, Girardi was appreciating Spencer's contribution much more now that he was gone. To Girardi's frustration, the CEP files still had not been located.

He'd caught only the last two innings of Jake's Tuesday game, and prospects were dim for him making any of this afternoon's contest, which was an away game up in north county. On the bright side, the bus ride would keep Jake occupied until around eight o'clock.

There had been some moderate good news. Jack Tremont had regained consciousness—at least in a manner of speaking. Girardi had gone to see him the prior afternoon, hoping that his mentor might be well enough to talk some business. Perhaps Tremont would explain what it was that had gotten him so worked up prior to his collapse. Was there a problem with CEP or another firm client? If so, Girardi and his partners needed to know about it.

But things at the hospital were not as he'd hoped. Although Tremont's eyes were open and he was breathing on his own, he was still heavily medicated and looked exhausted. There was a gash on the side of his head, and he supposed that Tremont must have hit his head when collapsing in his office. After a brief period of optimism, the sight of Tremont had dashed Girardi's hopes. Girardi now felt completely alone.

It was the beginning of the lunch hour, and a few parties were taking seats at surrounding tables. As he sat, sunglasses propped jauntily atop his head, two young women smiled at Girardi and the bolder of the pair invited him to join them at their nearby table. He politely declined and decided it was time to look over the resumes of lateral associates gathered by Cliff Conroy. As he scrolled through the resumes on his phone, he was approached from behind.

"You're here already?" said Elizabeth Stowe, offering no other greeting. "Didn't we say noon?"

"We did," Girardi said, getting quickly to his feet. "I came down a little early—I needed to get out of the office."

The two stood looking at one another. After two years apart, Girardi now saw his old associate with fresh eyes. She was petite, with golden brown hair, standing just above five feet. This morning she wore a simple blue sundress under a while cardigan. Back at the firm, she'd dressed expensively and her hair had been short. Now, her look was much more casual, and her hair was longer, falling almost to her shoulders. He also thought she'd gained some weight, a change Girardi quickly decided was flattering, for she'd been quite thin in her practice days. *She looks good*, he thought fleetingly as he pushed his mind to the business at hand.

"Thanks for calling me, Beth. I appreciate it."

Stowe reached into her bag. "Well, since I was coming down here today anyway for an appointment at St. Mark's, I decided to nose around my old electronic files. It turns out that I did have some documents on a memory stick on the *Trinity Hills* matter."

She handed him an envelope containing a stack perhaps an inch thick. "Here you go."

"That's great. What's in here?"

"I don't know."

Girardi's face fell. He'd hope that she might have some story to tell him about *Trinity Hills*.

"I can tell you generally what's there," she clarified, "some memos, correspondence, the usual stuff. These documents are from the early months of the case—that's when I was the most involved. Jack was lead counsel, of course, so he communicated most closely with the in-house attorneys. But I can tell you that *Trinity Hills* involved an expensive audit of a construction contract between CEP and the government."

"How expensive?"

"I'm not sure precisely—many millions."

"Do you recall the specific allegations?"

"Not really." Stowe shook her head. "I worked on lots of audits for Jack in those days."

Girardi nodded his understanding. "Have you heard of a matter called *Pope Electronics*?"

"No."

"Okay, well, I appreciate you tracking these down for me."

He smiled at her and then paused. They were both still standing, and it felt to Girardi as if Stowe might dash off at any moment.

"Do you have time for lunch? *Emilio's* is right over there," he said, pointing to an Italian restaurant popular with the Marshall, Lufton crowd.

"I don't have time for a sit-down meal."

Of course not, he thought to himself with a sigh. *Lots to do at the convent, I suppose.*

Though he felt mixed emotions, Girardi was happy to see Beth Stowe. He hated to see her go so quickly.

"How about a sandwich at *The Carvery*?"

Back when Stowe was at Marshall, Lufton, the pair had frequently shared *Carvery* sandwiches during their working lunches together.

She surprised him with a smile—her first of the conversation. *"The Carvery*? I miss that place."

Taking this as assent, Girardi took a few steps toward the stand. "The food is as good as ever—come on, it's my treat."

They walked together to the outdoor stand that boasted the best ham and roast beef sandwiches in Newport. The pair found a table off away from the others.

He sat looking at her as she dove into her sandwich. "The way our conversation went the other day, I didn't think I'd ever hear from you again," he offered honestly. "What changed your mind?"

She dabbed her lips with her napkin. "In thinking over what you'd told me, I realized that you must be under a lot of pressure right now with Jack in the hospital. I spoke to our superior, Sister Agnes, and she told me that I should help you if I could."

Thanks, Agnes.

"So," she continued, "I started looking at my files, and what I quickly concluded was that you shouldn't need to do anything on *Trinity Hills* while Jack is away."

"Why not?"

"Marshall, Lufton was hired to help CEP submit written responses to the government's audit allegations. That work was done years ago. There's a strong chance the matter has settled already. In-house counsel probably handled that. For the firm, the matter should be closed."

This sounded reasonable, but Girardi wasn't ready to put the matter aside. Right now, he was in charge of all the litigation in the office and he and didn't like being in the dark on *Trinity Hills*. He shifted around in his seat and took a bite of his sandwich. After he'd swallowed, he made an initial pitch, which he expected to be rejected.

"Is there any way I could pay you just to read these documents and write me a memo summarizing them? With your background on the case, you'd do a far better job than anyone else."

"No thanks, Mike," she replied carefully, her tone frank but respectful. "I'm not interested in legal work anymore."

He took another bite as the wheels continued to turn. "I can imagine," he ventured, "that a nun-in-training . . . or whatever you are, might have trouble accepting an outside job for pay. Am I right?"

Stowe hesitated and folded her arms uncomfortably. Full of his own thoughts, Girardi failed to read Stowe's body language. Taking her lack of a response as a yes, he pressed on.

"I might also imagine, however, that the center takes donations. It does, am I right?"

"This feels a little like a cross-examination with the yes-or-no questions, but yes, of course, we take donations."

"Then, I'd like to propose that you analyze the documents and I'll pay you in the form of a donation to the center. How does three hundred an hour sound?"

She shook her head at him in disbelief.

"Three-fifty? Gee, Beth, I didn't think you'd drive a hard bargain on the money."

"It's not that," she said quietly. "You shouldn't waste the money."

Despite this resistance, Girardi still believed that she might agree to help him.

"If you take on the project, you can help an old colleague—and make some money for a good cause. Why pass that up?"

"Because," she began to gesture with her fingers, "*one*, I'm not a lawyer anymore, and *two*, because you shouldn't waste your time worrying about *Trinity Hills*. As I said, those audit responses were submitted years ago. Why waste time and money on something like this when you obviously have more pressing matters to worry about?"

Girardi was a little surprised by Stowe's forcefulness. He was pursuing *Trinity Hills* on a hunch, but perhaps she was right—he might be worrying about it for nothing. And there was no doubt that he was swamped with other cases that needed his attention. Perhaps this was a dead end and he should just let it go. But if he did, he likely wouldn't see Stowe again.

Today's lunch reminded of the good old days when Stowe had been his primary associate at the firm. At least, they had been the good old days for him. A part of him wanted to ask her why she'd left Marshall, Lufton so abruptly, but he held back. They were having an enjoyable lunch and he did not want to spoil the mood. They settled into a thoughtful quiet as they finished their sandwiches.

"How is your son doing?" Stowe asked after some time.

Girardi, who had been deep in thought, found the shift in subject a bit jarring at first, but he went with the flow.

"Jake is good. He just turned seventeen. I gave him the truck we'd been restoring together. *That* was a gift that went over very well—he was dying to have his own wheels. He's still playing baseball, and hoping to play in college."

"Seventeen?" she repeated. "Wow, time really does fly. I remember when you'd bring him to the office on the weekend and he'd play video games on the computer."

Girardi chuckled at this and went on to say more about Jake's baseball and about their household routine. There came a natural break in the conversation. Stowe gathered the trash and threw it away, depositing the plastic trays in a special slot above the bin.

"I should be getting back," she said. "I need to swing by Costco. We have visitors coming for retreat tomorrow. It's a youth group from San Diego. Retreat weekends are always crazy."

"I should get back, too. Where are you parked?"

"I parked at St. Mark's—it's an easy walk from here."

Girardi had passed the church numerous times but had never been inside. He extended the envelope to Stowe. "Will you write me that memo, Beth? Please? I hate being in charge of Jack's cases and not knowing anything about *Trinity Hills*. You may be absolutely right that there's nothing to this, but it would ease my mind to have a memo from you. That way, if anything did come up, I'd know what I was talking about. Without Jack, I'm feeling all alone up there."

"If you're lonely, you should invite Mona to come in and do some typing," Stowe rejoined in a quick, sour tone. "She'll cheer you up."

Always with Mona, he sighed, wondering why in the world Stowe would bring up his former girlfriend out of the blue this way. Although Girardi hated to talk about his personal life, he decided to set the record straight.

"I broke up with Mona a couple of years ago, right around the time you left the firm, as a matter of fact."

Stowe's eyes grew large at this revelation. "You did?"

His thoughts moving quickly, Girardi began to wonder what had happened with Stowe's old boyfriend, an investment banker named Troy. Girardi had never really cared for Troy, a cocky Ivy League business school graduate. At one time, it had appeared to Girardi that the pair was quite serious. Despite his curiosity, Girardi did not ask about Troy.

"Will you write the memo? Your help would mean something to me."

"You are making it hard to say no."

"Then don't."

She took the envelope, but then handed it back to him. She fiddled with her hair for a moment or two and then rooted around her purse for her keys.

"You can keep those—I printed a set for myself."

She's still a lawyer, Girardi smiled to himself.

"I'll write you that memo," she continued, still looking into her purse and avoiding eye contact. "The center can certainly use the money. But I can't promise to finish immediately—we're busy at the center. I'm the only full-timer around the place under 65, you know."

"That's fine," Girardi replied. Although he was anxious to receive her analysis, he did not want to get into a tussle over the timeline. "Let's touch base sometime next week."

She nodded. "Alright—I guess I'll talk to you then." She extended her hand awkwardly, and he shook it. "Bye, Mike."

"Goodbye, Beth. Good luck with that retreat group."

8

Late the following afternoon, Mike and Jake found themselves stuck in Friday traffic southbound on Pacific Coast Highway. They were dressed in tuxedos, headed for a political fundraiser at the Ritz-Carlton in Laguna Niguel. The candidate? Jean Dewey-Martinez's husband, Jaime.

"I can't believe you talked me into this, dad. I feel like an idiot in this rental tuxedo. My coat sleeves are way too short."

Girardi, who was already annoyed with his son, felt little sympathy. "Coming along with your dear old dad was the least you could do, Jacob, after you took it upon yourself last night to stay out until past eleven on a school night without calling me."

"We just went for pizza to celebrate our win. Then Jeff's parents let us play video games on their huge flat screen. We lost track of time. Besides, I knew you'd be working."

"I was working at home, waiting for you. You know to be in by ten on a school night."

Girardi decided to say no more on the subject, at least for the time being. There was plenty more on his mind. He had two associates back at the office working busily, and he would have preferred to stay with them. But, in a meeting the prior afternoon, Cliff Conroy had strongly urged Girardi to take Jack Tremont's place at the event.

"Several of Jack's clients will be there," Conroy had said. "Jack generously purchased two tables on his own, it addition to the table the firm is sponsoring. You can host a table and let everyone know that everything is under control."

And so, Girardi had assented. He'd also insisted that Jake come along and keep him company, for he absolutely hated events like this. They were the most excruciating part of client relations for him. He would gladly take a client to a sporting event or to play tennis or golf, though golf was not really his game. But a formal banquet? Forget it. Girardi was never at his ease. In truth, he felt like a bit of a fake. *This is Jack's territory, not mine,* he always said to himself.

"So, Jake, I have some good news. I'm told that the judge and Andy will be at our table. Mitch's wife is out of town. *And,*" he paused for effect, "apparently, Cynthia Dewey-Martinez will be seated at our table. According to Cliff, who is the guru of such things, we are being specially favored by getting to sit with the daughter of the man of honor."

At this, Jake let out a snort. "Cyndy Martinez? That girl's a skank."

"Jacob!" exclaimed his father in surprise. "Don't talk like that."

"Sorry dad, but she goes to my school, remember? That girl is bad news. I doubt it will feel like much of an honor to sit with her. Word is she wants to be a reality TV star like the Kardashians. She has some YouTube channel, I guess. She and her friends dress like fools just to get attention."

There were conversations with his son in which Girardi felt entirely lost. They were happening more frequently lately, and he felt another one coming on strong. Luckily, however, he was spared this time by their arrival at the hotel. Girardi pulled the BMW up near the front door, careful to avoid the half-dozen other cars that had come in just ahead. The keys were taken by an energetic valet who turned out to be a schoolmate of Jake's. The two young men spoke briefly and shared a fist bump before the valet shoved the BMW into gear and tore down the winding driveway. *I can't look,* Girardi said as he averted his eyes and headed for the lobby door.

A pretty young blonde woman in a navy blue suit and high heels stood just inside the doorway clutching a clip board. She smiled up at Jake and asked if he needed directions. A little startled, he mumbled a few words before turning to his amused father for assistance.

"The Dewey-Martinez fundraiser, please," said the elder Girardi.

"Of course," she replied, still looking at Jake. "That's in the Crystal Ballroom. Just walk up these stairs to the mezzanine level. The ballroom will be all the way to the end on your left. There are signs posted to guide you."

"Thanks," Jake replied.

"Enjoy the event." After one last smile, she moved to assist the next guests.

"Wow, good job, man," his father teased when they were out of ear-shot, "she was cute."

Jake colored a little and said nothing, keeping his eyes down as he slowly mounted the steps. "She probably smiles at everybody."

"She didn't smile at me."

"Then she probably felt sorry for me in these lame clothes."

"No, sir. It's just the opposite—the ladies love a guy in a tux."

Jake walked a little taller now as they arrived at the ballroom and head-ed inside. The room was divided into two sections, one for the cocktail hour and another for the dinner.

"Dad, can I go outside and walk around the grounds? I promise I'll be back for dinner."

Girardi considered this request and reluctantly assented. "Sure, Jake, go ahead. Be back by 7:15. I'm sure I'll need a friendly face by then. Are you wearing a watch?"

"I have my phone."

"Okay. I'll see you at 7:15."

"Check."

"We're at table seven—got it?"

"Check."

As he watched his son head outside, Girardi felt a strong hand on his shoulder. It was Judge Best.

"It's about time, Mike," the judge bellowed. "Where have you been?"

It was apparent that Best had been at the party for some time, taking advantage of the hosted bar.

"Let's get you a drink," the judge continued.

"No thanks, Mitch, I'm good."

Early in his career, Girardi had observed up close the range of difficulties that can arise from drinking at a gathering like this, especially one with an open bar. Having internalized these lessons, Girardi almost never consumed alcohol at a firm or public event.

The two headed for a corner of the crowded room.

"Dewey-Martinez for Congress, huh?" Best offered dubiously. "That's the bright prospect that brings us together this fine night?"

"Yep."

"I wouldn't vote for him for dog-catcher. I don't believe he's really a conservative. These RINOs make me sick. What's the other guy's name—Jonas or something like that? They say he's the one to take on the Democrats in D.C."

Now that he had a lifetime appointment to the federal bench, Girardi noticed that Judge Best was even more inclined than before to speak his mind. Of course, he'd not been particularly reticent to begin with.

"They say Jaime has a decent chance," Girardi demurred. "In this part of Orange County it's all about the Republican primary. Whoever wins in June is a shoo-in for November."

"I can't believe he took on his wife's last name. What guy does that? Jaime *Dewey*-Martinez? She must keep his balls in storage somewhere for him."

In spite of himself, Girardi chuckled at this.

"Where's your lovely wife this evening, Mitch?"

Best frowned and hesitated for a moment. "She's in Napa at some spa with her girlfriends. I brought Andy along."

"Where is he?"

"Outside on the balcony, I think, talking to some girl. She looks like a professional—and I don't mean a doctor."

The old friends chatted for some time. A steady flow of guests approached the pair to say hello and exchange a little small talk. Most came by to speak with the judge, but a number also wished to shake hands with

Girardi. Although he disliked these events, he always did his best to play his part and to be pleasant. And the truth was, Girardi performed much better in these settings than he gave himself credit for.

When the two men were again alone some time later, Best gestured toward the bar.

"Have you seen that woman in the green dress? She looks like a circus freak. What happened to her face?"

"That's Miranda Perkins. She's assistant vice president and associate counsel at *Warner Brothers*."

Miranda Perkins was long-time friend of Jack Tremont. A divorced former beauty queen who had attended law school in her thirties, Miranda had not taken well to the process of aging. For a period, it seemed to her friends that she had undergone nearly every treatment and procedure known to man to hold back the forces of time. And for years, it had worked. But then, some time in her late-fifties there was that one procedure too many, and it all went awry. Her face no longer moved when she tried to smile—the distance between her eyes was not quite right. Her skin looked stretched and unnatural. But Miranda Perkins was a spirited and successful woman, and she soldiered on, apparently ignoring what she knew people must be saying behind her back.

"I'd better go and say hi to Miranda," Girardi said.

"You do that while I get another drink."

As Miranda left the bar with a martini in her hand, Girardi approached her. "How are you, Miranda?"

"Just fine, Michael, and you?"

"Worried about Jack," Girardi replied honestly.

"Good god, I know. Poor Celeste. I spoke with her on the phone the other day. They aren't sure if he's going to make it. I'm going to try and get down there to see them this weekend."

"I'm sure they'll appreciate it."

"So, tell me," she offered, changing the subject with a wicked little smile, "did you bring a date tonight?"

Miranda liked to flirt with Girardi.

"Yes, I did."

Her stiff face fell a little. "That's too bad. I heard that we're sitting together."

"Yes, table seven. But I think you'll really like my date, Miranda. We'll see."

Miranda seemed dubious. "Tell me, where's the guest of honor tonight? I haven't met him yet."

Girardi took the hint. "I think I see Jaime over there in the corner. Come on, I'll introduce you to him."

"Good."

"How are things over there at the studio?" he asked as they wove through the crowd. "I haven't seen anything from you in our office for some time."

"Oh Mike, you know the new normal. You guys kill us with those rates. Nowadays, we actually have to do some of the work ourselves." She stopped to take a gulp of her drink. "*God*, I miss the nineties."

They had now arrived at the side of Jean Dewey-Martinez. "Jean, I'd like you to meet Miranda Perkins—general counsel at *Warner's*."

"*Associate* general counsel," Perkins clarified as she extended her hand to Dewey-Martinez. "Don't kiss up to me, Michael, you know I hate that."

Girardi knew that Miranda loved it when law firm partners kissed up to her—it was one of the main perks of her job.

"It's a pleasure to meet you," the candidate's wife said with a gracious smile. "Come, let me introduce you to Jaime."

She plays the game well, Girardi thought of his law partner as he handed Miranda off and headed back in the direction of the judge. On the way, he met several more people, each of whom asked about Jack Tremont. The time passed quickly, and before Girardi knew it, the dinner gong sounded.

He made his way to table seven, which was up front and just to the right of the speaker's podium. As he arrived, he found everyone there but his son. Miranda Perkins took her seat next to Bruce and Eileen Duncan. Bruce was in-house counsel for a long-time client of Jack Tremont's, and

Miranda socialized some with the Duncans. Theirs had been a skillful seating match, which Girardi credited to Cliff Conroy.

Girardi sat down next to Eileen, unfolded his napkin and glanced over at the others. Judge Best and Andy were standing and talking with two women that Girardi did not at first recognize. The younger of the two wore a zebra print mini dress and black platform knee boots. Her face was elaborately made up, and hoop earrings dangled from her ears. Girardi deduced that this must be Cynthia Dewey-Martinez. It had been more than a year since he'd seen her, but she seemed to have aged at least five years in that time. *They grow up fast*, he lamented. He wondered for a moment why Jean had allowed her teenaged daughter to come dressed like this to such an important occasion for the family. *She probably can't fight every battle, so she let this one go.* Although he did not always care for Jean, he respected her dedication to her career and her family. She was a dynamo who got as much done as anyone he knew. When it came to teen child rearing, Girardi was inclined not to be overly judgmental.

Girardi then turned his attention to the woman standing next to Mitch Best. To his dismay, he realized that it was Michelle Bailey, the lawyer from the tennis club. She was dressed elegantly this evening in a black satin sheath dress and pumps. Her accessories were gold, and her makeup was simple but flattering. Although he was wary of her, Girardi had to admit that she was a striking woman.

As Andy and Cynthia took their seats, the judge tugged on Bailey's arm, motioning for her to take the seat next to him that had been saved for Jake. Girardi tried to get the judge's attention to dissuade him, but Best did not look in his direction. Bailey hesitated and pointed to a table in the back, but then slipped into the chair. She unfolded a napkin and began to eat the salad in front of her.

Unbelievable, Girardi fumed. *Where is Jake, anyway?* He grabbed his phone and quickly texted his son, wondering how he was going to remove Bailey from Jake's seat. It was plain that the judge was now engrossed in conversation with her. Andy and Cynthia also seemed to be hitting it off. In violation of his longstanding practice, Girardi took a frustrated gulp of the pre-poured glass of champagne in front of him.

As the entrees were arriving, Jake at last appeared. Girardi noticed right away the faraway look in his son's eyes. He stood and pulled Jake aside.

"You alright, son?"

"Everything's great, dad," he replied with a satisfied smile. Girardi was surprised by this answer, but with all that seemed to be unraveling around him, he was glad to see his son in good humor. Girardi glanced over to Michelle Bailey, who was buttering a piece of bread and striking up a conversation with Miranda Perkins. *She's settling in*, Girardi observed. He made a snap decision.

"Jake, I want you to take my place at the table. There was a little mix-up on the seating. That happens a lot at these banquets. I need to call the office anyway. I'll head outside. You eat—I'll grab something later."

"Are you sure?"

"I'm sure, son." Girardi then introduced Jake to the Duncans and Miranda, and excused himself to make his phone call.

An hour and a half later, Jake approached his father sitting at a table outside above the tennis courts. It was now quiet enough for them to hear the surf down on the beach below. Girardi had spent most of the intervening time outside on the phone with his two associates, each of whom was drafting a brief on a different matter for him. Between calls, he had come inside and stood in the back of the ballroom to listen to Jaime Dewey-Martinez's speech, which he'd found boring. In small groups, Jaime could be charming, but Girardi was never impressed by his public presentations.

Jake placed a plate of food in front of his father.

"Thanks."

"You're welcome. It was actually Miranda's idea about the food. She's funny."

"She is funny," Girardi replied. Apparently, Miranda had spoken enough with Jake for him to remember her name. *And*, she'd thought to send him out some dinner. This was good of her.

"Is it over?" Girardi asked hopefully.

"Pretty much—at least, the program is over. Some people are hanging out, eating their dessert or whatever. Andy and Cynthia headed down to the beach to . . . you know . . ."

Girardi very much did not want to know. Unwrapping his silverware, he dove into his meal and began wolfing it down.

"I guess I was starved."

"I guess you were," Jake laughed. Girardi could see that his son was still in good spirits.

"Did you have anyone to talk to in there?"

"Not really, but that's okay. I was thinking about Heather the whole time, anyway."

Heather, Girardi repeated to himself, skimming his mental file of female names he heard his son mention. He came up empty on Heather.

"Who's Heather?"

"Come on, dad, Heather from the lobby."

"Heather with the clipboard?"

"Exactly."

"She made an impression on you, huh?"

Jake leaned back in his chair and nodded. "There's more to the story than you know, dad."

"There's *always* more to the story than I know."

"I was outside wandering around before dinner, and who do you think was by the pool talking to some guests?"

"Heather?"

Jake affirmed this with a nod. *Now I know why he was late*, Girardi chuckled to himself.

"Did you talk to her this time?"

"I stood around for a while, minding my own business but also kind of keeping an eye on her without really keeping an eye on her, you know? When she was done, she came over and asked me if I was lost again."

"And what did you say?"

"I said that I was taking a look around—and guess what?"

"What?"

"Part of her job is guiding people on tours of the property. So, she said she'd take me the long way back to the Crystal Ballroom and show me some of the sights."

"Such as?"

"Do you see that gazebo over there? I guess a lot of people get married there. We also went by the spa and the gym. That's a nice gym; they had really good equipment. Then, we saw the mezzanine gift store and the coffee shop. And it was on to the ballroom."

"Did you get her phone number?" he asked warily.

"Oh no, it was nothing like that. She's old—maybe 22 or 23."

She's practically a senior citizen.

"I see."

"I didn't even really say much, but it was great, you know?"

"You just walked along with her and basked in the glow?"

Jake considered this for a few moments. "Yeah, I guess you could say that. She did kind of glow. Girls in high school aren't like that."

Girardi smiled as he observed his son. There was an innocence to the story that almost surprised him. Jake was seventeen, not the optimal age for enjoying a chaste encounter like this one, especially in today's culture. But, then again, he thought, maybe this was the optimal age. Miraculously, his son was not yet jaded about the world, or at least he did not seem to be.

Girardi knew that he was getting the "parent" version of the story, and that it would probably sound different to his teammates at school on Monday. But he liked the parent version.

As Girardi was thinking about all of this, he spotted Mitch Best down on the path along the tennis courts. Walking by his side was Michelle Bailey. Girardi felt a rumbling in his stomach.

"Jake, do me a favor. Take this plate back into the ballroom and wait for me there. I need to take care of something, and then we'll head home, okay?"

Jake nodded his assent and headed back to the ballroom as instructed.

Girardi raced down the steps and quickly caught up to the pair. "That was quite an evening, wasn't it?" he said rather loudly.

The others stared at him stone-faced and offered no reply. He was undaunted. "What did you think of Jaime's speech, Mitch? Interesting, huh?"

Bailey stared at Girardi in disbelief, and then turned to the judge expectantly. He said nothing for the moment.

"I think I'll go powder my nose," she said. "I'll be right back."

"I'll be right here," Best rejoined.

As soon as Bailey was out of earshot, the judge turned to Girardi. "Scram, Mike, I meant it. Everyone is a grownup here."

"But Mitch . . ."

"Don't but Mitch me. Why don't you be a parent and take your son home?"

Best was being obnoxious so that Girardi would leave him alone. Girardi had seen this trick many times over the years; his friend was really good at it.

"Why don't *you* be a parent and go find Andy?" Girardi rejoined.

"He's eighteen—he can do what he wants."

"Not with a sixteen year old."

Best appeared taken aback. "That girl was *sixteen*?"

"Yep."

"Holy cow!" he exclaimed with a whistle. "Now come on, Mike. Get out of here."

"I can't, Mitch. Have you ruled on that motion yet?"

"No," he admitted a little sheepishly.

"Then you have to stay away from her. This place is crawling with people who know you. Don't take this chance."

Bailey soon returned, looking disappointed that Girardi was still with Best. But Girardi did not care what she was thinking. He was determined to stick it out, and the others seemed to sense this.

"Maybe I should be going," she said quietly.

"It is getting late. Shall we go get the cars?" Girardi said, beginning to walk in the direction of the lobby. "Here, Michelle, give me your ticket and I'll take care of it."

She dug around her purse and produced the stub. Girardi texted his son to meet him out front.

When the trio arrived at the kiosk, Girardi paid for his parking and Bailey's. Best waited with Bailey. Girardi quietly gave the attendant an extra twenty to bring Bailey's car around right away. Girardi then stood a few feet away from the pair, keeping a close watch on them. When her silver Audi pulled up, the judge helped Bailey into the car and she drove away.

Girardi sighed with relief as his friend slowly approached him. But when Best reached the light, Girardi could see the ferocity of his expression.

"Fuck you, Mike."

"You're welcome, your honor. Have a good evening."

The judge then headed back into the hotel to look for his son. The BMW soon swung around, and a discouraged Girardi motioned for Jake to take the keys and drive them home.

9

Late Sunday morning, after a simple service in the chapel of the Emanuel Prayer and Retreat Center, Elizabeth Stowe met with Russ Greenway of Bethany Lutheran Church in San Diego to settle his group's account. He and three other adults had chaperoned eight pre-teens on a spiritual retreat weekend at the center. The group had hiked in the nearby hills, participated in workshops with local youth pastors, sung hymns by a campfire and attended worship services. It had been a full weekend, and the group was ready to head home.

Stowe herself was tired this morning and a little out of sorts. It had been a lot of work to look after the Bethany Lutheran group, and although she had genuinely enjoyed spending time with some of the kids, she'd found the adults to be unpleasant and demanding. What's more, her work on the center's finances and Girardi's memo had been neglected. These looming tasks weighed heavily upon her as she took her seat.

Greenway sat across the desk in Stowe's cramped office and wrote out a check. Tall and tanned, he was dressed this morning in a brown polo shirt, khaki shorts and a cap from the Torrey Pines golf resort in La Jolla. Greenway handed the check to her and stood quickly to leave. As she looked at the amount, she frowned and grabbed the Bethany Lutheran file.

"Did you make a larger deposit than the usual $200?" she asked, flipping through the handwritten notes of Sister Margaret and her own supplemental typed entries. One of Stowe's many projects at the center had been to convert all of the center's financial records into electronic form.

Greenway shook his head uncomfortably. "I don't think so."

Finding Margaret's scribbled notation of receipt of a $200 deposit, Stowe's frown deepened. "But this is a check for only $600."

"Right."

She swallowed hard, thinking of the three late-model SUVs out in the parking lot. "Let's see. You are a party of twelve. The suggested donation is $70 per day per person."

Although she well knew the total, she pulled out the calculator and ran the numbers, loudly narrating them. "Seventy dollars times two is, of course, $140. $140 times the party of 12 is $1680."

"You said 'suggested' donation, right?"

"Yes, but . . ."

"I specifically recall that back when I made this reservation in the fall, the sister told me that the center takes whatever visitors can pay. She made the pricing sound very flexible."

His face had by now colored, and his arms were crossed unhappily.

Stowe made no effort to hide her skepticism. "So, what you are telling me is that Bethany Lutheran cannot afford to pay even half of the suggested donation?"

"We did a fundraising carwash and this is what we raised. In fact, I've kicked in a hundred dollars of my own not including gas money. The kids worked hard on that carwash, and so did their parents. We are a busy church—we do a lot of good in the community."

"I'm sure you do."

Greenway resumed his seat. "I don't like your tone. This is your own fault. You all should be clearer about your prices. Besides, this isn't exactly the *Four Seasons*."

Stowe considered the center's balance sheet; they needed every dime they could get.

"You've imparted a valuable lesson here, Mr. Greenway. When we say that we will take anything a visitor can afford, we mean of course that if a group truly lacks the means to pay, we do not wish to deny them access to our programs. A place of God should be open to everyone."

Stowe was certain she was right, and didn't like the thought of someone like Greenway getting the best of her.

"Having said that," she continued, "when some groups pay the suggested amount or more, they help make it possible for others to come who might not have those funds. *Obviously*, that was not clear. I'll draft some better language so that we will avoid such confusion in the future."

"You do that," he rejoined huffily, standing once more.

Stowe stood also, giving him her best evil eye in the vain hope that she still might guilt him into writing another check.

"So, that's it, Mr. Greenway?" she ventured expectantly.

"Yes, that's it. What are you going to do, sue me for the money?"

I ought to sue you. Better still, I ought to sick Mike Girardi and the Marshall, Lufton crew on you. Then you'd cough up that $880.

"God's peace to you, Mr. Greenway," she said, trying, but utterly failing, to mean what she said.

"God's peace to you too, Ms. Stowe." He seemed to mean this even less than she had. "If I might make a suggestion? You should read some sacred scripture once in a while—you're not very generous of spirit."

Stowe was so taken aback by this that she had no rejoinder.

"Travel safely," she mumbled.

When he was gone, Stowe closed the door behind him, returned to her chair and burst into tears. On her desk were several vendors' bills that were already in arrears, and she had hoped to pay them down with the Bethany Lutheran funds. These vendors had long-time relationships with the center and so far had been patient. But Stowe knew that the reprieve would not last forever.

Sometime after the group's departure, Sister Agnes, the Superior of the Emmanuel Center, came knocking on Stowe's door. Today she was wearing a variant of her accustomed uniform, a navy blue turtleneck and matching corduroy jumper dress. The petite Agnes peered at Stowe through her huge glasses.

"Is everything alright, Elizabeth? You've been in here forever, and you didn't say goodbye to the children."

Stowe looked at Agnes and shook her head sadly. "Oh, Agnes, you won't believe it. They only paid $800."

Agnes shrugged and appeared unmoved. "Well, that's $800 more than we had this morning."

The younger woman was incredulous. *She doesn't get it.*

"Actually, it's *six* hundred more than we had this morning—they paid a deposit last fall." Then, she took a breath and tried to speak patiently. "But my point is that we need to do better on our collections than that. You know that we have bills to pay—*overdue* bills."

"The Lord will provide, child."

"But *we* must manage this place—*we* must pay the bills. How can people like Mr. Greenway call themselves Christians and then skip out on an obligation that way?"

Agnes studied her companion and shook her head. "You had words with him, didn't you?"

Stowe swallowed hard. "Yes."

"Why did you do that? Nothing justifies our being harsh with a guest."

Stowe was not yet ready to consider the possibility that she had acted wrongly.

"I had words with him to try and collect the rest of our money."

Agnes sat patiently and appeared to consider this. Unable to sit quietly, the agitated Stowe moved to fill the silence.

"We need to change our written materials and our policy. We've got to stop saying that we'll take whatever people will give us. No more wiggle room. I want everyone to sign a contract from now on when we accept a deposit. I know we need to have some language in there to protect our tax-exempt status, but that shouldn't be too difficult to draft. I have a law school friend I can call for help with that."

This was ground the pair had been over before.

"I have already explained that I am opposed to contracts, Elizabeth. Contracts are a product of the laws of this world. This world's laws do not concern us. This is not a matter of our tax status. If we stop saying that we'll take whatever people will give us, then we might as well close our doors. What would be the point of continuing? It wouldn't be right to insist on a certain amount."

"But Bethany Lutheran obviously could have given more."

Agnes ran her fingers over the cross around her neck. She seemed to be in no hurry to speak, and she chose her words with care. "Although it is no easy matter for me to debate with someone as intelligent as you are, my dear, I must disagree. The group from Bethany Lutheran gave us all that they could give—not a cent more or less. Giving all that one can give is not simply about one's pocketbook. It's about the generosity in a person's heart. Mr. Greenway gave us the opportunity to spend the weekend with twelve children of God, Elizabeth. That's a blessing. Twelve—did you consider that number? The twelve apostles?"

"Sure, and they even had their Judas in Greenway."

Agnes's expression bore her disapproval. "Your cleverness and sarcasm are not your finest traits, Elizabeth. They are evidence of a lack of humility in your heart."

Stowe was hurt and confused at being put on the spot this way. She considered offering up some argument in her defense, but then, just in time, she caught herself. She was here to learn from the sisters, not to argue with them. Humility, simplicity and patience were the hallmarks of Agnes's order, and Stowe understood deep down that there was room for her to improve in these areas.

Agnes, meanwhile, continued speaking. "Who knows how those twelve hearts were touched? Perhaps we didn't see the fruits of the visit, but others might. You told me yourself that you liked the girls you hiked with yesterday."

"I did."

"Then focus upon that. Mr. Greenway and the other parents brought those young people to us. That says something for them. They could have spent that money at the mall or the movies. But instead, they came here to encounter nature and the holy spirit."

"I can't think that way," Stowe confided. "I'm angry with those parents."

"Then the devil has triumphed."

Stowe became uncomfortable whenever Agnes mentioned the devil, which was fairly frequently. "I don't know about that . . ."

"I do. An angry heart is where the devil dwells. We can't do the Lord's work when we are angry."

"But right now we are in *this* world, and in this world money is required to do our work."

"There is a saying of the Desert Fathers. *If, wishing to correct another, you are moved to anger, you gratify your own passion. Do not lose yourself in order to save another.*"

Stowe shrugged at this.

"Elizabeth, I want you to lock this office door behind you and put the subject of money entirely out of your mind. This is Sunday—the Lord's day. Why don't you take a walk? Or plant some more flowers?" The old woman took Stowe's hand into her own. "Listen to me, child. I know that you only want to help me and the other sisters here. But the ways of the world are not the ways of God. We are obliged to do things properly, even if the balance sheet on that computer screen suffers. Besides, it's not the earthly balance sheet that matters—it's the Lord's. Try not to forget that as you stew over our books."

"You're probably right, Agnes."

"Pray on it a little bit . . ."

"I will."

"Come. Let's go have some lunch. Ida's chili will make you feel better."

■ ■ ■

On Sunday afternoon, Girardi arrived at the small conference room for a meeting with his two young associates, Tammy Thompson and Chas Cunningham. The purpose of the gathering was to discuss with them their draft briefs. With the loss of Randall Spencer, Girardi was now forced to deal directly with his less-experienced attorneys. Usually, their work was filtered through Spencer, and thus by the time it reached Girardi's desk, it had achieved a certain level of polish. That was certainly not the case with the two heavily-marked documents in his hand.

Thompson, who was small and thin, almost disappeared next to Cunningham, who was tall and weighed well over two hundred pounds. The two were opposites in more than just appearance. In Girardi's view, Thompson overdid everything—she talked too much, wrote briefs that were too long, and even dressed too elaborately for work. Cunningham, by contrast, had what Judge Best had once called "a low pilot light." He walked and talked slowly, and did just enough to get by. He'd played college football as a lineman at Nebraska, and Judge Best had hired him as a judicial clerk largely on that basis. Of course, it did not hurt that Cunningham's uncle was a United States Congressman. Best had put in a good word with Girardi and Tremont, who had decided to give Cunningham a chance as an associate.

Thompson was working on a brief for Girardi on one of Tremont's matters, while Cunningham had drafted one for Girardi's San Diego fraud case. In part as an educational exercise, Girardi had decided to meet with the two together so that each might learn from his comments on both briefs. In preparation, he'd asked them to read the other's work.

Girardi greeted them and thanked them for coming in on Sunday.

"I can only stay for an hour," Thompson announced at once. "My therapist says that I need to improve my work-life balance. I'm starting a yoga class today at four."

Apropos of this announcement, Thompson was wearing a stylish olive-colored yoga outfit that still had an overlooked price tag attached near the zipper of the hooded sweatshirt. Cunningham, in contrast, wore a faded red Cornhuskers polo shirt, shorts and sneakers.

Girardi took a deep breath and held it for a few seconds.

"Tammy," he exhaled, "as I'm sure you know, you are expected to bill a minimum of 2,000 hours per year."

"Yes."

"Well, to get there, an associate needs to work some nights and weekends. When the workload demands it, we are all expected to step up—period."

Thompson and Cunningham exchanged looks but said nothing. Girardi, meanwhile, was dismayed by the necessity of delivering this message. To him, what he'd said should be entirely understood by every attorney in the firm. Associates in the "good old days" did not complain this way—at least not to the partners. *Therapists? Yoga?* These had been all but unheard of back in his associate days, when people who spoke like this were labeled as nuts or weaklings and were weeded out. He recalled his conversation with Randall Spencer at the hospital. Spencer had said that times were changing for law firm associates these days. Perhaps the young man was right.

"Chas, let's start with your brief, okay?"

"Sure thing."

"Did you read it, Tammy?"

"Yes. I skimmed through it in *Starbucks* this morning while my boyfriend read the *New York Times* book reviews to me. He's so cute that way."

Girardi shook his head and swallowed the comment in his throat. *She has no filter.*

"So, Chas, what is the page limit on a brief like this?"

Cunningham of course should have looked this up before beginning to write the brief. Also, having recently been a clerk in federal court, he likely should have recalled this from his days in Judge Best's Chambers.

"I don't know exactly—maybe 20 pages?"

"The limit is 35 pages, Chas. And you've given me 12."

"It's a rough draft."

"It sure is."

Girardi went on to explain his comments in detail, and in fact, the news was not all bad for Cunningham. What there was of the draft was well-written, and there had been very few typos. After some preliminaries, Girardi got to the heart of the matter.

"You need to develop your story, Chas, especially in your description of the facts. Lawyers are storytellers. If you tell the story well up front, the judge will be disposed to rule in your favor before he or she even reads your legal analysis. I want you to expand this statement of facts—right now yours is only two pages long. It should be seven or eight pages long.

And remember, *every* fact must be accompanied by a citation to the record. They're not just going to take our word for things. Each fact must be substantiated."

He turned to Thompson. "I want you to think about those things, too, Tammy. But you sort of had the opposite problem from Chas. This draft is almost 50 pages long."

"Oh, right. Well, my personal style has always been to just get all of my thoughts down to begin with. Then I sort things out."

"You may need to adapt your approach. Legal writing is all about clarity and discipline. You need to discipline yourself *before* you begin to write. Maybe an outline would help. You have some good points in this draft, but they are completely buried. Your summary statement at the beginning should encapsulate the entire argument. Right now, your summary statement is not a summary at all, but just an introduction to the case. Scrap it. I want you to rewrite the summary statement first and show it to me by the end of the day. That statement should contain a roadmap for the entire brief. You can send me your re-draft as an email attachment and I'll have more comments for you by tomorrow morning."

He went on to give each of them several more tips. He tried to be positive and encouraging when he could be, and was firm on a few necessary points. At the end of the meeting, Thompson surprised Girardi.

"Mike, thanks. This is great. I've worked at Marshall, Lufton for a year and a half and this is the first time a partner has given me detailed feedback on my work."

Cunningham nodded his agreement.

"Jack just tells me I've done something wrong but never explains how to fix it," she continued.

"Yep," Cunningham interjected, "and now that Spence is gone, we're kind of screwed because he used to try and help us along. As for Jack, I'm afraid of him. I wouldn't ever ask him for help. I get freaked out whenever his extension comes up on my office phone."

Girardi looked at them both as he considered what they were saying. They looked like kids to him, not all that much older than Jake. *I must be getting old*, he thought ruefully. And then, there was Cunningham's comment about Jack Tremont. The idea of this big football player being afraid of the old man at first struck him as ridiculous. But then, Spencer had warned him that Tremont was being too hard on his people, and Beth Stowe had said the same thing. Girardi hated to admit it to himself, but perhaps he had lost touch with what was going on in the department. He knew this needed to change.

"Look," he said, "things are going to be tough around here for a while without Spence and Jack, but we can manage. If you have any questions or problems, come to me."

Thompson squirmed at this and looked over at Cunningham. "But Mike, you are so busy that we can't even get in to see you."

"You have to be persistent, Tammy. One call or visit may not be enough. Get in my face if you have to—that's your job."

The two young people again exchanged unhappy looks.

"I know that you two need guidance. I'll tell my assistant that you both get high priority for a while, okay?"

This seemed to meet with their approval.

"Oh, and Chas, if you can get this brief into shape, I'll bring you with me to depo. in San Diego, okay?"

At this, Cunningham perked up. "Really? That would be awesome."

He sounds exactly like Jake.

Thompson meanwhile looked left out. "Don't worry, Tammy. You'll have plenty of chances soon enough. That's the advantage of being on a short-handed crew. You two will get to do some stuff that's usually left to the mid-levels. Hang in there with me and you'll come out of the experience stronger for it."

In this way, the meeting ended on a relative high note. Girardi thanked them once more and then headed for his office to drop off his legal pad and pick up his jacket. He was on his way to meet Judge Best for a beer downstairs at *Emilio's*.

10

Girardi found Mitch Best in the *Emilio's* bar, watching a baseball game and wearing orange board shorts, a tank top and flip-flops.

"Thanks for coming down, Mike."

"Sure thing, Mitch," Girardi replied as he took a seat across from the judge. "I was a little surprised to hear from you after how things ended on Friday night."

"Shit, that was my fault. You were just trying to keep me out of trouble."

"That's true," Girardi allowed, surprised by Best's semi-apology.

"I thought everything over during my stand up paddle-boarding lesson."

Well, that explains the outfit. What will Mitch get himself into next?

"What's stand up paddle-boarding?"

"Good question—I didn't know either until the kids bought me a package of lessons down in Dana Point for my fiftieth birthday. Paddle-boarding is just like it sounds—you stand up on a wide board and paddle yourself around the bay. It's boring as hell, but I like the challenge of staying up there without falling. It's not as easy as it looks. Plus, it's beginning to be bikini season down there, so the views are spectacular. You ought to see my instructor."

"Good for you, Mitch. I'm glad you're motivated."

"So anyway, when I was out there today, I thought about our friendship."

Girardi was once more surprised, for his friend Mitch did not often share nostalgic reflections.

"Do you remember where we met?" Best asked.

"Sure," Girardi replied as the waitress brought him a glass of his favorite beer. The pair were regulars at *Emilio's*, and were accustomed to receiving attentive service. He nodded his thanks and continued. "We met on the first day of torts class—Professor Gunderson."

"That's right," Best replied, motioning for another beer for himself. "I still remember talking to you after class. I didn't know what the hell was going on, but I could tell right away that *you* did. I'd been in the Marines for four years. I remember thinking to myself, 'that little Italian guy is unassuming, but he knows his stuff.'"

"Gee, thanks Mitch, I'm flattered."

"You don't need me to flatter you—you graduated second in our class."

Girardi paused and reflected for a few moments. "You know, I really liked law school. I think that's when I finally got serious."

"There was nothing to do in Davis but study anyway—it was a cow town."

"Maybe so," Girardi chuckled, "but the law made sense to me. And I worked my ass off to get those grades. It was no cake walk."

"Like I said, I could tell right away that you'd do well."

This highlighted one of Mitch Best's most useful abilities—he was excellent at sizing up other people. He would never be the sharpest thinker or most articulate speaker in a room of lawyers, but he was a genius at evaluating people and forming strategic professional relationships. Girardi might have been the more intelligent of the pair, but he was not always so adept at judging those around him.

Taking a long sip of beer, Girardi allowed his mind to slip into reminiscences of their first year of law school.

"As I recall, you were also well-acquainted with the person who finished *first* in our class," Girardi laughed.

"That bitch," Best exhaled, "she ruined both of our lives. Without her, *you'd* have been first."

Over the years, Jennifer Pritchard's name had all but disappeared from Mitch Best's vocabulary, having been replaced by "the kids' mother" or, after a few drinks, "the bitch."

"Jenny was in our torts class, too," Girardi recalled.

"But that's not where we met her. It was at that mixer they had at the end of our first week of school."

"Yep," Girardi nodded, conjuring the scene in his mind's eye, "we were just sitting there drinking our beers and minding our own business . . ."

". . . like we are now . . ."

". . . and she came over and asked you to dance."

"I should have said no."

"Come on, Mitch, you were really crazy about that girl."

"I suppose so—it's hard to remember that far back."

"I still remember when the two of you won the first year moot court competition that spring. The partners were supposed to be selected randomly, but somehow she rigged it to get you."

"That was stupid of her."

"Well, you managed to win somehow. That was cool."

"So, what's the moral? Never marry your moot court partner?" Best quipped. But then, his expression grew more serious. "Jenny was a force of nature; she always knew exactly what she wanted."

"And that included you, my friend."

Best had married Pritchard in a small ceremony after their second year of law school. Girardi was best man. The marriage lasted twelve years and produced two children, Andy and Brianna. Pritchard, who had never remarried, was now a partner with a large Los Angeles law firm.

Always loath to remain for long on the subject of his children's mother, Best moved on. "You did moot court, too, didn't you?"

"Right. You married your moot court partner and I almost killed mine."

"What was her name, anyway?"

Girardi's mind was a blank. His first-year moot court experience had been disastrous, and he had always blamed his assigned partner. For years he had fumed about her. Now, he could not recall her name or the details of her face.

"I can't think of it," Girardi said, shaking his head. "But I remember what she was like. She had this gigantic chip on her shoulder and was always trying to prove herself. She could never just relax and have a conversation. The girls at Davis all seemed that way to me—too wound up."

"After that fiasco, you swore that you'd never date a law student."

"And I kept my word. It wasn't too difficult, either."

Girardi had carried some of this attitude with him into the working world. He worked well enough with female colleagues, but he rarely became friendly with them. In this regard, Elizabeth Stowe had been something of an exception.

"Do you remember when we went to D.C. together?" Best asked, changing the subject again.

"Of course I do."

Best was referring to the trip the pair had made years earlier to attend his confirmation hearing in Washington D.C. Girardi had served as the judge's personal counsel and had sat next to Best when he'd appeared before a Senate Judiciary sub-committee. This had been one of the high points of their careers, and they each recalled that trip with great fondness.

"We were a couple of regular dudes from Davis up there with the Ivy Leaguers," Best said, referring to his fellow district court nominees and many of the Senate staffers they dealt with on the trip.

"We acquitted ourselves well enough."

"That's because you prepared me," Best replied. "You made sure I didn't look like an idiot up there."

It was true that Girardi had insisted that Best prepare himself thoroughly for the hearings. And although the process was largely pro forma, he'd still been asked some tough questions. But, thanks to the preparation, Best had performed well.

"Beth Stowe helped a lot, too," Girardi recalled. "She went to school with those Ivy Leaguers, and she called some of her friends on the hill to learn the ins an outs of the process. She prepared me to prepare you."

"Who's Beth Stowe?"

"God, Mitch, what's the matter with you? We all had dinner together especially so that you could thank her. And she was at your swearing-in. Don't you remember?"

"Nope. Was she hot?"

Girardi shook his head in frustration. "Never mind."

Best gave his friend a wry smile and worked to recall Stowe. "I think I remember her—slight and scrawny, right? Short brown hair?"

"Kind of blondish brown hair—and it's long now. I saw her this week as a matter of fact—she looks good."

Best bugged out his eyes. "Wasn't she kind of intense?"

"Sometimes."

"Now I remember. She came from a well-to-do family, right? Come to think of it, Sophia suspected that there might be something going on between the two of you. She thought you were kind of familiar with one another. Women always pick up on that stuff."

Sophia, a publishing executive, was the judge's current wife. Girardi's relationship with Sophia was much different from that with Jenny Pritchard. There was so much history with Pritchard. Girardi had never bonded with Sophia, and he certainly did not like the idea that she had called him and Stowe familiar, whatever that meant.

"Beth and I worked together a lot in those days," Girardi demurred.

"My take on Beth was that there was an attractive woman in there somewhere, but she was trapped and couldn't get out." Best paused and offered a smile full of mischief. "*But then* Mona Phillips came riding up on her Harley and swept you away, so it didn't matter if you were familiar with Beth Stowe or not."

Girardi found this description of his life jarring and unpleasant.

"There was nothing between Beth and me, Mitch. Besides, she had a boyfriend. She was my associate, and a damned good one. I was sorry to see her go."

"What happened to her? Did she go off to make babies?"

"Not exactly; she lives in a community of nuns."

Best let out a hearty belly laugh. "That's a good one, Mike."

"I'm not making it up."

Best was incredulous. "I didn't really pick up a Mother Teresa vibe from her, did you?"

Girardi shook his head disapprovingly at the judge and decided to return them to their earlier subject.

"*Anyway*, you aced your confirmation hearing. That was a great week in DC. I'll never forget it."

"Me neither. I'm glad you were there with me."

"Me too."

A thoughtful quiet fell between the two old friends.

"You know, I thought I'd enjoy being a judge more than I do."

Girardi hated to hear his friend say this, but he was not entirely surprised. He had achieved a level of professional success most lawyers could only dream of, but still, Best was unsatisfied. Girardi feared that it might always be so with him.

"I know I have a ton of authority, and everyone pretends to be respectful to me. But the day-to-day job can be kind of boring. Some of trials are interesting, but most aren't. Most of my docket is criminal—drug stuff. With the sentencing guidelines, you might as well have a robot sitting in my chair most of the time. And don't get me started on those liberal pricks on the ninth circuit."

The judge had recently been overturned twice on appeals to the ninth circuit and was still sore about it.

"But you have a chance to do some real good, Mitch. Our system depends upon the fair and honest administration of justice. Nowhere is that more important than in the trial court. You have an important job."

Best nodded. "I know it, Mike. By the way, I talked to one of my clerks this morning. I'm going to deny that removal motion and send the case back to the state court. By noon tomorrow, Michelle Bailey won't have any more formal business in my courtroom."

Girardi was relieved to hear this. But yet, there was something in his friend's choice of words and expression that left Girardi apprehensive. He worried that the matter of Michelle Bailey was not truly closed. Before he could ask anything further on the subject, they were interrupted by Emilio himself checking on the pair.

"Will you gentlemen be staying for dinner?"

Best spoke up first. "I'm a free man."

"Jake's out with his friends, so I can have a bite."

"Do you want to stay here in the bar?" Emilio asked. "If not, there's a nice table outside for you if you'd like it."

"Let's go outside," the judge declared.

Girardi nodded his assent, and Emilio led them out.

The restaurant sat in a plaza in the shadow of the Marshall, Lufton office tower, just down the street from St. Mark's Church. The patio was festively decorated with potted plants and trees adorned with strings of red and yellow lights. On Sundays, the plaza was usually quiet, and so Best and Girardi had a section of the patio to themselves.

"Say, Mike, can I ask you a question?" Best ventured, after they'd settled in and ordered their dinner.

"Sure."

"What was it like to date Mona Phillips?"

"You know I don't kiss and tell, Mitch."

"How'd you meet her? It was at work, right?"

Girardi had long resisted questions about his relationship with Mona, which he viewed as private. But time had passed, and Girardi was now in a relatively relaxed mood.

"It was summer, and I was working on a trial. I was spending all day in court and then half the night at the office preparing for the next day. Mona was a late night word processor. She worked for a temporary agency."

"She didn't look like a word processor—she looked like Miss February."

Girardi shook his head. "If you're going to talk that way, then I'm dropping the subject," he warned.

Best made a buttoning gesture over his mouth. "My lips are sealed. Proceed, counselor."

"Thank you, your honor. Anyway, Jake was away with his mom for the summer, and one night Mona came into my office with a couple of beers. No one was around. God knows how many office policies we violated, but that's how we started."

Best brightened up at this and leaned forward confidentially. "You did it right there in the office?"

Girardi squirmed. "Sort of—not exactly." He finished the beer in front of him in one big swig. "She invited me for a ride on her Harley— I'm not kidding. We went zooming down PCH at three in the morning. That was outstanding."

Girardi leaned back and gave a satisfied smile at the recollection. Best for once sat quietly as his friend took a couple of bites of bread.

"Mona was a free spirit. I've always liked that kind of girl. She had no inhibitions. I thought I was pretty uninhibited myself. Boy, was I wrong about that." He chuckled. "But it wasn't just about the physical attraction. I learned a lot from Mona."

Best shifted in his seat, his skepticism obvious.

"Hear me out. Mona wasn't an intellectual or anything like that. But she could live in the moment and enjoy herself. She *never* had an unkind word for anyone. We both knew it wouldn't last forever, but I have no regrets. She was a decent person."

"You broke up during a trip, right?"

Mitch knows more of the story than I thought he did.

"I took her to Jamaica," Girardi nodded. "We had a great time, and on our last night, she sat me down for a talk. She went on and on about energy fields and the ocean and chi. I didn't understand much of what she said, but she talked like that quite a bit. After a lot of discussion, the upshot was that she had decided to stay in Jamaica. She thought she'd found peace there."

"Aw, Mike," Best offered sympathetically, "that sucks. You should have taken her to Cleveland."

"Mona also predicted that I'd find a nice girl some day and get remarried. I told her that she was a nice girl and she just laughed at me. Mona was always a couple steps ahead, pulling me along. Even at the end."

"And that was it?"

"That was it. Would you like to hear a funny coincidence? Beth Stowe quit while I was on that trip. No one bothered to tell me. When

I got back to my office, each case file had a memo on top explaining the status. All the work was caught up, but she never even said goodbye."

"Blown off by two women in the same week. That's got to be a record."

"I guess so," Girardi agreed sadly. "Anyway, as for Mona, I don't know if she's still in Jamaica or not. We lost touch. But wherever she is, I hope she's happy."

There was a long pause. Best raised his glass and grinned. "Here's to Mona and her enormous rack!"

Girardi rolled his eyes and raised his water glass. "Here's to Mona and her enormous zest for life."

"Cheers."

Girardi leaned back and folded his arms, his expression darkening. "You know the thing that surprised me most in the entire Mona episode?"

"What's that?"

"How strongly people reacted to it. My god. The other women in the office despised Mona and said awful things about her. And for good measure they treated me like the biggest scumbag on the planet. Mona took a temp job at another firm something like a week or two after we started seeing one another, so it shouldn't have been an ongoing issue in the office. But it was."

Although he'd tried to forget the fact, one critic had been Elizabeth Stowe.

"We were both single adults, for heaven's sake. It really shook everyone up to see Mona and me together."

"It was a little unusual," Best allowed.

"And then there were the guys."

The judge sat back in his chair, suspecting he was among the guilty.

"They treated me like the biggest stud on the planet."

"You were living the dream, partner."

"Funny thing was, the same guys also took it upon themselves to comment about Mona's body all the time. They showed no respect at all. Do guys mention Sophia's breasts to you very often?"

"Never," Best replied, obviously suppressing a sarcastic comment.

"The Mike and Mona Show apparently broke all the rules. I saw a side of the people around me that I didn't like." Girardi rubbed the back of his neck and continued. "But you know, I always liked Mona because it didn't feel like she was with me because I had money. We just were hanging out together."

Best labored mightily, but could not resist a rejoinder. "So, a hot girl and a middle-aged law firm partner hook up, and it's not mainly about sex or money? That's refreshing."

Girardi's expression darkened. "You just don't get it, Mitch."

The judged sighed. "No, I probably don't."

They were saved by the arrival of their meals, and the pair moved on to other subjects. As they ate, Reverend Mountjoy sat at a table on the other end of the patio with Hector and Sylvia Bea, two of St. Mark's most generous contributors. The Beas were considering making a special do-nation to support musical programs, including the endangered Evensong service, and the dinner was spent discussing various possibilities. It had been a long day, but Mountjoy was pleased with how the meeting had gone. As she and the Beas were exiting the patio, she heard a bellowing voice behind her.

"Susie Mountjoy, is that you?"

Startled, Mountjoy turned and saw Mitch Best standing from his seat and rushing toward her. The Beas frowned at the judge's beach at-tire and turned expectantly to Mountjoy for an explanation. Meanwhile, Mountjoy's mind struggled to adapt to the sight of someone she hadn't seen in twenty-five years.

"Mitch Best?"

"That's me."

She recovered herself and turned to her companions. "Hector, Sylvia, this is Judge Best of the U.S. District Court."

The Beas looked skeptically at Best as he extended his hand to them.

"Judge Best, this is Doctor Hector Bea and his wife, Sylvia."

"Pleased to meet you both." He turned to Mountjoy. "How did you know I was a judge?"

"I read it in the paper."

"Won't you join us, Susie?"

Mountjoy reluctantly assented, still reeling. "Let me walk the Beas out, and then I'll come back. But just for a few minutes."

Best returned to his table excitedly. "Mike, that's Susie Mountjoy!"

"I heard."

"We went to college together. I wonder what she's doing now?"

"From the collar, I'll bet she's a minister of some kind."

Best's remarkable power of sizing up others sometimes failed him when a woman was involved.

"Really? I totally missed that."

Mountjoy soon returned and was introduced to Girardi.

"So, Susie," Best ventured as she took a seat, "what's with the collar?"

Mountjoy shook her head. *He's still a child*, she thought to herself. *He dresses like a child, too.*

"Well, I'm an Episcopal priest, Mitch. I'm rector of St. Mark's just up the street."

Best was dumfounded.

"So," she continued, "how do you like being a judge?"

"It's great. How do you like being a minister?"

"The job's a little much sometimes, but I really do love it most of the time."

"Do you mind my asking how you got into that line of work? I remember you running around USC with your Daisy Duke shorts on . . ."

Mountjoy laughed at this in spite of herself. *Thanks be to God that I took the Beas out to the car. One mention of me in Daisy Dukes and they'll head over to St. Bart's with half of my congregation in line behind them.*

"I see you're still a Neanderthal, Mitch."

"Why, thank you, Susie. From you, that's a fine compliment." Best turned to Girardi. "The *Reverend* here was a bit of a feminist in college. She loved using words like 'patriarchy' and 'Neanderthal.'"

"Guys like you were good for business, Mitch."

Girardi grabbed his wallet and stood from the table. "I need to get going; you two should stay. It was a pleasure to meet you, Reverend Mountjoy."

He threw some money on the table and headed off. Best and Mountjoy remained for some time, sharing coffee and dessert and laughing about old times. In no time at all, the years melted away. Mountjoy was surprised by how quickly the two seemed to pick up where they'd left off.

Some time later, as she at last stood to leave, she surprised herself by asking him a personal question.

"Do you attend church?"

"No," he replied quietly. "Neither my wife nor I is particularly religious."

"Someday you two should come see the church. I'll give you a tour." She paused and looked up directly into his face. "A little bit of Jesus Christ might do you some good, Mitch."

Best appeared taken aback. "Still trying to make a better man out of me, huh Susie?"

"Guys like you can still be good for business."

The two were standing close to one another. Best reached down, placed his hands lightly on her arms, and planted a careful kiss on her cheek. "It was great to see you; you're still a beautiful girl."

Mountjoy looked up at Best in surprise. It had been a long time since anyone had called her a beautiful girl. It felt good. But the joy did not last, and soon she became needled with a familiar old sense of annoyance.

"You guys think that no matter how accomplished we women are, all you have to do is give us a compliment and we'll melt at your feet."

Best scowled down at her. "You're right, Susie. My mistake—what I really should have said is that you could stand to lose about twenty pounds."

Although neither of them was aware of the fact at the moment, this type of tension had cropped up fairly regularly back during their school days. In spite of herself, Mountjoy allowed the hurt to show in her expression. But, thinking of the collar around her neck, she took a deep breath, said prayer of forbearance, and refrained from retaliation.

"Bye, Mitch. Have a nice life."

The Reverend turned from the judge and left the restaurant.

11

On Monday morning, Mike Girardi arrived early at the office ahead of a very full day of meetings and conference calls. He stopped by Tammy Thompson's office and left a marked-up version of her summary statement. This second draft had been an improvement, and Girardi had modest hopes that the brief might turn out satisfactorily after all.

A short time later, he heard a rustling and looked up to find Thompson standing in his doorway looking sheepish.

"Hi Tammy—I must have just missed you. I left the mark-up of that document on your chair."

"Yes, I saw it."

"Good."

Girardi expected her to dash off, and wondered why she remained.

"Do you have some questions for me?" he asked.

She entered the room and gestured to the rust-colored expandable file in her hand. The color in her cheeks began to rise.

"Do you remember the email you sent around last week, asking us if we had any files in our offices on CEP?"

Girardi certainly did recall the message. "Yes."

"I'm sorry, but I ignored the message at the time because I'd never done any work for CEP. I was certain that none of the files would be in my office. It's the oddest thing, but . . ."

"But you *did* have something?"

"Yes. I found this on my credenza yesterday afternoon after you'd left.
The matter is called *Pope Electronics.*"

Bingo, Girardi thought to himself.

"Great, Tammy. Just leave the file here with me."

"You aren't upset?"

"No, I'm not. Files get misplaced sometimes. I understand."

Her relief was manifest.

"Are you *sure* this is everything you have?" he continued.

"Yes, I checked every folder in my office, twice. I wonder how in the
world that one ended up there. It was underneath a file I hadn't looked at
in weeks."

"The main thing is that you found it. You should probably get back to
work. Thanks, Tammy."

"I'll do that." She headed for the door and then turned back. "I
promise I'll write you a first-rate brief."

Girardi smiled at this. "Good."

When she'd left, Girardi flipped through the *Pope Electronics* file and saw
that there was not much to it. There were a couple of sheets of Tremont's
handwritten notes, indicating conversations with a CEP in-house attorney named Russell Yost. Girardi knew, and liked, Yost from a case he'd
worked on a few years back.

On one sheet, Tremont had written "call consultants," and on another, "need exhibits and printouts." There was no formal correspondence
in the file. The longest document was an official governmental Audit
Report, detailing the results of a review of a government contract to build
a prototype armored truck for the Army. The prime contractor was apparently an automaker in the Midwest, and Pope Electronics served as a
sub-contractor supplying an on-board communication system.

Although Girardi did not consider himself an expert on government
contracting law, he did have some experience in the field. He knew that
audits like this were a common part of doing business with the federal
government, and that contractors often hired legal counsel to prepare responses. Flipping through the dense report, he found that the auditing

agency was seeking from Pope Electronics a refund of several million dollars. While this struck Girardi as on the high end of audits he'd seen, he knew that government auditors could sometimes be quite aggressive. It was often the role of hired counsel to object to audit allegations with equal force.

Thinking back to his Thursday conversation with Elizabeth Stowe, he recalled that the old CEP matter, *Trinity Hills*, had also involved a government audit. Now he was even more anxious than before to receive her analysis of the old documents. Perhaps the two contracts were somehow related or involved similar allegations.

Replacing the Audit Report in the expanding file, he noticed a dirty manila envelope in the back. He opened the envelope and pulled out a messy stack of documents. Some were wrinkled and torn, others were upside down. Girardi tried to decipher them, but found that most of the sheets were computer printouts containing numerical data and calculations. Some had dates in the upper left corner indicating that they were several years old, while others were undated. On a quick review, he could not make out the calculations or discern whether or not these documents were even related to the Pope Electronics subcontract.

Marshall, Lufton had very clear policies on the maintenance of its paper files. It was never proper to leave documents in an envelope like this, let alone a dirty one. Girardi wondered both how the file had ended up on the bottom of a pile in Thompson's office and why it was in such bad shape.

As he flipped through the papers, a small single sheet dropped out of the stack and onto the floor. He picked it up and saw that it was part of a phone bill for a residence on Cherry Tree Lane in Huntington Beach. To his surprise, the account was in Jack Tremont's name.

Jack has a place in Huntington Beach? he said to himself in surprise. He'd never heard Tremont speak of owning any property in California besides his house in Corona del Mar. His children were grown and married and none of them lived in Orange County. Girardi placed the sheet on a clean corner of his desk and then spent a few more minutes perusing the papers before his phone rang. It was the in-house counsel on his San Diego fraud case. Girardi carefully placed the *Pope Electronics* file in the bottom drawer of his credenza and turned to his other work.

Girardi did not come up for air until shortly before noon. He was in the lunch room refilling his coffee cup and chatting with Jean Dewey-Martinez about her husband's fundraiser when Cliff Conroy came rushing in. The normally unflappable Conroy looked a bit flustered.

"Mike, can I have a few minutes of your time?"

Dewey-Martinez took the hint and headed back to her office, apparently not interested in hearing about whatever was bothering Conroy.

"We've got a situation," Conroy continued.

Use of language like this had contributed to Conroy's "CIA spook" reputation over the years.

"Let's go down to my office," Girardi offered, motioning with his Angels World Series mug for Conroy to lead the way.

When they arrived, Girardi closed the door and took his seat. Conroy remained standing, running his hand over his hair as he moved to speak.

"We received a fax from the court on the *Hoffman Medical* matter. The court . . ."

Girardi gestured with his open palm. "Wait a minute, Cliff. Slow down. I need to catch up." Girardi paused to think. "*Hoffman Medical* is one of Jack's cases. It's a dispute with a hospital about some allegedly defective medical equipment, right?"

"I guess so. I don't know the facts of the case. But the court has entered a judgment for the plaintiff because we apparently failed to respond to a dispositive motion."

Girardi's heart began to beat faster. This was every litigator's lurking fear—that an important court deadline would somehow be missed. Attorneys take elaborate measures to make sure this never happens. But, of course, even in a good firm, it does sometimes happen.

Girardi shook his head. "No way. There was no motion pending in that file. I just looked at it a week ago."

Conroy nodded knowingly. "It wasn't your mistake, Mike. It must have been Jack's or Spencer's. Apparently, those papers were due several weeks ago. The opponent asked for a judgment and the court granted it."

Conroy then handed Girardi the court's order. When he was finished reading, Girardi looked up into Conroy's face. "This is bad, Cliff."

"I know it is. Do you want me to call the court?"

Girardi looked at Conroy in disbelief. *Sometimes he forgets that he's not an attorney himself.* Girardi then stared back down at the court order. *Why did Cliff see this before I did?*

"No Cliff, it wouldn't be proper for you to contact the court. That's my job. I'll go in *ex parte* this afternoon and beg for mercy. Is the case file still in the small conference room?"

The small conference room had become Girardi's command center for Tremont's cases.

"The file should be there. I'll go and check right away."

"Can you bring it to me? Thanks." Girardi turned and dialed Tammy Thompson's extension.

I don't have time for this, he thought in frustration, looking at his calendar as he waited for her to pick up.

"Hi, Mike," Thompson answered brightly. "I'm working on those revisions you asked for. I should have something for you by the end of the day."

"That's not why I'm calling. I need you to come to my office right away. You'll need to prepare some *ex parte* papers—we're going to court this afternoon."

"We are?" she replied as if he had just informed her of an impromptu trip to China.

"Yes, we are. Get down here now, okay?"

"Okay."

Girardi quickly got onto his computer and hunted around for sample *ex parte* papers to show Thompson as a guide. A couple of minutes later, she entered his office right behind Conroy, who was holding the *Hoffman Medical* file. Girardi found the document he wanted in his computer directory and sent it to the printer. Next, he attached the file and emailed it to Thompson's account.

"Here's the file, Mike," Conroy said.

"Thanks, Cliff."

"So, do you have this thing under control?"

Girardi eyed Thompson and then squinted up at Conroy. He did not care for the office manager's handling of this little crisis so far, but now was not the time to say anything. Spotting the phone bill he'd found in the *Pope Electronics* file, he held it out to Conroy.

"Cliff, I found something of Jack's in a file today. Does he have a place in Huntington Beach?"

Conroy blinked in surprise as he looked at the sheet. "Yes. It's a condo—an investment property. I'll see that Celeste gets this. Thanks."

"You're welcome."

Conroy slipped out of the room and Thompson took a seat in the guest chair across from her boss, pad and pen in hand.

Looking down at the papers in front of him, Girardi began to explain what he needed from Thompson. He then looked up and was surprised by what he saw. Thompson was dressed this morning in a long yellow sweater over black leggings. Wrapped several times around her neck was a green scarf that appeared to be swallowing up her small head. With all that was on his mind, he had not particularly noticed the details of her outfit when she'd visited his office earlier in the day with the *Pope Electronics* file.

"Tammy, you'll need to change into your emergency suit before we head to the court."

"My what?"

Girardi rubbed the back of his neck as he felt the muscles there tighten. "Now that we live in the days of office casual, every litigator must keep a suit in his or her office for impromptu visits to court like the one we'll be making this afternoon."

"No one ever told me this, Mike. I'm sorry, but I don't have any other clothes here."

"Tammy, I think this is something you could have deduced on your own."

"But in a year and a half I've only been to court twice—and I've never even sat at counsel table."

Girardi took a deep breath and exhaled slowly. "Okay. Well, at least you can prepare the documents I need."

He proceeded to show her the sample he'd printed and gave her a short run-down on *Hoffman Medical*. Picking up the file, she promised to get right on it. As she reached the door, she turned to Girardi.

"You don't think this will work for court?" she asked sadly, pointing at her sweater. "This is an expensive outfit. Eighties-influenced styles are all the rage right now."

I'll have to give my sister the fashion bulletin. She'll be thrilled, Girardi thought in a fleeting moment of levity.

"Although it may be fashionable, your clothing today won't fly in court. At least not as an attorney with this firm. When you represent a client in a courtroom, you need to be conservative."

I've become one of the stodgy old partners I used to laugh at. He shook his head as Thompson spoke.

"If I get these papers done right away, I can zoom home and change. My apartment is just ten minutes from here. I've got half a closet full of suits, honestly, I do. I just don't usually have an occasion to wear them. Can I meet you down at the courthouse?"

Girardi hesitated. It would be good to have Thompson with him at counsel table to take notes and to show that a legal team was in place and ready to resume the case. Chas Cunningham was behind on his factual statement, and Girardi did not want to pull him away from the office.

"Okay, I'll meet you in the courtroom at 1:45. You've got to get these documents to me before you leave here; and you can't be late to court. Do you understand?"

"Absolutely."

At this, Thompson went off to create Girardi's documents. Girardi meanwhile went out to see his assistant about rescheduling his afternoon appointments. There was no telling how long he would be at the courthouse. Worse still, there was no telling whether the judge would withdraw the dismissal or not.

■ ■ ■

Girardi checked in with the clerk of Judge Richard Grossman at 1:40 in the afternoon and was told to take a seat in the gallery. Tammy Thompson blew in four minutes later, dressed in a conservative, well-tailored blue suit, gray turtleneck and gray pumps. Her hair was pulled back in a ponytail. Girardi nearly did not recognize her at first. *She actually looks like a lawyer,* he said to himself as he motioned for her to take a seat by him.

As it turned out, Judge Grossman was not anxious to speak with the Marshall, Lufton team on the *Hoffman Medical* matter. He allowed Girardi and Thompson to cool their heels for nearly three hours before finally calling them forward as the last order of business for the day. Girardi apologized profusely for his office's mistake and cited Tremont's stroke.

"I'm sorry, counsel," Grossman cut him off. "When did Mr. Tremont fall ill?"

"Nine days ago, your honor."

"Your papers were due more than three weeks ago. I don't see why his illness is even relevant. Your argument so far sounds a little bit like 'the dog at my homework.'"

Girardi took a deep breath and steadied himself. "Your honor, I honestly don't know what happened on this motion. I believe that my partner may well have taken ill some time before his stroke, but I have no proof of this."

Although Girardi genuinely believed this to be a possibility, the judge shook his head skeptically. Girardi then moved on to what he knew would be his best argument.

"*Please*, your honor, do not punish our client Hoffman Medical and deny them their day in court because of an oversight by counsel."

"It was a damned big oversight."

"I know, your honor, and I apologize once more on behalf of Jack Tremont and Marshall, Lufton. Ms. Thomson and I are prepared to take over, and I assure you that nothing like this will happen again."

This continued until the judge appeared to grow weary of torturing Girardi.

"Counsel, I could care less about your excuses or the reputation of your mighty New York firm. But, having said that, I also do not want to see your client denied an opportunity for a full hearing. And so, I'm going to order a sanctions hearing and reinstate the case. The sanctions will of course be paid by your firm and *not* your client. This is your one and only chance. Do you understand me, Mr. Girardi?"

"I do, your honor."

"Alright, then. You can go now."

"Thank you, your honor."

12

After wasting over an hour in rush hour traffic from the Santa Ana courthouse to Newport, Girardi arrived back at the office in a terrible mood. He had lost his entire afternoon to an issue that should never have been before the court to begin with. He had submitted himself to the whims of a grumpy judge who made the most of the opportunity to knock around a fancy, big-firm partner like Girardi. Worse yet, while he was in court taking this beating, valuable hours had been lost on other matters that needed his attention.

He plopped wearily down in his chair and placed on the desk his large coffee and *Carvery* roast beef sandwich. He tried to read the revised draft brief that Chas Cunningham had left for him, but it did not hold his attention for long. Restless, he called Mitch Best in the hopes of telling his friend the story of Judge Grossman. Girardi knew that Best would have the perfect thing to say about Grossman to make him feel better. Unfortunately, the judge did not pick up. With the cell phone still in his hand, he walked over to the window and stared out into the twilight. The sky was exceptionally clear this evening, and he could see the lights of the federal courthouse where Best's chambers were located. With the pair of binoculars he kept on his bookshelf, he looked toward Anaheim and could just make out a bit of the giant neon "A" in the Angel Stadium parking lot and the Matterhorn Mountain at Disneyland. For an Orange County guy like Girardi, this was the ideal view.

As the CEP work crossed his mind, he dialed Beth Stowe's number on a whim. When there came no answer, he hung up without leaving a message, feeling somewhat relieved that she had not picked up. It would not be right for him to nag her so soon. He returned his gaze outside and became lost in thought.

He considered Cliff Conroy and his odd handling of the *Hoffman Medical* emergency. Why had a fax on a litigation matter gone to Conroy instead of Girardi? The territory between attorneys and administrators was clearly divided, and Conway had poached. Was this a fluke, or was Conway monitoring Tremont's incoming correspondence? And how did the CEP file wind up in Tammy Thompson's office? Girardi knew that he was tired, and he reassured himself that there was probably a logical explanation for everything.

Girardi was pulled from these thoughts by a knock at the door. He looked over to see Chas Cunningham filling his doorway.

"I came to see if you had any comments on that revised brief, Mike."

"Not yet, Chas. I was in court all afternoon. I'll look at it right now."

"Do you want me to wait?"

Of course I want you to wait, Chas, he thought with annoyance. *You shouldn't have asked me that. Come on, man.*

"Yes, please wait," Girardi offered calmly. "I'll call you when I'm ready to give you my comments."

"While you're looking at the brief, I think I'll head downstairs and grab some dinner. You want anything?"

Girardi pointed at his sandwich. "No thanks, I'm good. By the way, Chas, have you pulled all the documents for Thursday's deposition?"

"Not yet."

"And how about the exhibits for this brief?"

Cunningham looked down at his shoes and shook his head in the negative. His reaction led Girardi to wonder if Cunningham would have done this work without the reminder.

"While you're waiting for me, why don't you start pulling the exhibits for this brief? Remember that each of our factual assertions must be backed up by something in the record. The court's not just going to take our word for anything."

"I'll start that right away."

"You can grab a bite first—but then start those exhibits. It's going to take me a while to get through this draft."

As Cunningham departed, Girardi forced his attention to the young man's brief and was soon disappointed by what he saw. While it still had a long way to go, Thompson's second draft had at least clearly incorporated Girardi's suggestions and demonstrated that she was listening to him. *I'm getting too old for this.*

Later, Girardi's cell phone rang. Eager for a distraction, he answered without even checking to identify the caller.

"Mike Girardi."

"Hello Mike, it's Beth Stowe."

Girardi was surprised. *She must have checked her dropped calls.* He felt needled with guilt for having disturbed her because of his own restless anxiety.

"Oh, hi Beth. You didn't need to call me back."

"I'm sorry I missed your call. I was in the common room with the sisters watching *Law & Order.*"

Girardi was struck by how chipper she sounded. *Law & Order? She really is in a different world,* he thought with a chuckle. *She's lucky.*

"Are you serious?" he asked.

"Dead serious—the sisters absolutely *love Law & Order.* The reruns are on all the time. One of my main contributions to the community is my ability to explain some of the procedural questions that come up on the show. Sister Agnes is keen on *Miranda* warnings, and Stella is always watching the chain of evidence."

Girardi laughed. "I don't know what to say to that."

"You should see how disappointed they are when I can't answer their legal questions. I never practiced criminal law, so I'm at a disadvantage."

"Next time you're in a jam, you can call me. I was a prosecutor for five years."

"Why did you call me, Mike? I still have a long way to go on those documents."

"I was looking at my schedule," Girardi explained, "and I wondered if we might put something on calendar to talk about those documents. When can I come and see you?"

There was a long pause on the other end. "You don't mind coming here?" she asked, sounding surprised.

"Nope. What's good for you?"

"Let me think. We have some people coming for day programs this week, but no one is staying overnight thank goodness. We have spiritual direction on Friday mornings. How about Friday afternoon?"

Girardi clicked a few buttons on his computer. Friday afternoon looked terrible, but so did every other day for the next two weeks. The main thing was that he had no court dates on Friday.

"Friday is fine—what time?"

"How about two in the afternoon?"

"That works." Wheels turning, Girardi thought that he might bring his work with him and head directly home on Friday after seeing Stowe at the center. Perhaps he could coax Jake to stay home for a Friday dinner with his old man.

"How's it going over there? Is everything under control?" Stowe ventured.

There was now a long pause on Girardi's end as he considered how to answer that question. Under almost any other circumstances, he would have responded with the standard, "everything is under control." But it was late, and he was tired. And everything was not under control.

"Let me guess," she prompted. "You had a rough day?"

"You might say that."

"I knew it. I could hear it in your voice. Are you still at the office?"

Girardi cringed a bit, for he prided himself on his ability to maintain a calm exterior under pressure.

"Yep, I'm still here, but it's not a big deal, really. Just a lot going on."

"Oh," she replied in disappointment. "I thought you were going to share some really interesting war story."

Girardi paused. "I thought you left Marshall, Lufton to get away from that kind of thing."

"It might surprise you, but I'm beginning to rack up some new war stories of my own here at the center."

"You are?"

"Just yesterday, I got into a tussle with a retreat guest in the office."

Girardi was stumped. "I assumed that everyone would be nice to one another at a place like the center."

Rather than respond to this, Stowe moved back a step in the conversation. "I left Marshall, Lufton because my own war stories became too much for me, and I realized that I wasn't cut out for firm practice. But I don't mind hearing other people's war stories. Come on," she coaxed, "there must be some interesting stuff happening over there. I can take it."

At this, Girardi shared the story of his afternoon in Judge Grossman's courtroom. He spoke in a monologue, describing everything from the arrival of the court's faxed order in the hands of Cliff Conroy to the banging of the gavel that had signaled Girardi's reprieve.

"That reminds me of the time Magistrate Judge Chavez chewed us out for being late on those discovery responses. Do you remember that? He was brutal." She paused. "I remember what you told me on the way home. 'Occasional public humiliation is just a cost of doing business, Beth. It's what they pay us for.'"

"I said that?"

"You sure did. You also reminded me of your theory that everyone has to play his or her role. Sometimes judges need to yell and scream so that the rules don't become too easily violated. And plenty of times lawyers fall on the sword and apologize for other people's mistakes. The main thing, you said, is that we should never take things personally. Business is business."

This all surprised Girardi, though he had to admit that his old advice sounded cogent and on-point.

"Well, did my sage words make you feel better?"

There was a thoughtful silence on the line. "That's hard to say. I'm not sure your advice made me *feel* any better. Intellectually, it always made sense to me. And, in turn, it helped me understand my job."

"But . . . ?"

"But, I never quite got the hang of 'business is business.' I tended to get wrapped up in my work and I took things personally. When opposing counsel lied to me, I took it personally. When a partner or a judge yelled at me, I took it *very* personally. Maybe that's why I wasn't a very good attorney."

This was a lot for the tired Girardi to take in, and he was certain that he had never yelled at her. "You were a terrific attorney, Beth. You may not have liked the work, but you were good at it."

Stowe chuckled. "You're just saying that so I'll do a good job with those *Trinity Hills* documents."

"No, I'm not."

"Well," she continued carefully, "I'm sorry that Judge Grossman was so tough on you. It was good of you to stand up for Jack that way."

"It's my job."

"Yes, but not every partner can do something like this properly. I'm sure you handled everything just right today. Jack's lucky to have you. He always has been. I've never thought he appreciated all you do for him. He might be a champion BS-er, but you're the skilled attorney."

"In a law firm, money often takes the place of appreciation."

Stowe let out a long sigh at this. "Money means so much in the firm . . . and so little here . . ."

The line became quiet once more, and Girardi decided to change the subject. "Well, since I told you my war story, why don't you share yours? What kind of trouble did you get into on Sunday?"

"You don't want to hear about that. Compared to Judge Grossman, it's silly."

"No, really. I could use the distraction. Tell me."

"The story involves money as a matter of fact."

Stowe proceeded to share her encounter with Greenway, and Girardi was predictably sympathetic.

"What a jerk. I'm glad you gave it to him; sounds like he deserved it."

"I thought so at first, too. But Sister Agnes took me to task afterwards."

"She did?"

"It's a long story, but Agnes was right about what she said. I should have held my temper. There's no room for anger in a place like this."

Girardi considered this. "I suppose that's true, but you were just trying to collect money the center needs to keep itself going, right?"

"That's right."

"Then I don't see the problem."

"I'm learning that 'business is business' does not fly around here." Stowe let out a long sigh. "The values of this place are different. It's one thing to know a set of values intellectually and a different thing entirely to put them into practice. I need to be gracious even with the Mr. Greenways of the world." She paused. "*Especially* with the Mr. Greenways. My parents taught me all of this as a child, but I didn't truly understand."

Girardi didn't know how to respond to these philosophical musings, and the paperwork on his desk seemed to call to him. "You know, Beth, it's great talking with you, but it's getting late. I should probably be going. I have an associate waiting for me."

"Okay. I'll see you at two o'clock on Friday."

"Right—see you then."

Girardi hung up the phone with his spirits at least partially restored. It had done him good to tell his story about Grossman and to hear more about the goings-on at the center. Each time he spoke with her, Girardi thought he detected more of the old Stowe coming through. And yet, some things had clearly changed, too.

Grabbing his sandwich, he forced his attention back to Cunningham's brief. At nine-thirty, Girardi called Jake to touch base and then sat down with Cunningham to review his brief. The young man took lots of notes and at least appeared to be engaged in the conversation. Around eleven, Girardi walked down to the parking garage with his associate and they both headed home.

■ ■ ■

In the office the following afternoon, Girardi was surprised to receive a call from CEP in-house counsel Russell Yost.

"Hello, Mike. How are you?"

"Busy, Russell, but everybody's busy. How are you doing?"

"Just fine. I'm calling on a matter that Jack was working on for us before his stroke."

"*Pope Electronics*?"

"That's right."

Thank goodness that file turned up yesterday, Girardi thought with relief. *At least I won't look like a complete idiot.*

"I took a quick look at the audit report. I take it that CEP owns Pope Electronics?"

"Yes."

"So, have you completed your internal investigation yet?"

Yost paused before answering. "Actually, Mike, I was under the impression that Jack was preparing a written response for us to submit to the government on *Pope Electronics*. He'd promised it to us last Monday. Our deadline with the agency is coming up and I'm empty-handed at the moment. It's making me nervous. Will you please find out about it?"

The familiar old discomfort that accompanied any consideration of CEP now swept over Girardi. There had been no evidence of any formal written product from Tremont in the paper file or on the computer system. In fact, there was no preliminary analysis memorandum either. In cases like this, with millions at stake, such a written analysis almost always preceded the drafting of a formal response to the government.

"You know, Russell, it's been a little crazy around here lately with me taking over for Jack. Let me look around and get back to you, okay?"

"Will you call me back as soon as you find anything?"

"Of course. Russell, may I clarify something?"

"Sure."

"Did Jack provide you a preliminary analysis memo? I don't recall seeing one in the file."

"No." Yost hesitated. "Jack just gave us a verbal evaluation."

Thinking of the lengthy and complicated allegations in the audit report, Girardi wondered how Tremont could possibly have given such a verbal assessment without written backup. In his experience, clients wished to have such a memorandum before deciding how to proceed. And counsel also desired a clear record of the advice given should any question arise in the future.

"No memo?"

"We didn't want to spend the money. You know how it is these days."

Girardi wondered if this explained the thin *Pope Electronics* file. Perhaps Jack and the client were trying to do something on the cheap. But there was no quick and dirty way that Girardi knew of to respond to a comprehensive audit report. *What was Jack doing?*

"I promise I'll find out whatever I can. I'll get back to you the minute I know something."

"Thanks Mike, I really appreciate it. Oh, and I'm sorry to hear about Jack. Is he going to be okay?"

"The reports I'm hearing are cautiously optimistic. It's time for me to go and see him. I'll give him your best."

"Yes, please do that."

"I will, and I'll call you tomorrow. Goodbye, Russell."

13

The following morning, Girardi met with Celeste Tremont in the Hope Hospital cafeteria. He bought her the breakfast special and grabbed a banana muffin and coffee for himself. As they took seats at a sunny table by the corner windows, Girardi observed the toll that her husband's illness had taken upon his companion. The usually glamorous and vibrant Celeste was dressed this morning in jeans and a faded University of South Carolina sweatshirt. She and her husband were fond of calling the school "the *real* USC." Celeste's gray-blonde hair was pulled back, revealing a face that was pale and sullen.

"So, tell me," Girardi ventured cautiously, "how is he doing?"

"Oh, Mike, it's hard to say. The doctor tells me something different every day or two, and I can't understand most of it anyway. Jack and I wait for the doctor all day and then he's in and out of the room in two minutes. He usually doesn't even sit down while we try and ask our questions." She shook her head. "I don't understand our medical system."

"You told me on the phone that they've moved Jack to a private room with less monitoring. That sounds like a good sign."

"Well, the doctors say he's stabilized, but he looks terrible to me. I hate to see him suffering so. He grunts and thrashes around in his sleep. When he's awake, he struggles to speak and it makes him angry. I do most of the talking."

Girardi hated to hear this, because he had come this morning with some very specific and important questions for Tremont.

"You said on the phone that he has physical therapy in the mornings?"

"Sort of—the therapist was in with him earlier; she's a sweet little Asian girl. Very patient. Jack's so weak that he can't get out of bed, but the therapist has him trying to move his arm and his leg. It's a start."

Celeste went on to share some more details of Tremont's hospital routine before changing the subject.

"How is everything at the office?" she asked.

"Hectic."

"Cliff told us that you had to go to court because of a mistake on one of Jack's cases."

Girardi was surprised and annoyed with Conroy for troubling Jack and Celeste with this information.

"It's all taken care of, Celeste. The judge gave me a hard time for a few minutes, but he let us back into the case. Nothing to worry about."

"That's good to hear. Thank you, Mike."

"Speaking of business, do you think Jack might be up to talking to me about a couple of cases? It's important."

Her expression clouded, and she wrung her hands with uncertainty. "You are welcome to try. He has his good moments, and you might get lucky. But, as I said, it's a struggle for him to say much. Please be realistic."

"Okay."

"And *promise* me you won't over-tax him."

"I promise."

"You know, his doctor warned him that something like this could happen—he was diabetic."

"I didn't know that."

"He just refused to take care of himself. I tried a thousand times to get him to diet."

"He works hard—it can take a toll."

She shook her head. "And even now he still won't let his mind rest. Cliff is here practically every day. Jack says he likes to see him, but I think Cliff upsets him."

This surprised Girardi. "What are they talking about?"

"Who knows? I usually take a walk when Cliff visits."

"Why don't you suggest to Cliff that he not come so often?"

Celeste's eyes grew large as she shook her head in the negative. "Oh, I couldn't do that. Jack wouldn't want me to interfere."

"Do you want me to talk to him?"

"*No*, please Mike. I shouldn't have said anything."

She crumpled up her napkin and then leaned back in her chair, staring worried out the window. In the fifteen years he'd known Celeste Tremont, he had never seen her like this before. Celeste was energetic and upbeat— always the center of attention. Now, she seemed like a small, tired old woman. At the same time, however, he had to admit that she was easier to talk to than usual. Gone were the dramatic stories and gestures. Despite the circumstances, a part of him liked this simpler version of Celeste.

"Are you taking care of yourself?" he asked.

She appeared surprised by the question. "Probably not. I'm here all the time. My daughter is trying to help me, but she's busy with her kids and we aren't all that close. My friends come and sit with me. And my sons visited last week," she paused an offered a rare smile at this. "I love my boys so much. But they had to fly home on Monday and go back to work. To tell you the truth, I feel alone."

"You don't have a minister or anything like that to help you?"

"A minister?" she chuckled. "I haven't attended church regularly since I was a teenager. Jack never had much use for religion, you know. I didn't think you did, either."

Girardi nodded.

"The truth is," she continued, "I'm afraid for Jack . . . and I suppose for myself, too. We've been together since college. My god, what would I ever do without him?"

"Try not to think that way, Celeste. He's getting great care here."

"I suppose so." She rubbed her face with her hands. "We rattle around that big house by ourselves. It's too much for us, and the mortgage is enormous. I think we should sell the Plantation."

"Sell the Plantation? That place is legendary."

Celeste smiled wanly. "I doubt we'll be throwing any more big parties there."

Girardi thought of the phone bill he'd seen in the *Pope Electronics* file. "Maybe you two could move into the condo in Huntington Beach."

Celeste looked puzzled. "What condo?"

Girardi blinked in confusion. He'd distinctly heard Cliff Conroy say that he would pass on the Cherry Tree Lane phone bill to Celeste.

"For some reason I thought you guys had a rental property up there," he bluffed. "It's a nice area. When Jack gets better, maybe you can look for a little place by the beach."

"I'd like to find something smaller, that's for certain."

Girardi rose from the table. "I think I'll go upstairs and at least say hello. Will you come with me?"

"No thanks. I'm going to stay here for a while and read my book. This is my favorite spot—I can see the blue sky from here. Jack's room is so dreary."

She reached up and embraced Girardi. "Thanks for the breakfast and the talk, Mike. It was good to see you."

"It was good to see you, too."

With a nod, Girardi left the cafeteria and headed for Jack Tremont's room, apprehensive of how he would find his old mentor. Riding up in the busy elevator, he watched the anxious families and harried hospital personnel enter and exit at each floor. On this longer-than-expected ride, Girardi was reminded of how much he had always hated hospitals. Despite efforts to repress them, his mind recalled hazy, distant scenes of distress.

Long ago, on a terrible Thanksgiving weekend when Girardi was a young boy, a station wagon carrying his maternal grandparents, an aunt and two cousins had been struck on the freeway in a rain storm. Girardi had been too young to comprehend what was going on. But he had been old enough to absorb the fear and anguish of his relatives during the weeks spent at the hospital. These unpleasant memories extended also to the attendant funeral masses. For as long as he could remember, Girardi had assiduously avoided hospitals and churches because of his painful associations from this period. He also never cared for Thanksgiving or turkey.

Bracing himself as he approached Tremont's doorway, Girardi stepped aside to let out a technician pushing a cart from the room. When the cart was gone, Girardi hesitantly entered and found Cliff Conroy sitting at his old mentor's bedside.

Conroy stood at once and offered his hand. "Good morning, Mike."

Girardi took Conroy's hand. "Hi, Cliff." Then, he turned to Tremont. "Hello there, partner. How are they treating you in this place?"

Tremont's eye's flashed. "Just . . . t . . . t . . . terrible . . ."

Girardi looked the big man over carefully and immediately perceived his distress and frustration. His gray hair was disheveled and there was a wild look about his features that almost frightened Girardi. The large bandage still covered the gash on the side of his head.

"He's having a hard time talking today," Conroy explained calmly. "I keep telling him to relax and rest. Everything will come back with time."

Girardi placed his briefcase on the floor and pulled a chair up next to the bed across from Conroy. "Cliff is right, Jack. You shouldn't push yourself too much."

Tremont squinted his shrunken eyes and tried to lean forward. "Work to . . . do . . . ," he said with effort.

Girardi picked up on this immediately.

"Are you thinking of any work in particular, Jack? Do you mean that we have work to do at the office?"

Conroy shot Girardi a look of disapproval. Tremont stared forlornly at Girardi but did not say anything.

"Mike has all of the work under control. Right, Mike?" Conroy offered.

Again the phrase that Girardi so disliked.

"Of course. But I wanted to ask Jack if there was anything in particular he'd like to hear an update on."

Girardi knew that this sounded far-fetched, given how weak Tremont seemed. He recalled also his promise to Celeste that he would not over-tax her husband. Again, there was a flash in Tremont's eye. It seemed to Girardi that he had much to say, but his ailing body held him back.

"Everyone is concerned for you, Jack. They all ask me to send their good wishes to you and Celeste."

Tremont nodded slightly at this as Girardi continued.

"I heard from Russell Yost at CEP just yesterday. He asked me to give you his best." Girardi paused and his eyes met Tremont's. "By the way, Jack, he was apparently expecting a written response from you for the government on *Pope Electronics*. I looked around, but did not find anything in the file or on the computer system. Did you write anything for him?"

Girardi watched Tremont carefully as the old man took in the ques-tion. He appeared to think for some time and at last shook his head in the negative. Girardi detected no special distress at the mention of *Pope Electronics* or CEP.

"Jean tells me that Jaime's fundraiser was a big success," Conroy in-terjected. "We missed you there. And, just as Mike said, everybody asked about you. Jean and Jaime asked me to specifically thank you for buy-ing those tables. She believes that he has a real chance in the primary. Apparently the district has never been represented by an Hispanic. Plenty of folks in the party want to see him win."

Tremont mumbled a few words of acknowledgment. It was plain that he was not ready for substantive conversation. Girardi resigned himself to this fact and joined Conroy in some small talk until the nurse's assistant came in to give Tremont his bath. Relieved, Girardi said his goodbyes and followed Conroy out of the room and toward the elevator. The pair moved along in tense silence and did not speak until they were alone to-gether once more in the hospital's main floor lobby.

"Mike, I can't understand why you asked him about that case. It's clear he's not ready yet."

Girardi took a deep breath before answering. "Russ Yost called me yesterday in a lather, asking for Jack's response to that government audit report. I can't find *any* evidence of a document like that in the file. I hated to disturb Jack, but I needed to ask the question. I'm the one in charge of his cases now. We don't want to be committing any malpractice if we can help it."

The pair separated for a moment as they exited through the sliding glass doors and met a crowd coming in.

"By the way, Cliff, Tammy found the *Pope Electronics* file in her office," Girardi commented as soon as Conroy was back at his side.

"Good." Conroy pulled out a case and removed a pair of designer prescription sunglasses, replacing his clear lenses.

They walked on until they arrived at Conroy's green Jaguar. The car was at least twenty years old, but it was in nearly perfect condition. Girardi's mind suddenly went to the phone bill he'd found in the CEP file. Conroy had said he would give the bill to Celeste, but Celeste seemed to know nothing about it. Girardi considered smoking Conroy out, but then he stopped himself. Even if Conroy had lied, what business was it of Girardi's if Tremont owned one rental property or a dozen? And Tremont's arrangements with Celeste were none of his concern either.

Conroy opened his door and slid in behind the driver's seat. "I'll see you later, Mike."

At this, Conroy left a bewildered Girardi alone to consider his next steps. He drove back to the office and when he arrived, Girardi's first call was to Russell Yost. His plan was to fall on the sword and admit to Yost that as far as he could tell, there was no written draft response on *Pope Electronics*. Girardi would also offer to analyze the file as quickly as possible. There might be enough time to write at least a preliminary response to the government. Girardi planned to suggest to Yost that he request some sort of extension from the government, citing Jack Tremont's illness.

Girardi felt his heart beating fast as he waited for Yost to pick up his line. To his disappointment, he learned that Yost was out at a meeting in the San Fernando Valley and was not expected back until the following morning. Girardi left a general voice message for Yost asking him to call back but not mentioning specifically the audit report. Girardi knew that he needed to speak directly with Yost on that subject. Girardi then turned to his other work, waiting for Yost's return call and worrying over what the CEP counsel would ask of him when he learned that Girardi was at present empty-handed.

14

On Wednesday evening at St. Mark's Episcopal Church, the Reverend Doctor Susan Mountjoy stood before fifteen congregants, leading them through the Evensong service. In attendance this evening were Hector and Sylvia Bea, who were still considering a donation to the parish's musical programs. The couple's college-aged son Francisco was with them. This was the family's first Evensong, and Mountjoy hoped to make a good impression with them.

Dressed in her plain black cassock, she began to chant the *Phos hilaron,* "O gracious light," with accompaniment from her black and white-robed choir. The sanctuary was dark save for the choir's small pin lights and a couple of dozen candles scattered on posts along the center aisle and on the altar. There was a warm, ethereal glow about the place. The ancient Christians had worshipped by candlelight, and Mountjoy favored liturgies that linked her congregation to the practices of the early church.

What's more, Mountjoy had always loved to chant. Yale Divinity School was known for its sacred music program, and this had been one of the reasons she'd chosen to attend seminary there. Standing now at the pulpit with a tiny reading lamp illuminating the book in front of her, she began to chant, placing a long emphasis on the vowels in the first line, *"Ooo . . . graaa . . . cious liiight . . .*

pure brightness of the everliving Father in Heaven,
O Jesus Christ, holy and blessed.

Now as we come to the setting of the sun,
and our eyes behold the vesper light,
we sing your praises, O God: Father, Son, and Holy Spirit.

You are worthy at all times to be praised by happy voices,
O Son of God, O Giver of Life,
and to be glorified through all the worlds."

After some meditative silence, the service continued with the reading of a psalm and Bible passage by a lay lector. There was then more time for reflection, for Mountjoy desired a prayerful atmosphere for the busy souls who made time for Wednesday evening services. Next, the choir and organist offered a beautiful rendition of the Magnificat. Sitting off to the side in the dark chancel, Mountjoy allowed herself to become momentarily lost in the beauty of the Virgin Mary's song. When things became trying for her, Mountjoy often found herself praying to Mary. It had always been comforting to have at least one feminine presence among the most holy.

On Sunday mornings, Mountjoy routinely stood at the back of the church after services to greet and shake hands with her parishioners and visitors. On Wednesday nights, however, it was her habit to dismiss the congregants from the pulpit. It was a weeknight, and everyone was anxious to get home, including the rector. She followed her usual practice this evening, and as the group filed out the back of the sanctuary, she set about quickly gathering her things and congratulating her choir on a job well done. As she was wishing the music director a good evening, she heard an out-of-place yet familiar voice from the foyer.

"Hector, Sylvia, it's good to see you again. Lovely service, wasn't it?"

Mary, Mother of God, it can't be. I must be imagining. She squinted toward the back of the church but could not make out clearly the tall stranger she'd noticed coming in part way through the service. It was even darker now, for her acolyte had doused all of the candles in the sanctuary.

Mountjoy strongly considered making her escape through the side door, but then she stopped herself. She needed to lock all of the church's doors, and it would not do to ditch a visitor this way. Lingering near the pulpit for a few extra minutes, she at last gathered her Evensong notebook and her courage and headed for the back of the church.

"Well Reverend, I must compliment you on that service. It was lovely."

"Thank you, Mitch," she replied abruptly.

"Are you just going to leave, Susie?" the judge asked in surprise as she moved past him and headed for the door, keys in hand.

"It's late and I'm exhausted."

"Would you like to go and get a bite to eat?"

He's got to be kidding if he thinks I'd eat with him after the way he acted at the restaurant on Sunday.

"I ate before the service."

"Then would you please stay and talk to me for a few minutes?"

Mountjoy very much wanted to send Judge Best away, but could not quite bring herself to do it.

"Okay, just a few minutes." She reached over and flipped on the lights above them and then motioned him to a pew. She took the adjacent bench and placed her binder next to her. Mountjoy was very fond of three-ring binders, and almost always had at least one with her. She took great comfort in the sense of organization, control, and regularity that came with a well-maintained binder.

The judge was dressed this evening in a charcoal gray pinstripe suit, crisp white shirt and red tie. She surveyed Best sitting with his long arm draped casually over the back of his pew, and thought he looked surprisingly comfortable. And in his business attire, he was entirely transformed from the goofy-looking guy in his shorts and flip-flops on the *Emilio's* patio. Years ago back in college, Mountjoy had secretly thought that despite his being a thorough-going Neanderthal, Best was in his own way an attractive man. To her surprise, she still found him so.

"So, what can I do for you, Mitch?"

"Gee, Susie, are you always so short with visitors? Aren't you supposed to be the face of Christ or something like that?"

Where did he pick that up?

"What brings you to St. Mark's on this fine evening, your honor?"

"I ran into a girl I used to know, and she told me that I could use a little Jesus Christ in my life."

"She was probably mistaken."

Best chuckled at this. "Maybe she wasn't. I looked this girl up, and it turns out that she's pretty hot stuff. She has a master's degree *and* a doctorate from Yale Divinity School. As if that were not enough, a few years ago she earned a certificate in music and liturgy from Cambridge. She's on all kinds of boards and committees, and she was even nominated for bishop."

"In Alabama. And she lost that election."

"So what, it's probably good that she lost. Who in her right mind wants to leave Newport Beach for Mobile?"

"Birmingham, actually, but we go where God calls us," she replied reflexively, though in fact she had spent many hours worrying and praying over this very issue during the months of her nomination. Her loss, though a disappointment, had in truth also come as something of a relief.

Looking at Best, Mountjoy paused before continuing, surprised that he seemed to know so much about her. "What did you do, hire a private eye to check up on me?"

"No, I just had one of my marshals do a background check in his spare time. You'd be surprised how much time those guys waste just sitting around the courthouse on the taxpayers' dime."

Mountjoy was taken aback. "Oh Mitch, you didn't!"

"Calm down, Susie. That was a joke. I mainly Googled you and made a couple of calls. Really, you should be proud of your accomplishments. You've done well for yourself."

Made a couple of calls? she repeated to herself. *Good heavens, why did he do that? And who did he call?*

"Why are buttering me up?" she asked suspiciously.

"Who says I'm buttering you up?"

"Tell me why you're here."

Best paused for a few moments and looked around the sanctuary. He shifted in his pew and then rested his gaze intently upon Mountjoy. "I suppose I'm here for two reasons. First of all, I wanted to apologize for my comment about your weight at the restaurant. That was childish and entirely inappropriate and I'm sorry. I didn't even mean what I said, for the record. I swear it won't happen again."

Mountjoy was a little surprised by this. "Alright, Mitch, I accept your apology."

"Really?"

"Yes."

"Are you sure? That was a little too easy. Maybe you'd like to insult me somehow just to make things even?"

"Since this isn't junior high, I don't need to insult you to get even. I'll just write something about you in one of the ladies' room stalls before Sunday. That'll square things up."

Best laughed heartily at this. "Sarcasm! Good for you, Susie. That's much better."

He's nuts, she thought as Best continued.

"I can't tell sometimes whether you have a sense of humor or not. You had one back when we were in school, or at least you sort of did. But you lost it when you got onto that feminist bandwagon."

"*Okay*," she interjected impatiently, "what's the second reason you're here?"

"I'd like to get some counseling."

Mountjoy laughed at this, assuming that this was another of Best's seemingly endless stream of jokes. But as she looked at him, an improbable look of hurt crossed Best's face. "Is that so impossible to believe, Susie?"

You've got to get serious, Susan. He's not joking around. Mountjoy looked up toward the altar and said a little prayer to Mary for patience and a generous heart. This was a prayer she offered with greater frequency these days.

"I'm sorry, Mitch. I'm just surprised, that's all. When I saw you at the restaurant, you said that everything was going well for you."

"Yeah, and you said the same thing. We were both BS-ing because we hadn't seen each other in so long. With strangers, we're supposed to say that everything is great and that we love our jobs and our kids are perfect and all of that nonsense."

Mountjoy wondered why Best would presume to offer commentary on her own circumstances, but she put this aside for the time being. As improbable as it was, here before her, in the guise of a long-lost friend, was a soul seeking her help. Despite her misgivings, she knew she needed to do her best for him.

As a pastor, Mountjoy had learned over the years to flip a little switch in her mind. She never knew in the course of her day when someone might suddenly want advice or comfort from her. It happened on airplanes, in restaurants and anywhere she wore her collar in public. And sometimes, as it had with Elizabeth Stowe and now with Best, it could happen at the end of the evening in Mountjoy's own sanctuary.

"So, something is bothering you?"

"My marriage is falling apart."

The words landed hard.

"Mitch, I'm very sorry to hear that. But I'm not a marriage counselor."

"I know that. I'm not interested in a marriage counselor. I went through that with my first wife. What a joke! That counselor was more messed up than either of us. Jenny and I knew what our problems were, but neither of us was willing to bend enough to make it work."

"But if you are having problems with . . . did you say her name was Sophia?"

Best nodded. "Good memory, Susie."

"If Sophia is interested in marriage counseling, you should give it another shot. Put that first experience out of your mind. Sophia deserves as much. I can make a couple of good referrals if you'd like. In my line of work, I make it a point to know qualified counselors."

"I'm afraid it's too late. My wife was offered a promotion with her magazine on the condition that she move to San Francisco. She took the job without even asking me about it."

This hit a nerve with the staunchly feminist Mountjoy. "What's she supposed to do? Turn a promotion down because *your* career is more important?"

The judge's face colored. "Shit Susie, why are you taking her side? I haven't even told you the whole story yet. Sophia went ahead and rented an apartment up there before she even talked to me about this. I found out because of the credit check they ran at the apartment building. The guy is not always to blame when a marriage goes south, you know."

"Don't swear in my sanctuary, Mitch."

Best assumed an expression and posture of contrition. "I'm sorry. It's just that you're the first person I've told about this. It's tearing me up and I don't know what to do. But before you tell me I'm wrong, I'd like you to hear more."

Mountjoy looked carefully at Best as she considered what to say next. "I still think this is a job for a good marriage counselor. But, if you want to speak with a priest, I know somebody in Santa Ana who would be perfect. Father Tim O'Brien. He spent some time in law school before seminary. We met at Yale. His parish isn't far from the courthouse. He's busy, but with a good word from me, I think he might agree to see you. Tim is really smart and he won't let you get away with anything."

The more Mountjoy thought about it, the more she liked the idea of sending the judge to Father Tim. They were each intelligent and accomplished men around the same age, and they might just understand one another. From the expression on Best's face, however, she could see that he was less than convinced.

"I don't want to see some Irish guy in Santa Ana. I want *you* to help me. It won't work for me to deal with a stranger. I trust you."

"I can't, Mitch. I wouldn't be right for you. In my professional judgment, you'd do much better working with a man."

"That's baloney, Susie. You always boil everything down to gender. I promise I'll tone down the smart-ass stuff. And I won't say anything about your appearance. The truth is, though, that you look great."

Mountjoy took a deep breath as she considered what to say next.

"To tell you the truth, the fact that we were friends a long time ago is a factor in my evaluation." She decided not to mention the issue of his sexist comments. "But even leaving that aside, you'd do better with a man. I'm confident about that. Trust me, I know what I'm talking about. I've been doing this for a long time."

"But the marriage is only part of why I'm here. I need something more in my life, and I'd like to learn about Christianity."

"Why?"

Best was quick with his rejoinder. "Why did you say that a little Jesus Christ might do me good?"

At this, Mountjoy again paused thoughtfully. In truth, she wasn't sure why she'd said this to him. Back on the *Emilio's* patio, the idea had suddenly come over her that a little evangelizing with Judge Best might help him. She'd spoken on impulse, which was unusual for her. But now, with even a bit of reflection, it was plain to Mountjoy that if Best wanted to explore the mysteries of the faith and find some solace, he'd have to do it with someone else.

"I think a little Jesus Christ would do everyone some good," she demurred.

Best looked at Mountjoy for some time, wheels turning, and changed the subject.

"You know, this Evensong service surprised me. It was a lot more subtle than I expected. You didn't even preach. Growing up I went to church off and on with my mother and brother, but that was at a Baptist place out in the sticks, and the sermon was the focal point. I'll never forget the preacher my mom liked so much—he wore white suits and drove this huge white Cadillac." The judge chuckled at the recollection, then returned to his point. "For your church, the liturgy seems more important."

Mountjoy was surprised that Best even knew this much of the terminology of the church. She chuckled. "Smells and bells—that's us."

"What do you mean?"

"That's a joke about Anglican liturgies. There were no bells or incense this evening, but we can go to town on that stuff sometimes. Some people find it to be too much."

"Holy smoke?"

She nodded and smiled knowingly. "Exactly."

"So you studied liturgy at Cambridge? How did that come about?"

"In my job here I accrue some sabbatical time each year. A few years ago, I spent a summer in England, exploring the roots of my church. It was such a great trip. A part of me thinks I could have stayed there forever."

Mountjoy paused and smiled as she conjured scenes from the journey in her mind's eye.

"At the beginning of the summer, I spent a few weeks in classes at the university. Then I traveled, visiting churches and cathedrals all over England and attending as many different types of services as I could. After that it was back to Cambridge for more seminars. At the end of the term, I wrote a paper. The professors really liked it. I wasn't sure that I'd enjoy a classroom setting at my age, but the truth was that I loved it. It was during a service in a small chapel in Cambridge that I got the idea for an Evensong here at St. Mark's. When I returned home, I met with my music director and she loved the idea. We applied for a grant to pay the musicians and went for it."

"A change of scenery can do a world of good, can't it?"

"It sure can," Mountjoy agreed, suddenly wondering what had prompted her to share all of these details from her sabbatical. "If I had the time, I'd take a stab at expanding the paper I wrote in England into a book. I've always wanted to write a book."

"Why haven't you?"

"There's no time."

"But everybody's busy. Really, what would it take to get a book project going?"

"The two things I lack," she replied helplessly, "time and money. I'd require some time away to write, and I'd need to hire someone to fill in for me. I have a retired priest who helps out occasionally. He's terrific, but I can't go to that well too often. And, my congregation hates unfamiliar substitute pastors. So, I'm stuck."

Best seemed not to know what to say to this. "Well," he offered, "it's great that you at least started a new service as a result of the trip."

Mountjoy paused and let out a sigh. "It was great for a while, but the truth is that I may need to discontinue the Evensong service."

"Why?"

"Look at the attendance, Mitch. I had barely more than a dozen. Our grant from the diocese was supposed to lead to new members for the parish, but by and large it's my regulars who show up on Wednesday nights. The grant has run out, and I can't afford to take up resources for such a sparsely-attended service. My musicians are very talented, but they cost money."

"I'm sorry to hear that. Down at the courthouse, I never need to worry about drumming up business. There's always more than we can handle."

"That doesn't surprise me."

"I was chatting with Hector and Sylvia after the service," Best continued. "They said something about possibly making a donation to support musical program. They are clearly admirers of yours."

"We'll see if that comes through. The Beas are generous people, but they support causes all over town. I've learned over the years that I can't count on anything until I have a check in my hand."

"It turns out that that Francisco Bea is interested in law school. I invited junior for a personal tour of the courthouse. He took me right up on it. I think he's coming on Friday."

"That was good of you, Mitch."

"No problem. I hope that donation comes through. This really was a pleasant service—more pleasant than I'd expected to tell you the truth."

After some more small talk, there came a natural break in the conversation, and Mountjoy stood to go. Best also rose slowly from his pew.

"Listen, Susie, can't I come back some time for that tour of the church you offered me?"

"You should see Father Tim."

"So, you're reneging on me? That doesn't seem right. Your bulletin says '*there shall be no outcasts*.'"

Mountjoy reached into her notebook and grabbed a blank piece of paper. She scribbled Tim O'Brien's name and contact information.

"Father Tim's your ticket, Mitch. You'll like him. Here's his information. I'll let him know I referred you."

Best made a face. "You won't talk to me yourself?"

Mountjoy folded the sheet of paper and closed her notebook. "I'll tell you what," she offered, handing him the paper as she moved to the door. "If you go and see Father Tim a few times and give the process a real chance, I'll give you your tour of St. Mark's after that."

"You drive a hard bargain."

"We ministers are a rough bunch," she rejoined with a laugh. Clutching her notebook to her chest, she extended her hand. She had no interest in another kiss on the cheek from the judge. "Good night, Mitch. I wish you well with your wife. I'll pray for you both."

Best shook her hand and headed slowly for the door. "Goodnight, Susie," he said back over the shoulder. "I'll see you around."

Mountjoy then turned off the lights, locked the door and walked alone to her car, hoping she'd done the right thing in pushing Best to see Tim O'Brien.

15

At the Emmanuel Center just after breakfast, Sister Agnes and Elizabeth Stowe headed to the east conference room for a conversation they had scheduled earlier in the week. Each anticipated full days ahead. Agnes had four spiritual direction appointments scheduled with members of the community, and Stowe needed to finish up her memo before meeting with Mike Girardi in the afternoon. As the pair sat down, Agnes took Stowe's hand into hers and offered a simple prayer, *Lord, open our minds and our hearts so that we may follow your intentions in all things. Forgive us our sins, known and unknown. We ask in the name of your Son, Amen.*

The pair then got down to business.

"When I saw Reverend Susan last week," Stowe began, "she asked me to prepare a report on the center's finances."

Agnes squinted through her large glasses. "I thought you saw her to talk about spiritual matters."

In her months at the center, Stowe had sometimes found herself uncomfortably in the middle between Reverend Susan and Sister Agnes. She admired both women and was indebted to each for guiding her so faithfully through this period of personal exploration and discernment. But as highly as she esteemed them both, the pair seemed to Stowe to be polar opposites, and she struggled to mediate between them.

"We *did* discuss spiritual matters," Stowe replied quickly. "And I also learned that there's going to be an important concert at St. Mark's a week from Sunday. She's hoping we all will attend."

Agnes merely shrugged at this. Things like symphony concerts were worldly matters that she usually preferred to ignore. Her mind and her heart were fixed on the center and its inhabitants and guests.

"About the finances," Stowe continued, worked up thanks to the two cups of coffee she'd gulped down with her breakfast. "I want to show you the format of the report I'm planning to write. It will have some charts and a narrative section."

"You don't need to show me that, Elizabeth."

"Yes I do. I want you to be fully informed of what's going on. Some day the Board of Overseers might want to discuss the report with you. I suppose the sisters back in Minnesota might see it, too."

"We don't need to discuss this. Your primary purpose for being here is not to study our finances. You're here to become closer to the Lord. Tell me, have you made any progress on your personal Rule?"

At the center, Stowe's title was that of Lay Associate, and she was to hold this position for a year. She had begun the prior October and it was now late April. During this year, Stowe was working to discern what she was to do in her professional life now that she'd left legal practice. At the same time, she and the sisters were working together to determine if Stowe would take the significant step of becoming a secular oblate to Agnes's order. Oblates were not monks or nuns. Rather, they were people from all walks of life—doctors, teachers, shop keepers, and homemakers who created voluntary bonds with a religious order. They continued their secular lives, but with a strong commitment to prayer and to furthering the ministries of their chosen order. For her part, Reverend Mountjoy believed that Stowe's true calling might well be to ordained ministry, and she hoped that this calling might make itself apparent through her work at the center.

In some orders like Sister Agnes's, an oblate was required to write a personal Rule of Life. Agnes had worked with a fair number of lay oblates over the years, and she had come to place great emphasis on the personal Rule as evidence of an oblate's spiritual understanding and bond with God.

"I have been gathering books and articles on personal Rules, Agnes, and in fact Susan loaned me a couple of books on the subject. I promise to read them carefully."

"Elizabeth, I know you love your books dearly, but your Rule should come mainly from your heart, not from things other people have written."

Stowe frowned, for this was ground they'd covered before. "But the books fill my mind *and* my heart, Agnes. Reverend Susan understands this."

"With all due respect to the learned Reverend Doctor," Agnes replied archly, "you don't need a stack of books to write your Rule. At most, you need three. Do you know which ones I mean?"

Stowe struggled to shift her mind to this new subject, for her thoughts the past few days had been captured by accounting spread sheets and Mike Girardi's *Trinity Hills* matter.

"The Bible?" she ventured, going for the sure bet first.

Agnes nodded. "What else?"

Stowe hesitated uncomfortably. "I'm not sure." Then, a thought crossed her mind just time. "The sayings of the Desert Fathers and Mothers?"

Agnes nodded her approval at the mention of her favorite literature outside of the sacred scriptures. Over the years, she had acquired various volumes full of these sayings. She also frequently shared Xeroxed copies of such sayings with center guests.

"And for an A plus, what's the third?" Agnes prompted.

Stowe was stumped. "What is it?"

"*The Rule of Benedict.*"

"Oh," Stowe replied without much enthusiasm.

"The Benedictine Rule has survived for over fifteen hundred years, Elizabeth, and it is full of wisdom. The Rule of our own order is based upon it. Benedict was influenced by the Desert Fathers, you know."

"Yes, I know."

The truth was that Stowe had read Benedict's Rule shortly after her arrival at the retreat center, and had not gleaned much from it. To her, the ancient rule seemed almost barbaric, with its extreme austerity and talk of corporal punishment for wayward monks. Stowe had soon put the book aside as largely irrelevant to her or the sisters' twenty-first century vocations.

"I promise I'll start working on my Rule when things settle down a little bit here."

"If you'd forget about that financial report, you might start immediately."

"But I can't forget the report. One of my main contributions to your ministry here is to provide support with the accounting."

"I disagree. Your main contribution to our ministry is simply being here with us. You contribute with your youthful energy, with your smiles and little jokes . . . and your explanations of criminal procedure."

Agnes had a way of blending humor with her serious points that often made the medicine go down a little easier.

"And my gardening?" Stowe asked hopefully.

"My word, I almost forgot—especially your gardening." The tiny nun smiled and turned toward the window, pointing down to the garden. "We all love what you've done."

Despite these kind words, Stowe was not to be turned from her main purpose so easily.

"*Please*, Agnes, hear me out about the report. You and the sisters do so much good here. But, if the finances are not straightened out, that good work might be jeopardized. What if you have to go back to Minnesota?"

"We go where the Lord calls us. He will always provide for our needs. If you cannot abide in that belief, Elizabeth, then perhaps you are not cut out to be an oblate of our order."

The hurt showed plainly on Stowe's face. She had not anticipated receiving such a rebuke from the sister in this meeting on the finances. "Do you really mean that?"

The nun's expression softened some, but her demeanor was still serious. "I do not intend to be harsh, child. But, by my way of seeing, these financial charts and reports are like worldly idols, put before you by the devil to distract you from your prayers and other good works."

Again with this talk of the devil, Stowe fumed, wondering what Reverend Mountjoy might have to say in response to this. The Reverend seemed to Stowe to be very comfortable with the subject of money—and she *never* said anything about the devil. Although she certainly had a spiritual side, Reverend Mountjoy struck Stowe as a woman very at home in the world.

"But I have promised the report to Reverend Mountjoy. She expects it."

"Then write the report if you must, but I have no desire to see or hear about it. Please spend as little time as possible on it. Just leave me a copy when you've finished. I have several other projects around here that need attention."

"Really?" Stowe was immediately intrigued by this, for she was at times frustrated that Agnes did not seem to trust her to do any of the center's spiritually-oriented work.

"Yes. When you are finished with your accounting work . . . ," she paused and frowned once more, "and this legal work you are apparently doing for Mr. Girardi . . . then we will discuss these new projects. Not before."

"Not even a preview?" she coaxed with a little smile.

"I'm afraid not."

Stowe turned back to the sheets in front of her and shook her head at the oppressive stack. "So, you do not want to see any of this?"

"No."

"I am to proceed on my own and deal directly with Reverend Susan?"

"If you must be troubled by this at all, then I think you'd best deal directly with her."

"Alright then."

Agnes was quick to change the subject.

"So, tell me about this project for Mr. Girardi. You worked for him at your old law firm?"

Stowe's stomach rumbled a bit at the question, for this subject was in truth much more difficult for her than that of the financial reports.

"Yes. I worked for two partners at Marshall, Lufton, Mike Girardi and Jack Tremont."

"Mr. Tremont the one who is ill, correct? I've been praying for him."

"He had a stroke two weeks ago."

"And how is he doing?"

"I don't know for certain, but my impression is that he is quite ill."

"I'll keep him on the prayer list, then."

You should be more choosy with the prayer list, Stowe thought.

"Mr. Tremont is not a particularly nice man, Agnes."

"And so he does not deserve our prayers?"

"I did not mean that . . ."

"Indeed, if he is not a very nice man, then perhaps he needs our prayers *more* than most do."

Stowe considered this for a moment. "That may be so, but I worked for the man for years, and I am confident that you would not approve of him if you knew more of him."

"Would I approve of Mr. Girardi if I knew more of him?"

Anges's questions this morning were sharper than usual. This last one caught Stowe off guard, and she pondered her answer for some time.

"I believe that you *would* approve of him. He is an excellent attorney, a devoted father, and a thoroughly decent person."

"I thought you disliked all of the people you worked with at the firm."

"Well, in the case of Mr. Girardi, I *do* like him and in fact I hold him in high esteem. My leaving the firm had nothing to do with him."

The truth was in fact more complicated that this, but Stowe did genuinely admire Girardi.

"You know how hard I've worked to move on. Things were difficult for me there."

"Then why did you agree to do this work for Mr. Girardi?"

"To tell you the truth, I refused at first. But then, I recalled you telling me that I should help him if I could."

"When you first mentioned this to me, I thought he'd simply asked you to look through some papers."

"That was true at first. But when I saw him to drop off the papers, Mike described how much he's struggling to keep up with everything now that he's covering for Jack Tremont. He asked for my help because I had expertise on a particular case that no one else did."

"Is that the only reason you accepted the work?"

"He's going to pay me in the form of a donation to the center." Stowe summoned her enthusiasm and smiled hopefully as she tapped the financial charts with her finger. "Isn't that great?"

"Is the money the main reason you took on this work?"

Stowe could see that Agnes was unhappy, but she could not discern which part of the scheme the sister most particularly disliked.

"The money was part of the reason I accepted. As I said, I also wanted to help Mr. Girardi."

"I don't think you should take any money from him. If the project is important enough for you to take time away from your work here, then you should not seek compensation for it."

Stowe was incredulous. "I'm *not* taking any money, Agnes. He's going to write a check to the center. It was *his* idea, but I think it was a good one. This will make up for the money we lost on Bethany Lutheran and then some."

"I don't want to hear about what we lost on Bethany Lutheran, and I don't want Mr. Girardi's money for the center."

Why is she being so stubborn?

"But we accept all sorts of donations."

"That money is freely given."

"So is this." Stowe's frustration was nearly boiling over, and she struggled to maintain herself with her mentor. "You always say that the Lord will provide. Isn't this an example of the Lord providing? I can help my old boss and raise money for the center at the same time."

"Do you feel fulfilled by this legal work?"

"No," she replied honestly.

"Does it do your heart good?"

Again with the heart.

"No; in fact . . ."

"In fact what?"

"In fact," Stowe repeated, then she hesitated, unsure how much to reveal. "There is a serious problem with this work."

"What kind of problem?"

"When I was at the firm, I discovered what I thought was misconduct by Jack Tremont. I was forced out of my job because of it, and I never told Mike what happened. In fact, aside from my parents, I've never told anyone about it. It turns out that the misconduct occurred on the very case Mike has now asked me to help him on. I'm convinced he has no idea what really happened. I'm not sure whether to tell him or not."

Agnes reached over and took Stowe's hand. "I'm sorry to hear that you are burdened this way. I knew something was wrong, but I didn't dream it was something like this."

"I've worried about all of this for so long. I thought I'd put it behind me . . . I don't know what to do."

"Surely you owe him the truth."

"What good would it do him? Jack Tremont was Mike's mentor—he really looks up to the man. It would hurt him to know the truth."

"But he's put his faith into someone dishonest."

"I know." Stowe folded her arms and nodded. "But then, there's also a practical reason for me to hold back."

"What's that?"

"I'm afraid that if the authorities were ever to become involved, Mike might somehow be blamed for Jack's wrongdoing. That man is extremely manipulative. It might be best for Mike to stay completely removed."

Agnes worked to take in all that she was hearing. "But perhaps he already suspects something and that's why he's asked for your help."

Stowe nodded. "I thought of that as well, and you may be right. But based on what he's said to me so far, I don't think he suspects anything as serious as illegal conduct on Jack's part. He says he needs to be on top of all of Jack's workload now that he's in charge, and that includes this *Trinity Hills* matter."

As she began to wrap her mind around the problem, Agnes asked for further information, and the two continued to hash out the matter until Sister Stella came to let Agnes know that her first appointment had arrived.

"It's up to you, my dear," Agnes said as she stood, "but I think you should tell Mr. Girardi what you know."

Stowe nodded and stood to embrace Agnes. The old nun then offered a closing prayer and went off to see her visitor, while Stowe headed out to her rooms to finish her memorandum for Girardi, relieved to have shared her story with Agnes but still unsure how much she would tell her old boss.

16

Early Friday afternoon, Girardi scrambled to wrap up his work in the office so that he could be on his way to the Emmanuel Center for his appointment with Beth Stowe. He had worked nonstop all week, and ahead was the task of finishing up the two briefs due for filing with the court on Monday. On Thursday, he'd been in San Diego at the deposition of his client's CFO. Although it had been a long day, he was pleased by the results. His witness had maintained a controlled, thoughtful demeanor and had certainly said nothing that would significantly harm their case. This was an instance, Girardi thought, where thorough preparation of a witness had clearly paid dividends.

Girardi had tried continuously to reach Russell Yost, but without success. Then, as luck would have it, he heard from the CEP in-house counsel just ten minutes before he needed to leave for the center. When his assistant rang in to announce the call, Girardi took it and asked Janice to phone the center and warn Stowe that he was running late.

"How are you, Russell? I've been trying to reach you since Wednesday morning."

"It's been busy here."

Girardi took a deep breath. *It's been busy here, too.*

"I understand."

"Listen, Mike, did you track down that response on *Pope Electronics?*"

Girardi hesitated for a moment but decided there was no point beating around the bush. "No."

"Did you speak with Jack?"

"I tried, but he's not in shape to talk business yet."

"Did he tell you *anything* about *Pope Electronics*?"

"No."

"And you have nothing in your files?"

"There's no formal response in the file. I'm sorry. It's my professional opinion that we should contact the government immediately and ask for more time based on Jack's illness. It might be uncomfortable, but it should work. I'm happy to write a letter or call the auditing agent myself. And of course, I won't charge CEP for my time at this stage."

There was a long pause on the line. "Do you have time to meet me this weekend?" Yost asked at last, ignoring Girardi's advice about the extension.

"This weekend?"

"Yes. I know it's unusual, but this is urgent. Jack's always been good about accommodating us on these things over the years."

Girardi wondered what this meant but did not ask.

"You could come over here to my office on Monday, Russell. Or, I could come to you . . ."

Yost cut him off. "Let's meet at the Newport pier early on Sunday morning."

"The Newport pier? I don't understand."

"I don't have much time now—I'll explain when I see you."

Girardi's mind started to spin. *What's going on?* He stalled for time to think.

"The truth is that I'm booked up most of the weekend. We have two significant briefs due on Monday afternoon. Let me look at my calendar. It will just take me a minute. I'll be right back."

Girardi put down the phone, leaned back in his chair, and mulled this over for a few moments. What had taken Yost so long to get back to him? And why in the world did he want to meet at the pier? Although Girardi had certainly encountered some odd and unexpected situations over the years, this was the first time a client had ever requested such a clandestine meeting as this. The whole thing sounded shady, and Girardi knew he needed to be careful. Thinking fast, he picked up the phone and offered a counter-proposal.

"I completely forgot that I'm supposed to have breakfast with someone down in Dana Point Harbor Sunday morning."

This was a white lie, but Girardi felt no compunction about it. "Since I'll be there anyway, and it's pretty secluded this time of year, what do you say we meet down at the harbor?"

Yost hesitated for long enough that Girardi feared he would balk. But then, he assented.

"Alright. I guess I can drive down there. I don't want it to be by the restaurants, though. That will be too crowded. Why don't we meet over by the replica tall ships at the Ocean Institute?"

Girardi knew the place Yost was referring to. "That's perfect. Shall we say ten o'clock?"

Yost again hesitated. "Yeah, that will be fine."

"Russell, can you give me even a small heads-up as to why you think a meeting like this is necessary? Do we need to go over the *Pope Electronics* audit report? Should I prepare that request for an extension from the government?"

"We don't need a request for extension. We need a full response with the backup data and we need it immediately."

"But there's nothing in our files—I don't have anything for you. It's going to take us time to conduct an investigation and come up with a formal response. Documents like that aren't finished overnight. I don't think we have any choice but to ask for an extension."

"Mike, forget the extension. We need to speak in person. Trust me that I wouldn't make such a request unless I absolutely believed it to be necessary."

"You've got me worried."

"I'm worried, too. I need to go. I'll see you at the harbor on Sunday at ten. Thanks."

Hanging up the phone and beginning to process Yost's call, Girardi stared out the window and let out a long sigh. In need of advice, Girardi decided to give his closest friend a call.

"Hey there, partner," Mitch Best intoned jovially as he picked up the line a few minutes later. "It's just another day in paradise here at the Ronald Reagan Federal Building and United States Courthouse."

"I feel as though I should salute or something when you say the name of your building that way, Mitch."

"Damn straight you should," replied the judge, who kept a large oil painting of the fortieth president in his chambers. "So, to what do I owe the honor of this call? Are you reinstating the Saturday doubles match you cancelled? Andy and I are itching to avenge our most recent loss. I'm looking forward to you buying *my* breakfast for a change."

"No, I'm sorry. I wish I were calling about tennis."

"Then what is it? You don't sound so good."

"First of all, let me say that this is all off the record . . ."

"You know what Mikey," Best interjected abruptly, "I need to take care of something. My new friend from the church Sylvia Bea is here with her son. They're about to go on a tour of the building, but I want to speak to them before they go. Can I call you back in a bit?"

Girardi was so consumed by his present worries that he barely caught the improbable line, '*my new friend from the church.*' Girardi never knew what his friend would say next—and that was part of the fun.

"Sure, but don't forget about me. I'll be waiting."

Best immediately hung up without saying goodbye. Fifteen minutes later, he called back. Girardi could tell he was outside on his cell phone.

"Shit, Mike," he began, "if you want to talk to me off the record, I wish you'd do it at *Emilio's* over a beer. But for sure don't *ever* call my office line. Have you heard of the PATRIOT Act and FISA for Christ's sake? Who knows what those pinheads at the NSA and Justice are listening to. I doubt they're monitoring anybody who actually might harm the country—that would be too scary for them."

The thought had not even occurred to Girardi. "Sorry about that, but is a cell phone any more secure?"

"Who knows, but I do have some extra security on this thing. Alright, so what's the trouble? Remember to leave out anything that I'd have to report because I'm a federal judicial officer. I've had to cut way down on the cloak and dagger James Bond stuff since assuming the bench," he joked.

Girardi proceeded to share the story of Russell Yost's request to meet him in Newport and his own counter-proposal.

"It was very clever of you to meet someplace you knew I'd be," Best said sarcastically, referring to his usual Sunday morning stand-up paddle boarding lesson in Dana Point Harbor. "I appreciate your thinking of me."

"Listen Mitch, I don't understand what's going on here, and I need advice from someone I can trust. If you don't want to be around Sunday, I completely understand. But I'd just feel better if you were there helping me keep an eye on things."

"Do you want me to dial 911 if anyone tries to stuff you into the back of an unmarked white van?" he laughed.

In truth, Girardi did not believe that he was in danger of physical harm. Or, at least he hoped he wasn't. He did, however, strongly suspect that something illegal was going on. Would Yost try and pull him in? Was Jack Tremont already mired in trouble?

Best's voice became serious once more. "Are you sure you have no idea why Russ Yost wants to meet you like this?"

"I swear I don't. There's so little in the file that I can't tell what's going on."

"Do you think Jack was involved in anything shady?"

"I don't want to think that way about Jack, but I can't rule it out. Russell said that Jack usually accommodates their requests like this. I didn't ask what he meant by that."

Best paused. "To tell you the truth, partner, I've never quite understood why you're so loyal to Jack Tremont. I've always thought that guy was a little sketchy."

"You have?"

"Yep."

Girardi began to feel defensive. "You never said anything to me about it before."

"I believe that I *have* hinted from time to time. You know how subtle I always am about everything, so you probably just missed it." Best paused to let his friend laugh at his irony, but there was not so much as a chuckle. "Seriously, Mike, I have raised the subject with you before. But I'm not interested in 'I told you so.' The point is, now's not the time to cling to any illusions about Jack Tremont. Don't let him or this Russ Yost get you into any trouble."

Girardi sighed in discouragement. "I know the ethical rules, Mitch, and I'm pretty good about abiding by them."

"I know—that's what makes you such a unique guy."

"I'm just hoping that this might still turn out to be a misunderstanding. I owe a lot to Jack, and if I can straighten this thing out for him while he's sick, then I'd like to do my best."

"Okay, partner. But I don't think you're listening to me. You've got to look out for number one here. Tremont's not putting his ass on the line meeting this Yost guy on the sly. He's in the hospital. If anything goes wrong, it will be on *you*."

"But it's only one meeting," Girardi demurred without much confidence. "It should all be fine."

"Alright," Best exhaled with frustration. "I'm here at the coffee cart now, so I'd better get going. I'm picking up coffee for everybody upstairs— that's pretty nice of me. I'm a great boss, don't you think? Why don't you call me early Sunday morning and we'll work out the details?"

"I appreciate it, Mitch."

"You're welcome. Talk to you later."

17

Girardi arrived at the Emmanuel Center an hour late. Sister Stella directed him to the east conference room, where he found Stowe reading over her notes.

"I'm sorry to be so late, Beth," he offered immediately, "but I did manage to pick us up some sandwiches from *The Carvery* on the way."

"No problem. I appreciated the call from Janice." She took the bags from him eagerly. "Wow, thanks for bringing sandwiches. I worked through lunch."

Glad I stopped for the food, he thought with relief. He'd been worried that the delay might bother Stowe, but she seemed just fine to him. There was suddenly a lot of energy in the room as Girardi removed the jacket from his brand new navy blue suit and placed it carefully on the back of his chair. He looked at Stowe with a smile. "Say, you got some sun since the last time I saw you."

Stowe looked at him quizzically for a moment and then touched her left cheek. "Oh right, I was out in the garden all day on Monday. It was overcast, but I burned anyway. Come here and I'll show you my handiwork."

Girardi walked around to the opposite side of the table and stood next to Stowe, who pointed down to the flower bed around the courtyard fountain. She explained the design to him, adding that she'd received a good number of compliments on her work.

Girardi was impressed. *She's so talented*, he thought with a swell of his old admiration for her. Then, he caught a whiff of her floral scented lotion. *She smells good, too.*

With some effort, he derailed the train of thought that might have continued naturally from these pleasant observations. *We're here for business*, he reminded himself, *serious business.*

"The flower bed looks good. I had no idea you knew how to garden."

Although he rarely mentioned it, Girardi was something of a gardening buff himself. His paternal grandfather had been an avid gardener and had taken the young Girardi under his wing when he had shown some interest. Girardi had fond memories of doing chores in his grandparents' yard and eventually being trusted with the secrets of cultivating grapes and tending roses. Although Jake was in charge of mowing the front yard, Girardi himself tended the garden out back. During the summer, when Jake was away with his mother, Girardi consoled himself on evenings and weekends by doing yard work.

Stowe turned to the cabinet and pulled out plates, plastic utensils and two bottles of water. Before Girardi's arrival, Sister Ida had brought in a carafe of fresh coffee and some peanut butter cookies. The pair sat and ate their sandwiches, chatting about Jake's baseball team and Stowe's future plans for a flower bed on the other side of the property. With his worries about Russell Yost and CEP, Girardi welcomed the opportunity to decompress.

When they'd polished off their sandwiches and several cookies, they got down to business. Just as she had at the beginning of the morning's meeting with Sister Agnes, Stowe shuffled the papers in front of her uncomfortably, unsure how to begin.

"Wow, this feels kind of weird after all this time."

It feels good to me, Girardi thought, recalling the good old days when Stowe had regularly reported to him on the research and fact-gathering that were a normal part of their legal practice.

"I'm going to divide this presentation into three parts. The first should be quick—it will cover background. Second, I'll explain the Trinity Hills contract. And then third . . . ," she hesitated, "I'll end with some separate post-audit information."

"Good," he said with a nod as he leaned over and pulled a legal pad from his briefcase. He recalled that Stowe's presentations were usually logical and to the point.

"Alright, as for the background, CEP was founded in the 1930s by two brothers, Charlie and Ernest Peck."

"Hence the name CEP," Girardi interjected knowingly.

Stowe hesitated before continuing. "Well, that's what the all the marketing materials say . . ."

"What else would CEP stand for?"

"It's kind of a funny story."

"How so?"

"On one of my trips to South Carolina for CEP, I encountered some project managers who were aficionados of company lore. They took me into the archives and showed me some old pictures of the Peck brothers and revealed that the company initials really stood for the Crooked Elm Partnership."

Girardi was skeptical. "They were telling you a tall tale, Beth. You know those southern boys love to BS."

Stowe shot him an exasperated look. "What does their corporate logo look like?"

"I have no idea."

Stowe dug through her paperwork and found a document on CEP letterhead. She handed the sheet to Girardi, pointing at the masthead. "What does that look like to you?"

"A tree."

"A bent tree—a crooked Elm. As the story goes, the Peck boys were always in trouble as kids. There was a tree on the family property where they liked to hide. They spent a lot of hours up in that tree, and apparently never forgot it."

"This is their official corporate logo?" Girardi asked in surprise, still staring at the sheet.

"The logo has evolved over the years, but the elm has always been in there somewhere. I'm told that at some point it occurred to someone in the company that the word "crooked" does not exactly engender public trust, so they stopped referring directly to the Crooked Elm. Officially, the Pecks started out as a small construction company, doing government-funded projects in South Carolina. My CEP contacts bragged that the Pecks also dabbled in bootlegging during Prohibition, but that, as you say, may have been a tall tale. In any event, the company remained small until the post-war housing boom, when they made a fortune building homes for returning GIs all over the country, including some in California. Although they apparently considered going public in the 1970s, CEP has always remained family-owned."

Stowe paused, and Girardi jumped in. "Didn't they go on a buying frenzy in the 1980s and early 90s?"

"They sure did. By that time, the original Pecks had died, and the company was run by Ernest's youngest son and several of the grandchildren. Jack Tremont went to college with at least one of the grandkids, and so he was in line to do some of their legal work during the expansion. CEP always kept its core construction interests, but it also got into power plants and retail clothing and even some oil and gas exploration. For a while, CEP was one of the largest privately-held companies in the southeast. But they over-expanded and ran into tough times. They've sold off a good number of their subsidiaries, and they are mainly a construction company again. According to some of their online promotional materials, CEP is now 'lean and mean.' It's been a wild ride for the old Crooked Elm Partnership over the years."

"And what about *Trinity Hills*? Where does the matter name come from?"

Stowe nodded. "Okay, if that was enough background, we can move on to part two. Trinity Hills is the name of a little town in the western Carolinas. It's situated in a valley between three small mountains, hence the name. In the late 1990s, the federal government proposed constructing a new complex of buildings in the area. CEP was one of the bidders on the contract. They submitted a proposal in 1998, I believe it was, but the government just sat on the bids and the project stalled."

Girardi shook his head in recollection. "Right, I remember this now. The government revived the project after September 11, didn't they?"

"Yes, and they also dramatically expanded its scope. The government invited the original bidders to resubmit proposals on an expedited timeline. Then, they opened up the bidding to newcomers, but no one else came forward with a complete bid. In any event, CEP won the bidding and was handed this huge new government contract. At the time, this was hailed as a big windfall for CEP."

"But it turned out to be a nightmare for them, didn't it?" Girardi said.

Stowe nodded. "*Trinity Hills* became mired in litigation almost from day one. CEP had barely broken ground before an environmental group sued the company and the government, claiming that the proper impact studies had never been completed."

"Marshall, Lufton didn't handle the environmental litigation, did it?"

"No—it was a big Washington firm."

"Did the environmental matter settle?"

"Eventually, but not without significant expense and delay."

Girardi made a couple of short notes on his pad. "What happened next?"

"CEP proceeded with the project, but they encountered problems at every turn. There were labor conflicts and cost over-runs and a stack of audit reports from various agencies asking for substantial refunds."

"And that's where Marshall, Lufton comes in?"

Stowe nodded. "CEP retained Jack to evaluate half a dozen audit reports and to prepare written responses to the government. I worked on three of these." Her expression now cloudy, she reached a typed document to Girardi. "Here's the memo I've written for you. It reviews what I've told you so far and goes on to summarize the documents I located in my electronic files."

"The ones in the envelope you gave me last week at lunch?"

"Exactly. Those documents were all related to the largest of the audit reports we worked on. The government sought a $10 million reimbursement for one particular piece of the contract. A part of the *Trinity Hills* complex of buildings was to be dedicated to an armed services joint training facility. This facility was apparently added to the project after 9/11. CEP put together a special bid package for the joint training facility, and although the government awarded CEP the contract, they turned around and *hammered* the company in subsequent audit reports. The government essentially came out and said that CEP had lied right and left in their bid for the joint training facility. I've never seen more strongly-worded criticism in an audit report. The auditors alleged that CEP was liable to the government for fraud, which can lead to triple damages."

"So this was a serious matter," Girardi commented.

"Absolutely. Some of the officials at the company felt unfairly singled out and were itching to fight back. I kid you not, some of them spoke about their distrust of the federal government as if the Civil War were still going on. They talked about the Crooked Elm days and how old Charlie and Ernest would never have stood for it. We worked with the company for months putting together a response, sparing no expense. I traveled several times to the Carolinas to interview witnesses and review documents." She paused and offered an aside. "As I recall, you weren't too happy with my being away because that meant I was slower to get *your* work done."

Girardi frowned and shook his head, not appreciating this little jab. "Was your written response any good?"

Stowe appeared surprised by the question. "I thought it was *quite* good if I do say so myself. We killed ourselves on that document. I expected that the government would at least shave off a few million from the allegations based on our response alone. Then, I assumed that the rest would be negotiated. We always knew CEP would have to pay something, but if we'd knocked off a third to a half of the claim, this would have been a tremendous result."

"And well worth a few hundred thousand dollars in attorneys fees," Girardi agreed.

Stowe nodded. "We finished drafting the response, and things were quiet for some time."

"But?"

Stowe fell silent and began arranging the documents in front of her into still-neater piles.

"That's pretty much the end of the record as far as my electronic files go."

For the past few minutes, Girardi had watched the slow but steady decline of his companion's spirits. She'd started out talkative and chipper, but now seemed grave and uncertain.

As he thought over her presentation so far, everything Stowe had said made perfect sense. There had been no big surprises, and Girardi felt much more on top of *Trinity Hills*. It all looked fine. But as Stowe stood and moved to close the conference room door, he knew that was about to change.

"But there's more to the story, I take it?" he ventured.

There's always more to the story.

She nodded, struggling for her words. She had held on to this secret for nearly two years and wasn't sure she was ready to let it out, for once she did, she would have no control over where things went from here.

"I'm not sure you're going to want to hear the rest . . . and I don't know how to explain it all to you so that you'll understand."

When she'd shut the door, she walked over to the window and stared down to the garden, arms folded. There was a long pause, and Girardi considered jumping in. Whatever she had to say, he wanted to get it over with. But still, he did not prompt her. The tension in the room continued to build.

"When we provided the written response to CEP's in-house counsel," she resumed at last, "I assumed they'd put the document on their company letterhead and submit it to the government exactly as we'd written it."

This did not surprise Girardi. "That's typically what happens, isn't it?"

"In my experience, yes."

"So what happened in this case?"

"Six months or so after the submission, CEP's in-house counsel forwarded to Jack a list of follow-up questions from the government. Jack was out of the office, and his assistant, not knowing any better, gave the package to me. Then I, also not knowing any better, decided to start working on responses to the government's questions. I did this without Jack specifically asking me to."

"But you assumed he would ask you, right?"

"Of course. By that time I knew more about *Trinity Hills* than Jack did. Or, at least, I thought I did. In order to get back up to speed, I reread the final CEP submission. I saw then for the first time that in-house counsel had made substantial changes to our draft. The problem was, the new material contained what I thought were substantial misstatements of the facts."

Here we go.

"Uh-oh," Girardi offered.

She turned back to him and nodded. "Uh-oh is right."

"And these were material misstatements?"

"Absolutely. They went to the heart of the government's allegations."

"So, you think the CEP submission was fraudulent?"

"Yes, I do."

Girardi began to speak deliberately. "But a fraudulent submission would carry all sorts of consequences. An attorney could be disbarred for such conduct."

"Disbarred or worse," Stowe agreed grimly.

"The company and its managers could be sued civilly and subject to criminal charges," he continued.

Stowe again nodded her agreement.

Girardi then ventured a question, suspecting that he already knew the answer. "Who was in-house counsel on this part of the *Trinity Hills* work?"

"Russell Yost."

"So, I assume you brought this to Jack's attention?"

She nodded.

"And, what did he say?"

Stowe wrung her hands, apparently conjuring the scene in her mind's eye. "Forgive me, but he said, quote *'mind your own fucking business Beth and forget about that audit report. I'll handle it.'*"

Girardi's heart fell at this. "So he knew about the fraud."

"It certainly seemed so."

"Oh Beth, I'm sorry."

"Me too," she replied, fighting back tears. "He literally snatched some of the papers out of my hand and made it clear I couldn't have them back. I'd never seen an attorney act like that before. I'd seen Jack angry plenty of times, but never like this. And I was just supposed to forget the whole thing."

That's why she quit, Girardi surmised as a period of ponderous quiet overtook them. In his effort to unravel one mystery, he had discovered the solution to another. *Jack's to blame for my losing Beth. Damn him.*

"Where was I when this was all going on?" he asked, again suspecting he knew the answer.

Stowe kept her eyes on the flower bed, her voice wavering some. "You were out of the office for weeks. You had a bunch of depositions on the east coast . . . and then, I think you were headed to the Caribbean . . ."

The Mona break-up trip.

"Did you consider reporting this?" he asked.

The question struck a nerve. Stowe whirled around to face Girardi, eyes flashing and cheeks red. "Of course I did! I considered all kinds of options, Mike. But after I calmed down and thought about the situation somewhat rationally, I knew that it would be almost impossible for me to prove the false statements by myself. I understood what was happening because I'd interviewed all the key witnesses and had analyzed the documents the company officials had given us. The story in CEP's written response was very different from the story they gave me in person. What's more, I think they fabricated evidence, but I can't be absolutely certain about that. The final submission included exhibits I'd never seen before. But still, if I'd tried to raise an objection, it would have come down to my word against theirs."

"So you walked away?"

So you ran away was what he was really thinking.

"Jack would have fired me if I hadn't quit. Cliff made this very clear. He came into my office and told me point-blank that I had no future at the firm. Then he threatened that I'd never get another decent job in the law if I complained. He also told me that you were planning to propose to Mona."

He found the reference to Mona jarring. *What did that have to do with anything?*

"I felt completely helpless and alone," she continued. "So, I turned to your work for a few days and got as much of it done as I could. You should have seen how Cliff hovered over me. He removed files from my office when I wasn't around. I was furious, but what could I do? At the end of that awful week, I left and never looked back."

There were so many questions Girardi wanted to ask, but he didn't know where to begin. Stowe held her place by the window. He thought she might cry, but she mostly kept her game face on. Girardi felt miserable as he sat and watched her for some time. The old regrets came upon him with greater force than ever. *Why didn't I try harder to find out why she left? Maybe this could have all been avoided if I'd just been paying more attention.*

But then, he wondered about Stowe's actions. Even if he had been away on a trip with Mona, why hadn't she simply called him? They had always communicated regularly when either one was out of the office, including on vacations. Why would she try and deal with something like this entirely on her own? He had considered himself not only her boss but her mentor—she should have come to him. *Why didn't she just call me? We wouldn't be in this mess now if she'd just called me.*

At a loss for what to say, Girardi reflexively grabbed his phone and checked his messages.

"Beth, do you mind if I go outside and make a quick call? Janice wants to touch base with me."

"Go ahead."

"I'll be back in a few minutes."

And with a small wave, Girardi headed outside.

18

On Sunday morning, an apprehensive Girardi drove to Dana Point, arriving at the Ocean Institute fifteen minutes early for his meeting with Russell Yost. Dana Point was named for nineteenth century adventurer Richard Henry Dana, who described his 1830s voyage from Boston to Alta California as a common crewman aboard the brig *Pilgrim* in the famous diary, *Two Years Before the Mast.* Dana Point had for decades been a low-key alternative to its trendier neighbors to the north, Laguna and Newport.

Girardi took a seat on a bench near the two-masted tall ship *Pilgrim* and watched a small crew of museum docents in period costumes standing on the deck, explaining the ship's history to a handful of visitors. The weather was typical for the spring, with the coastal sky overcast and the air cool. Girardi was dressed in jeans and a UC Davis pullover sweatshirt. A couple of hundred yards away from the *Pilgrim* was a small sandy strip at the base of the cliffs called Baby Beach. The water in this protected cove was so still that children could play without fear of dangerous currents. During the summer, Baby Beach was overrun with families. On off-season weekends like this one, by contrast, the area primarily served as a launching place for kayakers and stand-up paddle boarders. Mitch Best's class was getting under way, and Girardi watched his friend chatting jovially with his half-dozen middle aged male classmates and their slim, tanned young instructor Katie. Unbeknownst to the others, Best was keeping at least one eye in Girardi's direction.

The Dana Point Outrigger Club also had several teams of very fit kayakers on the beach, preparing for an informal race across the channel. The mixed-gender teams good-naturedly taunted one another as they prepared for the contest. Girardi watched the scene with considerable envy, wishing he had come to the harbor with Jake for some carefree recreation.

Girardi waited for Yost for half an hour, sometimes sitting and sometimes walking back and forth between the *Pilgrim* and its sister replica tall ship the *Spirit of Dana Point*. Back when Jake had been younger, he'd gone through a phase of fascination with tall ships and pirates. For three birthdays in a row, Jake and his father had taken a tall ship cruise on the ocean aboard the *Spirit*. To Girardi's disappointment, his son had grown out of this phase and never mentioned the tall ships anymore. Looking at the *Pilgrim's* square-rigged masts and white rolled sails, Girardi missed those days. *At least he still loves baseball*, Girardi consoled himself.

Girardi checked his phone constantly, half-hoping for a message from Yost calling the whole thing off. He phoned Yost shortly after ten, but there was no answer. If only the situation might turn out to be some simple miscommunication or misunderstanding. At ten-fifteen, Girardi began to suspect he'd been stood up, and he wondered how long he should wait. Best's class was to last until eleven, and the two planned to have breakfast after that. So, he decided to try and be patient. He dialed Russell Yost's number for a second time, but the line went directly to voicemail.

At last, Girardi saw Yost's black Lexus coming up the drive. He parked near Girardi's bench and was soon beside him. Yost, like Girardi, was in his mid-forties. He was of average height, with a stocky build and thinning black hair. He was dressed this morning in black slacks, a gray silk shirt and a black nylon jacket.

"Hello, Mike."

"Morning, Russ."

"Shall we walk?"

"Sure. Which way?"

Yost shrugged as he took a casual look around. "I don't care."

There were a few handfuls of people in either direction, but the two would be able to speak privately no matter which way they went. Yost pointed toward Baby Beach.

"I don't want to belabor this," Yost began, pulling a pack of cigarettes from his jacket pocket and deftly lighting one as he walked.

I had no idea he smoked.

"Would you like a cigarette?"

Although Girardi hadn't smoked a cigarette in at least twenty years, he was half-tempted to accept. "No thanks."

"The thing is, Mike, the company is in a jam with this *Pope Electronics* audit report."

"What do you mean by a jam?"

"Before Jack's stroke, we did some investigating and concluded that it would be tough to refute the government's allegations."

Girardi considered this for a moment or two. "I don't mean to sound old-fashioned, Russ, but maybe that means you'll have to pony up the money to the government," he offered with uncharacteristic sarcasm.

Yost shook his head. "We don't owe them the money, Mike. The allegations are unfair. Ever since *Trinity Hills*, the government has thought they could get away with pounding on us. It's terrible. Individuals have constitutional rights to protect against governmental abuse, but what about corporations? You know how it is. If the auditors poke around for long enough they'll always find *something*. Unfortunately for us, in this case, we're not in an easy position to exonerate ourselves."

Yost's comments had a familiar ring to them. Under circumstances far more routine than this, Girardi had encountered clients driven by a deep, unshakeable conviction that they'd been terribly wronged. And of course, in some instances, this was so. But such feelings of persecution also existed in cases where a rational analysis of the facts indicated that the client bore significant responsibility for their predicament. The profession had long filled its coffers on the basis of these emotional reactions by clients, but this dynamic bothered Girardi. Business was business, and he saw it as his job to convince his clients to analyze their legal position and assess their options rationally. If that meant settling a case or admitting liability under circumstances that did not yield substantial fees for his firm, then so be it.

In the present instance, Girardi immediately wondered how Yost had surmised that the allegations were unfair if the evidence gathered so far in the matter was weak. Girardi had read the audit report through twice. He had a fair understanding of the allegations, but had no idea what documents or testimony might be gathered to refute the government's allegations. Without looking at the company's records and interviewing key witnesses, as Beth Stowe had done on *Trinity Hills*, it would be impossible for him to assess the strengths of the government's claims.

"Jack was convinced that he could help us on this," Yost continued.

"Beyond just writing a normal response?"

Yost nodded.

Girardi shook his head. He recalled that the case file had been nearly empty, save for the audit report and the dirty envelope full of documents.

"But I told you that I have nothing like that in the file."

"This isn't the kind of thing that Jack would let just sit around in an office file."

"What do you mean?"

Yost stopped walking and faced Girardi, looking him squarely in the eye. "So, you really don't know?"

Girardi's mind went back to Stowe's story about the fraudulent *Trinity Hills* audit response, with which Russell Yost had been involved.

"I have no idea what you're talking about," Girardi replied, meeting Yost's gaze.

"Well," Yost hesitated thoughtfully, casting his eyes toward the paddle-boarders as he resumed his pace, "Jack knows some people he calls the Consultants.'"

Girardi recalled seeing a notation like this in Jack's file back at the office.

"Are they expert witnesses?"

"No, no. Just people who work behind the scenes to help a contractor like CEP come up with evidence to refute government audit allegations. They use more creative methods than your standard law firm attorneys."

"More creative methods?" Girardi repeated, thinking again of what Beth Stowe had told him about the *Trinity Hills* response. "You mean they *make up* evidence?"

Girardi began to consider the effort it would take for "the Consultants" to create out of whole cloth evidence that would be convincing enough to fool skeptical government attorneys and auditors. He knew from experience that it was difficult enough to get anywhere with evidence that was entirely legitimate. It would take a sophisticated and daring set of consultants indeed to pull off something like this. In twenty years of practice, Girardi thought he'd seen just about everything. But now he felt naïve.

Yost took a final drag on his cigarette, dropped it to the ground and stepped on it. "I'm not sure what the Consultants do exactly. For obvious reasons, I've never wanted to know. I've never seen or spoken with any of them. But, as I said before, we're in a jam with *Pope Electronics.* Jack promised he'd have something for us, no matter what it took. We're already into him for a lot of money on this thing . . ."

Girardi gestured with his hand. "Wait a minute. I've looked at the billings for *Pope Electronics.* They've been quite modest so far."

"I don't mean your firm's fees. Jack asked for money up front to pay the Consultants—several hundred thousand."

Several hundred thousand? Girardi repeated to himself in dismay as Yost continued.

"We need that response right away, Mike. We've already missed the first government deadline. They gave us a short extension, but that's running out, too. We cannot delay any longer."

"I don't have anything for you."

"That's bullshit," Yost said irritably, grabbing for his cigarettes and lighting another.

Girardi shook his head. Yost was behaving so unlike his usual self that it was hard for Girardi to know what tack to take with him.

"You think I'm lying, Russell?"

"I don't know who's lying to whom, but Jack promised us something, and we intend to get it. We've already *paid* the money. I'm not sure you understand how serious this is."

As the men reached the edge of Baby Beach, Yost turned them around and they headed back toward the *Pilgrim*. Girardi took a look over to the brightly-dressed Best, who was now up on his board and paddling slowly toward the tall ships. He was surprised to see how competent Best seemed—the judge was apparently catching on quickly to his new hobby.

"We're having a secret meeting in Dana Point on Sunday morning, Russ. I think I understand that this is serious. However, I need to make it clear that I have no knowledge of anything like what you're talking about. What's more, I have no intention of engaging in any unethical or illegal . . ."

Yost cut him off sharply. "Skip the CYA disclaimer. It's way too late for that now. Jack and Cliff are way in this, and therefore so are you and your partners."

Girardi hesitated at the mention of Conroy. "Cliff?"

"Cliff's usually involved in this kind of thing."

He makes it all sound so routine, Girardi thought in dismay as Yost continued.

"Mike, I'm still having a hard time believing *you* know nothing about this."

"I'm sorry to disappoint you."

"If word ever got out, your practice and your office could well be destroyed."

Girardi was reaching his boiling point. "So, now you're threatening me? We've known each other a long time, Russ. You know I don't lie to my clients or engage in the type of conduct you're describing."

"Sure, you're an Eagle Scout, Mike. But that's not the issue. You've been drawing your share of the profits every year just like the rest of your partners. If you've managed to somehow turn a blind eye to what Jack Tremont has been doing, that's still no excuse. You're *all* responsible as far as I'm concerned. I need that response by Friday at the latest."

"Or . . . ?"

"Or people a lot less friendly than me will start coming around. Trust me, I'm the nicest guy by far that you'll encounter in this process. For your own peace of mind, get me that document."

Girardi laughed at this. "Come on, Russell. Don't try and scare me this way."

"I'm telling you the truth. Ask Cliff."

"Why didn't you just ask him yourself? Why are you even involving me?"

"I deal only with the lawyers. I'd never communicate with someone like Cliff on an issue like this. How would that look? Jack has always been the company's person in matters like this, and now *you* are my person, Mike. It's too bad Jack got sick. You're going to have to contact the Consultants yourself."

"Even if I were inclined to do that, I have no idea who they are."

"Then find out who they are—fast."

"Look Russell, now we're going around in circles. I'm happy to speak with Jack one more time, and maybe I'll touch base with Cliff. But I'm *not* going to try and track down any 'Consultants' as you term them. That will have to be between you and Jack when he recovers."

They were soon back at the *Pilgrim*, and Girardi knew there was nothing more to say.

"I meant what I said," Yost offered as he headed for his car. "You need to do whatever it takes to get me that document by Friday—the future of your and Jack's practice depends on it."

"Goodbye, Russ."

Yost dropped his cigarette on the ground, got quickly into his car, and drove off.

19

When Mitch Best finished his paddle boarding lesson, he and Girardi headed up to *Cannon's* restaurant, which was situated atop the cliffs overlooking the Dana Point Harbor. Best loved the *Cannon's* Sunday buffet, and Girardi had suggested they debrief over brunch outside on the patio.

The early fog had burned off, and the view from up on the bluffs was spectacular. From their table, they could see down the coast past San Clemente to the sprawling Marine Corps base at Camp Pendleton. Two hundred feet directly below them were Baby Beach and the replica Tall Ships. The crowd had now picked up, and a steady flow of sailboats and motorboats moved in and out of the channel.

At a quiet table in the corner that was sheltered from the breeze, the two ordered coffee and juice and began to settle in. Best was wearing a blue themed sweatshirt over his shorts and t-shirt.

"*Old Guys Rule*, huh Mitch?" Girardi asked wryly, reading the writing on his friend's shirt.

"This is an example of my lovely daughter's sense of humor. She and Andy made a big deal out of my fiftieth birthday. Andy got me the lessons, and Brianna bought the outfits. They signed me up for AARP, too. Funny, right?"

"I'm lucky. It would never occur to Jake to do something like that."

"Yeah, he's a nice kid. Mine take too much after me, especially Brianna. But you know what? By the time she gets home from college for the summer, I'm planning to be an expert paddle-boarder. I'm hoping to convince her take lessons so the two of us can go out together."

"So, she'll be here for the summer?"

Best smiled broadly. "Yep. That internship at the Bowers Museum came through, thanks to Sophia. The best thing is that she'll live with me this summer."

Girardi noted that Best said that Brianna would live with *him*, and not with him and his wife Sophia. Girardi had suspected for some time now that there might be trouble in the judge's marriage, but he had not asked about it. The incident with Michelle Bailey at the fundraiser had heightened his concern, but still, he did not pry. Best would tell his story in his own time, and that suited Girardi just fine.

As Girardi considered this, the judge continued to describe his summer plans. "Bri and I might even carpool to work, because the museum's not too far from the courthouse."

Girardi was envious. "I hate the summer. Jake's always with his mother."

"You don't appreciate the little break? You're the full-time guy most of the year, partner."

"I don't appreciate the break at all. The house is way too quiet when Jake's gone. I know I shouldn't talk like this, but I'd like to see Jake stay home for college. The whole thing is going by way too fast for me. It seems like just yesterday Jake was dressing like a pirate for Halloween and begging me to bring him down here to see the Tall Ships."

Best smiled knowingly at this. "We have awesome baseball teams here in Orange County. I could see Jake at Fullerton or UCI. It would be win-win."

"It sure would . . ."

"Jake doesn't seem anxious to go away for college, does he?"

"Not yet. If the baseball thing works out, I might be in business to have him with me for a few more years."

"Is he still playing well?"

"It feels like forever since I've seen a game all the way through, but his stats are solid, and he's slowly getting accustomed to left field. He seems to have a good season shaping up."

"It's a big adjustment coming from the infield, isn't it?"

"It is, but his coach seems convinced that Jake's chances of starting in college as an outfielder are significantly better than they would have been at third base. This year he's mainly focused on improving his batting average."

Best shook his head. "Who knew there was so much strategy involved in this stuff?"

Girardi let out a long sigh and looked down toward the *Pilgrim*, recalling his meeting with Russell Yost. "There seems to be a lot of strategy to everything in this world."

"You're right," Best replied, pushing back his chair and pointing in the direction of the food. "Take for example the buffet over there. What do we get first? Eggs? Seafood? Made-to-order pasta? Fruit?"

Girardi chuckled. "This is your territory, my friend. I'll follow your lead."

The two went over and made their first assault on the buffet tables, returning and immediately digging in.

"So, how was your meeting?" Best quietly ventured some time later.

"Nobody tried to stuff me into a van," Girardi offered with a forced laugh.

"Yep. The whole thing was kind of boring from my vantage point."

"Good. I'm glad it was boring for you."

"Tell me what your friend Russ had to say."

Girardi proceeded to describe to Best the details not only of his encounter with Russell Yost but also his conversations with Elizabeth Stowe about *Trinity Hills*. The two then moved on to discuss Girardi's options, such as they were. One possibility was for Girardi to wash his hands of the matter and refuse to help Russell Yost, leaving everything to Tremont when he recovered. But this option did not suit Girardi. Not only did he think it incredibly unlikely that Yost would stop pestering him, but he also felt a duty on behalf of the firm to get to the bottom of the situation.

Another option would be for him to speak with Tremont and perhaps Cliff Conroy, postponing any immediate decision on what to do with Yost until he'd heard what the two had to say. After some back and forth with Best, this was the option that Girardi seemed to be favoring.

For his part, however, the judge came down in favor of an alternative that Girardi thought extreme, at least under the present circumstances.

"Listen, Mike, you really should consider talking to the US Attorneys. I know somebody in the Santa Ana office who's a former Marine, Charley Strong. He's a good guy and you can trust him."

Mitch knows everybody, Girardi thought as he shrugged.

"I wouldn't have much to tell your friend, and I have *zero* evidence. Beth seems convinced that the company lied in its *Trinity Hills* audit response, but she doesn't have firm proof. Russ Yost hinted very strongly that he's already paid for a fraudulent document to be submitted to the government on *Pope Electronics*, but he could certainly deny the whole thing later on."

Best considered this. "I haven't thought this all the way through, but, as far as your new matter goes, I guess it's not illegal to pay someone else to help you prepare something that you *might* turn around and use to commit fraud."

"It might be some form of conspiracy to commit fraud," rejoined the former prosecutor. "If Russ is telling me the truth, they've paid several hundred thousand dollars for someone to prepare a submission that is in all likelihood fraudulent."

"Maybe, but it would be a bitch to prove something like that without the submission of an actual false claim to the government. Russ Yost appears to be anxious to submit a false claim . . . but he hasn't been able to yet. At least not in the *Pope Electronics* case. That makes *Trinity Hills* a lot more important. You say you don't have *any* tangible evidence?"

"None."

"What about Beth? Would she tell the US Attorney about *Trinity Hills*?"

"I have no idea, but I'd hate to pull her into something like that."

"Too late, partner; you already *have* pulled her in."

Girardi grew ponderous, and Best returned to the buffet for some fruit and cottage cheese.

"Say, Mikey," the judge ventured when he resumed his seat, "do you think Beth might be holding out on you?"

"What do you mean?"

"Well, for one thing, she could have told you the truth about *Trinity Hills* right off the bat, when you first contacted her about it. Why did she wait so long to explain what happened?"

It was a question Girardi had already considered. "I'm not sure. I suspect that she just really wanted to put this all behind her. The memories are painful. Can you blame her for being reticent?"

Best seemed unsatisfied. "Do you think she's hiding out in the convent?"

"It's not a convent."

"Then what is it?"

"A prayer and retreat center."

Best's expression was blank, and Girardi moved to explain. "They run retreat weekends for church groups and provide spiritual direction for individuals."

"And Beth is studying with them to be a nun?"

Girardi hesitated for some time. "I don't think so." He shook his head sheepishly. "But I'm not sure what her position is."

"You aren't sure? Didn't you ask her?" The judge was incredulous. "How could you *not* ask her what she's doing in a place like that? Didn't you work together for four years?"

"I know it sounds strange, but things can be a little delicate with Beth sometimes. I'm doing my best to play it cool."

Best raised a suspicious eyebrow and then grinned. "There's something funny between you two," he offered, chomping on a big piece of cantaloupe. "I think Sophia was right after all."

Girardi fiddled with the pepper shaker. "Come on, Mitch. No conspiracy theories, please."

"No conspiracy theories? This whole thing with Jack and CEP is a giant conspiracy theory . . ."

"I know."

"I'm sorry, but Beth's story just doesn't add up for me," pressed the judge, who seemed much more interested in discussing Elizabeth Stowe than Russell Yost or his mysterious consultants. "She's an experienced litigator who allegedly stumbles across evidence of fraud. She raises the issue with a superior and loses her job over it. She goes to the trouble to make sure that her favorite boss's work is finished, but she doesn't tell him what's really going on? And even more unlikely, she doesn't take along with her *any* of the incriminating evidence from the file? Wouldn't any good lawyer in her position keep evidence of something like that?"

Girardi paused to consider what his friend was saying. "She told me that Jack took some of the documentation from her. She also said that Cliff watched her like a hawk and took some files from her office. He's like that. You should have seen how fast he got rid of all trace of Randall Spencer."

Best nodded his understanding. "Okay . . . but Beth probably at least had working copies of some of the documents. Did she say explicitly that she had *no* documentary proof of the fraud?"

"Mitch, I'm honestly not sure what she said. It was a lot to take in, and I wasn't trying to parse every word. But, now that you mention it, I don't think she made any definitive statement one way or the other."

"Last weekend, you told me that when she quit she left all of your work in neat piles on your desk, right?"

"Right."

"She sounds obsessive-compulsive to me."

Girardi nodded vigorously. "Almost all the good associates are at least a little that way. They're the only ones careful enough to make sure the work gets done properly. Beth was one of the most responsible associates I've ever had."

"Then I'll bet she found a way to bring along some souvenirs from *Trinity Hills*. You need to go back over to the retreat center and ask her about it, point-blank. No messing around. She might be sitting on proof that CEP submitted a false claim to the government in its *Trinity Hills* response. If she has that proof, you can take it to the U.S. Attorney."

"Don't you think she would have told me if she had documents like that?"

"Who knows? She's been giving you information in pieces so far. Besides, she doesn't know about *Pope Electronics*, does she?"

"No, she doesn't."

"Then she doesn't fully understand the urgency of your problem."

Girardi shook his head in doubt, wondering if Best could possibly be correct.

"Mike," the judge pressed, "is there any possibility that Beth was complicit in Jack's fraud?"

Girardi felt a flash of anger. "Of course not," he snapped. "Why would you even ask me such a thing?"

"I'm asking you because you need to look at this situation from every single angle. Even the unpleasant ones—*especially* the unpleasant ones."

"But not from the insane and ridiculous ones . . ."

Best leaned back and stretched his long arms over his head. "I have this friend . . . we've been pals for a long time, and I respect his opinion. Anyway, he says that when a guy is attracted to a woman, his judgment can go out the window. Sound familiar?"

"I take your point, Mitch, but Beth would *never* be involved in something like this. I'm absolutely certain."

"Okay, but you haven't wanted to believe Jack was involved, either."

"I've been slow to believe that Jack was involved in any wrongdoing, but I'm aware of how bad it looks. Still, I need to speak with him."

"Be careful there. You might be better off *not* hearing what Jack has to say. What if he incriminates himself and the firm? Then you'll have no choice but to go to the authorities."

"He probably won't do that, even with the state he's in."

"What about Cliff?"

"What about him?" Girardi rejoined sourly.

"Why don't you talk to him? You said that Russ Yost mentioned him."

"This is between Jack and me."

"But Jack may not even be well enough to talk to you. You work with Cliff every day. At least he's not sick. He might be able to help you."

Girardi shook his head in the negative. "I wouldn't trust a word that he said."

"That's a nice vote of confidence for your office manager. Isn't this profession of ours wonderful?"

"If I don't trust Cliff, why should I bother tipping my hand to him?"

"Because even if he lies to you, you might still learn something valuable in the process."

"Maybe," Girardi allowed, "but I'd rather deal directly with Jack. We've worked together for so long. I owe it to Jack to give him a chance to explain. I also owe it to him to try and help him if I can."

"I'm not sure you *owe* him anything."

"I'm still swamped with those two briefs, but they're due tomorrow afternoon. After that, I'll go see Jack at the hospital and decide what I'm going to do from there."

"You really should speak again with Beth."

"I need to think about that." He paused and looked the judge in the eye. "But I *promise* that I'll speak to your friend the prosecutor if the circumstances require me to. I appreciate the referral and the sound advice. I really do."

Best shook his head. "You're too loyal to Jack. Nobody in this world is loyal anymore."

"There are a few suckers like us out there, Mitch."

"Don't lump me into your group of saps and fools."

"Too late, you're in, partner," he smiled, grateful to have a friend like Best he could trust in these circumstances.

The judge pushed back his chair and gestured toward the buffet. "I'm going back in—you coming?"

Girardi nodded and followed his friend back to the dessert table.

20

Reverend Mountjoy stood at the back of the St. Mark's sanctuary shaking hands with the hundred-or-so parishioners who had gathered for the ten o'clock Sunday service. This was the second service of the morning. Toward the end of the line was Sylvia Bea, who was elegant as always in a green knit suit, matching purse and pumps. She and her husband were Episcopalians of the old school, wealthy, formal and cultured. They reminded Mountjoy of the church she had grown up in.

"I'm sorry to see that Hector is not here this morning," Mountjoy offered as Sylvia extended her hand. "I hope he's not ill."

"Oh, no. He's visiting with an old friend from medical school who is in town for a wedding. I tried to convince them both to come to church with me, but you know how it is."

"I understand," Mountjoy rejoined with a smile. She joked with her clerical colleagues that she smiled more on Sundays than the other six days combined.

"May I please speak with you alone for a few moments?" Sylvia asked.

"Certainly," Mountjoy replied, eyeing the short line behind Sylvia. "Shall I meet you by the fountain in five minutes?"

Sylvia nodded and went outside as Mountjoy turned to the couple next in line. In their early thirties, the pair was dressed this morning in sweatshirts, jeans and flip-flops; each had a matching recyclable coffee cup in hand. As far as the rector could tell, they'd tumbled out of bed just in time to make it to *Starbucks* and then on to church to catch the beginning of the sermon at ten-fifteen. Although she tried not to over-do it, Mountjoy could not help but notice which of her parishioners were chronic late-comers. And the coffee thing drove her crazy. Many of her colleagues believed that they were obliged to make church as comfortable as possible. But at the risk of seeming a fuddy-duddy, Mountjoy quietly clung to the notion instilled in her as a youngster that formality helped people approach church with a necessary sense of seriousness and reverence.

When Mountjoy arrived at the bench by the fountain a few minutes later, she found Sylvia holding two envelopes in her lap.

"I know you're busy this morning, Susan, and I don't want to monopolize your time. But I wanted to tell you that Francisco and I spent Friday afternoon at Judge Best's chambers. He's a delightful man, and such a charming host. I'd feared that we might be shuffled in and out in half-an-hour, but we were there for hours. We sat in on hearings, visited in chambers and toured the courthouse with the chief of the marshals. By the end of the day, I wanted to go to law school myself."

"And was Francisco also pleased with the experience?"

"Absolutely. He's going to apply for a summer internship with the court. I think the judge might put a good word in for him—but he warned us that there are no guarantees. They get lots of qualified applicants."

"I'm so glad that the visit was a success."

"So am I." Sylvia then cast her gaze out toward the parking lot. Mountjoy thought she seemed ill-at-ease, and wondered what was troubling her. And, although she knew better, she also could not help but wonder what was in those two envelopes.

"Susan," she ventured seriously, "I don't usually like to interfere in such things."

Oh boy, Mountjoy felt a swirl in her stomach. It was almost never good to hear such words from a parishioner, especially one as involved as Sylvia Bea.

"*But,*" Sylvia continued, "it seems that the judge does not have a home parish just now. In fact, I'm not even sure if he's an Episcopalian. But be that as it may, I think we should try and convince him to come here to St. Mark's. Wouldn't he be just perfect for the vestry?"

Mountjoy's mind tumbled at the idea of Mitch Best on what was essentially her church's board of directors. *That would be God telling me it's time to retire*, she thought to herself with a chuckle.

"We don't have anyone else like his honor, that's for certain."

"Well, I'm going to encourage him to come. I'm not a particularly skilled evangelist by any means, and I *never* want to push people. But, I sense that he'd benefit from having a strong parish home. I know how much the church has meant to our family over the years."

At this, the pair was interrupted by a call from Mountjoy's music director, who was standing at the side door of the sanctuary with her hands on her hips. Mountjoy had promised to comment on some of the arrangements for the concert coming up on Sunday.

"I'll be there in a few minutes, Sarah." Mountjoy then turned back to Sylvia. "I'm so sorry. Please go on."

"That's alright. There's just one more thing. My husband and I loved the Evensong service, and we'd like to make a modest contribution to the musical programs. You and Sarah do such wonderful work."

Sylvia handed one of the envelopes to Mountjoy, who slid it into a side pouch in her three-ring notebook. Mountjoy knew that it would be poor form for her to open it just then, unless Sylvia specifically asked her to, which she did not. The Reverend offered an embrace of thanks.

"Sylvia, this means a great deal to me. You and Hector have always been so generous."

"It's our pleasure to help where we can."

She's a gracious and modest woman, Mountjoy thought to herself in admiration as Sylvia reached the second envelope toward her. It was parishioners like the Beas who kept Mountjoy going.

"The judge asked me to give you this," Sylvia continued. "He shared with me that the two of you were friends back in college, and that you were the most intelligent person he knew there. I'm not surprised."

Mountjoy felt a surprising glow at this double compliment. "That's kind of you both—too kind, I'm afraid."

Mountjoy slipped the second envelope into the zippered pouch next to the first one and sealed the compartment. She chatted for a few more minutes with Sylvia, and then, thanking her once more, went off to find her music director.

■ ■ ■

Back at the restaurant in Dana Point, Girardi and Best were at last bringing their meal to a close. They had eventually managed to move on from the subject of CEP.

"Listen, Mike, I need to ask a favor."

"Uh-oh."

Best appeared surprised by his friend's reaction. He pointed down toward Baby Beach. "After taking part in this morning's special ops mission, I figured you'd be good for a return favor or two."

"I suppose so. What is it?"

Best reached for his wallet and pulled out a small envelope.

"I've got these tickets for a concert . . ."

Girardi jumped in. "No problem. How many do you want me to buy?"

For years, the two had purchased countless tickets from one another for their children's athletic and youth group fundraisers.

"This one's a little different . . ."

"How so?"

Best shifted uncomfortably in his chair, stoking Girardi's curiosity. From his friend's manner, he suspected that an interesting story might be coming, and he welcomed the distraction from his own troubles.

"Well, there's a church concert coming up at St. Mark's next Sunday night. It's kind of a big deal, and Sylvia Bea told me that Susie's really worried that the sanctuary will only be half-full. I bought half a dozen tickets and promised to make sure that six upstanding citizens show up for this thing. The butts need to be in the pews, so to speak."

Best handed Girardi two tickets and continued his unlikely explanation.

"So, I want you to scare up a date and be there with bells on. No biker chicks a-la Mona, either. It needs to be someone classy. Don't worry about the money—it's on me. And I think there will be a potluck afterwards in the parish hall, but Sylvia said we don't have to bring anything for that. They have a committee taking care of the food, I guess."

Girardi stared incredulously at his friend. "Wait a second," he began, waving his hands and laughing heartily. "You need to start at the top and give me the whole story again. For a minute there I almost thought you were inviting me to a church concert and a potluck . . ."

Best looked exasperated. "I'm not going to give it to you again. You heard me just fine the first time. You and a well-chosen guest next weekend at St. Mark's. That's all you need to know."

Girardi's mind worked quickly to recall their encounter with Susan Mountjoy and the Beas on the *Emilio's* patio.

"You're talking about Reverend Mountjoy's church? The priest we met last Sunday at the restaurant?"

"That's right."

"And Sylvia is the woman she was eating dinner with?"

Best nodded.

"How in the world did you get yourself roped into this concert?"

Best hesitated and looked a little sheepish. "Nobody roped me in. I volunteered. I guess you could say that I'm trying to get in good with the rector of St. Mark's."

Girardi again reflected upon their encounter with Mountjoy. "You knew her back in college, right?"

"She lived a couple of floors above me in the dorms. We knew a lot of people in common and ate together all the time in the cafeteria. You'll be surprised to hear this, but I was kind of a cut-up in school. Susie was the opposite—all-business with her nose in a book."

"Wasn't there some mention of Daisy Duke shorts?"

Best nodded. "Picture a tall, dark-haired, sort of coolly attractive girl who is dead serious all the time. That was Susie. Anyway, I was the only one who could make her laugh, though I had to work at it sometimes." He paused and chuckled. "I either made her laugh or I made her mad. I didn't care, though, as long as I got her attention. It was that kind of a deal. Kid stuff."

Girardi detected something different in his friend's demeanor that he couldn't quite put his finger on. "Did you date her?"

"Oh no. She was way out of my league."

"Way out of your league? That doesn't sound like you, Mitch."

"You didn't know me back then. I was a little overwhelmed in college, especially with all of those rich kids at USC. My origins were a lot more humble, you know, and I used to let that bother me. The Marine Corps helped me mature. I came out of there a lot more confident. It will be that way for your nephew, too. I'm sure of it."

The judge had spent an afternoon with Frankie Egan shortly after his enlistment, teaching him about Marine Corps lore and sharing some of his own experiences. Best had kept tabs on the young man through Girardi, and asked after him frequently.

"What was it like to see your friend after all these years?" Girardi asked.

"It was weird, to tell you the truth. Part of me felt like that dorky kid in the dorms again."

"Really? I'd like to see that."

Best ignored this. "It was good to see Susie. She's been very successful in her career." He paused thoughtfully and added, "but I'm not sure she's happy. I don't think she ever married, either. I wonder why not."

"I'm not sure anyone's happy—at least not anyone our age. And being married or not married doesn't seem to have much to do with it. Middle age is not much fun," Girardi reflected gloomily.

"I'm not so sure of that, Mike. Do you know what the author Trollope said?"

Trollope? Girardi repeated to himself, unused to hearing literary references from his friend. *What's with Mitch today?*

"What did Trollope say?"

"Trollope said that a man can't really love or appreciate a woman until he's middle-aged. That's an interesting observation, don't you think? There might be something to it."

With his current troubles, Girardi was not of a mind to grasp immediately the significance of what was being said. He merely shrugged as Best continued.

"I went to the Evensong service on Wednesday night. It was cool to see Susie do her thing. She's a commanding presence, and she can sing and chant beautifully. She kind of glowed up there in the candlelight. I wonder how she learned to do those things?"

"Probably in seminary."

Best looked skeptical. "Did we learn to be lawyers in law school? Of course not. To me, Susie seemed like a natural. We talked some after the service, and she told me that she'd like to take time off to write a book, but she can't do it."

Girardi smiled at the judge. "You seem a little in awe of her. Maybe I will come to that concert just to see you acting like a dorky kid around the Reverend."

"I want you to come, but you can't let on that you know anything."

"I don't know anything."

"Right, and let's keep it that way, okay partner?"

Confused, Girardi suddenly wondered if this was how Jake felt when he appeared puzzled by certain conversations among adults. He borrowed an apt phrase from his son.

"If you say so, Mitch."

"You'll come then?"

"Okay, I'll do my best to be there, but no promises about bringing a date. In fact, do you want the other ticket back?"

Best waved his hand. "No, no, that's okay. Besides, a successful stud like you should have no trouble finding a date." Best began to look around the patio. "We could probably find you one right here. Shall I make some inquiries?"

Best appeared to be about to engage a group of women across the way with whom he'd joked at the buffet, but Girardi grabbed his arm and stopped him.

"Geez, Mitch, knock it off. What's the matter with you?"

The judge laughed heartily, and there was a twinkle in his eye. "You'll think of a nice girl to bring if you put your mind to it."

■ ■ ■

After leaving St. Mark's that afternoon, Susan Mountjoy called on three elderly female shut-ins whose health prevented them from attending services. She gave them each communion and stayed a while to chat with them about the world's headlines and the goings-on at the parish.

She finally arrived home in the mid-afternoon. Mountjoy lived with her mother Lillian in her childhood Newport Beach home. The Spanish-revival home was small by Orange County standards, but it was extremely neat and well-appointed, for the Mountjoy women had very good taste. The now 80 year-old Lillian had been an English teacher before her marriage and then again after her divorce from the Reverend's father. There was no one Mountjoy admired more than her mother, and the two had always been close. Lillian and Mountjoy's younger sister Laura had encouraged Mountjoy to attend seminary at a time when relatively few women did so.

That morning, Lillian had attended the early service and then gone to breakfast with some friends. Mountjoy sometimes envied her mother's ability to form lasting friendships. This did not always come so easily for Susan. Mother and daughter sat down for tea and cookies, sharing stories about their respective days. After receiving the delightful news that there was a pot roast in the oven, Mountjoy retreated to her study to take care of some things before dinner.

Mountjoy's study was small but beautifully laid out. Unlike her desk at the church, she allowed no clutter on the oak table in the center of her study. The place was her intellectual and spiritual sanctuary. Three of the room's four walls contained built-in bookcases. A few religious paintings and icons were scattered about, most of which featured the Virgin Mary. There was a framed photo of Mountjoy and two Cambridge summer classmates on the corner of her table. The two women were pastors on the east coast, and Mountjoy made an effort to stay in touch with them.

She turned on her stereo and flipped to her favorite CD of Bach cantatas. Lighting three candles on her desk, she opened one of her old prayer books and worked her way slowly through the evening prayers. On busy days she sometimes found herself rushing through, but on Sunday afternoons, she made it a point to take her time.

Firing up her laptop some time later, she proceeded to respond to emails for half an hour before finally turning her attention to the notebook with the two sealed envelopes inside. Fingering them both and saying a little prayer of hope and thanksgiving, she opened the note from Sylvia Bea first. It was written on the heavy, salmon-colored stationery that Sylvia always used, and it bore her neat, careful script.

Dear Reverend Doctor Mountjoy,

In recognition of all the fine ministry you conduct for this parish and in the community at large, Hector and I have decided upon a gift to St. Mark's musical programs. Within this general rubric, please use the money in whatever manner you see fit.

With warmest regards and abiding admiration,
Sylvia Bea

Folded inside a blank sheet of salmon stationary was a check for fifteen thousand dollars. *Fifteen thousand dollars*, she rejoiced. This was more than she had allowed herself to hope for, and she offered another prayer of thanks before taking a few minutes to daydream about all of the good uses to which the funds might be put. By the time she was finished, she'd spent the money several times over in her mind and had a fine time doing so. For now, at least, the Evensong service could continue.

With a sigh of apprehension, she turned to the second envelope, holding it for several long moments. The envelope bore the seal and return address of the judge's court, and Mountjoy's name was written in thick black ink in Best's messy scrawl. She slit the top carefully with her letter-opener and as she unfolded the single-page note, she saw again the court's seal. It was an impressive presentation, she thought, lending a certain gravitas to the contents. The letter was dated the prior Friday.

> *Dear Susie:*
>
> *The Beas were here today, and Sylvia and I held the first meeting of the Susan Mountjoy Mutual Admiration Society. She told me about all of the good work you do for your people, and I'm genuinely impressed.*
>
> *With two kids in college, I'm not quite as flush as the Beas, but I'd like to make a small contribution myself. You should spend the funds where you'd like. However, I'd like to see you use them as seed money to get started on that book project of yours. Maybe you can hire some seminary kids to substitute in for you some Sundays.*
>
> *I have a call in to Tim O'Brien. We'll see if he has time for a sinner like me.*
>> *Mitch*

Mountjoy reread the note several times before picking up the check that had fallen face down on the desk. It was for a thousand dollars. She stared at the check for some time, not knowing what to think. *Why would he do this?* She wanted to believe that his motives were pure, and indeed she did not rule out the possibility. But nonetheless, she was uncomfortable. Was he under the impression that he could have her attention if he paid for it? The thought was repugnant to her, but yet, this was hardly the first time in her career that she had considered the issue. People donated to the church for all kinds of reasons and expected all kinds of rewards, earthly and otherwise. And although it was certainly not the case with all of them, some generous donors clearly believed that their needs should be prioritized when the rector allocated her always-scarce time and attention.

Oh Mitch, she sighed, *what are you up to?* She leaned back in her chair and ran her hand over the Book of Common Prayer as she pondered the matter some more. Although her discomfort lingered, there was another consideration. Since her summer in England, she had mentioned to plenty of people her desire to take the time to write a book. But Mitch Best was the first one to do anything to help her make that happen. He must have listened to what she'd said—this had to count for something.

As she was mulling this all over, Lillian knocked upon the study door. Dinner was ready.

21

At the Marshall, Lufton office on Monday afternoon, Girardi was holed up in the conference room that had become the war room for the two court briefs due to be filed that afternoon. Tammy Thompson stood at one end of the long oak table reviewing exhibits while Girardi sat at the other, proofreading the legal brief itself. For the most part, everything seemed to be in order. Thompson had put a great deal of effort and focus into this project, and the results showed.

Unfortunately for Chas Cunningham, who was doing some last-minute computer research in his office, the same could not be said for him. Girardi had spent the prior afternoon and evening re-drafting the legal argument section of Cunningham's brief. As a partner, Girardi was rarely called upon to do such work. Partners routinely guided and edited the work of associates, but rarely wrote briefs themselves. He was rusty and of course distracted by his meeting with Russell Yost and his worries about Jack Tremont. The project had been a struggle for him, and he could not wait to have these two briefs completed and filed.

As he attempted to focus now on Thompson's brief, the exhausted Girardi was interrupted by a firm knock on the conference room door. The room's walls were glass, and Girardi looked up to see receptionist Maria Raymond. He motioned for the pretty young woman to come in.

"Mike, I'm sorry to interrupt you," she began, sounding flustered, "but there's someone making a fuss out in the reception area."

"Maria, I'm sorry, but I don't have time to help you. You'll need to get Cliff."

"He's not in today."

Cliff is never around, Girardi fumed to himself.

"Then talk to one of the other partners."

The receptionist held her ground. "She asked for Cliff, but when I told her Cliff was out, she asked to see you. She says she's an old friend . . . and that she used to work here."

Thompson looked at Girardi in some surprise at this.

"Did you get her name?"

"No," Maria offered apologetically. "She wouldn't tell me. *Please*, won't you talk to her? I don't know what to do with her."

"Alright," Girardi relented, "I'll be right there."

He turned to Thompson. "You can go through the rest of this yourself. It looks good to me. As soon as you're done, go and spend some time with Chas. See how he's coming along."

A look of apprehension crossed her face, for she and Girardi both knew that Cunningham was struggling. The three had all remained in the office into the wee hours the night before and returned first thing in the morning. It would be a race to the wire to complete Cunningham's brief.

"I know," Girardi said in reply to her look, "just see if you can help him. I won't be gone long."

"Of course I'll help him," Thompson offered with as much optimism as she could muster. "Both briefs will get filed, Mike. Don't worry. Chas is really working hard."

In many instances, when two young associates in the same department were of similar seniority, they viewed one another as competitors. It was refreshing to Girardi to see that both Thompson and Cunningham appeared to go out of their way to support one another. He sometimes lamented that the kids today did not seem to have as much fire and toughness as their older counterparts. At the same time, however, he thought that they might just be more pleasant to deal with. Everything is a tradeoff.

Girardi thanked Thompson and hurried up to the reception area, stewing over the state of Cunningham's brief and cursing Cliff Conroy for his absence. When he arrived up front, Maria nodded and gestured to the door of a small conference room adjacent to the elevator.

"Thanks, Mike," she said as Girardi passed by.

"You're welcome."

Unlike most of the conference rooms in the firm, this one had no glass walls or doors. Girardi knocked on the door as he entered. The first thing he saw was a baby carrier and large blue diaper bag. Then, just a moment later, his astonished eyes fell upon Mona Phillips, his former girlfriend.

The blood left Girardi's head and he felt a little woozy as he took in the sight of his old flame holding an infant. It was surprising enough to see Mona after nearly two years apart and not so much as a post card or text message between them. It was even more of a shock to see the carefree woman with a child.

Girardi tried to estimate the baby's age and to do some quick math, but his mind was in no shape for the work. He was exhausted and confused.

Mona approached him and offered a hug with her free arm.

"Hi Mike, say hello to Gunnar."

Girardi patted her lightly on the back and then took a few steps away. "Mona—it's been a long time."

"It sure has."

"You're a mom now?"

The baby let out a little cry at this, and Mona lifted him up and sniffed his diaper. "I need to change him. Do you mind?"

"Do you want me to leave?" he asked uncomfortably.

"Not unless you're afraid to see a six month old wee-wee."

There was not a single human body part that Mona Phillips was afraid to mention in conversation, and wee-wees had certainly never been off-limits for her.

Memories of his time with Mona flooded his mind as he sat heavily in a chair near the door. While Mona went to work on little Gunnar's diaper, he was able to observe her appearance with some care. Back when they'd dated, Mona had routinely favored tank tops, snug jeans and leather jackets. Now, she wore a loose green sundress under an ivory cardigan sweater. It was quite a transformation. Her hair back then had been straight and bleached-blonde, but now it was light brown and wavy.

Watching her work, his eyes fell upon her breasts as they flowed out of the dress's loose bodice. Girardi had always thought that Mona's was the most perfect figure that he had ever seen. Despite the swirl in his mind, he observed that if anything, she was even more attractive now. He felt stirring inside him a muted version of his old passion for her.

"I didn't think they could get any bigger, but thanks to my little friend here, they did," Mona commented matter-of-factly as she sprinkled a little powder into Gunnar's fresh diaper.

"Excuse me?"

"My breasts—they're even bigger now thanks to the feeding. They make my back ache sometimes. Honestly, I feel like I'm carrying two bowling balls around all day."

She chuckled and then smiled apologetically, handing him the dirty diaper. "We probably shouldn't leave this in the conference room or Cliff will have the entire building fumigated. Would you take this to the men's room and dump it?"

It had been a long time indeed since Girardi had disposed of a little boy's diaper.

"Sure," was all he could say in reply. "I'll be right back."

Naturally, a group of several attorneys, including Huey, Dewey and Louie, had gathered in the lobby not far from the conference room door, hoping to learn what was going on inside. Girardi ignored them as he headed for the restroom with his bundle.

A couple of minutes later, he stood washing his hands and looking at his haggard face in the mirror. He was usually very careful with his appearance, but now he saw that his beard was unkempt and that he'd missed some spots shaving his neck that morning. There were dark circles under his eyes and his cheeks had no color to them. The pressure was getting to him.

As he threw some water on his face, Girardi forced himself to calm down. Of course this was not his baby, he assured himself. Mona had said that Gunnar was six months old. Six plus nine was fifteen. He went over that math one more time—six plus nine was fifteen. Their last time together in Jamaica had been two summers earlier, more than twenty months ago.

As he thought the matter over, he assured himself that Mona was not the type of person who would have a baby without telling the father. She was the most open person Girardi knew. On the other hand, it astonished him that she'd become pregnant so soon after their breakup.

With his bearings at least partially restored, Girardi rallied himself and headed back for the conference room. The same little group stood expectantly in the lobby, but Girardi once more acted as though he did not see them.

When Girardi entered the conference room, Gunnar was in his carrier playing with a little rattle as Mona hovered lovingly over him.

"So," Girardi began when he'd closed the door behind him, "Maria tells me that you came to see Cliff today."

Mona sighed heavily and nodded. "Yes, I did."

"What business do you have with Cliff?"

"Oh Mike, I have something to tell you, and it's going to make you angry. I hate to bother you with my troubles after all this time, but I don't have anywhere else to turn."

At this, tears began to streak down her pale cheeks. Mona was not one to cry easily, and Girardi could see the uncertainty in her expression. She grabbed a tissue and wiped her face with it. As she did this, Girardi noted that she was not wearing a ring.

"You're going to be really disappointed in me," she continued.

"Come on, you know me. I'm not a particularly judgmental guy."

"I know, but this is bad. Just let me tell you the whole story, starting at the beginning. And *please* try not to judge me too harshly."

Girardi hesitated, wondering what in the world Mona was about to tell him. He was busy, and did not have time for a long story. Besides, one thing needed to be cleared up right away.

"Listen, Mona, before you say anything else, do you mind if I ask who Gunnar's father is?"

"Jack."

"Jack who?"

"What's the matter with you, Mike? Jack *Tremont.*"

Girardi presumed he'd be relieved to hear any name besides his own. But in spite of himself, the news hit him hard. Jack Tremont? His gorgeous former girlfriend had a child with his senior citizen law partner and mentor? At first, his mind could not fathom it.

"I didn't think you even knew Jack."

"I met him at a firm party—remember the luau?"

Girardi certainly did recall the luau, which, for a host of reasons, he believed was the worst social event in Marshall, Lufton history. The firm hosted two big parties each year, one in the summer and the other at the holidays. The summer picnic always had a different theme and location. One particularly ambitious event had been a luau at a beach club. All manner of things had gone awry that day, and now Girardi had one more reason to curse the luau.

"Do you remember when the pig caught on fire?"

"Oh yes," Girardi replied quietly.

"And when they ran out of beer?"

He nodded.

Mona folded her arms at the recollection and let out a long sigh. "When we were together, you almost never invited me to any of your work parties. I thought I was missing out on something special. Boy, was I wrong."

"This life is not always what it's cracked up to be," Girardi conceded, summing up a lesson that had been sharply driven home in recent days.

"And Lizzy got mad at you at the luau for some reason or other. By the way, does she still work here?"

"Who?"

"My god Mike, do you have Alzheimer's? *Lizzy Stowe.* She's probably a partner by now. I always thought she was gunning for a corner office."

Girardi certainly did not like to hear Mona speaking of Stowe in this vein. Besides, the prediction about the corner office could not have been further from the mark.

"No, she doesn't work here any longer."

"Did she marry that tool Troy? You hated him if I recall correctly."

Girardi stared at her in surprise. "How do you remember so much about Beth Stowe?"

"How could I forget her? You used to spend more time with her than you did with me. And when she wasn't around you were always mentioning her."

"We worked together, Mona."

"I still remember the day of the luau so clearly. It was open seating, but you plopped yourself down in a chair right next to Lizzy. She spent the entire luau giving me the evil eye . . . and meanwhile, Troy was giving me another kind of eye, if you know what I mean."

Girardi had been a little fuzzy on some of the details of the ill-fated luau, but now he began to recall the particulars of that terrible occasion. He had rarely brought Mona along with him to firm events, preferring to keep his work and private lives separate. But the issue had become a point of contention between them and Girardi had made an exception for the luau.

"It's great to reminisce about old times," Girardi interjected sarcastically, "but you should probably tell me about Jack. We have two court filings this afternoon, and I don't have much time."

A small look of hurt crossed Mona's face, and she reflexively put her hand on Gunnar's leg and tugged it playfully. The baby obliged his mom with a smile and giggle.

"Jack called me a few days after the luau and asked to see me," she continued.

Girardi felt his anger rising.

"I refused," she said quickly. "He called me other times, but my answer was always the same."

Girardi folded his arms tensely. "What changed?"

"A few weeks before the Jamaica trip, he showed up at my job with a bouquet of lilies. He talked me into going to dinner with him. He was so charming."

"*Mona,* we were still together then. How could you see my partner like that behind my back?"

"I knew it was wrong, but I kind of got sucked in. No one had ever talked to me the way he did."

Girardi prided himself on being a pretty good talker when he made an effort, and he doubted very much that Jack Tremont had anything on him when it came to wooing a woman.

"So, when you broke up with me in Jamaica, were you lying about wanting to stay there?"

She shook her head sadly. "No. I thought that I might be better off staying away from both of you. I lived in Jamaica for two months."

"And then?"

"Jack came to see me."

I can't believe this, Girardi fumed. He recalled the talk he'd recently had with Judge Best about his relationship with Mona. *Wait 'til I tell Mitch. I said to him that Mona liked me for me. What a jackass I was.*

"Jack offered to take care of me if I'd come home with him. I didn't expect the two of us to get serious, but we did."

This was too much for Girardi.

"Serious? He knocked you up, Mona. He's got a wife—you aren't *serious* with him."

"You don't have to be cruel, Mike."

Girardi took a deep breath and labored to calm down. "I don't mean to be cruel, but you need to get real here. Jack's very ill."

"I haven't been able to find out a single thing about his condition. It's really bad, then?"

"His condition is quite serious. I saw him last week and tried to talk business with him. It's a struggle for him to speak, and I don't know his latest prognosis, but I suspect that only time will tell."

At this, Mona reached over and pulled the whimpering Gunnar from his carrier. She kissed him and whispered in his ear as she pointed to a colorful picture on the wall. After some time, she spoke up.

"I'm sure you won't believe me, but Jack and I love each other. I know it looks terrible, but I'm not just some girl he has on the side. Before he got sick, we were planning to be together."

I'm sure you were, Girardi thought cynically to himself.

"He wants to be a father to Gunnar."

Girardi remained skeptical, but he tried not to show it. Tremont was a grandfather several times over—and he'd never struck Girardi as being particularly interested in his children or grandkids. What were the odds that he was enthusiastic to play father to his mistress's six-month old?

"So, tell me Mona, why did you come here today?"

"Jack bought a condo for Gunnar and me in Huntington Beach."

Huntington Beach? That explains the phone bill. And it explains why Celeste didn't know about the condo.

"The place on Cherry Tree Lane?"

Mona opened her eyes wide in surprise. "How do you know about that?"

"It's not important."

"Yes it is important. Did Jack tell you about me?"

"Oh, no."

Mona paced swiftly around the room with Gunnar, apparently unsure if she should continue.

"Cliff takes care of the bills and they give me a little money each month for food and baby clothes. But Cliff hasn't been paying the bills lately and I'm running out of money. I begged him to let me see Jack, but Cliff has forbidden me to come near the hospital. I'm scared, Mike. Cliff won't say how Jack is doing, and I want to see Jack for myself. I think it would do him good to spend some time with Gunnar."

Girardi briefly attempted to conjure such a scene in his mind's eye. As far as he knew, Celeste spent every day at the hospital. She was a formidable woman, and there might be a terrible confrontation between Mona and Celeste. With all that Celeste had been through, Girardi feared that news like this might break her.

"I'm starting to get phone calls from bill collectors," she continued, "and I don't know what to do. I want to be a stay-at-home mom with Gunnar, but I might have to go to work. I can do that, but we couldn't afford to live where we are now on what I'd be able to earn."

She began once more to cry. "The idea of leaving Gunnar in day care kills me. We haven't been apart since he was born."

The baby, feeling his mother's tension, also began to sob. "No, no, Gun, don't cry. Mommy's fine." She began walking him around the small room. "He likes to keep moving. I can already tell that he's really smart and intuitive. But, unfortunately, he's a Scorpio—that means he will hold grudges and never get over things," she added worriedly.

"I'm a Scorpio." Girardi took some exception to the characterization of those born under the sign of the scorpion.

"Exactly."

Girardi folded his arms unhappily. "I don't put stock into any of that stuff."

"I know you don't—you're too rational for astrology. But I think there's something to it."

Girardi merely shrugged.

She kissed Gunnar's forehead, and as she did so, Girardi could not help but feel his heart warmed at the tenderness of Mona's attentions to her son.

"Look Mona, I'm sorry, but I'm going to need to get back to work. I really am swamped."

"You're always swamped—do you know how many times you said that to me when we were together? 'Hey baby, sorry, but I'm swamped here. I'll call you later.' It was the same message every time."

Girardi stared at her in surprise. "We always agreed that we were low-key—that we'd spend time together when we could."

"Yes, I know."

"In fact, *you* were the one who insisted from day one that we keep things casual—no pressure. That was your mantra, and I adopted it, too."

"That's true, but Mike, you were always *so* busy. After a while I figured out that our relationship was more important to me than it was to you. Jack really *wanted* me—that meant a lot."

As he took this in, Girardi wondered if Mona was trying in retrospect to justify her actions in taking up with Tremont. He wasn't buying it. But yet, it was probably true that he'd used his work to hold Mona at some distance. It had been a relationship they'd both said would not last forever. He allowed that it was at least possible that Mona had viewed things differently at the time.

"I suppose that's the life I've chosen for myself," Girardi demurred.

"Does it make you happy?"

"Does what make me happy?"

"The law."

"I thought it did—but lately, I'm not so sure."

"You know, Gunnar has given me a purpose in life—and I'm thankful."

Mona kissed Gunnar and placed him back in the carrier.

"Will you please talk to Jack for me? I want to visit him—quietly. I don't want to make trouble for him. Can't you help me get in to see him?"

"Oh Mona, I can't interfere that way. Celeste is a friend of mine."

Mona exhaled indignantly at this mention of Celeste. "But what about Gunnar?"

"You should talk to Cliff."

"Cliff is avoiding me—and he won't tell me anything anyway. He certainly won't let me see Jack. I'm considering driving down to the hospital this afternoon. Maybe it's time that Celeste knew what was going on. Let the chips fall where they may."

The prospect sounded terrible to Girardi. He held up a cautioning hand. "No, no, don't do that. Listen, give me a day or two. I have several things to discuss with Jack, and they're all important. If I'm able to, I'll suggest that he get in touch with you. That's the best I can offer."

Mona put her hand on Girardi's arm. "Thank you. You have no idea what this means."

"Please don't get your hopes up, but I'll try my best. Now, I really need to get going. Take care of yourself, okay? Leave your phone number with Maria at the desk. I'll be in touch when I know something."

He reached into his wallet, pulled out all of his cash, and handed it to her. She nodded her thanks and tucked the money into the diaper bag without making eye contact with him. As he watched her, Girardi was moved by the combination of pride and vulnerability she displayed.

Then he opened the door and took a couple of steps out.

"Maria will validate your parking."

And at this, Girardi made a bee line for the war room.

22

A few hours after parting from Mona, Girardi called Tammy Thompson into his office. To everyone's relief, the briefs had been filed. In the end, Thompson's brief had been quite good considering the circumstances. Cunningham's, in contrast, had gone out the door in rough shape. Girardi's efforts had of course saved the document from being a disaster, but it was nowhere near Marshall, Lufton's usual standards, and Girardi knew it.

To reward Thompson, and free up some time for himself, Girardi decided to send her to court the following morning on a status conference that Randall Spencer had been scheduled to cover.

"I'm going to court . . . alone?" she asked with big eyes. She was wearing a well-tailored brown pantsuit and a tan knit top.

"Yep," Girardi replied matter-of-factly. "You can handle that, right?"

He thought for a moment she might come around the desk and embrace him, but luckily she stayed put. Thompson was learning to tame her fashion excesses at the office, but not yet her exuberance.

"Of course I can handle that. This is great!"

"You shouldn't need to say much," he cautioned. "You'll mainly be there to listen and take notes, because we're a minor party so far and I want to keep it that way. But, there are a couple of things I want you to take care of while you're there."

Girardi proceeded to explain the procedural posture of the case and to describe what was likely to happen at the status conference. When he finished, Thompson assured him she'd take care of it.

"I probably won't be here tomorrow when you get back from court, Tammy, but leave a voicemail on my office line and let me know how it went, okay?"

"Okay."

"And what else are you doing for me this week?"

Thompson thought for a moment or two and then rattled off the half-dozen or so hot projects on her desk. In the rush to complete her big brief, lots of items had been placed on the back burner. It was now time to return her attention to them.

When the two had finished going over everything and Girardi felt satisfied that Thompson was on track for the week, he stood from his chair.

"Good work on that brief, Tammy."

"Thanks, Mike," she replied, rising also and heading for the door.

He suddenly recalled her prior comment in the small conference room about yoga class and her work-life balance. "You should go home and get some rest. You've earned it."

She paused and looked down at her legal pad. "I've got a couple more hours here at least. I want to get a jump on those discovery responses. After that, I'll need to read the file for tomorrow's hearing. I think I'll order in some dinner. Do you want anything?"

"No thanks, I'm actually heading out pretty soon. Good luck tomorrow."

Thompson nodded and left Girardi's office. *She just might be okay*, he allowed to himself as he walked out to the cubicle of his assistant.

"Janice, I've decided to take tomorrow off. I want you to cover for me. If anyone asks, just say I took a personal day."

"Okay, but you're due in court tomorrow morning on that status conference."

"Tammy's going to cover the hearing for me."

"She is?" Janice asked with obvious surprise.

"Yep."

They talked over Girardi's schedule for the rest of the week, then he returned to his office, quickly packed up his things, and wished Janice a good evening.

■ ■ ■

Pulling out of his office parking structure a short time later, Girardi made his way to Pacific Coast Highway and headed north in the direction of Hope Hospital. Once inside the building, Girardi headed straight for Tremont's room. Fighting the old anxiety that always plagued him in hospitals, Girardi kept his head down as he rode up in the busy elevator and then made his way down the lonely corridor. He summoned his courage as he approached the door of the private room he'd visited the prior week. Girardi had worked with Tremont for fifteen years, and all that they had shared was now riding on one conversation. Whatever happened, Girardi's central hope was that Tremont would be honest with him. With his heart nearly in his throat, Girardi knocked quietly and opened the door.

"Oh my!" came the startled cry of a plump elderly woman on the bed. Her head was wrapped in a white bandage, and her left arm was in a cast. She pulled up the covers with her good hand and stared at him suspiciously. "Who are *you*?"

Girardi's eyes grew wide in surprise and embarrassment. "I'm terribly sorry, ma'am. I must have the wrong room. I apologize for disturbing you."

He took several steps backward and left the room. On his way out, he checked the room number next to the door. Although he'd doubted himself for a moment or two, this was indeed the room where he'd spoken with Tremont and Conroy the prior week. *What did they do with Jack?*

He headed straight for the nurse's station, where several female members of the hospital staff came and went, ignoring him completely. Everyone was dressed similarly, and Girardi had no idea which ones might be the nurses or who was in charge. Still a little thrown by his encounter down the hall, Girardi stood quietly for a few awkward moments, hoping someone might offer to help him. But they continued their business as if they did not even see him. So, at last, he stepped forward and addressed a petite young woman wearing a floral smock and holding several clipboards.

"I'm looking for Jack Tremont."

She stared at him blankly. "Is he a patient?"

"Yes, yes," Girardi replied anxiously. "He was in that room just a few days ago," he said, pointing.

She consulted two of her clipboards and then shook her head. "He's not on this floor. Perhaps he was discharged?"

"I very much doubt it."

"Well, then you'll have to find a white courtesy phone and contact our switchboard. They have a current patient list."

At this, she turned from Girardi and began to speak with one of her colleagues. Left on his own, Girardi wandered down the hall toward the elevator and eventually found a white phone. On the third try, someone picked up.

"I'm looking for the room number of a patient of yours."

"Certainly," replied an efficient, professional female voice. "May I have the name?"

"Tremont, Jackson Tremont."

Girardi heard the sound of fingers typing on a keyboard. There was a long pause.

"I'm sorry, but I can't give out any information about Mr. Tremont."

"I don't understand."

"I'm sorry, sir, but I can't give out any information about Mr. Tremont."

Girardi shook his head in disbelief and tightened his grip on the receiver. He felt his neck muscles knot up. "I was here to see him last week. I'm his law partner, and I need to speak with him on urgent business. *Please*, I just need his room number. I'm not asking for information on his medical status."

To Girardi's frustration, the operator repeated the same phrase.

"Can you at least tell me if he's still here at Hope Hospital?"

"I'm sorry sir, I really can't give out any information about Mr. Tremont. Perhaps you might want to contact the family."

"Why can't *you* tell me about him? I've never heard of anything like this."

Still, she maintained her calm. "Sir, there are other calls ringing in. I wish I could have been of more help to you. Have a good day."

Click, and the line went dead.

Frustrated and confused, Girardi grabbed his cell phone and immediately dialed Celeste Tremont. Naturally, she did not pick up. He considered trying to throw his weight around with the hospital administration in order to glean some explanation of the situation, but he doubted this would be effective. An administrator might speak with him at greater length and offer him a cup of coffee and the appearance of some sympathy, but the basic message would likely be the same.

Next, he dialed Cliff Conroy's cell. There was no response. Another dead end.

Still standing by the white phone, Girardi tried to calm himself down as he considered this latest development. It had not even occurred to him that Tremont might have been moved without anyone telling him. And where did he go?

He thought over her language, which had been the same each time. *I can't give out any information about Mr. Tremont.* She had seemed practiced at the phrase, which Girardi suspected was the type of thing that might be said when a celebrity or public figure was a patient. But, successful as he was, Jack Tremont was still a regular citizen. Pacing around the hallway, Girardi's mind went to Russell Yost's veiled threat that if he did not get his document, rougher men would become involved. Had Tremont himself been threatened? Perhaps he'd been moved for security's sake. But if so, Girardi should have been told.

Then, his mind went to Mona Phillips and her threat to bring Gunnar to the hospital. Had Cliff acted to shield the Tremonts from Mona? Girardi would not put it past Conroy to do such a thing. If this were so, Conroy had certainly acted quickly. Girardi dialed the office manager's number once more, but there was still no answer.

His thoughts in a whirl, Girardi headed outside. When he reached his car, he wasn't sure what to do with himself. He'd assumed that by this time he'd know the truth about *Trinity Hills* and *Pope Electronics*—or, if not the truth, then at least Tremont's version. He hoped also to have dealt with the subject of Mona Phillips once and for all. But now, nothing had been accomplished, and Girardi was more lost than ever. He called Mitch Best's chambers, but his assistant informed him that the judge had left for the day. Girardi tried his cell, and when it went to voicemail, he left a message. There was plenty to do at the office, but he was exhausted and in no shape to work. And so, he decided to head home.

23

Later that evening, Jake and his father sat together in their living room watching a Lakers game on mute. Empty glasses, plates, and the remnants of a frozen pizza were arranged neatly on a tray on the coffee table. Jake was half-heartedly doing his math homework on the sofa while Girardi occupied an easy chair and brooded over his troubles. He was so tired that he dozed off a few times. They were both in lousy moods, and little was said between them.

Watching his son laboriously working his math problems, Girardi hated to see him in such poor humor.

"So," Girardi ventured, rubbing his eyes, "everything okay at school?"

"School's fine."

Girardi got to thinking about Morgan the vegan and wondered if there had been any developments on that front. *While I'm prying, I may as well go all in.*

"So, what's up with Morgan?" he offered casually. "You haven't mentioned her lately."

The young man's face darkened, and he began to tap the mechanical pencil on his book the way his father did when he was tense. There was a very long pause, during which Girardi held his breath.

"She's dating a college guy. I can't compete with that."

Jake then placed his worksheet inside the textbook and headed for the stairs. "I'm going to take a shower."

My son, the man of few words, Girardi thought admiringly. He had put it in a nutshell, and Girardi now grasped the essence of the situation. *I could take a page out of his book on verbal economy.*

Girardi turned up the volume on the television and tried to interest himself in the Lakers game. The Angels and Dodgers had the night off, and so he was stuck with basketball. He was soon dozing again, but was awakened later by the sound of a silver Lexus SUV with the vanity plate "VALTAXI."

Girardi opened the front door and waited as his sister emerged from the driver's seat wearing her favorite Rick Springfield shirt and carrying a large Tupperware container of lasagna.

"I thought you guys might like some food."

Although he and Jake had already shared a pizza, Girardi nodded enthusiastically. There was always room for Val's lasagna. The two went into the kitchen, where Val zapped the food in the microwave and Girardi grabbed a beer for Val from the fridge.

"Is Jake upstairs?" she asked cautiously.

"Yep."

"Good, because I need to unload. You'll never guess what happened."

"It must be pretty bad if you're wearing your original Rick Springfield shirt."

Val nodded sadly. "The vice-principal called from school today. Jesse's going to have an F and a D on her progress report."

"Jesse? She could get A's in her sleep."

"Apparently, she's stopped turning in her homework. I thought she was doing it every night. Nothing like this has ever happened with her."

"If it's just a progress report, she has time to turn things around before final grades in June."

"There's more. Jesse's going to spend a week in zero period detention for mouthing off to her choir instructor. Get this, *I* need to drive her an hour early to school *five* mornings in a row. They're punishing *me* for her smart mouth."

You had quite a mouth on you at Jesse's age, Girardi thought, recalling the seemingly endless battles between the teenaged Val and their mother.

"What does Stu say?"

"Stu suggested that I vacate the premises for a little while, so that he could talk to Jesse alone. I was thrilled. In fact, maybe I'll stay here with you and Jake for a few days. I'll let my husband drive that brat to school at six-thirty." She took a long swig of her beer. "If this were Frankie, I'd take charge. My son and I understand each other. But Jesse's always done better with her father."

"Do you want to eat in the yard?" Girardi asked. "It's nice out."

"Sure."

The two soon settled into cushioned chairs at Girardi's backyard patio table. Val, who hadn't seen the yard in several weeks, looked around and offered her brother a compliment.

"Mikey, your roses look amazing. I don't know how you do it. We pay our gardeners a fortune and our yard looks like crap. With all those HOA rules, I'm constantly getting violation notices for rules I've never heard of—it's crazy."

Girardi's backyard contained a brick patio area and two large swaths of grass. Dozens of blooming rose bushes were planted along the perimeter and in a neat alley between the two grass patches. Most of his plants were now in bloom, and as Girardi liked to say, early May was payoff time.

"You're so much like papa," Val offered, referring to their paternal grandfather. "Do you remember all of the flowers in his yard?"

"And the grapes," Girardi replied, pointing over at the arbor he'd constructed a few years earlier. "I wish I had his talent with grapes. I baby those vines along every year and the fruit still tastes lousy. Sometimes I dream about chucking it all and buying a little vineyard somewhere out in the country."

"With all the money you're stashing away in your mattress, you could probably do it."

Although Mike Girardi appeared on the surface to be a man with expensive tastes, in truth he was careful with his money. Over his twenty years of law practice, he had steadily amassed a significant portfolio of savings and investments, including two rental properties. Like many law-yers, he entertained fantasies of leaving the practice for a slower-paced, more fulfilling life.

"Papa always talked about having a vineyard," Girardi recalled.

"His yard practically was a vineyard."

"I know. I miss that house."

"So do I," Val agreed sadly. "And I miss them, too."

Given her mood, Girardi feared that Val might veer into maudlin rem-iniscences about their deceased relatives, but she didn't. For some time, she was uncharacteristically quiet as she ate her lasagna.

Girardi cast a careful glance toward the sliding glass door. Seeing no sign of Jake, he assumed a confidential, knowing tone. "I found out that it's a no-go with the vegan."

Val waved her hand dismissively. "Morgan? I know. She's got a boy-friend at San Diego State. She wasn't right for him anyway."

Girardi felt needled with annoyance. He thought that for once he had a scoop to share with Val. "You knew about this and didn't tell me?"

"I forgot. Besides, you've been scarce lately."

Girardi could hardly deny this. "I know."

Her mind in a whirl, Val moved quickly to a new thought. "You know, Mikey, I want to introduce you to a friend of mine—she's one of the moms at Jesse's school. Cheryl's not a bad looking gal when she makes an effort—and she's smart, too. She works really hard to make ends meet and to pay for April's tuition. And, naturally, her ex doesn't make his sup-port payments half the time."

"That sounds tough," Girardi demurred.

"So, would you like to meet her?" Val pressed, brightening at the idea.

"No thanks, Val."

"Why not? I told her about you, and I could tell she was intrigued."

Girardi felt the muscles in his neck tighten further. Describing her friend's financial woes and typical middle-aged emotional baggage, Val had said little to spark his interest. And "not a bad looking gal when she makes an effort" was not much of an endorsement. On this count, how-ever, Girardi knew from experience that his sister had a hard time praising the physical appearance of other women. So, it was possible that Cheryl was indeed an attractive woman.

"No thanks," he repeated. This time, he tried to be more firm, but he could see that she wasn't listening to him.

"You need to get back out there. What will you do when Jake eventually moves out? If you won't do anything about your love life, then *I'll* have to."

Val finished her beer and pointed at her shirt. "You know what Ricky says . . . *"you'd better love somebody, it's late . . ."*

She laughed and then started picking at the label on her bottle, caught up in her own thoughts. "What if Stu and I have a barbeque at our place? You know how much Stu loves to grill. We can get a jump on summer. It wouldn't be a set-up or anything like that. You could just say hi and see if any sparks fly."

See if any sparks fly, Girardi repeated skeptically to himself. *I doubt it.*

"I'm so busy right now, Val, that I have no time for sparks. This is the worst it's been at work in years."

There was so much more he could say on the subject, of course, but he left it at that.

"You work too hard at that that stupid job of yours, Mike. You know that's why Cassidy left in the first place."

It was difficult for Girardi's neck muscles to tighten any further, but they managed to. Girardi scowled as he picked up his plate and stood from his chair. This was now the second time in a few hours that he'd been criticized for working hard. He had let the matter go with Mona, but was not ready to do so with Val.

"That *stupid* job of mine pays for a lot of things, Val. Just like Stu's *stupid* company pays for your . . ."

"I know," she cut him off. "I don't need to hear that lecture right now."

"If I work too hard, then I certainly shouldn't be looking for a relationship right now, should I?"

Val stood from the table and followed him inside. "I'm sorry for mentioning Cass . . ."

The blackness remained about his brow as he rinsed the dishes and Val put them into the dishwasher. Then, he headed for the living room and brought in the dinner tray. The pair repeated the process with these dishes until everything was put in place.

"Listen," Val ventured at last, "I just hate to see you this way. You're lonely. I don't mean that you need to get serious with someone. Who needs that kind of a headache? I mean you should have some fun, like you did with Mona. *Please*, let me introduce you to Cheryl."

"I don't want to see anyone just for fun—I'm done with that."

Val pressed on without missing a beat. "Cheryl could probably be serious pretty quick, truth be told. Let's have her over—what could it hurt?"

She just won't stop. In his weary frustration and eagerness to end this line of conversation, Girardi let slip something that was not even fully formed in his own mind.

"Actually, Val, there might be a prospect on the horizon. I'm going to lay low and see where that goes."

"Who is she?" Val demanded breathlessly, taking a strong hold of his arm.

Seeing her reaction, Girardi immediately regretted his indiscretion. He thought of the mystery of Morgan the vegan and suddenly empathized with Jake.

"She's nobody I want to talk about, okay?"

"Is she a waitress somewhere? Or maybe a receptionist at the gym? Those girls are always hot." Val's brow knitted in disapproval. "Don't think we women don't understand why you guys like going to the gym so much."

Now Val was being annoying at too many levels to keep track.

"She's a lawyer, actually," he replied, his ire rising. "And she's very intelligent."

"A *lawyer*? Really?"

Girardi shook his head in dismay. "Is that what you think of me, Val? You think that I'm looking to date a gym receptionist? Those girls are Jake's age."

Val shrugged. "Don't get huffy, Mike, but you've always turned up your nose at the professional girls. Look at your track record so far—it's nobody with more than a high school diploma or a GED."

The GED reference was of course to Mona Phillips. *Always with Mona.*

"I'm glad you're keeping such careful records."

"Come on, Mikey, give me the story about the lawyer."

"There's no story to tell," he lied. "I ran into someone I used to work with. It was good to see her, that's all. Things are way too crazy for me right now. But I might try and spend some time with her down the road. I'm not interested in being fixed up—case closed."

Val consulted her watch. "Can I have another beer?"

"No, you can't. It's late, you're a lightweight, and you're driving. If you really want to stay, I can make us a pot of coffee. But . . ."

"But you'd really rather I stopped bugging you and went home."

"Something like that, yes."

Val untied the sweater from around her waist and pushed her arms roughly through the sleeves.

"I'm not sure I want to go home," she confided sadly.

Girardi softened. "It's going to be fine, Val. All kids go through phases."

"Jesse's never been in trouble at school. When the teachers talk to us, it's always to say how great she is. I'm stunned."

"Go home and talk to Stu. You two will figure this out together."

Val shook her head. "I'm always complaining about things, aren't I? How did that happen? I used to have so much fun . . . and now all I do is drag others down."

"That's not true at all. Most of the time you are making other people happy—and you are really good at it."

"Are you coming to Jake's game tomorrow?" she asked.

"Yep. I'm taking the day off. I have some things to take care of in the morning, but I plan to be at the game when it starts."

Val walked over to the sliding glass door leading to the backyard.

"Can I have a few roses to take home with me?"

"Of course."

Girardi obligingly went outside with his gloves and cutters and began to select stems from various bushes. Val silently followed him around the yard and at last spoke up softly.

"Can I have that one?" she asked, pointing to a full red bloom. "It's perfect."

"It's perfect now—but by the time you get up tomorrow morning it will be past its prime." He selected a half-open bud on the next branch over and assumed a philosophical tone. "You always want to look out for the ones that will last."

Val continued to follow Girardi along the path. "Will you tell me about your lawyer friend, please?" she coaxed at last. "I'm sorry I said all that about Cheryl and the gym girls. I won't tease you or be weird about the lawyer, I promise."

Girardi slowly revealed some facts about Stowe, careful to say nothing about *Trinity Hills* or why she had left Marshall, Lufton. When he'd finished, Val looked at him in surprise. "You really like her, don't you?"

He nodded.

"Then you should ask her out, Mike. Why not?"

Girardi paused from his work and looked Val in the eye. In the wake of his encounter with Mona Phillips, he could not help but conclude that he was a terrible judge of women. His marriage had ended in a blindsiding divorce and he'd lost a girlfriend to his sixty-year-old law partner. Obviously Mona was not the person he'd thought she was. How could he trust himself to choose someone after all that had gone on?

"It's complicated. She might not be interested in dating anyone right now."

Val paused to consider this. "I know it's politically incorrect for me to say this, but I think most single women are *always* looking for a good man to come along. This whole 'taking a break from dating' is usually BS. If she's as intelligent as you say, she won't pass you up because of the timing. How old is she?"

"Mid-thirties, maybe? A great age."

"A great age? For plenty of women, that's desperation time. Has she ever been married?"

"No—and Beth's not desperate."

"If you say so . . ."

"The timing isn't the only issue. The truth is that after all these years, I'm not sure I want to put myself out there that way again. I haven't done it since Cassidy—and that was twenty years ago."

"Mona doesn't count?"

"Mona was entirely different."

"I say you should take the initiative and ask Beth out to a movie or a ballgame or something low-key like that."

Girardi assembled his cuttings and wrapped them in a damp cloth for his sister to take with her.

"I'll think about it."

They chatted outside until it was entirely dark, and then Valerie reluctantly got into her car and headed home. Girardi went back inside and within ten minutes was asleep on the sofa.

24

At the gym, Girardi enjoyed his first swim in weeks. On the first few laps, he felt the strain, but he managed to work through it, and the swim did him a world of good. For forty minutes, he was nearly free from worries of Jack Tremont, Russell Yost, Mona and Gunnar, Frankie's deployment, and Jesse's progress report. He emptied his mind and thought of nothing but his stroke and the feeling of slicing through the water. Nothing relaxed Girardi more than a good swim, and he chastised himself for not making time to exercise during his recent work crises. As he headed for the locker room to change, he vowed to visit the gym no matter how busy he was at work.

Girardi then headed for Interstate 5, which would take him south to the Emanuel Center. He had surprised Sister Agnes the prior evening by phoning and asking for an appointment.

"I'm happy to meet with you, but I can't promise to have Elizabeth there. We'll see how she feels."

Sister Ida met Girardi in the lobby and showed him to the east conference room, where he found coffee and fresh cinnamon rolls.

Agnes and Stowe soon joined him. Girardi immediately observed that Stowe was more subdued than usual. She quietly poured coffee into three "Girls for God" mugs that had been a gift from Reverend Mountjoy. For her part, Stowe had spent a string of restless nights since Girardi's visit on

Friday, worrying about Girardi and wondering if she'd done the right thing by telling him about *Trinity Hills.*

After a bit of chit-chat, Agnes got them down to business. "Why did you come today, Mr. Girardi?"

He reached into his pocket, pulled out a personal check, and handed it to Agnes. Through her thick glasses, Girardi observed the nun's eyes growing wide as they fell upon the amount.

"This is a check for ten thousand dollars," she said in astonishment. "There must be some mistake."

Meanwhile, Stowe looked at her companions in surprise but didn't speak.

"There's no mistake," he assured them, hoping Agnes would accept the check without further question.

"I'm sure that she's a fine attorney, but Elizabeth worked for just a few days on that memorandum."

Stowe nodded her confirmation. "That's right."

"When I asked on Friday," Girardi continued, "Beth wouldn't tell me how many hours she'd spent on my project. She told me that she'd been happy to do the work for free, and she urged me to forget about the money."

By Girardi's estimation, Stowe had perhaps earned a third of the money based on the hourly rate he'd offered her. The remaining balance he'd thrown in as a gesture of support for Stowe and the sisters.

"I agree with Elizabeth," Agnes replied. "Tell me, why didn't you just do as she suggested and forget the money?"

Girardi took a hesitant sip of his coffee as he pondered his answer. There was something about Sister Agnes that made him feel as though she could see right through him.

"My son and I are fortunate enough have everything we need. This is an opportunity for us to support a worthy cause. You do some real good for people here. I want to teach my son something about giving back. Some day, when all of this trouble at work is behind me, I'd like to bring Jacob here for a visit."

In recent days, Girardi had thought quite a bit about the fact that neither he nor his wife had provided their son with any religious training.

They were not churchgoers themselves, and after some vague discussions when Jake was little, the two had completely let the matter go. Girardi now wondered if this had been a mistake. Perhaps some exposure to Christianity might do him some good. The choice would ultimately be his, of course. But as it stood now, Jake was going out into the world knowing nothing about faith or spirituality.

"Elizabeth told me you have a son. How old is he?"

"Seventeen."

"Ah, he is almost an adult then."

"To my dismay, yes," Girardi offered with a rueful smile. "The time has passed too quickly. It sometimes feels as though life is passing me by."

"You should of course feel free to bring your son here. We have several older youth groups scheduled to come this summer. He'd probably enjoy the chance to meet others his own age. Elizabeth, will you let Mr. Girardi know those dates?"

"Of course."

"Thank you."

Agnes stood to warm up Girardi's coffee. Before doing so, she folded the check and placed it carefully in the right pocket of her jumper dress. *That's a good sign*, Girardi thought hopefully as he helped himself to another cinnamon roll. With the check out of the way, his mind moved to the second of four items on his mental agenda, two of which involved business and two being personal.

"By the way," he ventured, trying to sound casual. "What is a Lay Associate?" He looked at Stowe. "I was on the website to get the phone number and I noticed that was your title."

At a loss, Stowe looked over to Agnes, who was usually excellent at explaining such things.

"In truth, it's a very flexible title," replied the nun. "In this case, Elizabeth has been our bookkeeper, landscape architect, youth coordinator, and criminal law consultant." Agnes chuckled, but Girardi did not join in, so she stood from her seat once more and decided upon another tack.

"Have you ever heard of a secular oblate?" she asked over her shoulder as she dug around some papers on a shelf in the corner.

"No."

"The word 'oblate' comes from the Latin for 'to offer.' A lay oblate offers herself to a religious community like this one, promising to spend time with us, to assist our ministry, and to follow our Rule of life to the extent possible. And always, an oblate must be obedient to the will of the Lord. Right now, Elizabeth is just in her discernment period."

This was a lot to take in, and Girardi was struggling with the jargon. "What is a discernment period?"

"It is a time of prayer and searching . . . for her and for the sisters. We must discern whether it is the Lord's will for Elizabeth to become a secular oblate to our order."

The Lord's will? Girardi repeated to himself skeptically, wondering how in the world the sisters ever reached a determination such as this. He wondered also if Stowe had now come to view her life decisions in those terms.

"How's that going so far?" he asked, hoping that Stowe herself would chime in.

"We must give the process the full year," Agnes demurred. "But Elizabeth is very dear to each of us here."

"What does a secular oblate do, exactly?"

"They live secular lives, but adhere to the values of this community as much as their circumstances will allow. In our order, we require oblates to write personal Rules of life and conduct. It is a very serious undertaking, and is meant to be a lifelong commitment. Some of the oblates are married, but without a partner's full support, it simply would not work out. I've seen prospective oblates give up because of unsupportive spouses."

"On the other hand," Girardi ventured, keeping his eyes fixed on Agnes, "a supportive partner might make it easier for an oblate to succeed. Isn't that right?"

Agnes folded her arms thoughtfully. "I'm not certain I'd look at it as a matter of *succeeding*, exactly," she corrected him gently. "But as long as a partner shares the same values and is willing to give the oblate the time she needs, then it can all work out nicely. Three of our lay oblates here are married women who live at a distance, and when they visit with their husbands, we enjoy our time with them almost as much as with the oblates themselves."

"That's good."

"When I was a young novice, I asked my director why some religious orders encourage participation by members of the laity."

"It's a good question—I've been wondering the same thing myself."

"I'll never forget her answer. 'Monasteries,' she said, 'are schools for love.'"

Girardi waited for Agnes to elaborate, but she didn't. "I'm not sure I understand."

"Neither did I. It took me years to figure it out. You see, we nuns consider ourselves to be married to the Lord. Lay women experience love in a different way, but all love springs from a common source. Lay women come here and share stories from their lives with us, and we in turn help them engage their hearts in spiritual communion with the Lord. This hopefully equips them to have stronger relationships in the secular world. We sisters are deeply enriched by our association with the laity."

Agnes reached across and handed Girardi two pamphlets about the order. "If you'd like to read more about it, you might find these helpful."

"Thank you."

"And here," she added, handing over one more stapled packet. "These are some sayings of the Desert Fathers and Mothers. You might enjoy them."

Girardi thanked her once more.

"I apologize," Agnes said suddenly as she glanced at her watch, "but I should excuse myself. I have a conference call with the sisters in Minnesota."

I didn't know nuns held conference calls.

"I understand."

"Perhaps you and Elizabeth might take a walk outside. The clouds should be burning off any time now. And if you're still here at lunchtime, you're welcome to stay and eat with us."

After a bit more conversation, Agnes took her leave and the two headed outside. Although Girardi was coming to like Agnes, he was relieved to at last be alone with Stowe.

"I certainly didn't expect to see you here this morning," she offered when they were out of earshot.

"You don't mind my coming, I hope."

She smiled. "Of course not. And I'm so glad that Agnes took the money. That was very generous of you."

"It's the least I can do after all that's happened."

They proceeded to walk around the large property, with Stowe from time to time sharing stories of the center's history. As Agnes predicted, the sun soon made its appearance. There were intermittent periods of quiet, where Girardi's mind wandered to all sorts of subjects. He thought quite a bit about his boyhood summers in his grandfather's yard, and the hours they'd spent together.

"You know, one summer, back when I was eleven or twelve," he ventured, "I listened to every Dodger game of the season on the radio. I don't think I missed a single game. One hundred and sixty-two sessions with the great Vin Scully. My grandfather listened to a lot of the games with me out in the yard on an old transistor radio. In some ways, that was the best summer of my life. We don't appreciate things when we're kids."

Stowe squinted at him. "What made you think to mention this now?"

"Gardens remind me of my grandfather, because he's the one who taught me how to garden."

"Why did you listen to all those games?"

"Because I was absolutely obsessed with the Dodgers. I knew *everything* about them—their batting averages, ERAs, winning percentages at home and on the road. I was a walking statistic machine. And remember—this was well *before* the Internet."

"Did you collect baseball cards?"

"I did," he nodded enthusiastically. "In fact, I saved most of my collection. I still have it somewhere at home, encased in protective plastic, of course. I haven't looked at my cards in years."

"Is your son a collector?"

"No. I could never get Jake interested in the cards. Now the kids follow their favorite players on Twitter and Instagram. A dozen paper cards and a flat stick of gum can't hold their interest for long."

"Do you still have your season tickets to the Angels?"

"I do—but because of work I've only been to one game so far this year."

"I haven't attended a game since we hosted the summer associates in that luxury box a few years ago—do you remember that? It was amazing. I had never seen cushioned chairs or a fancy dessert cart in a baseball stadium. That was an enjoyable evening. I have no recollection of who won the game, but the chocolate cake from that cart was the best I've ever tasted."

The idea flashed across his mind to invite Stowe to a baseball game with him. He had the seats. All they'd need to do was settle on a date. Jake would rib him, but he could handle whatever his son could dish out. He remembered Val's encouragement. Perhaps she was right—he should go for it.

But then, as quickly as it had come, his confidence left him. He recalled Val's comment about the gym receptionist. Was this what his family truly expected of him?

He thought of Jake and Morgan the vegan. They were the proper age for this kind of drama. He was much too old. It seemed to him that at his age, he should be able to invite someone to a baseball game without getting all worked up about it. What would it matter if she said no? But Girardi understood himself well enough to know that if she said no, such rejection would hurt him.

As a final blow to his scheme, a picture of Mona holding little Gunnar flashed across his mind, and he ditched the baseball game idea altogether.

"Speaking of firm events," he ventured, "do you remember the luau?"

Stowe's eyes grew wide. "How could I forget? That was hands down the *worst* Marshall, Lufton party I ever attended—and that's really saying something. Do you remember the pig?"

He nodded.

"And do you remember Mona's outfit?" she continued. "A bikini top and a pair of shorts four sizes too small. She could have stopped traffic in those clothes. I've always suspected that the cooks dropped the pig into the fire because they couldn't stop looking at Mona."

"I'm not sure you should blame Mona for the pig."

Stowe laughed good naturedly at this. "Probably not, but it's always given me great comfort to blame her."

"Why?"

She shook her head. "You wouldn't understand."

"At the time, I kind of assumed Mona didn't know any better," Girardi offered quietly. "She comes from a different world than we do."

"I didn't know Mona very well," Stowe allowed, "and, looking back now, I was probably too hasty in judging her. Do you ever hear from her?"

The question startled Girardi. A part of him considered telling her the truth, for he was still reeling from the news Mona had shared with him the day before. It would be a relief to unburden himself, and he was curious to know what Stowe would think of Mona's relationship with Tremont. But he quickly reconsidered, feeling it would be wrong to reveal such a confidence.

"I remember another outfit from the luau. There was this cute girl at my table in a blue sarong and purple flowers in her hair."

Stowe looked up at him in surprise. "I'm shocked that you remember what I was wearing. You'd be the only one," she added ruefully. "My date certainly had no eyes for me that afternoon."

Girardi recalled Mona saying the same thing about Troy. *Women notice everything; and they remember, too.*

"Do you still see Troy?"

"No—not for a long time. He moved to New York to take a job with a hedge fund—that was it."

"You didn't do the long distance thing?"

"No."

Girardi thought she might elaborate, but she did not. They walked on in quiet for some time.

"So, do you think you'll go through with the whole secular oblate thing?" he asked suddenly.

"Yes. I'm drawn to the idea of a lay oblate's disciplined life. I think I'd benefit from something like that."

"But you're already disciplined—look how productive you were at the firm. You can't do that without discipline."

"I'm talking about a different kind of discipline—moral and spiritual. That's what gets a person through difficult times."

"I see."

"You know, Reverend Susan doesn't seem so keen on the oblate idea. She has a different idea for me. Brace yourself." She paused for effect.

Girardi looked at her with interest. "Okay, I'm ready."

"She thinks I might have a calling to ordained ministry."

"To the ordained ministry? Wow, really?"

"So, you can't picture me in a collar?"

Girardi paused, lest he say the wrong thing. The idea was such a surprise that he didn't know what to think.

"Would you really go to seminary?"

"I don't know. It seems kind of strange to go to another professional school, doesn't it? It makes it seem as though I'm flailing around, trying to find something that will fit."

"Not necessarily. Plenty of people go back to school—we had some former doctors in my law school class."

"So did we."

"Can you imagine yourself doing the work of a minister?"

"I don't know. When I see all that Reverend Susan accomplishes, I'm not sure how she does it. I'm so impressed that she's dedicated her life to helping other people. I thought I might do that with the law, but look where I ended up."

"There are lots of legal jobs where you can help people, Beth. Have you considered those?"

"Yes, I have."

"For example, you'd be great as a public interest lawyer—your big firm experience would be an asset in that environment."

"You're right, but I just can't imagine myself doing litigation anymore. I didn't like that feeling of flipping the switch—one minute you're a nice person, the next moment you're engaged in combat. I hated that."

"Not all public interest lawyers litigate. It's a huge profession out there—there are a lot of law jobs you could do that you might find very fulfilling."

"Maybe so."

"I hate to see you give up on the law. I'm not just flattering you—you were good at your job. What happened with Jack was not your fault."

She shrugged.

"Just promise me you'll think about the public interest option."

"I will."

The two moved on to other subjects. By the time they arrived back at the center, it was lunchtime. Stowe managed, just barely, to coax Girardi into staying for the meal.

25

The sisters and Stowe gathered with Girardi for lunch in the dining room. At first, things were a little quiet, but with some prompting from Agnes, Girardi began to regale the ladies with war stories from his early days in the District Attorney's office. Recalling their fondness for *Law & Order*, he sprinkled in anecdotes on search warrants and Miranda warnings. The sisters proved eager listeners, and they exchanged knowing smiles at the obvious good cheer between Girardi and Stowe.

When the meal ended, the two headed back outside. Stowe put on the sprinklers to give some new plantings a good soaking and then took up the path toward the shed to put away some tools that had been left out by a group of volunteers that morning.

"I'm sorry that you have so much to deal with at work right now, Mike."

"Me, too."

"And I suppose I made it worse for you on Friday by telling you about *Trinity Hills*."

He looked at her in surprise. "Not at all. It's just the opposite. I need to know the truth about what's going on with all of Jack's cases. You were right to tell me. I'm just sorry that I didn't know about this two years ago. I hate it that we lost you that way. And I'm sorry that you've carried this burden by yourself for so long. The firm owes you an apology for what happened."

He reached out and took her hand into his as they kept walking. She returned the pressure with a squeeze of her small fingers, keeping her eyes on the path ahead of her.

"It's a relief to have told you."

Girardi thought back to his Sunday conversation with Mitch Best, in which the judge had urged him to make absolutely certain that Stowe had given him all of the evidence she had regarding *Trinity Hills*. Girardi did not believe for a moment that Stowe would hold out on him this way, and the last thing he wanted to do was anger her. They had shared a pleasant morning together, and he hesitated to rock the boat. At the same time, however, Best's advice kept nagging at him. This was the third of four items of Girardi's agenda, and he decided that now was the time to broach it. If he were to see the U.S. Attorney, he'd need to have all of his ducks in a row.

"Listen, Beth, while we're on the subject, I need to ask you something."

"Okay, ask away."

"Did you save *any* more documents on *Trinity Hills* besides the ones you've already given me?"

She looked up at him and frowned. "Even if I *did* have more documents, why in the world would you want them? You were not involved in Jack's fraud, and none of that was your fault. The firm has nothing more to do with the case now. Just move on. That's what I've tried my best to do. The more you dig around, the more responsible you'll become. Really, Mike, you should just forget about it."

This was not the answer Girardi was looking for.

"I can't just forget this, Beth."

"Why not?"

As they rounded a narrow bend in the path, Girardi let go of Stowe's hand and picked up his pace, unsure how much of the present predicament he should share with her.

"Because the problem is bigger than *Trinity Hills*," he revealed at last.

"What do you mean by bigger? Is it another matter for CEP?"

"I'd better not say."

"It's CEP, again," she surmised, struggling now to keep up with the fast-moving Girardi. "Why else would Jack have been looking at that old *Trinity Hills* memo when he collapsed? Are he and Russell Yost crazy enough to think that they can get away with something like this again?" She shook her head in dismay. "It's a good thing for the company's sake that Jack had his stroke—it will finally put a stop to this nonsense."

"I'm not so sure of that . . ."

"What do you mean? Of course this will stop now. I don't understand you." She paused as a look of disbelief crossed her face. "They don't expect *you* to help them, do they?"

Stowe was catching on fast, and Girardi knew that he needed to be careful.

"Beth, I really can't say anything more."

"*No way, Mike,*" she exclaimed, now red-faced and out of breath. "You can't let them drag you into this. The one silver lining in my leaving the firm the way I did was that you were shielded from everything. Promise me you'll keep your distance from Russ Yost."

Too late for that.

By this time, the pair had reached the storage shed. The lopsided wooden structure was ancient, and it looked as though a decent wind might blow it over for good. The single room was dark and cluttered inside, with the only light coming from two small, high windows.

"What are you going to do about CEP?" she asked as she carefully propped open the shed door.

"I haven't decided. I may need to see the U.S. Attorney. Mitch knows someone in the Santa Ana office."

"The U.S. Attorney? That sounds awful."

The prospect of telling the authorities about CEP was indeed miserable to Girardi. No lawyer ever wanted to become embroiled in an investigation like this, and being innocent would offer little consolation. As Russ Yost had indicated, the proceedings would damage Girardi's business and bring shame to Marshall, Lufton. And even if Jack Tremont were the one to blame, Girardi knew that he would not be shielded from the prosecutor's suspicion or his partners' scorn.

"I may not have much choice."

They put away the gardening tools, and Girardi headed back out into the sunshine. Stowe soon called out to him.

"Wait—will you help me with something in here?"

He came back in to find Stowe removing a dusty tarp from the corner. Folding the tarp and putting it aside, she began to pull out various old pieces of furniture and equipment.

"What are you doing, Beth?"

"Looking for something. Be careful—there are spiders in here. This place gives me the creeps."

He helped her put aside various old brooms, pots, lawn chairs and a broken umbrella. "You really should throw this stuff away."

"Agnes won't let me."

"If you just tossed it quietly, she'd probably never know," Girardi suggested. He was one who hated such clutter.

"There it is," she said at last, pointing to a gray banker's box. "Can you lift that out for me?"

"Sure."

It took Girardi a few moments to remove the debris around the box. He grabbed it and followed Stowe outside.

"What the heck is in here?" he asked.

She hesitated and then spoke softly. "It's what you asked for."

He could barely hear her. "What do you mean?"

She looked gravely up into his face. "It's the rest of what I have on *Trinity Hills*."

My god, Mitch was right, Girardi thought to himself in amazement. *She was holding out.*

"I don't have anything else. I swear," she continued, her voice rising. "*Please* take this with you. I can't stand having those documents here anymore. I half hoped it would rain hard enough to flood the shed and ruin them."

She lifted and tossed the box's lid to the ground, revealing the pristine stack of papers that she had snuck out of the Marshall, Lufton office in two of her assistant's shopping bags. She'd had these bags with her on the night she first met Susan Mountjoy at St. Mark's. The bags themselves were now tucked neatly along the side of the box.

"No such luck."

Girardi stood reeling from Stowe's revelation. First Tremont, then Mona and now Beth Stowe had misled him. Why couldn't anyone around him tell the truth? He bent down for a closer look at the documents.

"What's in here?"

"I don't remember exactly what I have—old interview notes, copies of the audit reports and responses, things like that. I snuck most of them out of the office on the day Jack yelled at me. Then, I mailed some of the papers to my sister's house. Although he watched me like a hawk, Cliff apparently didn't think to check the outgoing mail."

Girardi noticed a mild air of triumph in Stowe's voice as he recalled Mitch Best's words. *"Any good lawyer would find a way to keep documentation of fraud like this."*

"These documents should show some of the differences between the facts we initially gathered and the story CEP submitted in its response," she continued. "I have no idea what an investigator would say. It probably wouldn't be an easy case to make."

"I'll need you to go over this with me . . ."

"I know," she sighed, "but not today, okay? Please, just take the box with you for now."

"No," he rejoined sternly, thinking of Russ Yost's ultimatum. Things were coming to a head, and he needed answers now. This dithering around had to stop.

"There's no time for that. God, why didn't you tell me about these before?"

She folded her arms and a familiar look of stubborn defiance became set in her features. "Yelling at me won't do any good."

"I'm not yelling," he said coolly. "Let's get this over with. Review the documents with me today and then hopefully I can leave you alone for good."

At this, her defiance melted into hurt. "You don't care how this makes me feel, do you?"

Girardi was in no mood to deal with Stowe's feelings, and he wanted to nip this kind of talk in the bud. His voice fell into a lecturing tone. "A lawyer's job is *not* about feelings—it's about getting at the truth. You believed this when you started working for me." He paused. "And I think you still believe it now, deep down."

"The truth?" she laughed cynically. "If there's one thing your partner Jack Tremont taught me, it's that the legal profession has nothing to do with finding the truth. I'd rather be a Lay Associate here earning room and board for rest of my life than go back to a legal practice that was as dishonest as Marshall, Lufton's."

"Don't be a coward, Beth. *My* law practice wasn't dishonest—*our* law practice together was not dishonest. You ran away and hid out for two years because you couldn't face me—I thought you were braver than that. It's time to stop hiding."

"Who says I'm hiding? I'm happy here—I'm at peace."

"It doesn't look that way to me." Girardi shoved his hands into his pockets and began to pace around. So far he was getting nowhere, and he wasn't sure what tack to take with her. "Come on Beth, don't let the bad guys win."

"It's too late. The bad guys *have* won."

"Not quite yet," he muttered as he knelt on one knee and began to look at the documents in Stowe's box. He still expected her to help him, but to his dismay she just stood with her arms folded, watching him intently. The documents didn't make much sense to him, and he feared that it would take him forever to gain command of them. As he stared at a stack of incomprehensible handwritten notes, his anger boiled over.

"My career is going down the drain while you stand here in your garden deciding which piece of the story you'll deign to share with me today. I'm sick and tired of this."

"Then take your box with you, Mike. After two years of not hearing a word from you, I was getting a little tired of this myself."

"I see. So this is *my* fault? You want me to fall on the sword and take the blame because I'm not a mind-reader who knew that you'd run off to join some band of nuns and that you were hiding evidence of our client's fraud in the tool shed? *Really?* That's just . . . beyond absurd."

Tears began to stream down Stowe's cheeks. She turned from him and took several steps away. The look in Girardi's eyes showed plainly his uncertainty, for he did not want to argue with her this way or to hurt her. Nor did he wish to leave. He wanted to stay and go calmly through the documents with her. But what was he to do? His pride would not allow him to remain if she did not want him there, so he gathered the papers and tossed them into their box.

"Beth," he implored, "I need your help."

"I know you do, but I'm not sure I have it in me. This has been eating at me for two years—I haven't known what to do about it. Now you're thinking of going to the authorities and I'm still not sure I should have told you about this." She rubbed her eyes. "Believe it or not, I am trying to do the right thing here."

Girardi's heart began to soften. This could not be easy for her, and he knew he needed to show some sympathy.

"It was right to tell me—I needed to know. Now, you need to spend a little more time with me so that I understand what we have in terms of evidence. I don't have time to wait around anymore. Could we just sit down and spend half an hour on these? If you could even give me a general idea of what happened and identify for me the evidence you think was fabricated, it would be a huge help." He approached her and placed a hand on her arm; then he took her hand into his and looked her in the eye. "Let's forget what happened in the past and just move forward. I'm not angry with you, but please—I need you to help me now."

She shook her head in doubt but did not say anything. He just stood and held her hand for what felt to him like a long time. Anxious as he was to get to work, he did not rush her. Just as it was back at *The Carvery* when he'd first asked for her help, he suspected now that if he just hung in there, Stowe would relent. At last, his patience was rewarded.

"Alright," she said. "Let's go back inside and take a look."

■ ■ ■

To the perplexity of Agnes and the rest of the sisters, the now-somber pair returned with their box and were soon holed up in the center's east conference room. Girardi took the lead at first, laying out the documents in organized piles. Stowe was rusty, and it took her time to isolate the key evidence. The two carefully compared the original CEP *Trinity Hills* submission with the revised submission in order to find the fraudulent evidence. First, they identified several letters attached to the amended response that Stowe was certain she had not seen during her investigation. Girardi began to examine these carefully as Stowe returned to her stack and continued digging.

"Here it is," she said at last, holding up a stack of computer runs. "This was the evidence I thought was the most fishy."

"How so?"

"In the *Trinity Hills* audit report, the government alleged that CEP failed during the contract negotiating period to disclose certain information that would have led to a lower contract price."

"The law requires contractors to turn over *every* bit of data that could affect the price, right?"

"That's right," Stowe nodded. "These rules are in place to prevent the government from being cheated. CEP claimed in its audit response that these computer runs proved that the government was mistaken and that they *had* disclosed the data at issue in a timely fashion."

Girardi gestured toward the document. "What do these sheets purport to show?"

She reached over and pointed to a box in the upper right corner. "Take a look here. The CEP contract negotiator had an electronic account with the government negotiator through which pricing data was submitted via the Internet. These codes make it appear that CEP *did* submit these computer runs and that the government negotiator received them. If CEP could prove definitively that the government had the data in hand during the negotiations, they'd be in the clear. That's why this evidence is so valuable."

"May I have a closer look?"

Stowe slid the printouts across the table to Girardi, and to his astonishment, they looked familiar to him. His mind went back to the morning that Tammy Thompson had sheepishly brought him the missing *Pope Electronics* file. In the back of that file had been a dirty manila folder full of computer runs that looked very similar to these. He was nearly certain that some of those sheets contained the same box indicating electronic receipt by the government.

"In my *Trinity Hills* investigation," Stowe continued, "I *never* saw those printouts, but they were a key exhibit in the revised audit report. I had interviewed *everyone* on CEP's negotiating team and not a single person mentioned this submission."

"Could they have simply forgotten?"

She shook her head. "Not something this important."

"And you think that the documents were faked?"

"Yes." Stowe paused and let out a long, frustrated sigh. "But the problem is, the government's computer logs should easily reveal whether or not the data was received. It would be crazy for CEP to just make up a sheet and pretend that the data was submitted electronically if it wasn't."

"Then what do you think happened?"

"This sounds like a leap, but I think Jack must have figured out a way to hack into the government's computer system and insert such a record after the fact."

Girardi shook his head in the negative. "Jack can barely use his e mail; he could never have done something like this on his own."

"Then he had help."

Girardi's mind went immediately to his Sunday walk in Dana Point. Russ Yost had insisted that Jack employed consultants that helped on difficult audit cases. Perhaps these consultants had hacked into the government's database on *Trinity Hills*. Girardi wondered if they were doing the same again on *Pope Electronics*.

The two continued to discuss the documents for some time. The more they talked, the more strongly Girardi suspected that the *Pope Electronics* printouts would match the ones from Stowe's box. At last, he thought he had enough evidence to show Mitch Best's friend at the U.S. Attorney's office. He couldn't be sure what the prosecutor would think of such evidence, but that would be for the government to sort out.

Girardi began to plan in his mind how he might present the story to the prosecutor. It would be essential to explain everything as honestly as possible.

"Listen Beth," he said seriously, "if it turns out that I need to take these documents to the prosecutor, he'll want to know where I got them. I can't mislead him."

Stowe nodded as she began to gather her paperwork into piles. She was quiet for some time as she slowly replaced some of the documents in the box. "I'll come with you and explain these documents to him."

Girardi was hoping she would say this, but the uncertainty in her voice concerned him. "Are you sure, Beth? I need to be able to count on you a hundred percent."

"Yes, I'm sure. As long as we go in together, I know we'll be okay."

"And you're not holding anything more back? Is this really all you have?"

"Yes."

"Really? You can't sandbag me with the government. That would be disastrous."

"Yes, really. I swear it—that's it. No more holding out."

They made copies of the key documents. Then, he helped her put the rest of the papers back in the box, and they talked for a while before Girardi moved to leave. It was time to get to Jake's baseball game. He told her that he would call Mitch Best and then Charley Strong. If he was able to set an appointment, he would let her know the date and time.

"Will you walk me out?" he asked when they'd finished everything.

Girardi said goodbye to Sister Agnes and then the two headed outside. They stood out in the parking lot by his car and attempted to make some small talk. They had covered a lot of ground—much more than he'd anticipated. But still there was one last open item on his mental agenda.

Although item three had thrown him for a loop, he pressed on with number four.

"Mitch invited me to the concert this weekend at St. Mark's."

"Judge Best?" she asked quizzically. "What does he have to do with St. Mark's?"

"He and the minister went to college together—they were friends."

"The judge and Reverend Susan? You're kidding. They are such opposites."

"Apparently, they hadn't seen each other for years, and then we ran into her a couple of weeks ago at *Emilio's*."

"And he's attending the concert?"

"Yep, and he gave me two tickets. If you'd like to come with me, maybe we could grab something to eat afterwards. Mitch said there's a potluck, but it might be nicer to go out."

"Grab something to eat?" she repeated, struggling to take this in. "The two of us, you mean? Socially? Not just to talk about the case?"

Girardi assumed his best "it's no big deal" manner. "Yes, sure, it would be good to decompress. And there are lots of places to eat around the church."

"There's always *The Carvery*."

"I was thinking of something a little nicer than that."

Stowe looked at Girardi thoughtfully. "You'd have dinner with me, even after all that has happened?"

"Yep." He paused. "Would you have dinner with *me* after all that has happened?"

She smiled. "Yes, of course I would. I'd really like that, as a matter of fact."

"Great. Let's plan on it."

That wasn't so difficult.

"But I must warn you," Stowe offered.

Uh-oh. Come on Beth, let's keep it simple.

"The sisters may also be attending the concert. If so, I'll probably have to drive them. We could at least sit together at the concert."

The news about the sisters sounded like a significant logistical stumbling block, but he was not be deterred. "That shouldn't be a problem. We'll work something out. I'd be happy to treat for a cab for them to travel back and forth. Or maybe a town car if they'd like to travel in style."

"Oh, a cab would be fine, I think. Agnes would *not* approve of a town car. The truth is that they may not even be interested in the concert. I'll let you know closer to Sunday."

Girardi loaded the papers into his car and said his final goodbyes. He was about to drive away when Agnes came rushing out the front door.

"Mr. Girardi, please don't leave yet," she called.

By the time she arrived at the car, the nun was out of breath.

"What is it, sister?"

"I'm not sure. Your assistant is on the phone, and she's frantic to get hold of you. Please, won't you come inside and take the call?"

26

While Girardi was with Beth Stowe at the Emmanuel Center, Judge Best wrapped up his court business early and headed over to St. Jude's Catholic Church to see Father Tim O'Brien. The weather was lovely, and Best decided to make the 20 minute walk from the courthouse. When he arrived, he examined the old church's facade and heavy iron fence and did not see much that was welcoming or hopeful. Most of the buildings he'd observed along his walk had the same forlorn look about them. The church's small flower bed was choked with weeds, and fresh graffiti marked the announcement board, which was printed in English and Spanish.

The property was gated, lending it a fortress-like atmosphere. The buildings were arranged in a U shape, with the office facing the street and the sanctuary running along one side. A small sign indicated that visitors should use the intercom. Best noted the contrast with St. Mark's unlocked doors and open layout.

He rang the bell and a young voice came over the line. "Who is it?"
"Mitch Best."

The lock buzzed open. Best entered and found himself in the small, dimly-lit church office. A teenaged girl in a blue school uniform asked him to wait and ran off down the hall.

In a few moments, Best was greeted by a small, thin woman who appeared to be in her late forties. She wore jeans and a salmon-colored hooded sweatshirt. Her short brown hair was sprinkled with gray, and she wore no makeup. A small hand-painted desk sign read "Teresa Espinoza, Parish Administrator."

"You must be the judge," she offered with wide eyes as she placed some papers on her desk. She stood for a few moments looking the big man up and down. "We don't get many white people in here—especially not ones dressed so well. I'm Teresa. We spoke on the phone."

"Good to meet you, Teresa," he replied, extending his hand. "Thanks for getting me in to see the padre. It sounds like he's a busy fellow."

"He *is* busy. He works too hard and doesn't do a thing to take care of himself."

Best's doubts about this visit had mounted in recent days, and now that the moment was upon him, he almost welcomed an opportunity to postpone or cancel.

"If he's too busy, we can certainly reschedule," he offered quickly. "I can come back some other time."

"No, no, it will be okay. Come outside with me and we'll find him."

Best nodded and followed Espinoza down a poorly-lit corridor and out a side door into the sunny courtyard. As Best began to look around, he felt as though he'd entered another world. His guide pointed to a dozen well-tended raised gardening beds as she led Best along a path toward the back of the property.

"Father Tim runs a community garden here," she explained. "Our parishioners are so poor that they often can't afford fresh fruits and vegetables. We give most of our produce away, but we sell some of it at the farmer's market. The money we raise goes to the after-school program."

The fragrant smell of citrus beckoned the judge, who looked up to see that their path was lined with half a dozen orange and lemon trees. Two very mature fig trees stood in the corner of the property. From the street, one would never have guessed that this inner space was so pleasant.

Impressed by all that he saw in the courtyard, Best nodded with approval as they headed toward a concrete basketball court and several long picnic benches. Fifteen students from the junior high school up the street were scattered about. Some were playing board games or talking in small groups, while a few appeared to be doing their homework. A stocky red-haired man of around fifty hovered over a group of four girls, holding forth on the importance of properly diagramming an English sentence. He was dressed in jeans and an ancient Boston Red Sox long-sleeved T-shirt. He wore no collar, and Best would never have guessed that he was a priest.

"We run an after-school program for the neighborhood kids," Espinoza explained. "It's a safe place for them to be until their parents come home from work. Of all Father Tim's ministries, this one is closest to his heart."

"It's important work," Best commented. The two stood quietly for some time, waiting for Father O'Brien to approach them.

"Do you know Judge Tejada?" she asked suddenly.

"No. Is he here in Orange County?"

She nodded gravely.

"Then he must be a state court judge. I work in a different court-house." Best hesitated for a moment, not sure he wanted to go further. "Why do you ask about Judge Tejada?"

Espinoza's eyes narrowed. "My nephew got into some trouble last year. He's a good boy, but some of his friends are not. Anyway, when his judge turned out to be Mexican, we thought it would be a good thing. But he was very hard upon my nephew. I did not like that judge one bit. I think he was *harder* upon my nephew because we're a Mexican family. Why would he do that?"

"I don't know Judge Tejada," Best offered at length. "But I'll bet he was doing what he thought was right, given the facts of the case that were presented to him. That's his job."

"But my nephew is only nineteen. He's *never* been in trouble before. The judge treated him no better than a gang-banger. He sent him to prison for six months. He has a girlfriend and a little baby daughter to support—it wasn't right."

Best suspected it would do no good to continue on this tack. His mind moving quickly, he at first wondered how many families who came through his courtroom might have similar criticisms as to his own fairness.

He and his colleagues strove for impartiality, but did it seem that way to the families caught up in the system? Probably not.

Best thought next about the local business people he had met on a recent visit to the Santa Ana Chamber of Commerce. They described the terrible toll crime and poverty continued to take on their city and also spoke of their desire to give young people viable career and educational opportunities. Although he was a busy man, Best made a point of accepting as many such invitations as possible. It was always good to know people in the local community and to be aware of their concerns.

"When your nephew gets out, you can call me at my chambers. I may know some people who can get him a decent job."

"But now he's going to have a criminal record," she replied in frustration.

"I know, Teresa, but he can still get a job. I'd be happy to hook him up with a few contacts. I know some people down at the Chamber of Commerce."

She narrowed her eyes suspiciously. "Why would you help us?"

"Why not? You helped me get an appointment with the padre, didn't you? It's not a big deal to pass along some names and phone numbers. It sounds like your nephew could use a second chance. What he does with it is up to him."

"Thank you," she said softly, still sounding uncertain about the judge's offer.

"You're welcome," Best replied, wondering if she would indeed contact him. Mulling this over, he considered the alternative possibility of giving her the contact names now and letting her use them, or not, when the time came. He liked this idea better, and made a mental note to forward Espinoza the names of his local contacts as soon as possible.

"*Father,*" she called suddenly, bringing this interlude to an end. "Your appointment is here."

O'Brien frowned over at Espinoza and Best. Then, he turned back to the students. "Okay, try a few more sentences on your own. I'll be back to check on you in a little while."

O'Brien then approached his visitor as Espinoza headed back to the office.

"Thanks for making time to see me," Best offered. Half a foot taller than the priest, the judge was imposing in his navy blue pinstripe suit and maroon tie.

O'Brien looked the judge up and down for a few long moments, just as Espinoza had back at the church office. The priest's eyes lingered over the small flag pin on his lapel.

"So," he ventured with his thick Boston accent, "Reverend Mountjoy tells me that you'd like some counseling."

"That's right."

"Why?"

Best was surprised by the priest's tone, which sounded almost distrustful to him. He was no friendlier than Espinoza. *They should work on their hospitality*, thought the judge, who in truth was accustomed to being treated like royalty not only in his courtroom but also in many of his travels around Orange County.

"Well, I don't know how much Susie said to you . . ."

"She said plenty about you," he interjected sourly.

"I see," the judge replied patiently. He did not care for O'Brien's manner, but he was determined to stick this meeting out. Susie Mountjoy had urged him to come, and so he would make the best of it. If things went poorly, he would not come back. But today he would make a real effort.

"Anyway," Best continued, "she's an old college friend of mine. She told me that a little Jesus Christ might do me some good, and I think she might be right. I'd hoped that Susie might counsel me herself, but she thought you and I might do well together. And so, she encouraged me to come and see you. Here I am."

"What can I do for you, exactly?" he pressed in a clipped, impatient tone.

Best wasn't sure what to say. "I anticipated that you'd take the lead, father. I want to learn about Christianity."

"Are you Catholic?"

"No, no. I suppose I'm not much of anything when it comes to denominations." Although he did not fluster or embarrass easily, this was not an easy subject for Best. "My mother took my brother and me to a Baptist church sometimes when we were boys, but we never received any formal religious training. In fact, I was never even baptized as far as I know. My mother is dead, and so I can't ask her about it, and I doubt if my brother remembers."

O'Brien stood with his arms folded, looking intently at Best as he spoke. Although O'Brien could at times be quite empathetic, he did not seem to pick up on the judge's emotion at the mention of his family, nor did it appear to register that Best had made no mention of his father.

There was a long pause as the men remained standing in the courtyard. It was warm in the sun, but the priest did not seem to notice. Best considered ushering them over to a bench in the shade, but then decided against it. This was O'Brien's territory, and not his.

"In the gospels," O'Brien offered at length, "Jesus teaches that the last shall be first, and the first shall be last. Over the years, I've found that those born of wealth and privilege have the toughest time understanding Christianity. I used to work at a parish like Reverend Mountjoy's, but it wasn't for me. Too many rich people." He gestured to the children around them. "These kids have an intuitive grasp of the gospels because they suffer on a daily basis. Ours is a *profoundly* unjust society, your honor. Christianity is about creating justice for those oppressed by the system."

There was much in this for the judge to consider, not to mention some things he might take exception to. He, after all, was a powerful and unashamed representative of the system O'Brien was decrying. But Best was on good behavior today, and he did not jump on O'Brien. Weighing his words, the judge spoke at length.

"With due respect, father, although there are many things we could do better, I believe there is much for our society to be proud of. Our commitment to the rule of law and to freedom are an example to the world. The liberals can say whatever they like, but Reagan was right—we *are* a shining city on a hill."

O'Brien shook his head skeptically and kicked at a little rock on the ground with his tennis shoe. "Reverend Mountjoy warned me about you."

The judge was by now becoming weary of the priest. *Why in the world did Susie send me to this guy? And why does he keep calling her Reverend Mountjoy instead of Susan? They went to Yale together. Aren't they friends?*

"I wish I could have heard that warning," Best rejoined with a chuckle. "There are so many things she might have covered."

"She warned me about your politics."

Best folded his arms. "Is that so? That surprises me. I don't see what politics has to do with learning a little about the faith. You guys are big on lost sheep and prodigal sons, right? From what I understand, it's all about sin and redemption. I might just be a perfect fit for Christianity, at least on the sinning side of the equation," he joked.

But O'Brien did not break a smile. "In my view, social justice is at the heart of the gospels. It's not something that I would expect a man from your background to understand."

"A man from my background?" Best repeated, squinting and placing his hands on his hips impatiently. "I assume you mean my *privileged* background?"

O'Brien nodded. "When Reverend Mountjoy said you wanted some counseling, I was skeptical at first that I could help you. I think she believed we might get along because I spent some time in law school."

"At Yale, right? That's impressive, speaking of privileged backgrounds. I'm just a UC Davis guy myself."

O'Brien's eyes flashed at this. "My father was a common laborer and my mother cleaned houses. I have a lot in common with these kids. I was the first in my family to attend college. Law school was a mistake for me. I left after my first year and never looked back."

"I see."

O'Brien shifted his stance and refolded his thick arms. He had something of the manner of a boxer anxious for a bout.

"As I was saying, at first I wasn't sure how to go about counseling you. But I thought about it, and it occurred to me that it might do you some good to spend a little time with these kids."

This meeting was not at all what the judge had expected. Best let out a long sigh and cast a glance in the distance at the gleaming federal courthouse named for Ronald Reagan.

"Since coming to work in Santa Ana, I've certainly seen a different side of Orange County from what I had become accustomed to. It's been good for me. My colleagues and I talk about the issue quite a bit. We want to make a positive contribution to the neighborhood. I hate the thought that the courthouse is a place that a lot of the local people dread."

For the first time in the conversation, O'Brien nodded his head in agreement.

"So, would you like to meet some of the kids?"

"Sure, but give me the lay of the land first."

"What do you mean?"

"Which ones are your hopeless cases?"

"The hopeless cases are the ones who aren't here."

Best nodded. "That makes sense. Okay, who has the *best* chance of making it out of here some day and doing well?"

The priest pointed over at the table of students diagramming their sentences. "That would be the students at the homework table."

"It's mostly girls," the judge observed.

"I have the most hope for the girls, if they can stay out of trouble and stick with school. They don't get much encouragement at home, unfortunately. But they have much better study habits than the boys and will actually listen to what the adults have to say. If *any* of these kids make it to college some day, I suspect it will be them. We have several program graduates in community college now, and one at UCI."

O'Brien's pride in these students was obvious.

Best again nodded. "Okay. Then who would you say is on the fence?"

O'Brien considered the question for several moments and then pointed to a trio of boys around eleven or twelve years old. They were lounging on the basketball court, rolling a ball back and forth between them.

"What are their names?"

"I'll introduce you to them."

Best put up his hand. "No, no. Please, father. I'm more than happy to talk with them. But I'd like to do it my own way."

O'Brien hesitated uncomfortably, but then nodded his assent and began to point. "Alright. From left to right, that's Jesus, Hector, and Mikey."

"Okay. They're in junior high?"

"Yes."

"Are they decent students?"

"Decent, but that's all. Hector seems the brightest to me, but he's also an angry young man."

This did not faze Best. "Lots of young men are angry, father. And if they don't watch out, they grow into angry middle-aged men. There's plenty of that in this world."

"Hector's father and two older brothers are all in prison. He might not take very well to a judge."

"You never know; we'll see."

"Do they have a ring-leader?"

"Hector."

"Okay. I'll head over there. You should go back and check on the girls."

The judge walked slowly over to the basketball court. He slid off his suit coat and hung it on an exposed wire in the fence.

"Say, Mikey, toss me that ball, would you?" Best bellowed.

The shocked young man looked up at the judge with wide eyes and did as he was told. The judge dribbled the ball hard on the concrete and was disappointed to find it lop-sided. At the top of the key, he made a jump shot that bounced off the rim.

"Aw, *darn!*"

The ball rolled toward the smallest of the boys.

"Jesus, can you help me out? I need to try that again."

Jesus took his time, eventually retrieving the ball and tossing it to the judge. Best tried his shot again, and this time he made it.

"That's what I'm talking about! Okay, Hector, it's your turn." Best motioned for the young man to stand. "Why don't you show me what you've got?"

The boy looked at each of his friends and considered the matter.

"Do I have to?" he asked with unsure defiance.

The judge seemed entirely unfazed. "Nope, you don't have to. But I'd really like you to. Come on, we can play a game of HORSE or something. Jesus can be on my team. It will go quicker if we pair up. You and Mikey aren't afraid to play against an old dude like me, are you?" he coaxed.

There was a very long pause, during which Best feared he would do no better with the boys than he had with Father Tim and Teresa Espinoza. The trio continued to exchange uncertain looks. Mikey and Jesus kept looking to Hector, and it was plain to the judge that his decision would be determinative. The seconds ticked by slowly for the judge as he waited for the young man's verdict. At last, he stood.

"Okay," Hector offered with mild resignation as he tossed the ball hard to the judge.

The other two boys followed suit, and to the judge's relief, the quartet was soon engaged in a competitive game of HORSE. As time went on, the judge casually asked them some questions about themselves and shared some of his own story. The boys took well to the judge, playfully nicknaming him *jefe*, or boss.

Some time later, Teresa Espinoza and another woman brought out drinks and snacks for the kids. On her second trip from the kitchen, she carried a glass of cold lemonade for the judge, whose companions had left him to join the others at the snack tables.

"Thanks," he offered gratefully after a long gulp of his drink as he dabbed the sweat on his face with his handkerchief. "I needed that."

She nodded her acknowledgment and turned to go.

"Wait, Teresa, can I ask you a favor?"

Espinoza looked up at him and gave a wary nod. Best was coming to the conclusion that the kids at St. Jude's were easier to deal with than the adults.

"I need to get back to my chambers," he explained. "Could you pass along a message to the father for me?"

The priest had taken a handful of students with him to work in the vegetable garden.

"What is it?"

"I managed to talk Hector and his pals into coming to the courthouse for a tour."

"You did?"

"Just barely, but I did. It might help them to see the justice system from my side of the proceedings. Maybe you and the other kids might come along, too. Everybody's welcome, as long as we know how big the party will be in advance. My friend is chief of the marshals and he gives a *great* tour. Can you let Father O'Brien know that my executive assistant will be in touch to make the arrangements?"

"Yes."

"And can you be a contact person for my assistant? She's cool. Her name is Simone."

"Simone? Of course, I can be her contact."

Best wasn't sure what to make of Espinoza's crisp replies, but he was glad that she'd agreed to be their contact. Not only could she help arrange the visit, but Simone could pass to her the information for his Chamber of Commerce contacts.

Best walked over to the fence and grabbed his suit coat. In one last gulp, he finished his lemonade and handed her the glass.

"Thanks again for the drink. My office will be in touch, Teresa."

"Won't you go and say goodbye to Father Tim?"

"No, no. I don't want to bother him while he's working with the kids. Tell him I said thank you very much for the visit."

And with a last nod, Best threw his coat casually over his shoulder, waved goodbye to the boys, and went on his way. When he reached the street, he called Simone at the office to tell her about Teresa Espinoza. When he reached her, she had a surprise for him.

"Your honor, I received a call for you from Marshall, Lufton."

"From Mike?"

"No, the office manager, Cliff Conroy. He invited you to a funeral on Thursday—Jack Tremont is dead."

27

"Can I get you another scotch?"

Girardi squinted up from his phone as a buxom middle-aged waitress in a low-cut English bar maid's uniform leaned across the table to remove his empty glass. For the first time, Girardi vaguely noticed that her name tag read Marsha. The name tag was never the first thing anyone noticed about Marsha.

Business was slow in the bar at *Ye Olde Tavern* in Corona del Mar, and Marsha had been more than attentive to Girardi, even going to the trouble to bring him a complimentary plate of buffalo wings. The *Tavern* was not far from the Plantation, and Cliff Conroy had agreed to meet Girardi there after finishing a visit with Celeste Tremont to go over Jack's funeral arrangements. Conroy was running late, and Girardi had already polished off a beer and a scotch.

"May I have a couple of minutes to think about that drink?" he demurred.

The alcohol was beginning to affect him, and he felt numb. The weeks since Jack Tremont's stroke had been tense and painful, and Girardi wasn't sure how much more he could take. Looking around the dark bar, he saw several men sitting alone and drinking themselves into oblivion. At the moment, the prospect of some oblivion was alluring to him. Tremont had died before Girardi could talk with him about CEP and Mona—now he feared that he would never get his answers.

As he continued to wait for Conroy, he thought about Mona Phillips. She had taken up with Tremont and borne a son. Now, little Gunnar was fatherless. Had Tremont made any provision for them in his estate? Was there a court order as to the baby's parentage? As hurt as he was by her betrayal of him, Girardi hated to think of Mona and her son's precarious position. The road ahead would not be easy.

"No hurry, take your time," Marsha replied with an understanding nod. "Would you like some more wings?"

"No thanks," he said absently, studying the list of missed calls on his screen. For some time he'd been reading and responding to emails from clients and colleagues, and he had ignored the calls in an effort to concentrate.

Checking his personal texts, there was one from Val explaining that Jake was having a great game so far—two hits and a diving catch in left field. There was another from Beth Stowe encouraging him to hang in there.

Smiling as he read these messages over, Girardi called to Marsha. The situation was certainly bleak, but perhaps it wasn't entirely hopeless. "I'll have a cup of coffee—black."

"Coffee?" she repeated in surprise, walking back over to the table. "I don't serve much coffee in here. I'll need to make a fresh pot."

"I'm meeting someone . . ."

"What's her name?" she asked knowingly.

"It's not a her."

She squinted at him in puzzlement at the thought that she'd read him wrong. Marsha had been at this job a long time, and was normally quite good at sizing up her male customers.

"The way you've been brooding and staring at your screen for the last 45 minutes, I thought you were breaking up with your girlfriend or something like that. I get guys your age in here all the time telling me about their woman troubles."

Guys my age? Girardi repeated to himself. *What's that supposed to mean? You're no spring chicken yourself, Marsha.*

"There's a lot of drama going on out there," Marsha continued. "Women really do treat guys like crap sometimes—and for some reason, the more money a guy has, the worse he gets treated."

She paused. This was Girardi's cue. If he wanted to unload about his woman troubles, Marsha would be there for him, from now until her shift ended. And, hey, for a guy as cute as Girardi, she might be available after that. Marsha was careful not to spend social time with her customers very often, but once in a while she allowed herself an exception.

For his part, however, Girardi was not interested in confiding in Marsha, who continued speaking. "Once in a while one of my customers will tell me about his boyfriend troubles . . ." Her voice trailed off thoughtfully. "Did you say you wanted another scotch?"

"Coffee."

"Right—cream with that coffee?"

"Just black, thanks."

He returned to his screen and texted Val, asking about Jake's game. Val got right back to him, reporting that the score was tied in the bottom of the sixth inning. She also reported that Jesse was at home with her father, and that she was planning to take Jake to dinner after the game. She invited Girardi to join them. Jake was next up to bat, and she promised to text again in a few minutes. Val could pack a lot of information into her phone's character limit. *Technology is a marvelous thing*, Girardi thought as he texted a line of thanks to his sister.

His phone rang a couple minutes later.

"Mike, it's Mitch."

Girardi could tell immediately that his friend was worked up. "Where are you?"

"On the freeway—listen, do you have a few minutes? You won't believe the meeting I had with that padre. I'll probably spend extra time in purgatory for saying this, but he's an ass. I have no idea what Susie was thinking sending me to him."

"Jack's dead, Mitch."

There was a pause on the judge's end. "I heard. Do you know what happened?"

"I'm in a restaurant waiting for Cliff to come and fill me in."

"How do you feel about it?"

Girardi did not appreciate the question. "What do you mean? I feel terrible about it. How am I supposed to feel?"

"Taking a step back, this might make your other problem go away, right?"

"Do you think Russ Yost will back off?"

"He might."

Girardi was not ready to see any silver lining in Tremont's death, and his thoughts moved on quickly. He hadn't spoken with Best since Sunday, and Girardi had a lot to tell him. He wanted to share Mona's story, but he had to be very careful about what he said in public. So, he moved to another subject that was weighing on him.

"By the way, Mitch, you were right. My former associate was sitting on a stack of documents on that matter we've been discussing. I saw her at the center today."

Best whistled. "Holy cow. You've had a big day. Did you ask Beth out?"

Girardi wondered how Best could even think of this amid the rest of the news he was sharing. "What makes you so sure I was even considering asking Beth out to begin with?"

"Did she say yes?"

"Sort of—I think she's coming with me to the church concert. But the sisters may be coming, too, so I'm not sure how that will go." He changed the subject again. "It sounds as though you didn't like the priest?"

The animated Best went on to describe his visit to St. Jude's in some detail.

"So," Girardi ventured at the end of the judge's monologue, "will you just go back and see Reverend Mountjoy now?"

"Who knows?"

Out the small bar window, Girardi spotted Conroy's green Jaguar pulling into the parking lot off of Pacific Coast Highway. "Listen Mitch, I need to get going. Cliff's outside."

■ ■ ■

Over at St. Mark's, meanwhile, Susan Mountjoy was in her office stewing over the latest crisis there. Her sexton had up and quit on her in anger, leaving the place deliberately untidy. The job of a sexton is to look after the church building and grounds. Until a few years earlier, the St. Mark's position had been filled by Rufus Cornwell, who had served for twenty-five years until dying of a heart attack at age seventy. A lifelong bachelor, Rufus had taken little pay and yet served the church with distinction. He was something of an institution at St. Mark's and was thus nearly impossible to replace.

With her budget tight, Mountjoy had struggled to adequately fund the position. Since Rufus, five men had served for short periods. Now, she would have to find a sixth.

As she pondered her predicament, Mountjoy's office phone rang; it was Tim O'Brien on the line.

"Hello, Susan. How are you?"

"Hi, Tim. I'm okay, I guess. I lost another sexton today. The place is a mess, and we have a community concert coming up. A violinist from the Pacific Symphony is playing. I'm not sure what I'm going to do to get the place ready."

"You'll manage, I'm sure," O'Brien replied, not sounding particularly sympathetic. What amounted to a crisis at St. Mark's often sounded like no big deal to the pastor of St. Jude's. Never one for small talk, O'Brien moved on quickly to the main point of his call.

"Listen, Susan, I'm afraid that I may have offended your friend the judge this afternoon."

"Oh no, really?" Mountjoy replied with immediate concern. "What happened?"

"Well, before I get into that, I have to ask why you didn't think it was necessary to tell me about his background."

Wow, he's even grumpier than usual, Mountjoy thought. Ever since their days in graduate school at Yale, O'Brien had been a difficult personality. At the same time, however, deep down O'Brien was as loyal and generous as anyone Mountjoy had ever known. He was a man of deep faith who strove always to live his life consistently with his vision of the gospel message. It might not always be easy to deal with him, but Tim O'Brien was a friend worth having.

"I'm not sure I know much about Mitch's background, to tell you the truth. We were at USC together, but I don't recall where he came from before that."

"Well, he told some of the boys today that he grew up in a trailer park in the Central Valley. As the story went, he never knew his father, and his mother was an alcoholic. He told the boys that he understood how things were for them because he'd grown up the same way. He also said that if they stayed in school and kept out of trouble, they could be anything they wanted to be . . . because that's what America is all about."

Mountjoy shook her head in surprise. "Well, okay. I didn't know any of that about him, but if that's what he told the kids, it must be the truth. Whatever his faults, Mitch is a straight shooter, and he'd never make up something like that. But tell me, Tim, what does that have to do with you offending him?"

"Before I heard all of this, I told him that in order to learn about Christianity, he should start by interacting with people who had known suffering."

"Oh Tim . . . ," she scolded.

"I didn't know, okay?" he rejoined defensively. "You should have seen him when he first came out on the yard. He absolutely oozed privilege and authority. He even wore a flag pin for heaven's sake. Who does that?"

"He's a *Republican*, Tim. I warned you. What did you expect?"

"The judge is not just a Republican. I think he's a Republican on steroids. He quoted Ronald Reagan to me on a *barrio* playground with a straight face."

Knowing O'Brien's radical politics, Mountjoy could not help but chuckle.

"It's not funny, Susan," he continued crossly. "I know you deal with people like that all of the time in Newport, but I make it a point not to."

"We have all types of political views in my congregation. But, you know, we make it work. We focus our energy on being Christians, not Democrats or Republicans." She paused. "Tell me, did the judge act as though he was offended by what you said?"

"Not at first. In fact, he took me up on my offer to talk to the kids. He played basketball with them and even invited them to the courthouse."

"He did?"

"Yes. I did not personally care for your friend, Susan, but he responded to my challenge admirably. To my surprise, I think the kids liked him. They were certainly eager to tell me all about him after he'd gone. They seem interested in going to the courthouse, too. *That* surprised me even more."

"If he did so well with the kids, then how do you know Mitch was offended?"

"He left without saying good bye."

"Oh. I see."

"I'm sorry. I know you wanted me to help him, but honestly, the judge and I are not a very good fit. Maybe you should just go ahead and help him yourself. He seems to respect you."

Mountjoy expelled a regretful sigh. "He'd respect you, too, and vice versa, if the two of you got to know one another a little better."

"I'm not so sure."

"Okay, I understand. Perhaps I was wrong. I appreciate your taking the time to meet with him."

"No problem."

There came a lull in the conversation. "So, how are things at St. Jude's?"

"The same as always," he replied heavily.

"How are the gardens?" she asked, knowing of O'Brien's fondness for this subject.

"They're good. We're getting ready to plant a new bed. What do you say to coming down here one afternoon next week to help us out?"

"Oh Tim, I'd love to, but I'm swamped."

"It would do you good, Susan. Besides, you always like talking to the kids."

"They'll find me boring compared to Mitch."

"We've got a couple of new girls you'd enjoy knowing. They're smart and studious, like you. Why don't we say next Thursday afternoon?"

Although Mountjoy was busy, she found it hard to say no to O'Brien, especially since he'd taken the time to meet with the judge. She looked at her calendar, and found that she could likely squeeze in a little trip to Santa Ana.

"Okay, what about 3:30 a week from Thursday?"

"Perfect," he replied in surprise. "It will be good to see you."

"Likewise."

"Well, I'd better get going. I'm sorry again about the judge, Susan. I wish I'd done better with him."

"Me too, but sometimes it's tough to find a good fit. He's a unique case, but I'll think of someone."

"Okay. I'll look forward to seeing you next week."

"Alright. Thanks, Tim."

"Goodbye, Susan."

■ ■ ■

"How is Celeste holding up?" Girardi asked Conroy as he settled into his seat in the corner of the dark bar.

The normally immaculate office manager looked exhausted and disheveled, the strain of the present circumstances marked upon his features.

"Celeste is devastated. I can barely get her to say anything about the funeral plans. The doctor has her on sedatives—more sedatives than usual, I mean. She's leaving everything to me."

"When is the service?"

"Day-after-tomorrow, at the Lutheran Church in Irvine."

"Was Jack a Lutheran?"

"No, but they're the biggest church available. The sanctuary is lovely. I've been making calls all afternoon. An impressive VIP list is shaping up."

For a fleeting moment, it sounded to Girardi as though Conroy was simply planning another party with Celeste.

"I'm working on getting us some bagpipes. Jack loved bagpipes."

This was the first Girardi had ever heard of Tremont's fondness for this particular instrument. But then Girardi supposed that this was not the type of thing he would have discussed with his old mentor. In all their years together, it was the practice of law that bound them together.

"The reception after the service will be at UCI. Their development director and the symphony's fundraiser almost came to blows over who would host it."

"Why would they do that?"

"Jack and Celeste are big contributors, and so are their friends. This is a chance to hold a fundraising event disguised as a tribute. It's perfect for us because it's free. Thank goodness, because Celeste has been very worried about money lately."

The Tremonts, Girardi thought, had always been extravagant spenders, and there was never talk of sparing any expense for one of their gatherings. Conroy was letting details slip that he would normally keep to himself, and Girardi quickly chalked this up to the stress of the moment. Girardi wondered also how Mona and Gunnar fit into the financial picture. Jack had apparently purchased a condo for them and was covering the bills, some of which had recently gone unpaid.

"Mike," Conroy continued, leaning forward confidentially, "I need to ask you something important. Celeste would really like you to be one of the speakers. Have you ever delivered a eulogy before?"

The request hit Girardi hard, and as he reached for his cup, he suddenly wished he'd ordered another scotch after all. Girardi hated funerals, and the prospect of speaking at one sounded awful to him.

"No, I've never done a eulogy."

The doubt in his voice was obvious.

"But you speak in court all the time—it shouldn't be a problem for you."

"This is entirely different."

"You're his closest colleague and he really liked you, so you're perfect to cover his career. His son Robert and his daughter are also going to speak. Senator Pettigrew will deliver the main eulogy and focus on Jack's philanthropy. Pettigrew was a good get if I do say so myself."

"Sounds like you have it all covered."

"I'm trying. Here's to Jack," he toasted, raising his glass.

"Won't *you* speak at the service, Cliff?" Girardi asked. "You knew Jack better than any of us."

"No. I'm *not* a public speaker. I'm a behind the scenes guy." He paused reflectively. "In a lot of ways, this service is for Celeste and the kids, not for Jack."

"I suppose you're right."

Conroy laughed grimly. "It's not as though Jack will be watching down from heaven or anything like that."

Staring across the table at Conroy, Girardi thought that he was definitely not himself. Conroy never revealed personal information about the Tremonts, nor did he say anything that might put Jack in a negative light. Had he perhaps shared one or two of Celeste's pills?

Conroy went on to describe more details about the service, and Girardi did his best to listen attentively.

"When did it actually happen?" Girardi asked some time later.

"When did what happen?"

"When did Jack pass away?"

There was a very slight pause. "Yesterday afternoon."

"But I didn't receive word until this afternoon—why the delay?"

"Celeste insisted that I not tell anyone outside the family until today. She said she couldn't bear to speak with people until she'd gotten a little rest. But she still hasn't rested, and the only ones she'll see today are her kids."

Girardi turned this all over in his mind. "I was at the hospital yesterday afternoon. There was someone else in Jack's room, and I couldn't get anyone to tell me where he was. I wonder if he was already gone."

Conroy stared at his drink. "Jack wasn't at the hospital when he died."

"Where was he?"

"At the Plantation. Jack insisted upon being taken home over the weekend. He arranged for 24-hour care. I don't know how they were going to afford it. They were having some money troubles, you know."

Another reference to money.

"I don't understand why Jack would leave the hospital," Girardi said. "He wasn't up to something like that—what was he thinking?"

"He hated that hospital. Celeste thinks he gave up fighting and wanted to die at home where at least he'd be comfortable."

Girardi struggled to make sense of what he was hearing. In his view, Jack Tremont was not a man to give up fighting until absolutely all hope was lost. And although he had avoided the details of Tremont's condition, Girardi had been under the impression that if anything, his mentor had been improving slightly. It would have been a hard road forward, but Girardi had not believed that Tremont was ready to give up and die.

"I don't mean to make this about me, Cliff, but as his law partner, shouldn't I have been kept in the loop here?"

"I wasn't in the loop, either. Celeste and Jack made these decisions without consulting me. When I did find out, they impressed upon me that I was to be discreet. I respected that wish. Celeste has me involved now to make the arrangements. Just think—this is the last thing I'll ever do for Jack. It's hard to fathom."

"You'll continue to run the office that Jack built. That will be doing something for him."

Conroy shook his head in the negative. "I don't know about that. Huey, Dewey and Louie have wanted to get rid of me for years. This might be a good time for me to retire."

"Retire? What would you do? You work all the time."

"I've been saving my pennies. You all have paid me generously." Conroy's voice now assumed a far-away quality. "I might buy a little place on an island somewhere—play golf, read all of the books I've meant to get to but never did. Jack's illness has been a wake-up call for me. Life is short—and you never know when your time will be up."

Listening to Conroy, Girardi felt a surprising sympathy with him. They'd both spent most of their careers serving Jack Tremont. Now, their master was gone. For a time, both men would be lost without him. A short while later, Conroy prepared to leave. He reached into his coat pocket for his billfold, but Girardi stopped him.

"I've got this."

"Thanks, Mike."

"Listen," Girardi said hesitantly, "there's one more thing I need to ask you about before you go. It's sensitive."

"Then this probably isn't the place to mention it."

"Mona came to the office yesterday."

Conroy nodded. "I heard. What did she say?"

"Quite a bit."

"I'm sure."

"She said that Jack has set her up in a place with the baby, and that you'd been taking care of the bills."

"Mona agreed never to tell anyone at the firm about her . . . situation."

Conroy loved to use the word situation.

"So, you are paying her bills?"

"Jack was paying them, but I was writing the checks. Jack had a few indiscretions over the years, things you never knew about. But there was never anything like this. Jack used to say that he was in love with Mona—that she was everything to him. Good Lord . . . she was half his age. What an old fool he was." He paused and looked at Girardi. "Of course, I don't need to tell you about the effect that woman can have on a man."

"Does Celeste know anything?"

"Of course not," he replied fiercely. "We went to enormous lengths to keep this from her. And she is not to know now if I can help it."

"What will happen to Mona?"

"I have no idea."

"Did Jack make any provision for her?"

"Mike, forgive me, but Mona and her boy are the furthest thing from my mind right now. Jack is dead, and I'm planning his funeral. I don't know what the will says, or if he put aside anything for her. I rather doubt it, though."

"But Mona is all alone . . ."

"Yes, yes, my heart bleeds for her. Do *you* want to take care of her? I'm sure that could be arranged."

"Of course not."

"Then my advice would be to stay out of it. It's none of your business. I'm sorry to sound so callous, but you have no idea how difficult Mona made things for Jack—and for me." He expelled a long sigh. "Where did she come from, anyway?"

"What do you mean?"

"How did she first come to the firm?"

"A temp agency."

Conroy stared at Girardi. "God, that's right. Just think, the twist of fate of the agency sending us one girl instead of another. Things might have turned out very differently if there had never been a Mona Phillips."

Girardi nodded his agreement. "I suppose you're right."

"Never mind now; it doesn't do any good to think that way. So, tell me, can we count on you for Thursday?"

"You mean for the eulogy?"

"Yes."

Girardi nodded. "Sure. You say you want me just to cover his career?"

"That's right. No more than five minutes. It will be a piece of cake. This will mean the world to Celeste."

Conroy took his leave. Girardi then removed a stack of bills from his wallet, being sure to leave Marsha a generous tip, and headed outside.

28

At the Ronald Reagan Building the following afternoon, Judge Mitchell Best was on the bench, presiding over a tedious evidentiary hearing in a set of related criminal cases involving an alleged drug ring in San Clemente. The ring was thought to include members as young as eleven years old, kids the same age as the ones he'd visited at St. Jude's.

The judge was growing weary of what he thought were very weak arguments by the defense counsel. He looked up to the clock in the back of the courtroom and longed to call a recess. But it was not yet time, and if he called the break now, the session after the break would take forever.

"Your honor," droned on the little man with greased-back hair and an ill-fitting brown suit, "fairness dictates that the statements given to the police on the night of the San Clemente arrests must be suppressed."

"Counsel, do you have *any* relevant case law for me?" the judge asked impatiently. They'd been around and around on the point already.

"There's the *Rodriguez* decision I mentioned before," he offered weakly.

"That's from another jurisdiction—try again."

"Despite the fact that the case is from Arkansas . . ."

"Try again," Best cut him off.

This guy is such an idiot, the judge thought to himself as he looked over at the law clerk who was sitting in the courtroom taking notes. The clerk was a bright young Stanford Law graduate who happened to be the son of an old friend of Best's. It would be up to the clerk to write a memorandum and to talk the issues through with the judge prior to the issuance of his written ruling on the present evidentiary issues. Despite having a tendency to shoot from the hip in personal matters, Judge Best was not one to rule on important motions before they were carefully researched. Federal judges had generous stipends for law clerks, and Judge Best made the most of this resource.

As the lawyer fumbled around with his notes, his co-counsel whispered something to him.

"The *Stimpson* case is from the Ninth Circuit," he ventured, sounding as though he hoped that if he threw enough darts at the wall, one might stick.

Noticing the exchange between the lawyers, the judge leaned forward across the bench and pointed. "Is Ms. Patterson a ventriloquist, counsel?"

He had seen Supreme Court Justice Antonin Scalia do something like this once earlier during a visit to Washington D.C. Judge Best was an aficionado of the justice, who had been appointed by Best's hero Ronald Reagan. A rumble of laughter rose from the gallery. There always seemed to be people in the back of Best's courtroom, for he was known for putting on a good show.

While the lawyer struggled for an answer, Best's assistant Simone passed him a note. "Mr. Girardi is upstairs in room 628."

Best nodded his thanks to her.

"Okay, everybody, let's take fifteen minutes to regroup. If I were you, Mr. Byrd, I'd give Ms. Patterson a chance to talk after the break. It can't get much worse for you at this point. The court is now in recess."

Best exited the side door past his marshal. He moved quickly down the hall and up two flights of steps then down a narrow hallway to the conference room and opened the door.

"So, you made it, partner," Best said loudly, the tails of his robe flapping behind him as he pulled up next to his friend's chair.

Girardi nodded somberly, and the two were quiet for several moments. The judge could see that his friend was tense. Given the fact that he would shortly be meeting Assistant U.S. Attorney Charley Strong in that very conference room, Best could hardly blame him.

Early that morning, Girardi had compared the *Trinity Hills* and *Pope Electronics* computer printouts and found them to be nearly identical in form. With Russ Yost's deadline just a couple of days away, Girardi had decided to follow the judge's advice and tell the prosecutor everything he knew. He'd called Best, who had set a quick appointment with Strong. Things were now moving fast. Elizabeth Stowe had agreed to meet him at the courthouse and participate in the meeting.

"So, what's the plan in here?"

"Beth is supposed to meet me any time now. She's bringing the rest of the documents. We'll have some time to prepare before your friend comes in."

"Now remember, Mikey, you and I can't have any more conversations about this mess. Not a word. The matter is now going to be in Charley's hands, and I need to be entirely out of the loop."

"I know."

Best felt a pang of guilt for cutting his friend loose, but he had no choice. "I'm sorry, but any involvement by me could be tampering, and that's a no-no."

"I completely understand, Mitch. Don't worry. I appreciate your helping me as much as you have."

The judge heard a rustling behind him and turned around to see Elizabeth Stowe struggling through the door carrying an armful of papers and a heavy-looking briefcase. He hadn't seen her in two years and wasn't sure he would have recognized her if he'd run into her on the street. Her hair was now long, and she looked thinner than he remembered. Or, on second thought, perhaps she had gained a little weight. He couldn't say for sure, but he knew that something was different.

Girardi meanwhile jumped out of his chair and brushed past the surprised judge to get to her side.

"Can I help you with that bag, Beth? It looks heavy."

"Thanks," she said, managing a little smile.

"You look great," Girardi said softly. The compliment was intended for Stowe's ears only, but the sharp judge of course heard him.

"It's my old uniform," she replied. "When I was getting dressed I remembered what you used to say—that a lawyer putting on a suit for court is like a medieval knight strapping on a coat of armor."

Girardi shook his head. "I don't remember ever saying that."

"Trust me, you said it more than once. I used to wear a suit almost every day, but this morning I had to root around the closet to find a coat of armor that would fit. I've gained a few pounds since my Marshall, Lufton days."

"Well, you look great to me."

Stowe placed her small hand on his arm for a few moments and smiled as he showed her to a seat next to his. Girardi then poured her a cup of water from the carafe on the table. The judge meanwhile watched them carefully, sizing up the situation. Among her many talents, Judge Best's soon-to-be-former second wife was an astute reader of body language. Based on the lessons she had taught him, Best could see that there was what Sophia would call "very favorable" body language between these two.

My god, that's pathetic, Best lamented to himself. *He's practically melted into a puddle at the sight of her. What happened to him?*

Stowe took something from her bag and placed it carefully into Girardi's hand, covering his fingers with her own. "Agnes wanted me to give these to you. They're her Italian grandfather's rosary beads. She and the sisters are going to pray for us this afternoon."

Girardi looked at the blue beads in surprise before putting them into his pocket. "It can't hurt, I suppose."

As all this was going on, the judge felt a little left out. He approached Stowe and extended his hand with a smile.

"It's nice to see you again, Beth."

"Likewise, your honor."

"Your honor?" he repeated. "No, no. We don't need to be so formal. It's Mitch."

"Alright." She paused awkwardly. "Um, I passed the ladies' room on the way in. Before we get started, I think I'll go and powder my nose. Please excuse me."

"Of course."

As soon as he thought Stowe was out of earshot, the judge approached Girardi and punched his arm playfully.

"Geez, I feel like the third wheel on a date with you two. Did you see that body language? She's really into you."

The humorless Girardi meanwhile began to look at Stowe's documents. "I only wish we were on a date somewhere. I hope your friend Charley doesn't go too hard on us. God, I can't believe it has come to this."

"Charley has to do his job, Mike, and that will include asking some tough questions. He has to be skeptical in his line of work. You know— you were a prosecutor yourself."

"I know, but I don't want him to badger Beth."

"Beth will be fine."

"I hope you're right."

"I *am* right. Listen, I'd better get back downstairs and keep the wheels of justice grinding along. Good luck."

"Thanks, Mitch."

The two shook hands, and Best departed the room, waving down the hall to Stowe as she returned from the ladies' room.

Girardi and Stowe remained on the sixth floor of the federal building for the next several hours, not emerging until dusk. Charley Strong interviewed the pair together and then spoke with each individually. A young paralegal from his office took notes, and portions of the interview were recorded. It was a grueling, testy ordeal, and the two were certainly put through their paces. While mostly maintaining a cool, matter-of-fact demeanor, Strong made it a point to mix in the occasional question meant either to trip up or anger his subjects. Although they showed their frustration from time to time, both Girardi and Stowe managed to maintain their professional demeanors as well as could be expected.

When the day's ordeal was finally over, neither Girardi nor Stowe knew what to think. In truth, they were overwhelmed. The two were experienced litigators, but they'd never been through anything like this. They decided to walk to a nearby Mexican restaurant for dinner. Although they tried to avoid mentioning CEP and Charley Strong, the subject of Tremont's funeral came up soon after they'd ordered their meals.

"I can't believe I have to deliver Jack's eulogy tomorrow. I have no idea what to say without making myself a liar or a hypocrite. Maybe I can still back out."

Stowe took a sip of her iced tea and nodded sympathetically. "I understand where you're coming from, but I don't think you should back out. Take the high road and focus on the positives."

"I'm a little surprised to hear you say that, given what we just went through across the street."

"Agnes and I had a long talk about everything this morning. She stressed over and over how important it will be for us to forgive Jack Tremont."

"Jack put our careers in jeopardy—I'm not sure he deserves forgiveness."

"That's exactly what I said, but Agnes insisted that forgiveness is necessary for our own hearts to begin to heal. She says that forgiveness is at least as beneficial to the forgiver as the forgiven. When you think about it, it makes sense."

"I'm a long way from there right now, Beth."

"Me too, but it's something to shoot for. Agnes is so wise—I wish I were more like her."

Her voice trailed off, and the pair was quiet for some time. At last, Stowe spoke up again. "Listen, as far as the eulogy goes, why don't you tell some stories from the old days? You've always said that Jack was your mentor—that he shaped your view of legal practice more than anyone else."

"What a joke," Girardi interjected miserably.

"No, it isn't a joke. I know how important that is because you were *my* mentor."

Girardi could not help but smile a little at this as Stowe continued.

"When I had no clue what it meant to practice law, I watched you to figure out what this job was all about. Even the comments about the coat of armor—it all meant something to me. Jack may not have turned out to be the man you wanted him to be, but he still gave you a lot. Focus on that."

"How can you even think of this now? Aren't you exhausted?"

"I'm tired, but I'm also hyped up. It's going to take time to settle down." She reached over to her briefcase and pulled out a yellow pad. "In the meantime, why don't we take a crack at outlining that eulogy?"

"You're going to help me?"

"Sure, why not? What words or phrases come to mind to describe Jack as a lawyer?"

Girardi folded his arms. "Nothing that I can repeat in front of a lady."

"Come on, work with me here. Think back a few years before this mess—what would you have said about him when I was still at the firm?"

Girardi struggled for something to say in response to Stowe's question. At length, he spoke up. "Jack always stressed preparation and toughness . . ."

"Never take anything personally . . ."

"Business is business. Jack used to say that litigation is a game. The objective is to outsmart the other guy."

Stowe nodded. "I remember back during my 2L year, Jack took the summer associates to lunch at the *Clubhouse* in Costa Mesa. He sat at the head of the table and told war stories the entire time. Meanwhile, we, saps that we were, hung on every word. He told us that litigation was a chess game . . . the key is to be thinking at least three moves ahead of your opponent."

Girardi sighed heavily. "He was fond of chess metaphors."

Stowe jotted down some key phrases on the top lines of the page. "These can be your themes. Now, try and think of a few stories to illustrate them."

"I honestly can't think of one story right now," he protested.

But Stowe stuck with it, and through the rest of the meal, they traded anecdotes about Jack Tremont and selected a few that might be appropriate for the eulogy. Although Girardi did not understand it at the time, the exercise was a first step on the road to coming to terms with the loss of his mentor.

On her pad, Stowe dutifully recorded bullet points summarizing the anecdotes. When Girardi had paid the bill, Stowe tore the top sheet from her pad, folded it and gave it to him.

"Here's your outline. If you don't have time to type something out, you can deliver the eulogy from these notes."

Girardi nodded gratefully and placed the sheet carefully in his coat pocket. "This reminds me of when you used to prepare me for a court hearing."

"I know—and half the time you didn't stick to the script anyway," she replied with a knowing smile.

They headed outside and as they reached the crosswalk, Girardi looked both ways and took Stowe's hand protectively into his own.

"Let's go," he said when the way was clear.

"For years now," Girardi ventured when they'd safely reached the other side, "I've wondered what it would be like to have my own shop."

"Really?" she asked with obvious surprise. "You seem so comfortable as a big firm partner."

"I'm not comfortable with it anymore. Smaller practice intrigues me, but I don't like the idea of working alone. My legal practice has always been collaborative—that's one of the best things about a good law firm. I might be able to swing it, though, if I had another good attorney with me."

As he said this, Girardi looked expectantly to Stowe.

"You almost sound like you're offering me a job."

"Would you take one if I did offer?"

"I still have five months to go with Agnes. She told me today that I have the makings of a first-rate oblate." Stowe paused. "She probably said so because she feels sorry for me."

"I don't think she feels sorry for you, Beth."

"Well, I won't be looking for a job for a while. I want to focus as much as I can on my work at the center."

"That's okay; nothing will happen right away. But, I'd like you to at least think about it. It's all just in my head for now. I wouldn't be able to do anything until the investigation is over."

"And from what Charley Strong said, that could be six months to a year."

"Or more," he added glumly.

"Then again, it might be less. Good old Charley might find that we are not worth the taxpayers' resources. Even though my heart was beating in my throat most of the time up there, I honestly felt that we were boring him."

Girardi nodded. "I know what you mean. Prosecutors today want headline-grabbing cases . . . I'm not sure this qualifies."

They arrived at the stairwell of their parking structure and ascended the steps, still hand in hand.

"I have been entertaining another fantasy," he offered.

"What's that?" Stowe asked with wide eyes, tightening her grip on his hand.

"A vineyard."

"Oh." Her hand relaxed once more and she scolded herself for letting her mind run away with her.

"My grandfather always dreamed of owning a vineyard. It might be cool to have a few acres in the hills somewhere, making really good wine . . ."

"You want to be a farmer?" she teased.

"Not a *farmer* . . . a viticulturist."

"Ah, that sounds much better."

They arrived at Stowe's car, which was parked at the opposite end of the row from Girardi's. The lot was dark and there was not a soul in sight. In the dim glow of her cabin light, he watched her place her briefcase on the passenger seat. As she turned to him, he brought his arm around her waist and kissed her on the forehead. Without hesitation, she smiled and wrapped her thin arms around his neck.

"You were great today, Beth. I should never have called you a coward."

Stowe let out a thoughtful sigh. "I think we did okay up there. It seemed as though they believed us . . ."

"We did the best we could."

"I just wish we knew what was going to happen next. The thing I hate most is the uncertainty."

Girardi nodded his agreement and managed a smile as he brushed a few strands of hair from her face. "Do you want to catch a movie?"

"A movie—*now?*"

"Why not? I'm wide awake and I could use a distraction. Jake's with his aunt overnight, so I'm a free man."

"Where would we go?"

"We could head to the Irvine Spectrum and catch the ten o'clock shows."

"They have twenty theaters—I'm sure we could find something. A movie? I have no idea how you even thought of that. Okay, I'm in."

Stowe smiled brightly up at him, and he thought she looked beautiful in the dim light. He brushed her left cheek with his fingertips and kissed her ear. Girardi had waited for this for a long time, and he felt a rush as he began to caress her hair and to kiss her neck. There had been so much turmoil, and all of that emotion was coming to a head.

Holding her close, his companion smelled so sweet and felt so good. His fingers glided up the small of her back. He thought Stowe might gently signal for him to stop, but she seemed to be as caught up in the moment as Girardi was. Perhaps that movie could wait.

As he continued to kiss her, Girardi heard a muffled noise behind him and suddenly felt the shock of a searing pain in the back of his neck and his shoulder. He heard Stowe cry out his name, and then, he blacked out.

29

"Mike, are you listening to me? Mikey, come on. I'm talking to you."

Girardi opened his eyes to see a fuzzy, red-faced Mitch Best hovering over him. The room spun around him and he could not gain his bearings. He was lying on a bed, and Best was sitting on the edge of it, leaning in close to Girardi's face. Looking around, Girardi saw a bright panel of fluorescent lights that hurt his eyes, and so he closed them once more.

"*Mikey,* I really need you to stay with me."

Girardi mumbled something that Best could not make out. All he wanted to do was go back to sleep.

"You need to speak up, partner. I can't hear you."

"I don't know where I am, Mitch."

"Sure you do—I just told you a couple of minutes ago. We're at UCI Medical Center. You've had a little mishap, and the doctor asked me to keep you talking until we make sure you're okay."

Although he tried to concentrate on what his friend was saying, Girardi's mind drifted. "Am I in the hospital?"

"Yep."

"What happened to me?"

"That's what I'm trying to find out. Do you remember what you did yesterday?"

Girardi stared at Best and shrugged. As he moved his arm, he felt the tug of a line hooked to a machine behind him. Girardi became aware of a dull ache in the back of his neck as he tried to concentrate on what Best was saying to him.

"Mike, you told me before that you worked out in the morning at the gym. What did you do after that?"

"I went to work."

This was something of an educated guess on Girardi's part, but he could sense the urgency in his friend's voice and he wanted to play along and give him what he wanted.

"Great! What did you do after that?"

"I don't know what I did, Mitch. I can't remember."

"Did you come see me in Santa Ana?" the judge hinted.

"If you say I did."

The ache in Girardi's neck soon grew into a full-blown throbbing pain. "I'm sorry, but I'm confused and I'm not sure how to help you. I feel so tired. Can I maybe just sleep? This feels like a dream anyway . . . am I dreaming?"

Judge Best drew a patient breath and shook Girardi on the arm.

"You can rest in a little while, Mike. The last few hours are a mystery, and you can help us clear things up. Now, let's try again—you remember what you did yesterday?"

As the conversation wore on, they covered the same ground over and over until Girardi began to recall pieces of his day. Eventually, he could remember without prompting his trip to the gym, his swing by the coffee shop for a scone, his morning meetings at the office and even his conversation with Best and Stowe in the courthouse confer-ence room. But his memories faded out some time in the middle of his interview with U.S. Attorney Charley Strong. Everything after that was a blank.

When the doctor came in, Best eagerly gave her his report. "Dr. Gupta, he's doing better. He remembers most of his day—and he knows who he is and all of that."

Dr. Gupta stood by the bed and began to examine Girardi. She spoke softly as she ran through simple tests of his perception and motor skills. She looked into his eyes for a long time and asked him plenty of questions as she worked.

"So, who is this big fellow in the room with you?"

"That's my friend Mitch. He's a judge."

"He is a good friend indeed. He's got the entire hospital staff working on your case."

Gupta, who was the hospital's vice-dean of medicine and chief of staff, managed to say this matter-of-factly, without any sarcasm. While it might have been a slight exaggeration, the worried judge had in fact not been shy in throwing his weight around to make sure Girardi received plenty of attention.

"How long have you known the judge?" she continued.

"Since law school."

"Where did you two go to law school?"

"Davis."

"Ah, my husband graduated from the medical school there."

As she spoke, she continued her examination. Girardi liked her gentle, comforting manner.

"Two doctors in the family, huh?" he asked, managing a weak chuckle.

In saying this, Girardi wanted to project some sense of command of the situation. Girardi hated to feel vulnerable, especially with strangers.

But despite these efforts, the truth was that Girardi had absolutely no command of the situation. He was in terrible pain and had no idea what had happened to him. He was mainly along for the ride, straining to focus and respond to what Judge Best and the doctor said to him.

"That's right," Gupta responded. "Two doctors in the family. And my daughter is pre-med at UCLA. That will make three. My son, though, wants to be a lawyer. He's the black sheep. Does your shoulder hurt?"

"It's killing me," Girardi admitted. "My neck, too."

She loosened his gown and examined the wounds on his shoulder and neck. Judge Best meanwhile paced the room anxiously.

"I'm sorry, Mr. Girardi, but the strongest thing I can give you now for the pain is Tylenol. I need to make sure that there's no brain injury first."

"Brain injury?" Girardi repeated in alarm. Best stopped his pacing and approached the bedside.

Gupta remained calm. "From what I can deduce, it appears that you were struck with some instrument on your neck and shoulder. They caught you on the back of the head, too, but luckily they grazed you there. Before I clear you, however, you'll need an MRI and some other tests, because the symptoms of brain trauma can be easy to miss. I believe that your amnesia is a result of shock, and thus your memory should return naturally as you rest and recover. But I can't be sure. I'll want my colleagues in the neurology and psychiatry departments to see you—that's standard practice in a case like this." She turned to Best. "We must be thorough, isn't that right, your honor?"

"If the tests are clear, does that mean he's okay?"

"If the tests are clear, it would be a very good sign. We doctors are very much like you attorneys today. We *never* state things in terms of certainties. My general counsel would kill me if I ever promised a patient anything. But it seems to me that all in all you were very fortunate this evening, Mr. Girardi."

Girardi caught no more than half of what she said, and he hardly felt like a lucky man. Still, he sensed that the doctor was trying to be encouraging. "Thank you, doctor."

"You're welcome."

Gupta then left the room, and Best shared the good news that he had finally tracked Jake down at Val's house and that the two of them were on their way to the hospital. It was the middle of the night, but Girardi had little idea of the passage of time. Half an hour later, Val and Jake arrived. The judge made sure to brief the two on the situation before they saw Girardi. Best emphasized with Val the importance of remaining calm, but he was not sure she'd be able to do it.

With tears streaming down her face as she approached his bedside, Val leaned over and hugged her brother. "Oh, Mike," she exhaled.

"Hey, Val, thanks for coming down. Don't worry, I'm fine."

Val exchanged a skeptical look with Jake.

"I guess somebody robbed me," Girardi offered hazily.

"The judge says they took your car, dad. Did you get a look at them?"

"I can't remember anything about it—it's so frustrating."

Val placed a soothing hand on her brother's arm. "Don't work yourself up Mikey. It's just a car. Besides, you were getting tired of the BMW anyway. You should think about what to get next."

"Maybe a Prius," Girardi joked.

Jake eagerly weighed in, for he enjoyed the subject of cars. "A Prius? No way. Maybe a hybrid SUV."

"Hybrid SUV? Am I a soccer mom?"

"What's wrong with being a soccer mom?" Val interjected, feigning hurt.

"I know," Jake said triumphantly, "a Tesla."

The trio thus fell into a conversation typical in the hospital—upbeat on the surface, cordial and careful. Everyone was trying to act as though everything was okay, but of course everything was not okay. After chatting with her brother for some time, Val seemed to settle down. She left the room to call her husband with a report.

"How was school, Jake?" Girardi ventured to fill the vacuum from Val's departure.

"School was kind of boring, as usual."

"And practice?"

"Coach let us out early."

Jake moved to the seat beside the bed that his aunt had occupied. Girardi took a careful look at his son. While he said little, the worry on the young man's face was plain. Despite the fact that Girardi was in a lot of pain, his mind was slowly beginning to clear, and he was concerned for how Jake was taking all of this. Girardi summoned his strength so that he would seem alert.

"How did the Angels do tonight?"

"They lost."

"Who was pitching?"

"Wilson—but it wasn't his fault. He only gave up two runs. The team has just stopped hitting all of a sudden. Trout went zero for four."

They continued on in this fashion until a technician came in to announce that it was time for Girardi's MRI. Girardi waved goodbye to Jake as the assistant wheeled him out of the room.

■ ■ ■

"Keep your mouth shut in here, Lizzy, do you understand?" ordered the unseen speaker behind Elizabeth Stowe. She was blindfolded, and her wrists were bound securely with a sturdy length of cloth.

"Yes," she replied quietly.

As she stood in the small space, Stowe thought that this voice was familiar, but under the strain of the present circumstances she could not place it. As her captor departed, Stowe heard him lock the door and followed the sound of his steps until they faded away.

Alone at last, Stowe desperately tried to calm herself down and to take stock of her situation. Aside from a few bumps and bruises, physically she was fine. In the parking garage across from the federal building, men had come upon Girardi and Stowe by surprise. In what seemed like an instant, they had taken her things, bound and blindfolded her and placed her roughly in the back of what she thought was an SUV. Terrified, she had no idea what had become of Girardi.

After traveling for perhaps half an hour, mainly on the freeway, the SUV stopped and the occupants exited, leaving Stowe alone in the back seat and saying nothing to her. She struggled with the binding on her wrists but could not loosen it, so there was nothing for her to do but wait. Thinking of Sister Agnes and Reverend Mountjoy, Stowe strained to calm her mind and to offer a prayer for strength.

After some time, they continued on. At the next stop, Stowe was led by the arm out of the SUV and down a short flight of stairs. They paused at one point, and she thought she heard the sound of a gate being unlocked ahead of them. The gate swung open, and they walked on until at some point she was pulled up over what seemed like a barrier of some kind. Her right leg did not clear it at first, and one of the men roughly pulled it up and over. She cried out in pain, but they ignored her.

Now that she was alone, Stowe began to calm down. The floor seemed to be swaying beneath her, and she surmised that she was on a boat. She thought she heard the creaking of the vessel as it rubbed against the dock. What in the world was she doing on a boat, she wondered. Why had she and Girardi been attacked? If it had been a robbery, there would have been no reason to take her. What did her captors plan to do with her? And what had become of Mike Girardi?

As she was thinking over her predicament, Stowe was startled by the click of the key in the lock. In a moment, someone was over her removing the blindfold and the binding from her wrists. The room was dim and she could not see much. The person moved so quickly that for a moment she imagined that she was being freed. But it was not so.

"You need to lay low in here and not say a single word or make a single noise. Your safety depends upon it, and I'm not going to tell you twice. I'm the only friend you've got around here, but if you make these guys mad, I won't be able to help you."

"Why am I here?"

"You brought this upon yourself because you and Mike would not leave well enough alone. Do as I say and keep quiet."

Do as I say and keep quiet, she repeated to herself. Stowe had a thousand questions, and she barely managed to suppress the urge to begin asking them.

The man left her and locked the door once more. As he did so, Stowe strained to place the voice. Obviously, it was someone who knew her, or thought that he did. The only people who ever called her Lizzy were old Marshall, Lufton colleagues. She could not remember how the practice had started, but the name had stuck with everyone but Girardi. To him, she had always been Beth.

Lying down on the bunk bed, Stowe shook her head in amazement as she at last placed the voice—her captor was former Marshall, Lufton associate Randall Spencer.

30

Judge Best paced around the nearly deserted hospital corridors in an impatient, almost fierce mood, not knowing what to do with himself. He made several trips back and forth between the downstairs lobby, Girardi's room, and Dr. Gupta's office. Although Girardi was getting the finest care available, the judge could not settle down. He fretted over his friend's MRI and mulled the sketchy details of Girardi's evening.

Just before going to bed, Best had received a call informing him that Girardi was at the UCI Medical Center. The judge had rushed to the hospital. While in the car, Best had spoken with Charley Strong on the phone and learned that Girardi had been found in a garage near the federal building. Girardi's car, briefcase, and phone were gone, but his wallet had still been in his pocket. Strong also told him that Beth Stowe was missing. Her car was still at the garage but there was no sign of her there. She had not made it home to the Emmanuel Center.

Strong had explained that FBI agents were already working on the case and that one would be placed outside of Girardi's hospital room as a precaution. They were in the process of tracking down surveillance video from the garage where Girardi had been found and analyzing the physical evidence at the scene. Strong had reassured the judge that they were doing everything possible to locate Stowe.

In terms of theories, the investigators, working alongside the local police, thought that the incident might be a carjacking. They were well aware, however, of a possible link to the CEP investigation. In his own mind, Best was convinced that Girardi had been targeted because of his visit to Charley Strong that day. What were the odds that this was a co-incidence? Although he still believed his advice to involve Strong had been sound, the judge felt terrible that it had likely landed his friend in the hospital.

The judge was worried not only about Girardi's test results but also about his friend's mindset. Upon learning of Girardi's amnesia, he and Dr. Gupta had agreed together that Girardi should not be told about Stowe's disappearance until it was known that his own condition was stable. So, Best had kept quiet on the matter and ordered the others to do the same. Charley Strong's FBI agents had been persuaded by the doctor to hold off their questioning of Girardi for a few hours.

Exiting the elevator, Best was startled to see Susan Mountjoy standing before him. She was dressed in a peasant top, jeans, and a blue cardigan. In this outfit, she looked younger than she did in her dark suits and cleri-cal collar.

"Oh Mitch, there you are," she exclaimed, offering him a hug.

"Here I am."

"Tell me. How is Mike doing?"

"We're waiting on some test results. He's certainly doing better than when I first got here, but he still can't remember what happened to him. How did you find out about all this?"

Mountjoy hesitated. "Can we find a quiet place to talk?"

The judge nodded. "I know just the spot."

The two headed down to the private conference room of Dr. Gupta.

"We don't belong in here, do we?" Mountjoy asked uncomfortably as she read the "chief of staff" sign on the door.

"No, no, it's fine. Dr. Gupta offered the room to me."

Mountjoy looked at her companion and sighed. "I guess you really are a big-shot, Mitch."

"In this case, I'm just lucky. I'm on an advisory board at UCI. We sit around and BS over breakfast four times a year. They like to integrate the disciplines, and I always sit between the dean of medicine and some guy from the school of humanities—a Marxist historian." Best rolled his eyes. "The historian is dead wood if you ask me, but I like the dean. He's Dr. Gupta's boss. As soon as I heard about Mike, I called the dean and he asked her to come down here and look at him for me. He assured me that she's the best."

The Reverend shook her head. "That's being a big-shot."

Best was in no mood for compliments. "You can call it whatever you want, but I'll gladly use the connections I have to help my friends when they're in trouble. I'd do the same for you, Susie."

"I know you would."

The pair took seats across from one another at the conference room table, and Mountjoy moved to speak.

"Sister Agnes from the Emmanuel Center called to tell me that Elizabeth never made it home from the courthouse. Agnes has no idea what happened to her and she's absolutely frantic. I'm starting to feel a little frantic, too. Someone from the FBI came to the center to interview Agnes, but they didn't stay very long or tell her much. *Please*, Mitch, won't you explain what's going on?"

"They found Mike in a parking garage in Santa Ana next to Beth's car. His car, briefcase and, phone had been taken. There was no sign of Beth."

"Do the police think it was a robbery or a carjacking?"

"They think that those are possibilities," the judge replied dubiously.

"But . . . ?"

"But, Mike and Beth were at the federal building to talk to the prosecutor about some trouble on a case. I think that's why they were targeted."

"I don't understand."

Unsure how much he should reveal, Best provided her a general explanation of the situation.

"So, the problem stems from a case that Elizabeth worked on at her old firm?" she clarified.

Best nodded. "I can't say much, Susie, but they're involved in an investigation, and it's possible that they were targeted because of that investigation."

"What in the world is being investigated? Are Mike and Elizabeth in some kind of legal trouble?"

"I don't think I can say at this point."

"Why not?"

"Because it's all confidential."

"I'm a minister—can't you tell me? There are privileges that protect me—I know there are. I won't tell anyone the details. I swear I won't."

Best found it difficult to resist her pleas. "I'm really sorry. Trust me, I'd love to unload right now, but I'm obliged to keep my mouth shut."

"They're looking for Elizabeth, aren't they?"

Best nodded. "Of course."

"Will you at least tell me if you hear anything?"

"Yes."

Mountjoy folded her arms and stared out the window into the black night.

"I can't believe that Elizabeth is out there somewhere in danger. It's terrible—we can't do a thing about it. I feel so helpless."

"Me, too."

"I remember the first night I met her. Two summers ago—she showed up out of the blue at Evensong. Kind of the way you did last week."

"What happened?"

"I chatted with her a few minutes and she went away. I didn't think I would see her again. But, a few months later, to my surprise, she called me. We had tea and soon afterwards she began to attend St. Mark's. She's been with the parish ever since."

The pair fell quiet. Mountjoy dug into her purse and pulled out a small leather-bound book. She flipped through the well-worn pages and began reading to herself. Intermittently she would shut her eyes and silently move her lips. *She can pray,* the judge thought with some envy. *I wish I could believe there was somebody up there listening.*

Brooding over the present circumstances, the judge could not dismiss from his mind one particular nagging thought—perhaps Beth Stowe had disappeared because she was cooperating with Russell Yost or one of the mysterious consultants working for CEP. Had she lured Girardi into some kind of trap? He hated to think this way, but nonetheless, he had mentioned the idea to Charley Strong, who had not seemed to put much stock into it. Strong had spent the afternoon with Girardi and Stowe and had found them both to be credible. Nonetheless, Strong had promised that they would look at the case from all angles.

Best was drawn from these grim reflections by a deep sigh from Mountjoy.

"I don't know if I can believe in this anymore," she said quietly.

"Believe in what?"

"This," she said, waving the book in front of him.

"What is that, the Bible?"

"It's the Book of Common Prayer."

"I don't understand, Susie."

Mountjoy was silent for a long time. "For years I've come to hospitals to offer words of comfort from this book. I've prayed with patients and families . . . I've anointed the dying . . . blessed newborns. The language I use often comes directly from this book, and the Holy Spirit is at the center of each one of these encounters—I have always known it. Even in the worst cases, I've always felt a divine presence. I don't feel it now, and it scares me."

At this, Mountjoy began to cry. Best came around the table and led her over to the sofa. They sat down and he took her hand into his, not sure how to comfort her. He felt almost as hopeless as she did and he yearned for comfort himself.

Best reached for the prayer book, flipping through it with his free hand. He tried to make sense of what he read, but it was all a jumble to him.

"How does this thing work, anyway?" he asked at last, closing the volume and placing it on the arm of the sofa.

Mountjoy wiped some tears from her cheeks and looked at him quizzically. "What do you mean how does it work?"

"What does a Book of Common Prayer do?"

"You flip a switch and it gets up and dances around the room," she offered with desperate sarcasm. "It's powered by tiny batteries in the spine. I have one at home that plays *When the Saints Come Marching In.*"

"Okay, Reverend, thank you very much." Best let go of her hand.

"What do you want me to say, Mitch? Good heavens, it's a prayer book. You *pray* with it."

Best took a deep breath and made his own petition of sorts for patience. "Remember, I'm new to this religious stuff. I haven't been to church regularly since I was a kid. The world is falling apart around us, and I'm asking a sincere question here. Do you mind telling me how the prayer book works without being such a smart-ass? My goodness, are you like this with your parishioners when they're in trouble?"

Mountjoy opened her eyes wide in surprise at this reproach from the judge. She was accustomed to delivering scoldings but not to receiving them.

"Of course not."

"Then why I am I the lucky butt of your sarcasm?"

To Best's dismay, Mountjoy chuckled at the question. "Because I *can* be this way with you, Mitch. It would never do for me to be a smart aleck with the people in my parish. I'm naturally a bit sarcastic, but I've somehow managed to suppress the tendency over the years. It's a necessity in my job. I've suppressed it so well that I almost forgot about it. But you, my friend, bring it right out of me."

"Gee, I'm honored."

"You should be. Back in school, it was the same way. Do you remember how we used to argue in the dining hall?"

"Not really," Best bluffed.

"Yes, you do. Nobody else would take me on when I was spoiling for trouble. But I could always count on you. We argued about everything. I didn't understand it at the time, but you were braver than the others. I respect that about you."

"Why the heck did I put up with that abuse from you, anyway?"

"I suppose it had something to do with the Daisy Duke shorts . . ."

Best conjured a long-ago scene in his mind. "I think you're right about that."

"We were just kids back then, weren't we? Everything was so innocent. I miss those days. Don't you?"

"Not for a second."

Mountjoy seemed surprised by the judge's firmness. "Why not?"

"Because I'm not one to look backwards. I'd much rather think about tomorrow."

"No regrets?"

"Something like that." He looked at her seriously. "Were you religious back in school? That was a long time ago, but I don't remember you mentioning it."

"I've been religious my whole life. But in school, I probably didn't talk about it that much. I loved college and all the new things I was learning. My faith then was steady, but more in the back of my mind than the front."

"All that feminist, anti-patriarchal malarkey was in the front of your brain, as I recall."

With effort, she decided to ignore the malarkey comment. "That and plenty more. I was a double-major, you know."

"Yes, smarty-pants, I know." He shook his head. "How did you decide to go to seminary?"

"I took a few years off after college. I considered getting a PhD in history or even women's studies. But then I became more involved at my church, and one of my mentors told me that he thought I was called to ordained ministry. That was an exciting time in the Episcopal Church—all kinds of new possibilities were opening up to women. I eventually applied and received some scholarship money to attend Yale."

"That's where you met Father Tim?"

Mountjoy looked at Best uncomfortably at the mention of the priest. "Oh Mitch, I'm sorry about that."

"About what?"

"Pushing you to see him—I heard that your meeting didn't go very well."

"News travels fast, I see."

She nodded.

"Actually, it wasn't that bad. I was impressed by what the padre is accomplishing for those kids at St. Jude's. He's clearly a passionate guy—I can appreciate that."

Mountjoy listened carefully, waiting for the other shoe to drop. She knew well Best's ability to cut others down to size, especially when he felt insulted or threatened.

"I don't think I'll go back to see him anymore," Best continued, "but that's okay. I'm glad I went down there—it was good for me to see what's going on in the neighborhood."

To Mountjoy's relief, that was the end of the matter. Improbably, the sense of doom about the pair began to ease some. She reached for the book and opened it to the contents.

"Here, let me show you how this works."

"Okay," Best replied warily.

"My first tip is that you should never call it the Book of Common Prayer because you'll sound like a rookie. It's the BCP."

"BCP?"

She went on to explain the prayer book's history and to describe how ministers and lay people used it in worship and prayer. When finished, she handed him her Book of Common Prayer.

"Here—keep it."

"No, that's okay," he protested, holding up his hand. "I can buy my own on Amazon."

"I have lots of BCPs at home and at the church. In fact, I've been collecting old ones for years. You can trace the development of our church through those books."

"So, when you write your book, will you discuss the BCP?"

"*If* I write that book," she corrected him.

"No, Susie, *when* you write it. If you can get yourself into the mindset that it will happen, then it really will. It's called visualization, or some such thing." He winked at her. "I learned that watching Oprah."

In spite of herself, Mountjoy laughed. Then, she let out a long sigh.

"Oh Mitch, I was supposed to meet Elizabeth tomorrow. We were going to talk about her work at the center. I enjoy those meetings so much. She's a good person. I think she may have a calling to the ministry."

Best now felt a secret surge of guilt for distrusting Stowe. It was plain that not only Girardi but also Susan Mountjoy thought well of her. But despite this strong endorsement from the Reverend, doubts nagged him.

"You know her pretty well, then?"

"I know her very well."

Best nodded. "She'll turn up by tomorrow, safe and sound."

"I certainly hope so."

"Me, too. Poor Mike will be beside himself if not. He's a little sweet on her, you know."

Mountjoy shook her head. "No, I didn't know."

"I think she likes him, too."

"I doubt that. If Elizabeth was interested in someone, I think she would have told me."

The judge shrugged. "If you say so. But I saw them together today at the courthouse. They were touching each other more than necessary and sharing little jokes. Honestly, it was a little nauseating."

"Oh Mitch, where's your sense of romance?"

Best shook his head. "I've never been the romantic type."

"I'm not sure I am either. But we women are supposed to be romantics."

"How come you never married, Susie?"

Mountjoy opened her eyes wide at the question. "Why would you ask me that so bluntly?"

"Because I want to know the answer. Would you prefer that I beat around the bush?"

"Maybe," she nodded. "The art of subtlety is lost on you, isn't it?"

Best laughed. "Mostly."

"There's no simple answer to your question. It wasn't a direct decision on my part. I just never was with the right person at the right time, I suppose."

"It sounds like you might have been close . . ."

"I was close."

"And?"

"And someday I'll tell you more about that."

Although he was curious to know more, the judge decided not to press her further.

"Will you pray with me, Mitch?" she asked a few moments later.

Best looked at her uncomfortably. "I don't know what to do . . ."

"Just take my hand and bow your head," she ordered firmly.

Not sure he was being given much choice, the judge did as he was bidden. Mountjoy's fingers trembled as they locked with his, and as she began to speak aloud, her voice cracked. Soon, she found her rhythm.

"Oh good and gracious Lord, please be with your servant Elizabeth . . . shield her from danger and calm her fear. Bring her back to us safe and sound. Be also with Michael . . . guide the hands and minds of the doctors who are treating him. Strengthen his family and calm their fear so that they may show him the love and support he needs to recover. Be with Mitch as he continues to show his friends remarkable care and concern. Lord, you have certainly blessed me with the renewal of my friendship with this fine man. Help him as he begins in earnest to find you. Finally, Lord, strengthen me as I strive to do your good work. Be with me, envelope me in your abiding love . . . let me know that you are walking beside me. I am always your servant. Amen."

31

As Dr. Gupta entered the room, tablet computer in hand, Jake and Val stood anxiously by Girardi's bed to hear her report. She had everyone's full attention. After a few preliminary disclaimers, she got to the heart of the matter.

"I have some good news for you, Mr. Girardi," she began, tapping the computer screen. "Your tests looked clear. There are a few small things I want to watch, though. We'll keep you here under observation at least through the morning. Dr. Stein will take over the case for me. If he is comfortable with your progress, he will probably discharge you in the afternoon."

The relief in the room was palpable. Valerie had begun to cry the moment Dr. Gupta started speaking. As Jake comforted her, he brushed a tear from his own eye.

"That's great news, doctor," Girardi said. "Thank you."

"You're welcome. Now, it's time for you to rest. If I give you something for the pain, you'll go to sleep in short order."

After a short conference, it was agreed that Val and Jake would go home. Girardi insisted that Jake should go to school in the morning. It was a game day, and he could not play if he did not attend classes.

"I'm fine, son. You heard what the doctor said. I'd feel better knowing you were in class."

"Shouldn't I come back and pick you up? I can miss one game. It's no big deal."

Jake *never* wanted to miss a game. His willingness to do so was one more indication of his concern for his father.

"I'll take care of it," Val interjected. "You should go to school."

Girardi nodded his thanks.

"When you come back in the morning, could you please bring me a dark suit?"

"A suit? Why?" she repeated in surprise.

Girardi nodded. "Jack's funeral is in the afternoon. I think I'll be out of here in time to attend."

"Forget it—you're not well enough to attend that funeral. When the doctors discharge you, I'm bringing you to my house for some rest. Period."

"But I'm supposed to deliver a eulogy. I have no idea what I'm going to say, but if the doctors let me out, I want to try and make it."

Rather than argue with the patient, Val relented for the time being, and she and Jake headed home. Thanks to the promised painkillers, Girardi soon drifted off to sleep.

■ ■ ■

Judge Best was awakened in the morning by the ringing of his cell phone. He'd spent the past several hours sleeping on Dr. Gupta's conference room sofa, with his phone and Mountjoy's Book of Common Prayer resting near his head. After receiving Dr. Gupta's favorable update on Girardi's condition, Best had seen Susan Mountjoy to her car. He had been planning to leave himself, but changed his mind and headed back inside, reading himself to sleep by going through the psalms in Mountjoy's prayer book. He had wanted to see Girardi in the morning before Charley Strong's FBI agents descended and told him that Beth Stowe was missing. Best believed that Girardi should hear the news from him and not a stranger.

On the telephone line was Charley Strong. To Best's disappointment, Strong had little to report. Beth Stowe had not been located overnight.

There were apparently a few leads from the crime scene that the agents were following up on, but Strong was vague about them. Strong also told the judge that his agents were on their way to see Girardi. Best thanked him for the call and headed quickly toward Girardi's room, pondering how he might break the news.

Checking the rest of his messages as he walked, he was surprised to find a text from Michelle Bailey, whom he hadn't seen since the Dewey-Martinez for Congress fundraiser.

"The *Blanding* case has settled! I'm in Santa Ana this morning—do you have time for breakfast?" The message ended with a winking emoticon.

As the judge considered this unexpected invitation, he knew that Girardi would not approve of him seeing Bailey, even though the case that had originally brought her to his courtroom had apparently now settled. But still, he was tempted. Here was a gorgeous girl who was obviously attracted to him. Someone to share a little fun with no strings attached. His friend Girardi had done this with Mona—perhaps now it was the judge's turn. There were times when he longed to push back against the structure and constraints his life imposed on him. With his wife estranged and both of his kids in college, the judge craved a little fun.

He typed his reply quickly, lest he lose his nerve.

"Sounds great, but am busy today. Dinner tomorrow night?"

When Best arrived at Girardi's room, he found him sitting up in bed. Physically, he seemed much more himself, and the judge surmised that the rest had done him good. But as he stood beside the bed and looked his friend in the face, Best could see that Girardi was troubled. He was reading a yellow piece of paper covered with writing in a feminine hand. Best did not know it, but this was the eulogy outline that Stowe had written for Girardi at dinner the night before. On his bed table rested Agnes's blue rosary beads, which had been found in his pocket after the attack.

"Beth was with me when this happened, wasn't she?" Girardi asked, leaning forward and dispensing with anything like a greeting. There was a distrustful, angry look in his eye.

"Yes, she was. And now she's missing—but Charley Strong's people are looking for her. They will find her, Mike. I'm absolutely certain of it."

In saying this, Best wished to summon in Girardi every possible bit of optimism. Girardi meanwhile leaned back against the pillow in surprise.

"I thought you were going to say that she was here at the hospital. I was bracing myself for you to tell me that she was hurt."

Best shook his head in the negative and watched Girardi's wheels turning. He was quiet for some time. Then, he started.

"I'm getting out of here," Girardi declared, pushing away his covers. "I'm going to look for her."

"Forget it, Mike."

"I can't forget it. Charley Strong doesn't care about finding Beth. I need to do it myself."

As he spoke, Girardi swung his legs around, eased himself out of bed and moved past Best.

"Are you gonna run around town with your butt hanging out like that?" Best asked, pointing to the open back of Girardi's gown. He hoped his friend might laugh, but he did not.

"If I have to."

"Slow down, partner," Best rejoined, placing a firm grip on his friend's arm. "I think Val took your old clothes home—she's bringing fresh ones this morning."

"Fine, then I'm leaving the minute Val arrives. Can you call her for me and tell her to hurry up?"

"Sit back down, Mike. You've got to be patient. The doctors need to look you over to see if you're okay to leave. Besides, the FBI agents will be here any time now to take your statement. We were able to hold them off last night, but it's time you talked to them. If you have any ideas about where Beth might be, tell them. You won't do anybody any good running around pretending you're Superman."

"I can't just sit here knowing that she's out there somewhere, Mitch. I'm responsible for all this."

"They are professionals—they will find her. You need to get your rest."

"I got my rest—I'm fine."

"No, you're not fine. You're in the hospital."

Girardi ignored this, taking hold once more of the yellow piece of paper. "I remember now. Beth and I had dinner after the interview. She insisted on helping me outline a eulogy for Jack. After all we'd been through, she still wanted to help me."

Best nodded his understanding.

"Despite the miserable afternoon we had with Charley Strong, Beth and I had a pretty nice dinner together, considering the circumstances."

"I know you like her, Mike. She's a cute girl. But you need to stay focused and objective right now."

Girardi looked seriously up into Best's face. "I don't just like her, Mitch. My feelings are deeper than that. And she's more than a cute girl."

The judge could see that his friend was in earnest. "Okay, well, I'm happy for you Mike."

"Happy for me?" Girardi snapped. "I have no idea who has her or what they might do to her. Don't you see why I need to get out there? If it were someone you cared for, wouldn't you feel the same way?"

Best knew his friend had a point. "I probably would feel the same way—then you'd be the one talking sense, telling me to slow down and be careful." The judge paused and considered what Girardi was saying. "Do you have some idea where Beth might be?"

Girardi was quiet for some time—long enough for Best to think he was about to reveal something significant.

"No. But if I have a little time to think, maybe I can figure out something."

"Fine, but just do your thinking here in your nice cozy room for now. They'll probably spring you in a few more hours anyway."

Girardi looked helplessly at his friend. "This scares me, Mitch."

"Yeah partner, me, too."

Best's mind went to his conversation with Susan Mountjoy in the conference room. "Susie was here at the hospital last night. She showed me the BCP."

"The what?"

"You're a rookie," Best rejoined, sounding confident enough to teach a Sunday School class at St. Mark's. "The Book of Common Prayer. It contains all sorts of stuff—psalms, prayers, orders of service . . . things like that. Susie uses it each day to do morning and evening prayer. I guess she thinks it's important to have some sort of spiritual routine in your life. When this mess is over, I might give it a shot. I read through some of the psalms before falling asleep. They were pretty interesting. Good old King David had a lot of drama happening in his life."

Girardi looked at his friend in disbelief. "Are you serious, Mitch? I thought you had even less use for religion than I do."

The judge paused, trying to make sense of his own feelings on the subject. He knew that he could sometimes wax on about the evils of organized religion. This had long been something that separated him from his politically conservative friends and colleagues.

"I'm not going to pretend I've had some big conversion a-la Saint Augustine. But when I was with Susie last night we prayed together. Well, she prayed and I listened. But that prayer was very moving. I don't know how to describe it, but she managed to pray for you and Beth and me at the same time. It was seamless—connecting all of us. She also prayed for strength for herself. For a moment there it was as though she opened up, and I could see straight into her soul."

Girardi looked at the judge uncomprehendingly. "Straight into her soul?"

Best sensed his friend's skepticism and immediately backed off. "Forget it, Mike. I don't have the words to describe what I mean. It was just a feeling."

After some awkward silence, Girardi spoke up. "There's something I haven't mentioned to you that I found out the other day."

"What is it?"

"If I explain, you can't say 'I told you so.'"

Best leaned forward, happy to change the subject. "I'm intrigued. What is it?"

"Mona showed up at work on Monday."

"Mona Phillips?"

Girardi nodded.

"What is she up to these days?"

"She's a mom—of a six-month-old little boy. The father is Jack Tremont."

Best could barely believe his ears. *"No shit! Really?"*

Girardi nodded grimly. "He set her up in a place in Huntington Beach. Apparently Celeste doesn't know about it. Now that Jack is dead, I have no idea what will happen to them."

"Mona and *Jack*? When did they start up?"

"Around the time I took her to Jamaica." Fiddling with his blanket, trying to get comfortable, he slowly continued. "So, it turns out that Jack was responsible for *both* Mona and Beth leaving me. I feel like such a fool."

"Counselor Tremont was even more of a bastard than I gave him credit for. Stealing Mona behind your back that way—unbelievable." He paced around the room. "Why would she leave you for Jack? That's crazy— you're a stud and he was a fat old dude."

"She claims that Jack cared about her more than I did."

Best laughed heartily at this. "A real love story, huh?"

"I know it sounds weird, Mitch, but I almost believed what she said the other day. In a way, maybe Jack did care for her more than I did. They had a child together—that's a close bond. And Mona's crazy about her son; she said that being a parent has given her a purpose in life."

Best folded his arms and stared at Girardi. "Mike, you're still too trusting, especially where women are concerned. Even now, after all that's happened, you're buying into the crap she's feeding you. What's the matter with you? You need to wise up. You didn't give her any money, did you?"

Girardi ignored this last question.

"Maybe you're right, Mitch. But, you know, despite all that has happened, I don't want to become a person who can't trust anybody. What kind of example would that be for Jake? What kind of life would that be?"

Best sympathized with Girardi but had no easy answers. The two sat together for some time, making small talk until the arrival of the FBI agents. The judge went outside and called his assistant Simone, asking her to cancel his morning calendar at the court. There was no reply yet from

Michelle Bailey. He decided to go home for a little rest. He was planning to be in Irvine that afternoon for the funeral of Jack Tremont.

■ ■ ■

Elizabeth Stowe had been left alone all night in a tiny cabin that consisted of two bunk beds, a table that pulled down from the wall, and a small toilet and sink. Alone in the dark, she had experienced a range of emotions—terror, confusion, boredom, anger and small glimmers of hope. She longed for the familiarity and safety of her home at the Emmanuel Center. That, and the hope of seeing her loved ones, got her through the night.

In the morning, she was awakened by the click of the lock on the cabin door. A silent guard had opened it just long enough to toss in a newspaper and a bag containing two plain bagels and a packet of cream cheese. He had come and gone so quickly that she did not see or speak to him. She devoured the food immediately. At first, she was too upset to read the paper. It rested on the floor where it had landed, mocking her with its normalcy. Eventually, she managed to read some of the articles, and the activity brought her comfort. Never before had she so valued reports on the prior night's baseball games or previews of summer movies.

Taking a break from the paper some time later, Stowe rummaged around the cabin, and in the drawer below the bottom bunk found the floor plan of a yacht named *Checkmate*. According to the plans, the vessel was roughly 60 feet long and had been built in Massachusetts in the mid 1990s. Stowe suspected she was aboard *Checkmate*. Studying the plans, she located the stateroom, kitchen, pilot house and the bunkroom. This was where she believed herself to be. Out the small porthole above her, Stowe could hear the sounds of other boat engines and even some voices in the distance. She deduced from this that she was in a harbor. Given the distance she'd traveled from Santa Ana the night before in the SUV, she guessed this was either Newport or Dana Point.

As frightened as she was, she also understood that things could be worse. She was being fed and left alone. She assumed that Randall Spencer was seeing to her decent treatment. How in the world was Spence wrapped into all of this? She thought back to the days when he'd been a summer associate with the firm and she'd been his mentor. Stowe had always liked Spence, and it seemed almost unfathomable that he was now one of her captors, albeit so far a relatively benign one. If only she could talk to Spence, perhaps he might explain everything to her and even let her go. But she hadn't seen him since the night before. He had warned her to keep quiet, and although from time to time she felt the urge to start banging on the walls and shouting at the tiny porthole near the ceiling to get someone's attention outside on the docks, Stowe so far had done as Spencer ordered. All there was for her to do was wait.

32

When the minister called his name, Girardi was so lost in thought that he did not immediately stir from his pew. The choir had just finished an appropriately melancholy rendition of the twenty-third psalm, and Girardi was trying to make sense of all that had happened in the weeks since Jack Tremont's stroke. Everything in his mind was a jumble, and to make matters worse, his neck was killing him. He told himself that he just needed to get through this funeral, and then he would be free to go and find Beth Stowe, wherever she might be.

The judge elbowed him and whispered in his ear. "Mike, it's your turn up there."

Dazed, Girardi rose from his seat in the reserved section of pews at the front of the church. As he made his way slowly up to the pulpit in the large, light-filled sanctuary, he nodded to Cliff Conroy, who was pacing anxiously in a small alcove and wearing a Bluetooth earpiece. To Girardi, he looked like the event coordinator at a society wedding. Girardi passed Celeste Tremont and her family in the first pew. Celeste was wearing an enormous black straw hat that hid her face entirely from view. It appeared that she was sobbing into a handkerchief, and one of her sons was leaning over to comfort her.

When Girardi reached the pulpit, he stood facing the multitude. The gleaming white and gold casket was mercifully closed. A great spray of lilies was draped over the casket, and scores of elaborate flower arrange-ments were scattered about the sanctuary. As Conroy had predicted, sev-eral hundred mourners were in attendance, and it was standing room only. Many were strangers to Girardi, but there were plenty of familiar faces, too. Off to one side, the attorneys and staff from Marshall, Lufton occu-pied several pews together. Huey, Dewey and Louie sat with their spous-es. Hugh McDaniel was predictably stoic, while Jean Dewey-Martinez was elegant and alert as always. Louis Cox looked like a peevish child ready to throw a tantrum. Some things never change.

Nearby were three partners from the New York office who had made the trip to California. Even former Orange County associate Randall Spencer had come. Girardi had not seen the young man since their conversation at the hospital on the morning of Tremont's stroke. Spencer was sitting be-tween big Chas Cunningham and petite Tammy Thompson. Seeing these two, he wondered if they were on top of all their work at the office. He made a mental note that after the service, he should check in with them.

Girardi spotted Russell Yost in the crowd with some others from CEP. And to his surprise, he saw that Mona Phillips had come and was standing in the back holding Gunnar close to her.

In this surreal moment, Girardi was at a loss for how to begin his eu-logy, and he forgot all about the yellow sheet of notes in his pocket. He cleared his throat and surveyed the somber, expectant faces before him. *Say something, you dummy,* he urged himself.

"As I look at all of you gathered here this afternoon," he began, his voice shaky and lacking its usual confidence, "I realize that what I say here doesn't really matter all that much."

He heard someone cough in the back and saw several people up front squirm in their seats. Girardi became aware of an uncomfortable vibe in the large room. He had not yet established a connection with his audience, and he was completely winging it. What he was about to say was as much a mystery to him as it was to the rest of the crowd.

"The fact that so many of you took time from your busy lives to honor Jack's memory is a testament to the impact that he and Celeste have had upon each of us personally . . . and upon our community at large."

Looking around as he spoke, Girardi saw several people in the front pews nod their heads in agreement. He locked eyes with Judge Best for just a moment, and his friend gave him a nod for encouragement. These small positive signs helped Girardi to settle himself. He removed the now well-worn yellow sheet from his breast pocket, unfolded it and placed it before him deliberately. "Stay positive," Stowe had written in large letters across the top.

Laboring to push from his mind his concerns for Stowe, Girardi cleared his throat and then delivered the only laugh line he had planned in advance.

"Seeing so many attorneys in attendance today, I suspect a few ambulances will go unchased this afternoon on the streets of Orange County."

There were a few small sympathy laughs about the room, mostly from the non-attorneys. The joke had come to him in the hospital, and it had seemed funnier to him then, when he was still on a strong dose of painkillers. Now, given the reaction, he wasn't so sure.

"Like so many in our profession," he continued, "I went to law school because I didn't know what else to do with myself. I wasn't good enough at math to be an engineer . . . and I couldn't stand the sight of blood."

This was met by some knowing nods and a few more chuckles.

"But that was not the case with Jack Tremont. Jack was *born* to practice law. I'll never forget the first time I saw him in court—it was a revelation for me. This was back in the earliest days of Marshall, Lufton's Orange County practice. I was on a team at the District Attorney's office working a complex fraud case. We thought that we had this particular defendant nailed, but all of that changed when Jack flew in from the East Coast for a pre-trial hearing. What chance, we thought arrogantly, did a New York lawyer have in a Santa Ana courthouse against local prosecutors?"

Girardi paused for a moment to let the suspense build. "There were three of us from the District Attorney's office in the courtroom and just Jack on the other side, but Jack ate us for lunch. He was brilliant. He knew the facts of the case better than we did, he somehow seemed to know the law better than we did, and, most importantly, he clearly wanted to win more than we did. Before we even knew what hit us, a sure conviction became a mediocre plea bargain. I knew that in Jack I'd glimpsed the kind of practitioner I wanted to be—prepared, focused, and full of desire."

Now, in truth, for the sake of dramatic presentation, Girardi had enhanced a few of the facts of the story. There had likely been only two prosecutors in court, for there were rarely instances where public resources allowed three attorneys for one hearing. What's more, Tremont may have had an associate with him. But, what Girardi said was essentially the truth, and it went over very well with the audience, which at last seemed to be with him.

Girardi put one hand in his pocket as he scanned the list of anecdotes on Stowe's yellow sheet. Now, he was feeling comfortable up there.

"Jack liked chess metaphors," he continued, again seeing some nods in the crowd. "He was fond of saying that a lawyer always should think three moves ahead of his opponent, and that he should have a surprise or two up his sleeve, just in case."

Everyone in the first row nodded their agreement.

As Girardi said this, something clicked in his mind. *My God,* he thought to himself as he glanced over at the casket covered in lilies, *Jack is still three steps ahead of us.* Startled by the thought, he lost his place for a moment or two, but luckily, the audience did not seem to notice. Forcing himself to continue with his eulogy, Girardi's mind worked in the background and slowly began to unravel the mystery.

Girardi went on to share two more stories of Jack's legendary legal prowess. When he finished, Girardi left the pulpit and approached Celeste, who quietly thanked him for his "wonderful words." Both of Tremont's sons shook his hand heartily. The family, at least, seemed to be pleased with Girardi's remarks.

He then resumed his seat next to Judge Best as the bagpipes began to play a musical interlude.

"Well done, Mike," Best whispered. "You had me worried at first."

"Mitch, I need your keys."

Girardi was of course without a car, and the judge had driven him to the service.

"My what?"

"Your car keys," he said, laboring to keep his voice below the music. "I think I might know how to find Beth."

"Then tell that to the FBI—this place is crawling with agents, you know."

Girardi looked imploringly at the judge, who let out a long sigh and relinquished his keys. With the prize in hand, Girardi decided to play it cool, waiting for a few minutes before standing and heading in the direction of the men's room. If possible, he hoped to leave the service without anyone even noticing he'd gone.

Girardi spent a couple of minutes in the men's room and then quietly headed out toward the parking lot. He moved quickly, and did not notice anyone following him. Anyone, that is, aside from Judge Best.

"Go back inside, Mitch," Girardi ordered when the judge arrived at his side. "This might get dangerous."

"If it's dangerous, then shouldn't you let Charley's agents handle it?" the judge rejoined as Girardi opened the driver's seat door. "Besides, you're still doped up on those painkillers. I don't want you to smash into any of these European luxury sedans—especially not with *my* car. You'd better let me drive."

Best stepped forward authoritatively, and Girardi handed him the keys. In truth, Girardi was glad for the judge's company, for he had no idea what was to await them on their journey.

"Where are we headed?"

"The Plantation."

"The Plantation?" Best replied in dismay as he backed out of his spot. "Why? There's no one at Jack's house."

"I think there just might be someone pretty important there."

"Who?"

"Jack."

The judge slammed on the brakes. "Mike, are you feeling okay? You *do* know that you just delivered his eulogy, right?"

"I know it sounds crazy, but I think Jack may have staged all of this to make us think he was dead."

He gestured back at the church and continued. "And Cliff must be in on it. When we met the other night at the *Tavern*, Cliff's explanation of

Jack's death didn't ring true to me. But I couldn't put my finger on what the problem was."

"Why would Jack do something so crazy?"

"I'll tell you my theory if you keep driving, okay?"

The judge reluctantly nodded and continued toward the exit. "Should we take MacArthur Boulevard?"

Girardi nodded and resumed his analysis, which he was still piecing together as he spoke.

"I think it all comes down to money. On Tuesday, Cliff let slip that Jack and Celeste are having substantial money problems. One of the obvious issues involves Mona—Jack was spending a lot of money to support her and the baby. Mona told me that the bills haven't been paid lately. At the firm, Jack's business has been down for years, but that hasn't appeared to stop him from spending as much as ever. I didn't think much of it at the time, but at the hospital Celeste said something about selling the Plantation."

"Okay, Jack's in debt. I don't understand why this is significant."

"Russ Yost says he paid several hundred thousand dollars for the fraudulent audit response. That money was of course intended to pay the consultants, but I suspect that Jack kept the money for himself."

"He's not crazy—guys like that would want their money."

"He probably thought of it as a loan—as money he could keep for a while before passing it on to the consultants. Maybe he misjudged the timeline. He'd worked cases like this before—sometimes government audits can drag on forever. If I'm right, Russell is waiting on an audit response that he thinks he's paid for, and the consultants are withholding delivery because they want their money. If this is right, then Jack is getting squeezed from both sides. He probably doesn't have the money anymore. That pressure, plus the risk of getting caught engaging in something illegal like this, may have been enough to trigger this stroke. He might fear that he'll never be free of this mess. The only way out is for him to pretend to be dead."

It seemed for a few moments that Judge Best was at a rare loss for words. "Alright, Mikey. I'll drive you down there. But if nobody's home, then we're taking you straight to Val's for some rest. Got it?"

"Sure Mitch."

As they rode along, Girardi turned around every few minutes in an effort to see if anyone was following them. As far as he could tell, they were travelling alone. In reality, however, this was not the case. In the wake of the pair's departure, no less than three cars also left the church parking lot. Two of them, a sedan and an SUV, were headed in the same direction as Girardi and Best. The third vehicle, the yellow Prius of former Marshall, Lufton associate Randall Spencer, headed south toward Dana Point Harbor, where the yacht *Checkmate* was docked.

In less than a quarter hour, Best pulled onto Poppy Lane, not far from *Ye Olde Tavern* in Corona del Mar. Tremont's home was situated on a large lot toward the end of the small street.

"Mitch, look!" Girardi exclaimed, pointing to an alley running between the Plantation and the home next to it. "That's an ambulance. Did it come out of Jack's place? I think it did, but I'm not sure."

"Sorry, Mike, I'm not sure, either. Do you want me to park on the street?"

Girardi paused for a few moments and considered their options. "Even if he's alive, Jack is probably still really sick. He might need an ambulance to get around," he reasoned out loud. "Follow the ambulance."

At this, Judge Best let out an unexpected belly laugh as he made a U turn at the end of the block.

"How can you possibly be laughing?"

"Your lame joke from the eulogy—don't you remember? You said that some ambulances would go unchased because all of the lawyers in Orange County were at the funeral. And here we are now, a couple of lawyers, ditching the funeral to chase a real live ambulance."

"Don't get too close," Girardi ordered as they turned onto Pacific Coast Highway and headed south.

The ambulance moved slowly and did not activate its emergency lights or siren. Best settled into following a good distance back. The ambulance was big and easy to see, and so the judge did not need to follow too closely. Unbeknownst to the pair, the sedan from the church was still following them, forming the tail of a slow-moving little caravan.

"Where the heck are they going?" Best wondered aloud.

"There's a hospital in South Laguna, but it's old. I doubt Jack would go there."

"We don't know for sure that it's Jack, Mike."

"Who else would leave the Plantation in an ambulance? The whole family is in Irvine. If Jack wanted to get out of town undetected, this would be the perfect time to do it. Everyone he knows is at the funeral."

"But if he were leaving, wouldn't he be headed for the airport, which is in the other direction?"

"Not necessarily. Who knows what the plan is? Maybe he's headed for Mexico."

"Mexico? Well, we don't have enough gas to make it to Mexico."

"Let's just be patient and follow the ambulance."

"Okay, partner, if you say so. But when this wild goose chase is over, we're taking you home to get some sleep." He looked over at Girardi and shook his head. "I have no idea how you talk me into stuff like this."

■ ■ ■

Randall Spencer returned from the funeral and re-boarded *Checkmate*. He found the hired crew preparing for the vessel's imminent departure. When everything was in order, he headed downstairs and entered Elizabeth Stowe's cabin.

"Come into the other room with me," he motioned, showing her quickly out of the tiny cabin and into a more spacious stateroom.

Stowe looked at him incredulously as she did as he asked. She seemed startled and jumpy. The calm she'd managed to achieve earlier in the day had now left her.

"You doing okay?" he asked almost apologetically after he'd entered the stateroom behind her and closed the door.

"*Spence*," she cried, grabbing his arm, "I don't understand what's going on. *Please* explain it to me."

"Lizzy, I only have a couple of minutes to spend with you, and so you need to listen to me very carefully. We are set to depart in less than half an hour. If I can sneak you off the boat beforehand, I will."

"Oh yes, please . . ."

"Be quiet," he barked. "Look, the plan wasn't for you to be taken like that. It was a mistake. They were supposed to scare you, that's all."

"Who wanted to scare me?"

Ignoring her question, Spencer moved to a cabinet and removed an orange life vest. He handed it to Stowe.

"You need to put this on and keep it on. If I can't get you out before we take off, I may need to do it later."

"You mean when we're out at sea?"

"I don't know. For now you need to go back into your cabin and stay quiet. The others don't know that I'm trying to help you. If they find out, you'll be entirely on your own."

"When will you come?" she asked as she fumbled with the straps on the vest.

"I have no idea. You're going to have to be patient. Now come on, you'd better get back to the cabin where you belong."

"But I don't want to go back—that little room is driving me crazy."

"I know, but we don't have any choice."

He opened the door, took a careful look around, and ushered her back into the bunkroom.

"You just need to hang in there, Lizzy. I'm doing my best."

And with a click of the lock, Stowe was sadly returned to her captivity.

33

Best and Girardi continued to follow the slow-moving ambulance as it crawled south along Pacific Coast Highway in increasingly heavy afternoon traffic. They passed through Laguna Beach and Dana Point, glimpsing the Ritz-Carlton where they'd attended Jaime Dewey-Martinez's fundraiser. Their own pursuers, still undetected, also kept pace some distance back.

"It would serve us right if that stupid ambulance turned out to be empty," Best offered glumly.

"Do you think that rather than picking Jack up, they may have dropped someone off at the Plantation?" Girardi asked quickly, recognizing that his analysis of the situation had contained various leaps. He shrugged and pointed ahead toward the ambulance. "Never mind now. Let's stay the course."

When they were less than a mile from downtown Dana Point, the ambulance made an unexpected turn onto a small side street called Green Lantern.

"That's the way to *Cannon's*," Best said.

Girardi held his breath as he watched the ambulance move slowly along the side street and past the restaurant. Because the street eventually led to a dead end, he surmised that the ambulance must be nearing the end of its journey. It turned left onto the narrow, winding Cove Road leading down to the harbor. Once down at sea level, the ambulance passed the replica tall ships and crossed over to an island that ran the length of the harbor's breakwater. The ambulance moved to the tip of the island and backed into a parking spot at the Dana Point Yacht Club guest docks. Best eased his sedan into a public parking spot a few hundred feet away.

So far, it had been just another lazy spring afternoon in Dana Point Harbor. There were a few older couples and moms with baby strollers walking along the bay. There was a slight breeze, and the temperature was perfect. Everyone was relaxed in the harbor, and no one seemed to be in a hurry.

Girardi and Best watched as the two ambulance drivers headed to the back of the vehicle and swung open the doors. They wheeled out a stretcher and carefully guided it along the sidewalk to a gate leading out to the yacht club's guest slips.

"That's Jack!" Girardi exclaimed, leaning forward in his seat and pointing. "I was right. Do you see that?"

Best was not as certain as his friend that the form on the stretcher was indeed Jack Tremont. They were simply too far away to tell for certain. But it did appear to be a large old man with silver hair like Tremont's.

"It might be Jack," the judge allowed.

The stretcher was met at the gates by a tall, thin young man dressed in dark pants, a while polo shirt, and white cap. Girardi presumed that he was a crewman on one of the vessels docked nearby. The crewman opened the gate and the ambulance attendants proceeded to wheel the stretcher down the gangway and alongside a yacht. The patient was lifted aboard and carried inside, out of Best and Girardi's sight. The ambulance attendants then nonchalantly wheeled the empty stretcher back to the vehicle, stowed it in the back, and drove off.

"I'm going in there," Girardi declared.

"No, Mike. Just wait. We'll call Charley Strong. The agents will take care of this, whatever is going on in there."

Best grabbed his phone from the glove box and scanned the directory screen for Strong's number.

"There's no time. Look at the crewman running around the deck," Girardi pointed. "They're getting ready to take off."

302 PAMELA A. KELLEY

"But you have no idea what you'll find on that boat."

"I need to talk to Jack right away—maybe he knows where Beth is. You should stay here and call Charley. He'll want to know that Jack is still alive."

Not interested in further debate, Girardi hopped out of the car and walked with a measured pace toward the dock gate. He didn't want to draw too much attention to himself. When he arrived, he turned the gate's handle and found it locked. Frustrated, Girardi looked around, but at first did not see anyone. He tried the handle again and shook it this time, but still had no luck.

"What's the matter—you forget your key?" called a feminine voice from the deck of a small boat some distance away.

"Something like that," Girardi replied, smiling as his eyes fell upon two women, perhaps in their late thirties, wearing bikini tops and cut-off denim shorts. One was a brunette, the other blonde. The brunette's long hair was pulled back in a careless ponytail and she wore large sunglasses. Her body was lean and athletic and her skin was leathery, the product of a lifetime of surfing and sunbathing without proper sun protection. She and her friend were listening to the country music station on a small boom box. Two wet suits hung from the mast to dry.

"Do you want some help?" asked the brunette.

"That would be great," Girardi replied, laboring to turn on the charm enough to get himself inside the gate.

She slowly rose from her beach chair and took a long swig of her beer. Nothing about her suggested that she was in a hurry. As she drank, she managed to stand at just the perfect angle for Girardi to admire her figure.

Some time today, please, Girardi thought to himself impatiently and she rooted around for her flip-flops. At last, she located them behind the cooler and headed for the gate.

"You want a beer?" she asked as she opened the door and ushered him inside. "If we could get that tie off and a drink or two in you, you might just relax. You seem a little tense."

"Thanks," Girardi forced another smile. "I need to go see a friend of mine on that yacht over there. If you're still here when I'm done, I'll probably be ready for a beer."

"We'll be here," called the blonde from her chair, pushing back the cowboy hat from her brow and flashing him a smile. *Mitch should have come down here with me*, Girardi thought fleetingly as he moved past his rescuers. *These two would be right up his alley.*

Girardi waved his thanks to the ladies and headed toward the yacht. Taking a deep breath, he stepped boldly over the side and onto the aft deck. The uniformed crewman who had met the stretcher looked quizzically at him but did not say anything. The young man moved around Girardi as he unfastened the series of ropes that secured the boat to the dock. Girardi then heard the roar of an engine and a shout from the pilothouse inside. In what seemed to Girardi to be little more than an instant, the boat pulled away and headed up the channel, toward the mouth of the bay.

Not knowing what to do, Girardi remained where he was and strained for a glimpse of Judge Best or his car. From his present vantage point, he could not make out either one. Suddenly, Girardi had the sinking feeling of a man who was entirely on his own. Had the judge left already? If so, where had he gone? Perhaps to summon help? Or had something happened to him?

Summoning his courage and pushing these concerns from his mind, Girardi entered the yacht's main cabin and found Jack Tremont reclining alone on a sofa. His old mentor was indeed still alive, though he looked terrible. His face was ashen, his big body weak and unmoving.

"Mike," the old man rasped, "I certainly did not expect you to come see me off." He paused and chuckled. "By the way, thank you for the eulogy, I thought you did a fine job. I liked everything but that ambulance-chasing joke."

So, he was listening to the whole service, making fools of everyone there, Girardi thought in disgust. *No wonder Cliff looked so anxious.*

"Yep," Girardi offered with a cool nod, "if I could take one thing back, that ambulance joke would be it."

Tremont smiled triumphantly. "It's not often that a man gets to listen in on his own funeral. Cliff had it broadcast for me." He gestured to a pair of earphones that now rested around his neck. "I'm told that the church was packed. I guess everyone is headed now to UCI for the reception. I wish I could be a fly on the wall for that little party. Imagine those shameless fundraisers, capitalizing on my supposed death like that to try and shake money out of my friends. I'll bet there's a special circle of hell for fundraisers."

Right next to the circle for scumbag lawyers.

Tremont labored to reach a glass of water on the table behind him. Girardi stepped forward and handed him the glass. Even under the strain of these circumstances, he was determined to remain as calm as possible. Since the earliest days of their practice together, Tremont had emphasized that lawyers should never show weakness. He despised weakness. Girardi had eagerly absorbed his mentor's lessons, and now they would be put to the test.

"Where are my manners?" Tremont ventured. "Please sit down."

As Girardi took a chair not far from the sofa, he noticed a tall, well-built man in a black knit polo and dark slacks standing up in the pilot-house with the captain. There was a gun holstered on his belt. Girardi concluded immediately that the man was Tremont's bodyguard. *Oh, great,* Girardi thought. *He must be the muscle. Of course there has to be muscle.*

Looking out the window, Girardi saw the tall ships *Pilgrim* and *Spirit of Dana Point* disappearing in the distance behind. For a fleeting moment he recalled Jake's birthday cruises aboard the *Spirit*—what would happen to his son if any harm befell Girardi? Val and Stu would look after him, he reassured himself. And of course there was Jake's mother.

Girardi forced these troubling thoughts from his mind as the yacht moved quickly toward the open sea. *I hope Mitch went to get some help.*

"So," Tremont continued, "you found me out, Mike. I'm impressed, I really am. You've always been a sharp guy."

"I don't understand all of this, Jack."

Tremont shook his head sadly. "I've had a great run, but all of that is over now. I needed to disappear—to go off and live out whatever time I have left."

"Where will you go?"

"Pardon the phrase, Mike, but if I told you I'd have to kill you." Tremont gestured toward the bodyguard, but the threat did not ring true to Girardi. Would his law partner really kill him over what had transpired?

Girardi doubted it. Something in him believed that Tremont was bluffing. He might be an all-around bastard, but Tremont was not a killer.

Tremont leaned forward. "Would you like something to drink?"

"No thanks."

"You might as well be civil and have a drink with me. What could be the harm in that?"

"Alright," Girardi relented.

Tremont pointed to the small kitchen area behind him. Girardi went over to the refrigerator and grabbed a can of Pepsi.

"I can't believe you betrayed me that way with the U.S. Attorney," Tremont scolded as Girardi resumed his seat. "What were you thinking?"

Girardi took a sip of his drink and squinted at Tremont, laboring to conceal his incredulity at the accusation. He also wondered how Tremont had learned of his visit to Strong.

"I thought you were dead," he rejoined coldly.

"But to go to the authorities? Why drag my good name through the mud that way? That Lizzy put you up to it, didn't she? It's her fault that this whole thing unraveled."

Girardi once more fought not to react in anger and thus give himself away. Where were these accusations coming from? Why would Tremont feel the need to put him on the defensive now? Girardi wondered what possible use there could be in blaming him or Beth Stowe. Tremont was entirely responsible for the present circumstances.

"No one put me up to anything. I looked at the matter rationally and concluded that there was no other choice."

Tremont coughed into his handkerchief. "We *always* have choices, Mike."

Girardi considered this. "That may be so. You certainly chose to betray your partners by committing fraud against the government. We've busted our tails to build that practice, and you have destroyed all of it."

"You're the one who went to the authorities. Everything would have been fine at Marshall, Lufton if you'd just kept quiet."

Girardi leaned forward in his seat. Things were escalating. "Jack, you created this mess, and then you bailed out, leaving me to clean it up."

"Bailed out?" Tremont repeated, shifting his weight angrily. "I had a stroke that almost killed me. I didn't plan the damned stroke."

Girardi could summon no sympathy. "You should have told me the truth. Then I might have been able to help you find a way out of this mess. Going to the prosecutor was a last resort. I wanted to protect you, and to help you."

"That's very touching," Tremont rejoined sarcastically. "After all I've done for you, I expected you to be loyal."

In spite of himself, Girardi felt a tinge of guilt at this.

"And I expected you to be honest with me," Girardi rejoined, looking down to the floor and lowering his voice. "I suppose we both expected too much."

As he said this, something of Girardi's true disappointment came through, and his old mentor seemed to sense this. Despite the extreme circumstances they faced, this was very personal for both of them.

"Mona came to see me this week . . ."

There was a long sigh. "Oh yes, I know."

"You're very well-informed for a dead guy."

"Indeed, I am. So, what do you think of the idea of Mona and me?"

"Just a couple of crazy kids in love—I think it's great."

Tremont began to cough again, and Girardi could see that the old man's energy was running out. It took a great effort for him to speak, but he persevered. "Making love to Mona was unbelievable—I've never been with anyone like her. I'm sure you miss it."

Girardi again shook his head at Tremont, who seemed determined to use what little vigor he had left to hurt him.

"Things kind of ran their course for Mona and me, Jack. It's not a big deal—she's all yours."

Tremont looked at him in disbelief. "So, you're going to pretend that it doesn't bother you? I stole your girlfriend right out from under your nose. I *beat* you, Mike." Tremont's coughing continued until the man could barely speak. "I'm a better lawyer than you, a better husband . . . ," he paused to heave and then continued, "a better lover . . ."

"You're the man, Jack," Girardi cut him off. He was anxious to take some control of the conversation while Tremont still had some energy left. "Now, listen to me. You have to focus. I need you to tell me what you know about Beth Stowe. She has disappeared. Do you know where she is?"

"Is that all you care about?" Tremont whispered angrily. He shook his head and grunted. "She was always a pain in the ass."

"Where is she, Jack?"

Tremont opened his mouth, but all he could muster was a tiny, pathetic gasp.

"Tell me what you know," Girardi pressed.

"Let me rest," the old man begged, throwing his head back on the cushion and closing his eyes.

Almost bursting now with anger and frustration, Girardi looked around and saw that the bodyguard was still at his place with the captain. The guard kept an eye on Tremont and Girardi but did not come inside. The crewman on deck was putting cushions on the outdoor chairs, acting as though this was just another cruise. Girardi doubted that the crew knew what was really going on aboard *Checkmate*.

It was all so surreal. A part of him wanted to jump on Tremont and shake the information out of him, but with the bodyguard so close, he knew this would be futile. Not knowing was else to do, Girardi summoned his patience. Leaning back his chair, he decided to bide his time.

34

Judge Best frantically dialed his telephone as *Checkmate* motored past him on its way out to sea. He managed to raise Charley Strong on the third try.

"Charley, it's Mitch Best."

"Judge! Are you in Dana Point?"

Best paused in surprise. "How the hell do you know that?"

"It doesn't matter."

Charley Strong possessed a personality at least as formidable as the judge's and he immediately took control of the conversation. "I need you to drive over to the Harbor Patrol Station to meet my agent. Do you know where that is?"

The station was less than a half-mile from Best's present position near the yacht club, and the judge was familiar with the area.

"I know where it is."

"Okay, get going. You can tell me the story on the way."

The bewildered judge did as he was asked, making the short drive to the other end of the island and sharing his story as quickly as possible. He related Girardi's theory about Tremont faking his death and described their trip from the church out to the Plantation and then down to Dana Point.

"The ambulance attendants wheeled Jack Tremont onto a boat at the guest docks."

"Are you sure it was Tremont?"

Best hesitated. "Mike seemed sure—I couldn't tell for certain, but it sure could have been him. Mike went aboard and the damned thing took off like a shot. It's already left the harbor. I lost sight of it."

"Did you get the name?"

"*Checkmate.*"

"How big was it?"

Best had for years fantasized about buying a boat, and he knew something about them.

"It was good-sized. I'd say that it was a yacht, maybe 55 or 60 feet long."

"What color was it?"

"White—with blue detailing."

"What direction was it headed?"

"To the southeast—down the coast."

"That's a big help. Great job, your honor."

Best now pulled up at the Harbor Patrol Station. Exiting his car and scanning the docks, he spotted a red patrol boat with several officers talking excitedly on deck and preparing to take off. Four of them wore the trademark forest green of the Orange County Sheriffs, who regularly patrolled the county-run harbor. Three of the sheriffs were men and one was a woman. A fifth person wore an FBI windbreaker and cap.

"What do you want me to do now?" Best asked Strong.

"Do you see the patrol boat?"

"Yep."

"Great. Keep me on the line and head down there. I want to speak with Agent Bayless. Can you get her on the line for me?"

"Agent Bayless is a girl?" asked the intrigued judge.

"Yes, and she's the best."

Pumped up with the excitement of the moment, Best raced down the walkway in his dark suit and approached the crowd of officers.

"Hey everybody," he called, his face red and his breath a little short. "I'm Judge Mitch Best."

The group stopped its conversation and turned to Best in surprise.

"Which one of you is Agent Bayless?" he continued. "I've got Charley Strong on the line for her."

Out from the center of the crowd came a tall, fit young woman wearing an FBI cap, windbreaker, and sunglasses.

"That's me," the agent replied, making her way quickly to Best and extending her hand for the phone.

For a moment, the judge stared at Agent Bayless in disbelief. There was a glimmer of recognition, followed by a wave of doubt. *It can't be her,* he thought. He forgot all about the telephone as he stared at the impatient agent before him. To his astonishment, it was the woman he knew as Michelle Bailey.

"May I *please* have the phone, your honor?" she pressed.

"You're an FBI agent?" he asked incredulously, handing her the phone.

She nodded and walked away from him as she began to speak with Charley Strong. Standing beside the patrol boat, Best's mind flooded with recollections of his encounters with Michelle Bailey. From the moment he had first glimpsed her at counsel table in his courtroom, he had been captivated. She was smart, athletic, charming, and so beautiful. It had been all he could do to dismiss her case from his court, but thanks to Girardi's stern warning, he had done it. They'd sat together at the Dewey-Martinez fundraiser, and he often wondered where things might have led had Girardi not again interfered. Then there was that morning's text. Just one message had been enough to summon all of his desire for her. Now, standing and watching this vibrant young woman speaking excitedly on the phone, Mitch Best felt like a foolish old man.

After a few moments of conversation with Strong, Bayless shouted to the sheriffs. "Let's go."

One of the sheriffs unmoored the boat as the pilot prepared to depart. Best stood on the dock watching them, not sure what to do. No one had invited him along, but then again, no one had excluded him either. Agent Bayless still had his phone and showed no sign of giving it back. Best hesitated, then leapt aboard, hitting the deck with a loud thud just as the boat pulled away. The officers looked to one another in surprise, but no one said anything at first. Agent Bayless continued her conversation with Charley Strong as the boat headed straight for the breakwater.

"Here, your honor," said a young sheriff who looked to Best to be barely out of high school, "you'll need to wear a life vest."

"Thanks," he mumbled unhappily, removing his suit jacket and strapping on the vest.

"I'll take your coat downstairs and hang it up," she offered patiently, handing him a sheriff's department cap. "And you might want to wear this. That glare can really get to you."

"I appreciate that, deputy."

Best hesitated and then called after the young redhead. "What's your name?"

"I'm Deputy McShane, sir."

"Tell me, Deputy McShane. When did law enforcement get taken over by girls?"

McShane laughed good-naturedly and shrugged. "I couldn't say, your honor. I've only been out of the academy for three years."

When Agent Bayless had concluded her conversation with Strong, she handed Best the phone without making eye contact and headed for the front of the boat to consult with her sheriff colleagues.

"What the fuck, Charley?" Best bellowed into the phone as he paced around the aft deck. "You sent an FBI agent into my courtroom pretending to be a lawyer?"

Several of the sheriffs stared at the irate judge, but Best could not have cared less.

"She *is* a lawyer," Strong rejoined calmly.

"She *is* a lawyer?" Best stared at Bayless as the wind buffeted his red face. "Oh wow, that's just swell—good for her. I feel much better now."

"You have to understand, this wasn't my investigation. I didn't know a thing about it until recently. My colleagues and I can explain everything when the dust settles, okay? I *promise* that we can explain everything."

"Damn straight you're going to explain. Somebody's ass is going to be in a sling over this, Charley. I promise you that. Under *no* circumstances is it okay for you guys to send an agent sniffing around me undercover. Especially the way she went about it."

As he said this, his eyes followed Bayless.

"Hey Michelle," Best called, "you still want to have that meal you offered?"

Agent Bayless did her best to ignore the judge.

"You've got to calm down," Strong implored. "And don't hold this against Michelle, Mitch. She was just doing her job."

"Just doing her job? What the hell are you guys doing down there? Is this how you're spending government resources in the post-9/11 world? Shouldn't you be tracking ISIS cells or something? Really, Charley, you've got to be kidding!"

"Please calm down and I'll try and explain. The truth is, DOJ and the Defense Department have been investigating Jack Tremont and CEP for over a year now." He paused. "When Mike Girardi and Beth Stowe came to see me yesterday, they didn't tell me much that the government didn't already know about *Trinity Hills*."

The judge struggled to make sense of what he was hearing. "How is that possible?"

"The federal auditors discovered over a year ago that CEP's *Trinity Hills* response was falsified. Someone managed to hack into the Defense Department's database after the fact to make it appear that CEP had submitted certain information during contract negotiations. It was a very sophisticated job, and when Defense brought this to DOJ, they immediately launched a criminal investigation. Under pressure, Russell Yost testified in a sealed statement that the response had been prepared by Tremont and a group of consultants Yost had never met. DOJ wanted to shut down the consultants, and so they set up a sting operation."

"A sting? You're kidding."

"*Pope Electronics* is fake—there's no such case. It was fabricated to draw out Tremont and his consultants. From what I'm told, the plan seemed to be working. Tremont didn't appear to suspect a thing. He agreed to hire the Consultants to prepare an audit response with falsified evidence, just as he had in *Trinity Hills*. DOJ gave Russell Yost the money to pay the Consultants, and everything seemed to be on track. But then, Tremont got sick. The investigators considered calling off the whole thing, but too much had been invested, so they decided to move forward. That's when Yost began to pressure Mike Girardi. All along, their main objective was to find the Consultants. Girardi was essentially a pawn."

"A *pawn*? Do you know how miserable you've made him with this? Not to mention the danger you've put him in? You shouldn't drag innocent people in that way."

"Sometimes it's hard to tell who's innocent and who's guilty."

"It's not *that* hard," Best exhaled in frustration. "So, tell me, how did *I* get pulled into all this?"

"Mike Girardi was Tremont's closest business associate, and you're Girardi's best friend, Mitch. It's not hard to connect the dots."

"Connect the dots to what, for Christ's sake? Mike had no idea this was going on until Tremont had the stroke. And when I got wind of it, I told him to come to you. Don't you people need evidence before you go after folks this way? Who the hell signed the warrants? And you'd better not tell me it was one of those special FISA court panels, because this has nothing to do with terrorism."

"Actually, your honor, there is a possible connection to terrorism."

"What do you mean?"

"This is all strictly classified, but as it turns out, several ongoing terrorism investigations have involved some sophisticated forged evidence and computer hacking. The investigators believe that Tremont's consultants may be involved. These guys are good and they seem to have their hands in all kinds of things. That's all I can say."

None of this was enough to satisfy Best at the moment, and he was about to resume his tirade, but the static on the line was getting louder—his cell coverage was giving out.

"You need to stay focused," Strong continued. "Right now Agent Bayless and the others are going to find your friend. By the way, do you have any reason to think that Elizabeth Stowe might be aboard *Checkmate*?"

The patrol boat picked up speed as it left the protected waters of the channel and entered the open ocean. The craft began to rock along the waves, and Best could barely hear now.

"I don't have a clue where Beth Stowe is."

"Okay. Well, thank you very much for your help. You be careful out there."

"Yeah right, Charley. Have a nice day," he offered sarcastically.

"You too, your honor. We'll sit down for lunch sometime soon."

As the line went dead, Best in his fury turned and heaved his telephone into the ocean, following its long arc until it disappeared into a foamy swell. He paced around the deck and after some time Deputy McShane approached him with a soothing smile.

"Your honor, the sergeant asked me to take a statement from you."

If it had been anyone but McShane, Best would have let them have it with both barrels. But the young deputy reminded him of his daughter, and so he made an effort to restrain himself.

"I don't want to give any statement."

"I know you're upset, sir, but it might help us find your friends safely. *Please*, it won't take long—and it really would help us."

"I already told Charley Strong all I know."

"Yes, but it would help for you to tell me again."

Best looked at the young sheriff and shook his head in helpless defeat. "Alright, McShane. What do you want to know?"

35

Back aboard *Checkmate*, Girardi sat quietly in the main cabin and watched as Jack Tremont thrashed and murmured on the sofa, trying vainly to rest. The bodyguard remained at his post near the captain at the controls. Looking out the window, Girardi could see that they were travelling southeast, keeping the shoreline in sight. Wondering about their destination, he thought that his guess to Judge Best about Mexico might have been on-target.

Tremont's breathing continued to grow louder, and Girardi wondered how much longer the old man could keep going. Endeavoring to take a step back and evaluate his situation, Girardi suspected that if he remained calm and didn't cause any trouble, there was a chance that Tremont would take him along to Mexico and eventually let him go. Tremont also might well die on the journey, putting an end to everything. He knew that it was cold-hearted to hope for this, but thanks to his last conversation with the old man, Girardi was past caring about Tremont.

His greatest concern remained for Beth Stowe, and he continued to wonder if Tremont had been involved in her disappearance. His time aboard *Checkmate* had led to a number of revelations, but he still had no idea where Stowe was.

The ponderous quiet was broken by the sound of a speedboat outside. Loud footsteps came bounding up the stairs, and to Girardi's shock,

Randall Spencer appeared before him, still in the suit pants, white shirt and blue tie he'd worn at the funeral.

What the heck is Spence doing here? He quit three weeks ago because he couldn't stand Jack.

"Wow, Mike, it's a regular Marshall, Lufton reunion, isn't it?" the young man offered ironically as he hurried to the window.

"Weren't you at the funeral?"

Spencer nodded. "I was there, but when you and the judge left, I figured it was time for me to go, too. Nice job with the eulogy, by the way."

"Spence, what the hell is going on?" Girardi pressed.

"Now's not the time for an explanation—we've got trouble."

Spencer pointed out the window, and the two men watched as a small craft circled the yacht in an aggressive maneuver apparently intended to get *Checkmate* to stop. As the unmarked speedboat closed in, Girardi made out four men in dark clothing on the deck. At first, Girardi hoped that this might be the authorities, but his heart soon sank. The men appeared to be carrying automatic weapons, and from the way they were acting, Girardi doubted they were the police.

Over a loud bullhorn, a man with a southern accent ordered the yacht to stop. He fired a gunshot into the air to punctuate his command. The speaker was a man named Arthur Beckwith. Hearing the familiar, terrifying voice, Tremont raised himself from the sofa and swore.

"What's going on, Jack?" Girardi asked.

"They've found me."

"Who?"

The old man's shrunken features betrayed his fear. "The Consultants—they've come to kill me." Tremont then called to Spencer. "Tell that captain not to stop. And then go below and get the girl. Maybe we can use her for leverage."

"What girl, Jack?" Girardi interjected with alarm.

Tremont ignored the question.

"Is it Beth? Have you had her all along? God, what's the matter with you?"

Spencer dashed downstairs and soon returned with Stowe. She looked frightened and disheveled, but to Girardi's relief, she also appeared to be unharmed. An orange life vest covered the dark suit she'd worn the day before to see Charley Strong. Her hair was a tangled mess and her feet were bare. There was a large bruise on her right calf.

"Mike!" Stowe exclaimed with wide-eyed relief the moment she saw Girardi.

"Keep quiet, Lizzy," Spencer offered calmly but firmly. The young man motioned for Stowe to sit on the floor next to Girardi in the main cabin. Then he motioned to the bodyguard. "Neither of you move—Sam will be watching you."

As the speedboat continued to whiz around the yacht, growing closer with every pass, Tremont conferred with Spencer and Sam in a huddle around the sofa. Girardi meanwhile tried to reassure Stowe. He smiled and nodded at her when he thought the others weren't looking, and was pleased when at last he coaxed a cautious smile from her. He longed to put his arm around her—to kiss and comfort her. She was so close now. But all he could do was sit there. It killed him to see her looking so frightened, and he silently cursed his own powerlessness.

"Are you okay?" he ventured at last, when he thought the others weren't watching.

She nodded. "You?"

He also nodded but kept his eyes on Sam. "Just hang in there."

"I can't believe Jack's alive."

"He fooled everybody."

"Who is it outside?"

"The Consultants."

"What do they want?"

Girardi hesitated. "I think they want their money—Jack didn't pay them. You need to keep quiet and be attentive, okay?"

"Okay."

"Everything is going to be fine."

Just as he spoke, someone from the speedboat fired a second volley of warning shots, this time over the yacht's aft deck. Girardi threw his body over Stowe's to shield her while the others dove for cover.

"Tell the captain to keep going," Tremont ordered with all the energy he could muster. As he spoke, his body shuddered.

Spencer ran up to the pilothouse and tried to convince the frightened captain not to stop, but it was no use this time. He had already begun to power down the engine. When *Checkmate* came to a stop, the men from the speedboat tied their craft alongside the yacht. Four men dressed in military-style protective gear and carrying automatic weapons rushed aboard and quickly took charge. Each wore a dark mask that covered everything but his eyes and mouth. They were a fearsome bunch, and no one, not even Tremont's bodyguard, dared challenge them. Everyone's hands were quickly bound.

Stowe let out a cry as one of the men lifted her roughly to her feet. Arthur Beckwith approached her.

"What's your name, ma'am?" he asked in the southern drawl that under other circumstances might have been charming.

The frightened Stowe looked to Girardi, who nodded that she should answer.

"Elizabeth Stowe."

"Is that so? Well, Jack has more friends here than I expected. I know Mr. Girardi already. Tell me who the rest of these men are."

Girardi did not recognize Beckwith's voice and wondered how this stranger knew him.

"The only one I know is Spence," she replied softly, pointing apologetically at the young man.

Beckwith turned from Stowe to Tremont.

"Who are the others, Jack? And don't screw with me."

Tremont struggled to sit up straighter on the sofa. "God, Beckwith, why are you doing all this? It's way too much. They're just crewmen— they don't know what's going on. And Sam provides security for me."

Beckwith pointed his weapon at Sam and laughed heartily. "Security? A lot of good he'll do you." Then he called to his men and gestured toward Sam and the two crewmen. "Take those three downstairs and lock them up."

He turned to Tremont. "Where's your money, Jack?"

"What makes you think I have any left?"

The man pointed his weapon at Stowe. "Tell me or I'll shoot her."

Stowe let out another frightened cry, and it was all Girardi could do to resist charging Beckwith. But such a move would have been suicidal, and so he kept his place.

"Tell him, Jack," Girardi urged.

Tremont pointed to a drawer below the sofa.

"Down there," he mumbled.

"The key?"

"It's in my pocket."

At Beckwith's signal, one of the men reached into Tremont's pocket and roughly pulled out the key. Then he emptied the drawer's contents and gave them to Beckwith.

"How much is here?"

"Close to a hundred thousand."

"It's a start, but you owe us a lot more than that. I think you're holding out, Jack. Where's the rest?"

"That's it, I swear."

Beckwith ordered two of his men to search the yacht and then he approached Randall Spencer. Girardi was relieved to see him move away from Stowe. Beckwith shoved Spencer to the ground and then bent down over him.

"Where's the rest of Jack's money?"

"I don't know anything about his money."

"I don't believe you—where is it?" Beckwith pressed, ramming the butt of his weapon into the young man's chest.

Spencer gasped. "I swear I don't know . . ."

"Beckwith, god, *stop*," Tremont urged through a heaving cough. "You can search this boat from stem to stern and you won't find a thing—that's it. That's all the money I have in the world. Take it and *please* leave me to die."

"Give me a break, Jack. You already tried that once. You'll probably live longer than the rest of us."

Looking at Tremont, Girardi doubted very much that this was the case, but he could understand his captor's skepticism. Beckwith began to pace around the room, pausing before each of his captives and staring menacingly into their faces. When he reached Girardi, he began to speak.

"Mr. Girardi, I admire you for figuring out that Jack here was pulling a fast one on all of us. If it weren't for you, we wouldn't have known until too late."

Glad I could help, Girardi thought as he silently held the man's gaze.

"Do *you* know if Jack has any money aboard?"

Girardi shook his head slowly in the negative and braced himself to be beaten like Spencer. But Beckwith merely stared at him through the slits in his black mask. It occurred fleetingly to Girardi that this clothing made him look like a ninja from one of Jake's video games.

"I don't understand something," Beckwith continued. "Why did you even come aboard to begin with? Why not just let your old partner go?"

Girardi considered his response for a few moments. "Because Jack betrayed me—I wanted some answers from him."

In saying this, Girardi hoped not to reveal that he had any special attachment to Stowe. He feared that a man like Beckwith would use such knowledge against them.

"Did you get your answers?"

Girardi shook his head. "Not really."

"You're Jack's partner. What happened to our money?" Beckwith asked Girardi. "The CEP people paid him from what I understand."

"I have no idea—I had nothing to do with *Pope Electronics*."

Again, Girardi braced himself for an angry response, but it did not come. As unlikely as it seemed, he sensed that Beckwith wanted more than just the money he thought he was owed. Like Girardi, he wanted answers from Jack Tremont.

Beckwith looked back and forth between Tremont and Girardi. "We held up our end of the bargain—all we wanted was our money. It didn't have to come to this. Don't you have anything to say for yourself, Jack?"

"I've said all that I have to say—go ahead and kill me."

"Not until you've given me every dime you have stashed on this boat—do you understand me?"

Tremont heaved a terrible cough. "There is no more."

Beckwith rushed at Jack and raised his rifle as if to strike the old man, but then he stopped.

"Why don't you hit me again?" Tremont offered defiantly, pointing to the bandage on his temple. "I think *you* caused my stroke by hitting me in the head that night in the car."

Everyone in the room looked to Beckwith in surprise. Girardi's wheels began turning. Back in the hospital, he had observed the gash on Tremont's head and assumed it had come from a fall during the stroke. But now he claimed that Beckwith had attacked him, Girardi wondered if there was anything to it.

Moving away from Tremont in anger, Beckwith smashed a flower vase on the kitchen sink board with his weapon.

"Lou, have you found anything yet?" he called to one of his men.

"Not yet."

Beckwith then left one of his men in the main cabin and headed over to the speedboat, where he carefully secured Tremont's money. As Girardi watched Beckwith through the window, he thought he heard a helicopter in the distance.

Beckwith heard it too, and following the sound, he rushed to the aft deck and saw a large Coast Guard chopper approaching from the north. He rushed back onto the yacht and called to the men who'd gone below to search the cabins.

"We've got to get out of here, now," he exclaimed. "Grab them."

The three guards hustled Girardi, Stowe, and Spencer over to the speedboat and pushed them aboard. Beckwith himself tried to lift Tremont but he needed the help of two others to carry the big man over. Then they untied the speedboat from *Checkmate*, fired up their engine and took off.

Girardi watched the Coast Guard chopper bank and begin circling overhead as the red Harbor Patrol boat approached at full speed. As Beckwith's men shouted and scrambled to organize themselves, two of them carried Tremont to the small compartment below. This left only Beckwith and one other up on the deck. As Girardi considered the life vest Stowe was wearing, a plan formed quickly in his mind.

With Beckwith preoccupied by the chopper above, Girardi made his move. Doing his best to grab Stowe and to shield her from the guard with his body at the same time, Girardi shouted and tried to pull her up and over the low railing. With his hands bound, it was not easy.

"Jump, Beth, jump!"

"I can't."

"Do it! The patrol boat will pick you up."

She stumbled slightly and banged her already-bruised leg hard against the side of the boat. Then, somehow she managed, with Girardi's help, to get herself up and over the side. The move took everyone by surprise. Beckwith arrived just seconds too late, and took his anger out on Girardi by striking him on the back and knocking him to the deck. But for the moment, Girardi did not care, for he believed that now Beth Stowe would be safe.

Stowe splashed hard into the ocean and immediately took in a mouthful of saltwater. She was tossed around in the speedboat's wake for some time. When the water settled, she began to wave her arms in the direction of the patrol boat that had just whizzed past.

"*Holy cow*," exclaimed Sergeant John Pedrosa, commander of the patrol boat, who had done two tours of duty in Afghanistan with the National Guard. "We've got someone overboard. It looks like a girl."

Bayless looked at him sideways at his use of the term girl. "Let's go grab her."

"Roger that."

Pedrosa signaled to his pilot, who quickly brought the patrol boat around and headed straight for the spot where Stowe was bobbing on the ocean surface. Pedrosa was about to send one of his men into the water, but Agent Bayless waved him off.

"I've got this." She threw off her jacket, sunglasses and hat. In her black tank top and nylon workout pants, she was quite a sight as she grabbed a buoy and dove into the water. When she reached Stowe's side, Bayless tried to reassure her. "Don't worry, you're safe now, Ms. Stowe. Everything is going to be okay. Hold on to the buoy and come with me."

Bayless guided Stowe over to the harbor patrol boat, and Judge Best and Pedrosa carefully lifted Stowe over the side. Then, they pulled the agent aboard. For a few moments, Best stood face to face with Bayless as he held her arm long enough to make sure she had a solid footing on the deck. He stared into her face and opened his mouth as if to speak. But then he shook his head sadly and turned away.

Rallying himself, he brightened as he stepped toward Elizabeth Stowe. "Beth, it's great to see you in one piece . . ."

To the judge's surprise, the distraught Stowe extended her arms and moved to embrace him. She was soaking wet, and so, soon, was Best, but he did not care. There was little else for Best to do aboard the patrol boat, and he turned his attention to looking after Stowe. He knew that this was what Girardi would want him to do. The judge led her to a bench at the rear of the boat and sat down next to her.

"Oh, Mitch," she said, pointing toward the speedboat. "Mike's still over there. He threw me over the side. Did you see it?"

"I did."

"I wish he would have jumped, too."

The judge attempted humor. "That suit cost him a fortune—he probably didn't want to ruin it in the saltwater. I thought you landed in the water pretty gracefully. Too bad we don't have that on tape—we could post it on YouTube."

Stowe had no answer for this.

"Tell me, Beth, is Mike doing okay over there so far?"

"I think so."

The patrol boat made a sweeping U-turn and resumed the pursuit. Sergeant Pedrosa soon approached Stowe and offered her a blanket. The judge helped to wrap it around her. Then, Pedrosa knelt down on one knee so that he'd be at her eye level.

"Ms. Stowe, I'm Sergeant Pedrosa with the Orange County Sheriff's Department. You can call me John."

"Hi, John."

"I need to go over some things with you."

Before getting to the tough questions, Pedrosa wanted to establish a rapport with Stowe and to see how coherent she was.

"Do you know where you are?"

She nodded.

"Tell me."

"I'm on a patrol boat with Judge Best. I was taken yesterday from the courthouse parking structure."

"And where have you been since you were taken?"

"Locked in a bunkroom aboard *Checkmate*."

"Are you hurt?"

"Just my leg . . ."

Pedrosa looked carefully at her lower calf, which was bleeding some. "How did this happen?"

"I banged it last night, and then a second time on the side of the speedboat when Mike tossed me over. My ankle is starting to hurt now, too."

"I'll get McShane to bandage it for you. She has medic's training."

"Thank you."

"Now, I need to ask you about the situation on those two boats, okay?"

She nodded.

"*McShane*," he barked, "can you get over here and take some notes?"

The young deputy came immediately with her pad and pen. Agent Bayless interrupted her conversation with the Coast Guard chopper's pilot and came over, standing directly behind McShane to listen in.

"As far as you can tell, Ms. Stowe, how many people were on board *Checkmate* when it left the harbor?"

She counted them off with her fingers. "Jack Tremont, Mike Girardi, Randall Spencer, a bodyguard and the two crewmen."

"The crewmen?"

"I believe it was just the two—the older was apparently the captain and the younger one also wore a uniform. I'm not sure what his job was. He looked as frightened as me, poor fellow."

"Tell me what happened when the speedboat arrived."

Stowe did her best to describe the chaotic scene aboard the yacht when the Beckwith and his men came aboard.

"Were all four of the men carrying weapons?"

Stowe nodded.

"What kind?"

Stowe shrugged helplessly. "I don't know anything about guns. They were big."

"Were they automatic weapons?"

"Probably."

"Was anybody shot or injured?"

"No one was shot, but they knocked Randall Spencer down and roughed him up. He seemed to be in a lot of pain."

"Did you get a good look at the men?"

"Not at all—they wore masks and did not take them off."

"Can you think of anything that would identify any of them?"

Stowe thought about this. "Jack called the leader Beckwith—he and Jack seemed to know one another. And Beckwith called one of the men Lou, I think. Those are the only names I remember hearing."

"Did you say Beckwith?" Bayless interjected with great interest as Stowe nodded. "Is Beckwith a first or last name?"

"I don't know. He spoke with a southern accent."

"Do you know anything about Beckwith?"

Stowe again combed her memory. "Mike told me on the sly that the men were consultants that Jack worked with to defraud the government."

"Did you learn anything else?"

"Beckwith spoke mostly about money—and his men were searching the boat to find it. Beckwith said that he'd done his work and that he simply wanted the money he was owed."

"I've got to call Charley Strong right away," Bayless declared, leaving Pedrosa to wrap up the interview.

"You've been a big help," the sergeant said soothingly. "I'm sure we'll have questions for you later, but for now let McShane take you below."

"Will you come with me, Mitch?"

Best smiled at this. "Sure, Beth, I'll be right there."

36

Girardi, Tremont, and Spencer were holed up in a tight compartment below the speedboat's deck. They were continually tossed about the claustrophobic space as the speedboat skimmed the waves outside. Their wrists were still bound, and for the most part they were left alone by Beckwith and his men, who were fully occupied above trying to elude the helicopter and vessels now pursuing them.

Although his own back and neck were killing him, Girardi focused his energy on Spencer and Tremont. The young man was in terrible pain from Beckwith's blow, and he was convinced that several ribs were broken. Tremont, meanwhile, came in and out of consciousness. Girardi tried to keep the old man going and even convinced one of the guards to let Tremont have some water.

Girardi and Spencer conferred with one another over their situation, but neither could think of a concrete plan of escape.

"These guys are insane," the young man complained.

"We're just going to have to sit tight for now." Girardi let out a frustrated sigh, struggling to make sense of Spencer's motives. "How did you get involved in all this, anyway, Spence? You quit the firm that morning in the hospital."

"Cliff called me a week ago, offering a lot of money if I'd help Jack. I thought they wanted me to do legal work, but they mainly wanted help getting him out of the country. Janet freaked out when I quit, and I knew it wouldn't be easy in this economy to find another job. I thought I could make some extra cash." He exhaled loudly in pain. "My ribs are killing me."

Girardi felt Tremont's shaky hand clutching his arm.

"Mike," he wheezed, "I need to talk to you—I'm dying."

"You should save your breath, Jack. We need to rest up in case there's a chance to get out of here. We might have to act quickly."

The old man tightened his grip. "I don't have much time left—you need to listen to me. I want the baby to be recognized as an heir to my estate."

Girardi looked over at Spencer, who did not appear to know what Tremont was talking about.

"You mean Gunnar—Mona's boy?"

Tremont exhaled loudly. "Yes."

"Did you make any formal provision for him in your will?"

"How could I? Celeste would have found me out. I had no idea this would happen to me."

Girardi knew this was no time for an ethics lecture, though he was itching to deliver one.

"What are you talking about?" Spencer interjected.

"Jack's a baby daddy."

"What?"

Girardi turned to Tremont. "If you haven't made any provision for the baby, there's nothing we can do about it now. You just have to hope we make it out of here."

"That's not true—I can still change my will. You two will be my witnesses."

"It's too late."

"It might not be too late," Spencer interjected. "Do we have any paper? We could do a written codicil. With two attorneys as witnesses, it might stick, even under these circumstances."

The young man crawled around the space looking for something to write on. He found a pen but no paper. Girardi refused to help him at first, thinking that the two of them had lost their minds. They ought to be focused on trying to escape rather than eleventh-hour estate planning. But Spencer seemed determined to help Tremont. Despite his pain, he searched the entire space, then returned to his spot exhausted, having failed to locate any paper.

"Do you have anything to write on, Mike?"

Girardi struggled to pat his pockets and felt a single folded sheet. It was Beth Stowe's outline of Tremont's eulogy. *That's appropriate.*

Spencer then huddled with Tremont and patiently discussed the old man's intentions with him. They talked about Jack's other heirs and how his will and trusts had been structured. To Girardi's surprise, Spencer even made an effort to determine if Tremont really was of sound enough mind to make these proposed changes.

He's got the makings of a great lawyer, Girardi thought to himself. *Why would Spence risk ruining his career for some quick money? And to help Jack, no less? He hates Jack.*

Spencer tried to get Girardi's input on the will amendment, but to no avail.

"You draw it up and I'll witness it," was all Girardi would allow.

At last, Spencer did his best to memorialize the old man's intentions on the back of the yellow sheet. It wasn't easy with his hands bound, but he managed to scribble out some basic provisions. Tremont signed and dated the document with his shaky hand. When it was his turn, Girardi quickly skimmed the text and added his initials. He wanted nothing to do with it, but did not know how to refuse.

Spencer then added his own signature and folded the paper. "Who should hold it?"

Girardi shrugged indifferently. "I'm not liking anybody's chances of getting off this boat alive, so I can't say."

"I want you to take it, Mike," Tremont said, "and give it to Cliff. He'll know what to do."

"Cliff's in jail by now," Girardi rejoined coldly. "I'd have to give it to Celeste or one your kids."

Girardi stopped himself from saying that Celeste might well be in jail at the moment, too, depending upon her role in Tremont's faked death and upon how quickly the authorities were acting back on land.

Tremont exhaled sadly. "Do whatever you think best."

A few minutes later, the hatch opened up and one of Beckwith's men came rushing in. He grabbed Spencer roughly and pulled him up to the deck. The young man squirmed and shouted his protest, but to no avail. Girardi assumed that they would soon return for him, but then the hatch slammed shut—a short reprieve from the inevitable.

Tremont placed his shaking hand on top of Girardi's. "I always loved Celeste—she was the love of my life. Please tell her I said so."

"Should that be before or after I tell her about Mona?"

"Don't be cruel to me now, just give Celeste my love."

"I don't want to hear this. Like I said before, you should save your energy. If I make it out of here, I'll pass that paper on, but no personal messages."

"I'm sorry for all I put you through. You've been like a son to me, Mike. Neither of my sons went into the law, and I haven't been close with them since they were boys. *You* understood me—that was plain from your words at the service today. I know I should have said so earlier, but that eulogy meant a lot to me. I *do* have a heart, you know."

Girardi doubted this last point.

"*Please*, Mike, I'd like us to part as friends."

It was a surreal moment, and Girardi maintained a stone-faced silence. Although Tremont likely *was* dying this time, Girardi could summon no sympathy, and the mode of their parting meant nothing to him.

Like the flip of a switch, Tremont's demeanor changed and he leaned angrily into Girardi's face. "Why won't you accept my apology?"

Girardi scooted away from him. "It's too late for apologies, Jack. If you're really dying, then you might want to try praying." He looked upward. "Maybe that's an audience willing to show you some mercy."

"No Mike," the old man replied, his voice now clear. "I have no illusions that there's anything beyond this world. I've had a great run, but it's over for me now. Prayer is for people who are too weak to cope with the finite nature of this life."

Girardi considered this grim assessment and conceded that for much of his adult life he'd believed something similar. But now, the old man's harsh words were enough to make him reconsider. Had Jack lived his life this way because he assumed there was no higher power or Judgment in the end? Despite his skepticism, there was something in Girardi that believed in an ultimate reckoning of things.

To comfort himself, Girardi pushed these thoughts from his mind and reflected instead on his boyhood summers out in his grandparents' backyard. He and his grandfather had worked in the garden and listened to ballgames on the radio by the hour. And he'd been fortunate enough to share that love of the game with his own son.

As Girardi thought about Jake's future, Tremont was overcome with a fit of coughing.

"You want more of your water?"

"No; I think I need to rest now."

■ ■ ■

Charley Strong and his colleagues wasted no time in assembling resources to pursue and capture Beckwith and his men. Because of the fugitives' possible ties to terrorism, the mission was given the highest level of priority.

The harbor patrol boat was soon sent back to Dana Point with Stowe and Best aboard. Several Coast Guard vessels were deployed, and Sergeant Pedrosa and Agent Bayless were brought aboard one of them to remain part of the mission, though they were now little more than observers. In a briefing, they learned that as luck would have it, a team of Navy sailors and Marines was in the waters off of Camp Pendleton conducting anti-piracy training exercises. The unit was part of a multi-national task force being assembled to fight piracy in international waters.

Lieutenant Colonel Joseph Wakefield, commander of the anti-piracy unit, was placed in charge of the Beckwith mission. The forty-year-old

Marine had recently returned from a tour of duty that included multiple encounters with Somali pirates in the Gulf of Aden. It was decided that the Coast Guard would share jurisdiction with the Navy and Marine Corps over this quickly-evolving mission.

After leading their pursuers on a zig-zag course for nearly two hours, Beckwith's boat unexpectedly powered down around dusk. Although Wakefield did not know the reason, the truth was that the speedboat, which had been commandeered on the fly in Dana Point, had simply run out of fuel.

It took some time, but Colonel Wakefield eventually raised Beckwith on the radio. Beckwith made several immediate demands, but Wakefield would have nothing of it. Wakefield introduced himself and explained that it was the government's policy not to negotiate with terrorists and that he'd been informed by his superiors that no exception would be made in this case. Wakefield's sketchy initial briefing on those aboard the speedboat had suggested that even Beckwith's so-called "hostages" were criminals themselves fleeing from the law. The subtlety of Girardi's innocence had been lost in the rush of time.

"If you surrender now and don't harm anyone, you won't be hurt. But if you test us, you'll be sorry."

The irate Beckwith pointed his gun at Spencer's chest.

"I'll blow this kid away, colonel, you just watch me."

"That would be a mistake. Murder under these circumstances will certainly make you eligible for the federal death penalty. It's my understanding that no one has been seriously injured today. Am I right about that?"

"I'm not telling you anything."

The sky was now dark, and one of the Coast Guard vessels trained a bright light onto the speedboat's deck. Unhappy with how the conversation was progressing, the colonel tried another tack. He ordered his men to dim the lights and set about trying to establish a rapport with Beckwith.

"I was in Somalia recently. Do you know that most of those Somali pirates are teenagers? It's unbelievable. They're scared kids in way over their heads."

"Why would I possibly care about that?"

"Because I want you know that I'm aware that not every situation is what it appears to be on the surface."

"You just got through calling me a *terrorist* a few minutes ago."

"I'm not a lawyer," Wakefield rejoined, "I'm just a Marine. It's not my job to put labels on people. I trust our justice system to sort out the truth. Maybe you should trust it, too."

Beckwith laughed heartily at this. "Are you aware of the line of work I'm in?"

"Vaguely."

"I doubt Lady Justice will think much of me," Beckwith continued.

"You're surrounded and you have no means of escape. Surrender is your only option."

"I could go out in a blaze of glory and take some people with me—maybe a few of your Marines. Some of them are probably scared teenagers, too."

"I don't think you want to do that."

"Why not?"

"Because you're an intelligent man, Beckwith, and you know how to assess the situation and make your calculation."

"Is that what you're doing?"

"Maybe it's what we're both doing, but I'm playing with a lot more cards than you are."

The conversation continued on in this vein for some time until the colonel handed the radio over to a Coast Guard Lieutenant who also had experience in hostage negotiations. They thought that perhaps a change of personnel might do some good.

While the colonel had been on the radio, his men were below deck preparing a briefing on a mission plan to take control of the speedboat. Just a few hours earlier, the men had been conducting drills involving the boarding of hostile vessels. Now, they were planning to do the real thing.

Using PowerPoint, Marine Corps Major Ahmed Khani laid out a rescue and recovery plan that involved two four-man teams, Alpha Group and Beta Group, approaching the craft on separated inflatable boats under the cover of darkness. Colonel Wakefield and his Coast Guard counterparts discussed the plan and made a few alterations. When the briefing was finished, they sent the plan up the chain of command for approval by superiors back on land and began to wait.

Meanwhile, in order to keep Beckwith guessing, Wakefield adjusted the lights from the Coast Guard ship every few minutes. At the same time, he kept an open line of communication with Beckwith.

"I want to speak with your hostages," Wakefield informed Beckwith some time later, "bring them to the radio."

"Why?"

"So that I know they're unharmed."

By now, Wakefield had learned that at least one of the hostages was likely innocent and that another was an ailing old man. He was eager for a firmer understanding of the state of things on the speedboat.

"What's in it for me?" Beckwith rejoined, motioning for his men to go below and get Girardi and Tremont.

"What do you want?"

"I want a boat to take me out of here—no questions asked. I just drive off into the night."

Although Wakefield would never agree to such a thing, he saw an opportunity to use the demand to his advantage.

"And if I did this for you, you would release the others unharmed?"

"Yes."

Wakefield looked at his colleagues in surprise. "Let me see what I can do. Now, I want to speak with the others."

"We're getting them."

Beckwith's men opened the hatch meanwhile and called for Girardi and Tremont to come up.

"Get up here, *now*," one of them barked. "Both of you."

"He's dead," Girardi said simply.

"Dead?"

"Check his pulse—he died about fifteen minutes ago."

One of the men came down into the compartment and soon confirmed the fact, which was relayed to Beckwith. The men grabbed Girardi roughly and brought him to the front of the boat.

"Tremont's dead," Beckwith shouted into the radio.

"Do you mean you killed him?"

"*No*, we didn't touch him; he died down below with Girardi."

"Then put Girardi on the line."

Beckwith did as he asked.

"Mr. Girardi, I'm Colonel Wakefield. Can you confirm Mr. Tremont's condition?"

As the colonel asked the question, the Coast Guard ship cut the lights that had been shining on the deck. This did not cause Beckwith particular concern because the lights were changing constantly anyway. His men grabbed and turned on a pair of flashlights, shining one on Girardi and Beckwith, who were standing very close to one another.

"Jack Tremont is dead, colonel."

"How did he die?"

"We were below deck—he just drifted off. He'd been ill for weeks."

"And are you injured, Mr. Girardi?"

Beckwith grabbed the radio from Girardi before he could say any more.

"That's enough, that's enough. See, I told you I didn't kill anybody. Colonel, I want you to get that boat we talked about. We can't keep screwing around like this. You need to take some action or there will be consequences."

Girardi remained next to Beckwith and tried to hear the conversation over the noise of the circling helicopters. In the glow of the flashlight, Girardi perceived Beckwith's anger and desperation. He seemed like a man about to snap, and Girardi doubted that Wakefield or anyone else would be able to get through to him.

"If I obtained the boat for you," Wakefield replied, "would you expect to take your men along?"

"Of course."

"I'm not sure we could accommodate that. What if you went alone?"

"I'd at least want to bring one . . ."

As Beckwith was speaking, a strong arm emerged from the dark and pulled Girardi down to the deck. "Don't move," a young Marine whispered into Girardi's ear. Shocked, Girardi did as he was told.

Major Khani, wearing night vision equipment, moved silently on Beckwith, throwing the ringleader's weapon into the ocean and taking him down before he even knew what hit him. The other two men in Khani's Alpha Group subdued the guard closest to Beckwith and disposed of his weapon.

With the two flashlights now rolling on the deck, there was almost no light as the Bravo Group boarded and took the other two guards and Randall Spencer. When these three were secured, they went below and searched the cabin. All they found was Tremont's body.

It was all over in what felt to Girardi like an instant. Not a shot was fired—the mission had gone precisely as planned.

Major Khani, a man of few words, radioed Wakefield. "We're all clear here, sir."

"Report, major," Wakefield barked.

"Six men captured alive on deck—one dead below decks."

"The old man?"

"Roger."

"And your men?"

"All fine, sir."

Wakefield exhaled with relief. "Good work, major."

"Thank you, sir."

37

On Sunday afternoon, Girardi sat alone in the quiet bar area of *Emilio's*, in the shadow of the Marshall, Lufton office tower. He was drinking an Arnold Palmer and watching the Angels on the big screen. He and Jake had been to the game the night before to see the Angels beat up on the Texas Rangers. The pair had watched and scored every pitch, and it was the happiest Girardi had been in weeks.

Judge Best breezed in and headed straight for Girardi's table. He was wearing a dark green polo and black slacks. His hair was still a little wet from the shower he'd taken on a quick swing by his house.

"Thanks for coming over, Mitch."

The pair shook hands. They had spoken on the telephone several times since their big adventure but had not visited in person.

"No problem, partner." Best lowered his voice confidentially. "The truth is, you saved me from Susie."

"Are you sure you *want* to be saved from her?"

Best leaned forward eagerly. "She called and asked me to help her set up for the concert. Her maintenance guy quit on her last week, you know."

"I didn't know."

"Anyway, when she called, I figured, how hard could it be?"

"And?"

"And the woman is a slave-driver. I swept out the sanctuary, washed the parish hall windows and helped the ladies put out tablecloths and centerpieces for the potluck. She wouldn't even go with me for a coffee break. If you hadn't called, Lord knows what I'd be doing now. I barely had time to go home and clean up. No wonder the old sexton quit."

Despite his complaining, Girardi could see that Best was in good humor. Thinking over the judge's history all the way back to first year moot court in law school, Girardi observed that his friend never seemed happier than when he was being bossed around by a woman. Provided, that is, that he found her attractive and worthy of his attentions.

The past several days had been difficult for the judge as he had attempted to sort out the particulars of the Justice Department's decision to include him in their investigation. So far, he had not been entirely satisfied, even though the Attorney General had called personally to apologize, vowing to look into the matter and provide a full explanation.

"Do you mind my asking where things stand between you and the Reverend?" Girardi ventured.

"Beats me."

"And you're okay with the uncertainty?"

Best winked. "I'm thinking of testing the waters tonight."

Girardi wondered what this meant, but decided not to ask as he spotted Emilio approaching the table.

"Would you like a beer, your honor?"

"No thanks—just some iced tea, unsweetened, if you have it."

Emilio did not bother to conceal his surprise, for he and his staff had served these two countless afternoon beers over the years. "You're on the wagon now, too?"

"No, no. I'm headed over to church in a little while," Best attempted to explain. "St. Mark's Episcopal, just up the street."

Now the man was really perplexed.

"Can we get an order of bruschetta?" Best continued. "I'm starving."

"Coming right up."

"Great, Emilio. You're the best."

As Emilio walked away, the judge turned to his friend. "So, where were you when you called me? It almost sounded like the mall."

Girardi nodded. "It *was* the mall."

"I thought you refused to go to the mall."

"I had to make an exception. My son has some events coming up, including his mom's wedding. We bought him a suit."

"Holy cow, I forgot all about the wedding. Sorry, partner."

"That's okay," Girardi smiled good-naturedly. "With all that's gone on lately, Cass's wedding has almost slipped into the 'no big deal' category. Last night, Jake asked me again to come with him to the wedding. I think I will go with him after all."

"Really? I thought you were dead set against going."

"Not anymore. I'm sure it won't be easy when the time comes, but I should be there for her."

"That's big of you, Mike. I think you should be there for *Jake*—it's going to be weird for him to see his mom get married again."

Girardi nodded. "Beth said the same thing when I asked her about it on the phone."

"You and Jake will do fine."

"I know—by the way, the *Diamondbacks* are playing at home in Phoenix that weekend, so we'll try to take in a game or two while we're there."

Best's face then filled with mischief. "If you go to Cass's wedding, then you can turn around and invite her when you and Beth get hitched."

"Whoa, let's not get ahead of ourselves—Beth and I haven't even had a proper first date yet."

"I could hook you two up at the courthouse any time you want. If you want a church wedding, Susie can perform the service—and I'm free to be your best man if you need one. We've got all the bases covered."

"You're my best friend, Mitch, that's for sure. I want to thank you for all you've done for me lately, especially looking after Beth the way you did on Thursday. You even stayed with her at the hospital while they put the cast on. I appreciate that more than you know."

"No problem—Beth and I are pals now. I friended her on Facebook yesterday, as a matter of fact."

Girardi nodded knowingly. "You should hear what nice things she says about you."

"I was glad to help her out. You should have seen her reaction when we got the call that you were safe—she cried her eyes out. Of course, I was emotional myself. Anyway, I could see that she really cares for you, Mike."

"I care for her, too."

Best and Girardi watched the game for a while, and in the meantime Emilio brought the iced tea and bread, along with a fresh Arnold Palmer for Girardi. When the game went to commercial, Girardi spoke up.

"I spent two hours with Charley Strong and his people yesterday."

"I know. I was with them the day before."

"Not for two hours."

"No, more like ten minutes. They were 'your honoring' me all over the place, those two-faced assholes." Best wadded up his napkin in anger. "You know what bothers me most about the whole thing?"

Girardi suspected that he did, but did not venture a guess. "What?"

"The whole deal with Michelle. Good Lord, I one-hundred percent believed that she was into me. What an idiot I am—you'd think I would know better at my age. *You*, on the other hand, had her number from the start."

"I wouldn't say that I had her number. It never occurred to me that she was working undercover. I just thought she was flirting with you to gain some advantage for her client."

"Well, whatever your reasoning, I owe you, Mike. You saved me from a terrible mistake."

"No problem."

Best took a big swig of tea and forced his mind to another subject. "What did Charley tell you yesterday?"

"Not much that we didn't already know between us. *Pope Electronics* was a sting operation, and Jack fell for it. So, apparently, did the Consultants. Russell paid Jack using government funds, but Jack was desperate for money, and so he kept it for himself. Then, he got sick. We think Beckwith saw Jack shortly before his stroke and threatened him, but that hasn't been confirmed."

"And Cliff? How much did he know about all of this?"

"Charley thinks that Cliff was in the dark at first. Russell Yost, despite what he told me in Dana Point, *did* try to pressure Cliff for the document. Cliff told him to kiss off. But Cliff got pulled into the plan to fake Jack's death, so he could be looking at jail time for fraud."

"What about Celeste?"

"Jack apparently talked her into the idea of staging his death and then running away. They were planning to meet in Mexico—they had a little place down there none of us knew about."

"What's going to happen to her?"

"I don't know."

Best's cell phone rang. Girardi chuckled at the ring tone—*When the Saints Come Marching In.*

"Hey, Susie. How's it going?"

Mitch programmed a ringtone for her? It's more serious than I realized.

Best frowned as he listened to Mountjoy. "How late will they be?"

There was a pause. "Fifteen minutes is no big deal," he offered optimistically. "You can get up and tell jokes while everyone waits."

Girardi watched Best with great interest.

"Okay, maybe *I* can get up there and tell jokes. Yes, yes, I understand. I'll be right there. We just need to pay the bill." He hung up. "Gotta run—the violinist is running late. Susie's on the verge of a meltdown."

Girardi smiled at his friend. If the situation were reversed, he knew that Best would ride him for being too beholden to his lady friend. He would observe that Girardi's leash must hurt from being tugged on so hard. But Girardi held his tongue. He could see that the judge was enjoying himself, and he didn't want to spoil the mood.

"You go on ahead. I'll pay Emilio and see you over there in a little while."

"Thanks, Mike, you're the best."

■ ■ ■

Over at St. Mark's, the judge found Susan Mountjoy standing on the front steps wearing a burgundy-colored knit dress and matching jacket that she'd purchased just the day before on a "retail therapy" trip to the mall with Elizabeth Stowe. She had intended only to accompany Stowe and help her pick out something to wear to the concert, but while looking around, she'd decided to treat herself as well.

"Wow, you changed your clothes. You look great, Reverend."

"Thank you kindly, your honor."

"Has the violinist arrived yet?"

"She's supposedly five minutes away. I think I'll go and call her." Mountjoy patted Best on the arm and turned from him.

"Wait, Susie, before you go, I need to ask you something."

"Not now, Mitch, I have too much to do. We'll talk after the concert."

"I can't, remember? After the concert I'm headed straight to the airport. I'm going back East to help my daughter move out of her dorm room."

"That's right, I forgot." She leaned forward and surprised him with a kiss on the cheek. "Thanks for all of your help today—have a safe trip."

"I'm not done yet."

"Okay," she replied, laboring to hide her impatient anxiety. She had a couple-hundred patrons filling her sanctuary and a principal violinist running late. She would not be able to relax until the performance got under way.

"Bri and I fly home on Thursday. And then on Friday evening I'm set to give the keynote address at the *Federalist Society* conference."

"The *Federalist Society*? Is that the conservative lawyers' group?"

"Exactly." The judge stared at Mountjoy and hesitated. "The conference is up in Simi Valley at the Reagan Library. Have you ever been there?"

"No."

"Well, I was wondering . . . would you like to come with me? They have one of Reagan's old Air Force One jets in a big glass hangar—it's really cool. I could arrange an after-hours private tour of the library if you'd like one."

Mountjoy appeared dumbfounded at first. "You do know that I'm a lifelong Democrat, right?"

"Sure, and I like you anyway."

"That's magnanimous."

"Now that I'm a judge, I'm no longer a partisan."

Mountjoy looked skeptical, but the judge was sufficiently focused on his purpose that he barely noticed.

"I'm afraid that I wouldn't fit in with the *Federalists*, Mitch."

The judge had anticipated this response and was ready with his answer. "In a lot of ways, you fit in better than I do. You're intelligent, you love tradition, and you're classy. That's really the vibe of the *Federalist* group. Plus, I'll bet plenty of those guys were raised Episcopalian. Your church wasn't always so left-wing, you know. Honestly, I think they'd really like you. And, you might just like them, too."

"Keynote address, huh?" Mountjoy was impressed that her old school friend had done so well for himself. "What are you going to talk about?"

"I'm not sure yet. They gave me some general title about the rule of law . . . blah, blah, blah. I have a lot of thoughts on the subject you know, especially after what's happened lately."

Mountjoy shook her head in concern. "You wouldn't talk about Michael and Elizabeth's case, would you?"

"Probably not in so many words," Best replied, sounding uncertain.

Mountjoy's wheels were turning. "It's Friday evening, you say?"

"That's right. We'd need to leave by around three o'clock because it's a long drive up there through L.A. traffic."

"Okay—why don't you pick me up here at the church at three?"

Best could barely believe his ears, for he'd prepared himself to be turned down. "Really?"

"Yes, really. It sounds like fun. I'd like to see you in action with your *Federalist* buddies."

"That's great."

"But you don't expect me to pretend to be a Republican, do you?"

"Absolutely not. I just want you to be you. You being you is pretty great in my book."

Mountjoy was coming to enjoy these little compliments from the judge.

"Have a safe trip, Mitch, and I'll see you Friday."

She patted him on the arm, gave him one more kiss on the cheek and moved away, waving as she headed for the parish hall.

■ ■ ■

Girardi arrived at St. Mark's just in time to see Stowe and Sister Agnes pulling up in a cab. Stowe struggled some with her crutches as Mountjoy helped her with her handbag. Girardi meanwhile approached Agnes, and the two stood aside to speak privately.

"Oh Michael, I'm pleased to see you looking so well."

"Thank you, sister. How are you?"

"I'm quite well, thank you, now that we have our Elizabeth back safe and sound."

Agnes paused for a moment and exhaled in frustration. "My word, she is a terrible patient—the worst I've ever seen. She simply refuses to rest—they went to the mall yesterday, you know."

"It's probably a good sign that she wants to stay busy, right?"

"She has a troubled heart, Michael, *and* a broken ankle. She should rest."

Girardi nodded his head and stuck his hands into his pockets. "Oh sister, I almost forgot to give you these." He pulled out the blue string of rosary beads. "Thank you for loaning them to me."

"I want you to keep them."

"No, I couldn't keep them."

"Do you know how to use them?"

Girardi thought about bluffing, but then shook his head in the negative.

"You keep the beads," she urged, "and someday perhaps Elizabeth or I could show you how to use them. If not, I still want you to have them as a token of my thanks for finding our Elizabeth and keeping her safe."

At this, Agnes brushed a tear from her eye.

"I wish I could have saved her without breaking her ankle—I feel terrible about that."

Agnes had heard the whole story several times over and was quick to reassure him. "You removed her from danger and allowed her to give the police the information they needed. It was the right thing to do. I'm certain of it."

Although Girardi had not seen Stowe since that day, they had spoken on the phone for hours and she had repeatedly said the same thing. Logically, he believed that he had done the right thing. But still, the fact that she'd been hurt bothered him.

"Will you keep the beads, *please?*"

It was hard for Girardi to refuse Agnes. "Yes, I will. Thank you."

"You're welcome." She smiled. "Now, I should get inside and find my seat. The Reverend Doctor was kind enough to save us places in the reserved section. You should go over and talk to Elizabeth."

"I will."

"And by the way, I'll be taking a cab home right after the concert. You and Elizabeth should go and have a bite to eat—then you can bring her home."

"You'd be welcome to join us," he offered.

The little nun smiled knowingly. "That's kind of you, but I'd best keep to my plan. Please just don't keep her out too late."

"I won't."

Girardi then headed for Stowe, kissing her on the cheek and motioning her toward a bench near the courtyard fountain. She banged around with her crutches, struggling to settle herself comfortably.

"How are you doing?" he asked with concern. After a pause, he continued. "You look great, by the way."

"Thank you. Reverend Susan took me shopping and helped me find a sweater and skirt that match my blue cast perfectly. I think I might just be starting a new fashion trend."

Girardi was surprised by the look of Stowe's cast. "When I was in junior high, I broke my arm falling off my skateboard. I just had an old plaster cast—not this fancy blue stuff."

"I've never broken a bone before."

Girardi's face fell at this.

"No, no," Stowe rejoined quickly, "they told me it's not a bad break. I shouldn't need the cast for more than six weeks if I play my cards right.

So, you broke a bone skateboarding—were you trying to perform some trick?"

"Hardly. I was just a bonehead. I wanted to cross the street against the light and so I rushed and tripped."

"You could have been run over," she offered with concern.

"Nope, I didn't make it out into traffic. I fell in the gutter. Jake loves that story. He's heard it a million times but he still laughs every time I tell it."

"How is Jake doing?"

"He's great. His baseball team at school is tied for first place and headed for the playoffs."

"Good for him."

Girardi hesitated uncomfortably. "My sister is having a barbeque for the players and parents on Jake's team—kind of a pre-playoffs pep rally. One of the team moms apparently talked her into hosting. Val loves a party. Would you come with me?"

Stowe frowned. "Is it too soon for me to come to a family event? Perhaps you should ease me in."

"Ease you in?" Girardi chuckled. "Val was ready to come over here with me today to meet you and Agnes. I wouldn't put it past her to show up at the center next week."

"She's welcome anytime."

"You should definitely come to the barbeque. I don't know the other parents very well. The whole thing would be a lot more enjoyable for me if you were there."

"It would? That's nice."

"We're also celebrating some good news. My nephew Frankie, Val's eldest, has been deployed for five months. We just learned that he'll spend the last six weeks of his tour on Okinawa, which should be a heck of a lot safer. It's a big relief."

"That's wonderful news."

"So, will you come next Saturday?"

"Will you come and pick me up? I can't drive with this cast."

"Absolutely."

"Then yes, I'll come."

A quiet fell over the pair and Girardi changed the subject. "I think Agnes is worried about you. Tell me really, Beth, how are you doing?"

Stowe paused. "I'm not sleeping very well at night, and I'm restless in the daytime."

"I know what you mean about feeling restless. I haven't been able to sit still, either. But I'm lucky that I have no problem sleeping—I can sleep under almost any circumstances. I've been like that since I was a kid."

"You *are* lucky."

"Maybe you should talk to a counselor—what you went through was very stressful."

"No more so than what you went through," she rejoined quickly. "I'm not sure I want to see a counselor, but Reverend Susan is coming for another visit tomorrow. We had such a nice time together yesterday. She's helping me to put all of this in perspective. And so is Agnes. I'm surrounded by love—I'm lucky." Stowe leaned forward and touched Girardi's arm. "And I'm so glad you're here for this concert."

Girardi took her hand. "Me, too."

Stowe fought back a tear. "Things haven't entirely sunk in with me yet."

"What things?"

"That we're safe, and that the worst of this is behind us."

Girardi nodded his understanding. They sat together quietly for some time soaking in the peace and joy of the moment. The sun was warm and there was a gentle breeze. After all they'd been through, it was a relief for them to be together this way.

"Do you know where you want to go to dinner later?" he asked at last.

"How about the *Carvery*?"

"The *Carvery*? Don't you want to go somewhere fancier? I'll take you anywhere you want to go—maybe someplace down by the water?"

"No. I think of the *Carvery* as our special place now."

Girardi was looking forward to treating himself to a nice big steak, but he simply chuckled, looking on the bright side. "If we go there, we can afford some dessert afterwards."

"Maybe we could go down to the pier for some ice cream."

They heard Mountjoy begin her introduction of the program.

"I don't suppose it would be okay for us to ditch the concert and go straight to dinner?" Girardi ventured.

Stowe smiled as she considered the idea for a moment or two, but then she shook her head. "Oh no, we promised Susan and Mitch that we'd been here. We should stay—this concert is important to Susan; we should be here for her."

"That's true. I suppose we'll have plenty of time afterwards."

"All the time in the world."

Girardi stood with a nod and helped her with her crutches. And with a quick kiss, they headed off to the sanctuary.

THE END

ABOUT THE AUTHOR

 Pamela A. Kelley practices law with her husband William J. Kelley, III, at Kelley & Kelley in Irvine, California. An Orange County native, she graduated from Yale Law School in 1992 and litigated complex civil cases at the firms Chadbourne & Parke and Riordan & McKenzie in Los Angeles.

Kelley also lectures at the University of California, Irvine, her undergraduate alma mater, on civil rights law, constitutional law, the legal profession and legal ethics. She lives in Laguna Niguel, California.

Made in the USA
Columbia, SC
16 August 2020